"You have what I've always wanted."

Louisa looked as surprised as if Emmet had announced he carried rain in his back pocket. "Really? I can't imagine."

"Family. Siblings." His voice had thickened, but he couldn't help it. "I always felt lonely growing up alone." Abandoned.

She looked away, her gaze seeking the far edge of the field. "You know what I want?"

"No. What?" Whatever it was, he wished he could give it to her.

She paused for a beat. Two. Shuddered as if a chill had raced across her shoulders. She tried to speak, but her voice caught.

It obviously meant a lot to her. And his heart softened with such a protective urge that it was all he could do not to pull her into his arms and hold her close, keep her safe.

"For it to rain." Her voice rang with determination. "I pray for it every single day."

He knew without a doubt that wasn't what she'd started to say. Disappointment stained his insides. What was she afraid to admit she needed?

Linda Ford
and
Dorothy Clark

The Cowboy Father
&
Frontier Father

LOVE INSPIRED
INSPIRATIONAL ROMANCE

LOVE INSPIRED®

INSPIRATIONAL ROMANCE

ISBN-13: 978-1-335-50824-9

The Cowboy Father & Frontier Father

Copyright © 2020 by Harlequin Books S.A.

The Cowboy Father
First published in 2012. This edition published in 2020.
Copyright © 2012 by Linda Ford

Frontier Father
First published in 2011. This edition published in 2020.
Copyright © 2011 by Dorothy Clark

Recycling programs
for this product may
not exist in your area.

For questions and comments about the quality of this book,
please contact us at CustomerService@Harlequin.com.

Love Inspired
22 Adelaide St. West, 40th Floor
Toronto, Ontario M5H 4E3, Canada
www.Harlequin.com

Printed in U.S.A.

CONTENTS

Linda Ford lives on a ranch in Alberta, Canada, near enough to the Rocky Mountains that she can enjoy them on a daily basis. She and her husband raised fourteen children—four homemade, ten adopted. She currently shares her home and life with her husband, a grown son, a live-in paraplegic client, and a continual (and welcome) stream of kids, kids-in-law, grandkids, and assorted friends and relatives.

Books by Linda Ford

Love Inspired Historical

Big Sky Country

Montana Cowboy Daddy
Montana Cowboy Family
Montana Cowboy's Baby
Montana Bride by Christmas
Montana Groom of Convenience
Montana Lawman Rescuer

Montana Cowboys

The Cowboy's Ready-Made Family
The Cowboy's Baby Bond
The Cowboy's City Girl

Christmas in Eden Valley

A Daddy for Christmas
A Baby for Christmas
A Home for Christmas

Visit the Author Profile page
at Harlequin.com for more titles.

THE COWBOY FATHER

Linda Ford

If God so clothe the grass, which is today in the field, and tomorrow is cast into the oven; how much more will he clothe you, O ye of little faith.
—*Matthew* 6:30

Dedicated to the memory of my father, who was widowed with six children during the Depression and fought to provide for them so they weren't taken away. He succeeded despite the harsh realities of that era. Through it all, his faith survived and grew, and when he later remarried, he was able to pass that strength, faith and hope on to myself and my siblings born to that second marriage.

I thank God for the godly example he lived.

Chapter One

Louisa Morgan paused before the battered door of the Hamilton house. She'd prayed for an opportunity to earn money to help pay the medical bills—bills accumulated on her behalf. Influenza had struck many over the winter, but Louisa had been particularly ill with infection raging throughout her body. The doctor, meaning to be encouraging, said it was amazing she was alive and she should be glad. She was. Truly. But the illness had cost her something very precious...the ability to have children.

She vowed daily she would not let her disappointment turn into bitterness. She would enjoy what God still had in store for her. There was much to be grateful for...the ability to walk about and breathe in the spring air, the chance to continue her studies. She might have been content to keep on with her self-studies at home and not consider looking for a job, except she'd seen Mother slip cardboard into her shoes to cover the worn soles. She'd been about to confront Mother and insist she buy a new pair, but she noticed the pile of bills on the desk and knew Mother wouldn't buy anything until they were paid.

From that day, Louisa had prayed for a way to earn some money. Unfortunately a depression held the country in its grip. Able-bodied men were out of work. Many of them rode the rails or worked in government-run relief camps. Why would anyone hire a woman with no experience and a history of ill health when there were strong, family men eager to do any available job?

Then the teacher at the local school had asked her to tutor a bedridden little girl.

This job was truly an unexpected blessing and opportunity.

Still she did not knock.

A blessing it might be—and she had no doubt it was—but she had not expected to be thrust into a position that mocked her dreams. Dreams of a child of her own, a family and home of her own. Things she could never have now.

If she stood here long enough, she'd change her mind about the opportunity and answered prayer, decide it was only cruel mockery and walk away. *Lord, I believe You are in control and have opened a door for me in answer to prayer.* Pushing determination into her limbs, she knocked. Her heart battered against her ribs in determined anticipation.

The door opened. Louisa stilled her face to reveal none of the surprise she felt at the sight of the man in the doorway. He was stocky yet gave the impression of strength and authority. He had a thick mop of dark blond hair. His eyes looked as if they smiled, even though his expression revealed only wariness.

She'd expected an older man. A widower, she'd been told, and for some reason she'd imagined someone like old Mr. Knowles, who had married late and lost his wife to some unnamed illness a couple of years back. Mr. Knowles was bent, his hair almost gone except for a comb-over that caught in the wind, should he remove his hat. Mr. Knowles's face resembled a pale orange.

The man before her looked like someone used to being outdoors. The clothes he wore bore no resemblance to the broadcloth suit jacket and shiny trousers Mr. Knowles wore. No town clothes on this man, but a yoke-fronted shirt and soft denim jeans. Louisa knew he'd left his ranching life to bring his little girl home to recover from her broken leg.

The little girl was why Louisa was here. "Miss Ross, the teacher, said you need a tutor for your daughter." Adele Ross had said Mr. Hamilton insisted he approve the tutor she recommended. "I'm here to see if I'm —" Suitable. The word stuck in her throat. She wasn't suitable. She knew that. She had no formal education, unless one counted the few months Judd Kirk had tutored her last summer, before he married Louisa's sister, Madge, and moved to a nearby farm.

No formal education. No experience. A history of poor health. And barren. The word thundered through her head.

However, she was not here as a marriage candidate. She simply needed the job. She had no intention of letting her emotions become involved in any way. That would only lead to deeper sorrow.

"My name is Louisa Morgan, and I think I can provide your child with adequate tutoring."

"Miss Morgan." His voice was deep and gravelly. "I'm pleased to make your acquaintance. I'm Emmet Hamilton, as I'm sure you know. Please come in and we'll discuss the position." He stepped aside and indicated she should enter the house.

She tucked courage under her heart, strength into her legs and crossed the threshold. It took a moment for her eyes to adjust to the dim interior. Something brushed her ankle and she pressed her fingers to her mouth, stifling a squeal of alarm. It was only a cat, and she sighed.

"Auntie May is very fond of her cats. If you have an aversion or dislike of them, best you say so right away."

"I'm quite fond of them." She bent and stroked the big gray cat that meowed at her feet. Suddenly cats sprang from every corner until six crowded around, demanding attention. Louisa chortled at their antics. "Well, look at you guys. Aren't you pretty little things?"

"They're a nuisance."

She straightened and met his eyes, wondering if he objected to his aunt's pets, but she could read nothing in his expression. Seems the man had learned to hide his opinions rather well. Or perhaps he found it inappropriate she should spare the animals attention. Despite the continued demands of the cats, she determinedly ignored them, hoping it would prove her seriousness.

"Have a chair." He pointed toward a wingback chair in maroon upholstery.

She sat and glanced about. The room was crowded with furniture—three armchairs, a sagging brown sofa, at least eight little tables, their tops cluttered with knick-knacks. And not only the sort of pretty decorations one would expect. Among ornaments of birds of various colors and in various poses there were also china and wooden cats, bits and pieces of hardware, a doorknob, a lantern, books, dog-eared catalogues and magazines… Would she do the same as she grew older? Fill the lonely places that called for children with pets and possessions?

"Goodness me, boy." May Hamilton burst into a doorway on one side of the room. "Bring the miss into the kitchen where it's warmer."

So the cold in Louisa's bones wasn't just nerves.

She half rose then subsided, waiting to see what Mr. Hamilton intended to do.

He nodded. "Come along then." His eyes said far more though. They said he found his aunt both amusing and endearing.

Louisa relaxed marginally and followed Auntie May into a warm room as crowded with furniture and odds and ends as the front room. The whole place had the appearance of many projects on the go or abandoned at some point.

Auntie May studied Louisa. "Hello, my dear."

"Hello, Miss Hamilton."

She snorted. "Since when does anyone call me Miss Hamilton unless they are about to present a bill? I'm Auntie May. Always have been. Always will be. Now park yourself and talk to my nephew while I pour us tea."

Louisa "parked" on one of the mismatched chairs crowding around the table, as if Auntie May normally fed a large family instead of being on her own most of the time. Louisa had heard how she'd taken in her brother's son after his parents' untimely death and finished raising him. But he had left before Louisa and her family moved into the community. He'd returned a week ago with his injured daughter. Some suggested he came back so Auntie May could care for the child, but Louisa said where else would one go but back home if they needed help?

Auntie May nudged her way through a swarm of cats to set cups of tea in front of Louisa and Emmet. "I know Emmet will have hundreds of questions to ask you before he accepts you as tutor to little Ellie, but Emmet, let me say this. I've watched Louisa these past few years. I've seen her overcome challenges and emerge stronger and sweeter and kinder for them. I'm here to say you couldn't do much better than her."

Louisa's face burned with embarrassment at the praise. But at least Auntie May hadn't gone into detail about the challenges Louisa faced. Thankfully, only her family and Doc knew of her greatest challenge. One she must face with dignity and faith every day of her life.

"Thanks, Auntie May. I'll certainly take your opinion into consideration."

"Of course you will. Now come on, all of you." She spoke to the cats running after her as she stepped into the porch. "I've got some food ready." The meowing made conversation impossible until the door closed behind them.

Emmet laughed. "My aunt and her cats."

Louisa, twenty years from now—the local cat lady. "She'd be lonely without her pets." Auntie May was slightly eccentric but a good soul. There wasn't a person she wouldn't help, and the entire community knew it. The thought cheered Louisa marginally.

"Shall we get down to business?"

Louisa nodded, her tension returning tenfold.

"There are things I need to know about you."

"I understand." She'd tried to guess what questions he'd ask and how she'd answer them.

"First, what sort of training and education do you have that qualifies you to teach my daughter?"

She'd rightly guessed that would be uppermost in his mind. "I'm sure Miss Ross explained my education."

"I'd like to hear it from your lips."

"I do not have university education. Nor have I attended Normal school." If finances and health allowed it, she would love to go to Normal school and train to be a teacher.

"I see. And yet Miss Ross feels you are well educated. Tell me, formal training aside, what qualifies you for this job?" His voice was low, his look insistent.

Apart from the fact that it's the only one I've been offered and I need the money? "I did well in school and have continued my education since. Mostly I am self-taught, but last year my mother hired a tutor with a teaching degree and he helped me. I have a strong background in English, Greek, the arts and history."

"I see."

She wondered if he did. She must prove she could do this job. "I am also uniquely experienced for a situation such as your daughter's. I spent three winters unable to attend school. I kept up my studies while at home. I learned how to work on my own and how to amuse myself while confined to bed."

He studied her, then sighed. "Unfortunately, Ellie is used to being outdoors, riding her pony, climbing trees, running across the fields. School has always been a necessary evil in her opinion. I don't think she is going to find contentment in quiet activities."

"Does she have a choice?"

"Not at the moment. What else can you tell me about yourself? How old are you?"

"I'm twenty. Almost twenty-one."

"I would have taken you for much younger."

She squared her shoulders and tried to look wise. Realizing how silly her reaction, she had to steel herself not to chuckle.

"I assume you are only passing time until you marry."

"You, sir, assume incorrectly." He could not possibly know how his words hurt. For that she was thankful. "Marriage is not part of my plans." No man would want her, nor would she marry if one did momentarily profess love. It wouldn't be fair to deprive a man of children. Besides, wouldn't he grow to resent her? Better to remain single than take such a risk.

He gave her narrow-eyed concentration.

She refused to blink before his study, instead choosing to try to decide what color his eyes were. Green? Blue? Just when she'd decided on one, they shifted to the other. Ah. She'd learned something that might be useful in the future, should she get the job. His eyes changed color with his emotions. He had gone from green-eyed doubt to blue-eyed relief. For some inexplicable reason, it pleased her to have learned this tiny bit of information.

"Are you saying you have no beau?"

"I am indeed." She fully intended to protect herself from further pain by avoiding anything but friendship with any man.

"Daddy. Where are you?" A young, demanding voice called from a room past the kitchen.

The smile on the man's face made Louisa blink. The man looked as if the sun had come out and the sky turned blue at the sound of a little girl's voice. He was obviously very fond of his daughter. "I'll be right there."

Her eyes stung. Her father had loved his daughters in such a fashion. It had been almost four years since his passing, but she missed him as though it was yesterday.

"Would you like to meet Ellie?"

"Yes, please." Did this mean she had the job? Or would if she could relate to his daughter? *Please, God. Give me wisdom.*

"Come along."

She followed him into the adjoining room. A china cupboard and sideboard, groaning under a collection of mismatched dishes, took up most of one wall, but in the middle of the room stood a bed, raised to elbow level on blocks. A blonde child lay on the bed, her chocolate-brown eyes watching Louisa with unblinking interest.

"Who are you?"

"I'm Louisa Morgan." She glanced toward Emmet, but he stood back, observing her. Apparently he meant to see how she would handle the situation on her own. "And you are Ellie Hamilton."

"So?"

"Ellie?" Her father's voice carried gentle warning. "Be polite."

The little girl gave Louisa an unrepentant stare, then smiled at her father. "Okay, Daddy."

"Good girl." He stepped forward. "Her cast goes from here—" he pushed the blanket to show a cast up to her chest "—and down to here." This time he lifted the bottom of the covers. Only her toes peeked out. "So you can see she can't move around much."

"I'm sorry, Ellie. It can't be much fun." Louisa reviewed what she knew of the child. Seven years old. Motherless. Had fallen out of a tree and broken her leg.

"It's not any fun. I hate it." Crossing her arms over her chest, she put on a full-blown pout.

"It's necessary so your leg will heal." Emmet's voice was tight. It must hurt to see his child like this. "Even as it's necessary for you to continue with your schoolwork. Which is why Miss Morgan is here."

"No. I don't want to. Don't make me." The child screamed and cried at the same time. "Please, Daddy, don't make me."

Emmet stepped to Ellie's side, cradled her face between his palms. "Hush, sweetie. Don't upset yourself like this." He crooned wordless comfort.

Ellie wrapped her arms about Emmet's neck and pulled his face down to rest on her cheek.

Louisa turned away, her throat clogged with emotion at seeing his gentle pain over his daughter. Feeling his helplessness. Understanding how Ellie felt. How often had Louisa had to watch life move on while she observed from the sidelines? *Lord, all I want is a job, but perhaps You have something more for me here.* She would follow God's leading, but she would keep her heart under lock and key.

Emmet extricated himself from Ellie's grasp. "You'll be okay. I need to talk to Miss Morgan for a minute, then I'll be back."

"Then will you play with me?" A quiver in her voice tore at Louisa's resolve. The poor child. If she got the job of teaching her, she would do everything she could to make the days pass quickly with fun activities.

"Miss Morgan?" Emmet indicated she should follow

him. He led her through to the front room. "I don't want Ellie to hear us."

She sat while he went from one side of the room to the other, his strides long and hurried.

"I'm sorry. I can't imagine how you feel."

"No, you can't." He ground to a halt and jerked his thumb toward the room where his daughter lay. "It's my fault—"

"How can you blame yourself for an accident?" She ached to explain that sometimes things just happened despite our best efforts. For no good reason. A person simply had to accept it and move on. The only other choice was to be angry and bitter. Not a pleasant alternative, to her way of thinking.

"I should— Never mind. It has nothing to do with the job." He sat down and faced her. "I need to get Ellie into a routine of sorts as quickly as possible." He sighed deeply, as if he regretted the decision he must make. "Miss Ross spoke highly of you. Let's see how you do with Ellie. If you're still interested in the job…"

At first all she cared about was getting paying work, but seeing the child, witnessing their affection, sensing the frustration in both of them…well, now she *wanted* the job. "When do you wish me to start?"

He laughed, his face suddenly years younger. "Is tomorrow too soon?"

"I'll have to get lesson plans and advice from Miss Ross but tomorrow is fine."

"I hope you can make her happy."

"I'll do my best." Though she knew a person, whatever age, was only as happy as they chose to be. But she could imagine getting Ellie to laugh, seeing Emmet smile at his daughter's cheerfulness.

It wasn't until she stood on the street, smiling with anticipation, that she realized she was imagining all the things she could never have—teaching a child in the safety of home, sharing the pleasure with a man.

She'd strayed wildly from her intention of guarding her emotions. This was only a job, she scolded herself. A child who needed to learn. Nothing more.

Now all she had to do was face Mother and inform her of her decision. She already knew how she'd react. Warnings she would make herself sick. Advice that she must take care of herself. But Louisa was tired of being coddled, of being careful. It certainly hadn't prevented her from getting sick in the past. From now on, she intended to enjoy every bit of what she could squeeze from life. Certainly she knew her limitations. But no amount of hard work would make her barrenness more… or less…than it already was.

An ache the size of Alberta lay tightly tied and buried in a secret corner of her heart—where she would make sure it stayed.

Chapter Two

Emmet closed the door softly behind Miss Morgan's departure and stared at the wooden slab. She was much too young and pretty to be...what? Young and single? Not planning marriage? Most certainly a temporary condition. No doubt she waited only for the right man to show up. Not that it mattered one way or the other to him. He no longer sought after dreams such as marriage, home, success.... All that mattered now was taking care of Ellie. And he had failed badly in that area. Something he intended would not happen again. Nothing must divert him from caring for her.

"I hope you're going to let Louisa help Ellie."

His aunt's voice thankfully jerked him back from the dark trail his thoughts headed down. He turned to meet her intent look.

"She's a good person."

"She starts tomorrow."

"Good for you. I was afraid you'd see her pretty face and immediately count her out."

"Now, why would you think that?" He purposely kept

his voice soft. Sometimes Auntie May responded better to a gentle warning.

But not always.

"I know you, boy. You've been hurt too many times. And now you've locked your feelings in a deep vault someplace."

How wrong she was. Not that he hadn't tried exactly that. But he'd failed miserably. He'd never felt anything as deeply, as frighteningly real as when he'd found Ellie hurt. "My feelings are not buried. I care about Ellie. So much it hurts."

A cat jumped to a table next to Auntie May and leaned over in an attempt to get her attention. Several things clattered to the floor.

Auntie May scooped up the cat and retrieved the fallen objects. "I don't mean Ellie. Of course you love her. She's your flesh and blood. But don't you think she needs a mother? Just as you need a wife—a partner?"

"I've already tried that, remember? And it ended with Jane dying." Like everyone he cared for. His parents. Even his pet dog. "Ellie is enough for me."

"She can't be, you know. A man needs a wife."

He snorted. "This from a woman who never married." He considered her. "Are you saying you regret that?"

She chortled. "I have you and Ellie. And my pets." She scrubbed the heads of four cats sitting at her feet. Then she gave him a look full of both challenge and regret. "I loved once."

"You did? What happened?"

She shrugged and buried her face in the fur of the gray cat in her arms. Seemed the animal was the favored of the bunch, or perhaps the most demanding, as it always ended up being held. "Didn't work out."

"Why?" In the dozen or so years he'd lived here, she'd never once hinted she had loved someone. Nor expressed regrets at being single. Did the man die? Seems death stole a lot of people.

"I've been happy. Nothing to complain about, but take it from me. Cats aren't the same as humans."

"No kidding."

"They're more loyal for the most part, however."

Emmet considered the statement. Had Auntie May's love interest been disloyal? The idea only reinforced his decision. "Auntie, I'm sorry your love didn't work out. But you say you've been happy. That's more than many can claim, and likely all any of us can expect. I'm content with my life. I have Ellie and you." He bent to pat two furry heads. "And the cats."

"I always wanted more for you. I wanted you to have the things I didn't."

"You're sweet, but I had a wife. She died. But she gave me a daughter. Do I deserve anything more?"

"I don't know what any of us deserves, but God, in His mercy, blesses us anyway. My concern is you've shut your heart to more. Likely wouldn't take it, even if God sent it your way."

Emmet didn't want to argue with her. Didn't have an argument to offer. He had all he wanted. Anything else would only invite more pain. Auntie May was right. He had barred his heart.

A crash rattled from the kitchen. No, it was Ellie's room. Had she fallen? Hurt herself while he stood two rooms away making silly conversation? He would never forgive himself if—

He crossed the room in long strides and hurried to her bedside, Auntie May at his heels.

Ellie's covers were rumpled, but other than that she looked in one piece.

"What was that racket?" he demanded.

Auntie May continued past the bed. "I'd say this would explain the noise." She held up the shattered base of a lamp. "Now, I wonder how that ended up on the floor."

"I bumped it," Ellie said, "trying to get something to play with." She put on a pretty pout. "Daddy, you said you'd come back and play with me."

"I was on my way." He shouldn't have lingered talking to his aunt about things that didn't matter.

"I'll clean this up." Auntie May brought a broom and dustpan from the kitchen. "You go ahead and amuse your daughter."

"Thanks." He caught Ellie's eyes and tilted his head toward his aunt, silently signaling her.

Ellie smiled sweetly. "I'm sorry for breaking your lamp, Auntie May."

"Goodness, child. Don't you fret about it. Accidents happen."

His daughter made him proud. "What would you like to do?"

"Ride my pony."

He chuckled. "I guess you would, but how do you think he'd feel with a big white stiff body on his back? Wouldn't he be frightened?"

Ellie giggled. "He'd kneel down and dump me off."

"I expect he would."

"Is that lady going to be my teacher?"

"Miss Morgan? She's coming with lessons tomorrow."

"Do I have to do schoolwork? Please don't make me."

He hated doing so, but surely it was the best thing for

her. "It will help you pass the time and you'll be able to keep up with your friends at school."

"But Daddy, all my friends are where we used to live. I have no friends here." Her bottom lip quivered. "Why did we have to move?"

"I'm sorry, Button. But I couldn't take care of you and run the ranch."

"Betsy could look after me."

Anger surged up his throat at how Betsy had looked after his daughter. He'd arrived home early to find Ellie on the ground, screaming in pain with a broken leg and Betsy absent. She'd gone to a nearby homesteader's place—a single man—and left Ellie on her own. From all accounts, not an unusual occurrence. Seemed he was the last to discover it. Shouldn't he have been the first? "I didn't much care for the way Betsy watched you."

"Miss Morgan is very pretty, isn't she?"

Far too pretty to be single. But that mattered not to him in the least. "She's passable, I suppose."

Auntie May, mussing about in the kitchen, snorted loudly. Emmet chose to ignore it.

"You might like her better than me."

"Oh, Ellie." He pulled a stool close to her side and cradled her in his arms as best as the body cast allowed. "I will never like anyone better than you. Not so long as I live."

"You promise?"

"I promise." He held her close a moment longer, then she squirmed free.

"Tell me a story."

"I'm not much good at storytelling."

"Tell me about Grandma and Grandpa."

He sucked in air. All she knew was they had died

when he was nine. He never talked about them. It was another life. This was his life now. "How about if I tell you about the night you were born?"

"Okay." She sounded less than enthusiastic. Perhaps because she'd heard the story before.

So he tried to up the drama and suspense of that long-ago night when the doctor had come in the middle of an October snowstorm and the electricity had gone off. His little daughter had been delivered by flickering lamplight. And he'd fallen smash, dash in love with his tiny girl. "I loved you from your first breath, and I will love you until my last breath." He squeezed her gently.

Ellie giggled. "Daddy, you're silly."

"Silly about you."

"Then you won't make me do schoolwork?"

Emmet laughed, pleased at her wily ways. "You'll still have to do schoolwork." He scooped up the gray cat and put it on the bed beside Ellie. "You play with the cat while I do some chores." He didn't intend to sit around and let Auntie May do everything. He'd noticed a number of neglected things he planned to take care of while he was here.

Later, after he fixed a broken step and cleaned out weeds blown around the back shed, he returned to play with Ellie.

"I wish you would stay with me all day."

"I wish I could too, Button. But I can't." Having Louisa Morgan spend a few hours each day with Ellie would make it better for both him and his daughter.

Next morning, Emmet waited at the front door for Louisa to arrive. He'd had a restless night, wondering if he did right by Ellie, forcing her to take lessons while confined to bed. But Louisa said she'd spent time in a similar situation. Had she been ill? It was hard to believe. She looked in perfect health.

A battered-looking car, a Model A, wheezed to the front gate. Louisa stepped daintily from the vehicle. She moved as if she anticipated what life had to offer. Her cheeks glowed. Her skin was like pure silk, and curly dark hair framed her oval face. A dark pink dress with a flowery pattern accented her chinalike complexion and swirled about her legs as she turned. If she had any physical flaws, he did not detect them, and if she suffered any chronic illness, it didn't reveal itself in the way she moved.

She leaned into the backseat and pulled out a satchel so heavy it required she use both hands to set it on the ground. Then she dragged an awkward board out, set it beside the satchel and bent to extract some lengths of wood.

All this to teach Ellie a little reading, writing and 'rithmetic? He stepped outside. "Can I give you a hand with those things?"

She sent him a smile full of gratitude that sneaked through his defenses and delivered a king-size wallop to a spot behind his heart.

He sank a mental fist into the area and pushed it into oblivion. "Seems you're serious about this tutoring business."

She laughed. Music seemed to fill the air. He glanced around to see if a door was open, if someone was playing the piano. All doors were closed. He shifted his gaze to the trees. Birds sang an accompaniment to the sound. He concluded the music came from Louisa's laugh. "I like to do a good job."

"I'll take the bag. It looks heavy." He grunted as he hoisted it from the ground. "Did you bring bricks?"

Another musical chuckle. "Just books. Some Adele— Miss Ross—loaned from the school and some I brought from home." She tucked the longer pieces of wood under one arm and tried to tackle the bigger piece, but it was almost as big as she.

"I'll take that. What is it?"

She turned it to show the other side. "A blackboard. My brother-in-law, Judd, made this tripod. See, the legs extend so I can write on the board then raise it so Ellie can see it from her position in bed. Isn't that clever?"

"Oh, very."

She chuckled. It seemed everything amused her, pleased her.

Obviously, he thought with a shade of bitterness, she had not encountered major difficulties in her life.

They struggled toward the house and dropped the items on the floor.

"Is that all?"

"Yes. Thanks for helping."

They stood in the doorway to catch their breath. "We sure need rain." Clever conversation, Emmet mocked himself. But what did it matter? He was only being polite.

"Rain, an end to grasshoppers, better commodity prices. So many things. I know my sister thinks the government should fix the country's problems, but I prefer to trust God. He'll change things when He sees fit. In the meantime, I will trust Him for my daily needs."

Her faith sounded nice. But would she trust if everything she valued was snatched away? Would she say God was treating her fairly? Would her faith falter? But he didn't want to talk about trials and how they affected one's faith. His own hung on by a tiny thread. "I neglected to ask about your family. Do you come from a large one? Tell me about them."

"I have two younger sisters. Madge is a year younger. She married Judd last fall. Sally is two years younger. She lives at home as do I, with our mother." She paused a beat then went on. "My father died four years ago. I still miss him." Her voice thickened.

Emmet stilled an urge to squeeze her shoulder. "My parents died eighteen years ago and I still miss them."

"Oh." Her lips formed a little circle, and her eyes widened. "I thought it would get easier with time."

"It gets easier. Just never goes away."

"I remember him at the silliest times. A certain hymn will bring tears to my eyes. Or the smell of molasses cookies, which he loved. Or—" She shrugged. "I suppose it's the same for you."

It was a question, even though she didn't voice it as one. But he remembered very little about his parents. "I leave it in the past."

Her eyes widened even more. "You mean you purposely try to forget about them?" She didn't wait for an answer but provided her own. "Although I miss my father, I wouldn't want to forget him or all the wonderful memories I have. Nor the lessons he taught."

"I suppose time has dulled my memories." He didn't want to dwell on it any longer. "You must have moved to this area after I left."

"We bought the farm two miles from town eight years ago."

"Ah. I left nine years ago."

"Daddy!" Ellie's voice wailed through the house.

Emmet chuckled. "She's been waiting patiently all morning. Seems her patience has run out." He again picked up the bag and board and trooped through to Ellie's room. Several cats, seeing the unfamiliar items, hissed. Two backed into a corner and continued to hiss and arch their backs. Four skidded from the room.

Ellie laughed. "Scaredy-cats." But her laughter died and her eyes grew wary at all the equipment Emmet and Louisa dragged in.

"Where do you want this?" Emmet indicated the blackboard.

Louisa looked around. Stood beside the bed. At the end and then on the side farthest from the door. "This would be ideal—" Except for the bookshelf, the table and the wooden chair in the room, all of which were loaded with Auntie May's belongings.

"I'll move this stuff out of the way." He shoved it into the far corner, crowding the china cabinet. "Auntie May doesn't believe in throwing things out."

He wondered at the way the sunshine left Louisa's face and her eyes grew stormy.

"I suppose she finds comfort in being surrounded by familiar objects." She kept her back to him as she cleared the top of the table and lifted the bag onto it, but he thought he detected a tightness in her voice he hadn't noticed before. He put it down to tension at getting the room organized for teaching.

He set up the tripod, adjusted the blackboard on it then stepped back. "Looks like everything is set. I'll leave you to it." He edged toward the door, reluctant to leave them.

"Daddy, where are you going?" Ellie reached out, as if to stop him.

"I'll be close by. If you need me, you only have to call." The door was inches away, but he didn't step through.

"We'll be fine," Louisa murmured, then pulled a reader from the bag and directed her attention to Ellie. "Miss Ross sent the whole set of grade-two readers so you can show me which ones you can read."

Ellie sent Emmet a look rife with pleading and accusation. He hoped she would understand he was only doing what was best for her.

But she understood the knowledge would provide poor comfort.

Chapter Three

Louisa watched Emmet's departure, feeling the same frightening desperation she heard in Ellie's voice. *Don't leave us. I don't know what I'm doing.* Adele had laid out the lessons and told her what to expect. "The first thing to remember is the child may be resistant to the whole idea of having to do schoolwork while in bed. Find a way to pique her interest and curiosity."

Sounded so easy when Adele said it. But she could do this. Louisa drew a brave breath and began. "First, I'd like you to tell me what things you like. That way we can make your lessons as interesting as possible."

Ellie gave her a stubborn stare. "Can you bring my pony so I can ride?"

Louisa laughed softly. "I think that is outside my power. What games do you like?"

"Hide-and-seek. Racing. Climbing trees. We can't do that either, I suppose." Ellie boldly challenged Louisa with her words and her expression.

"You're quite right. So let's think of something you *can* do and enjoy."

The child made a most unladylike sound. "There isn't anything to enjoy while I'm stuck in bed."

"Do you like reading?"

"Hate it."

"Do you like stories?" Louisa held up two storybooks she'd enjoyed when she learned to read. The books were well-worn. "These were my two favorites at your age. They've been read over and over by myself and my sisters."

A flicker of interest. Good. "You've got sisters?"

"Two. Madge and Sally."

The interest died. "I've got my daddy." She grew fierce. "He'd be lonely without me."

"I'm sure he would. He's fortunate to have you."

Ellie nodded.

"Just as you're fortunate to have him. Now, shall I read a story to start with?" Ease into the lessons, Adele had advised.

"I guess." Her lack of enthusiasm was slightly dampening, but Louisa chose to ignore it, opened the book and began to read. She loved the rhythm of the words, the comfort of the familiar story, but she closed the book at the end of chapter one. "We'll read more later, but now it's your turn to read to me." She handed Ellie the primer Adele thought she would be reading from by now. "Can you read me the first page?"

Ellie fixed Louisa with a stubborn frown and made no move to open the book.

Louisa flipped the pages to the first story. "Start here."

Ellie didn't even shift her eyes to the page.

"Ellie, please read this."

Ellie lowered her eyes, skimmed the page and closed the book. "I can't."

"Why can't you? Is it too hard?"

"I can't remember."

Louisa sighed. "What do you remember?"

"Falling out of the tree and landing wrong. You should have heard my leg. It snapped. Like this." She clicked her tongue to imitate the sound. "I tried not to cry, but my daddy was gone."

"Gone? Where?" Was this what he meant when he said it was his fault?

"Out working. We own a ranch, you know. He was checking the cows."

"I see."

"So now I have to lie in bed in this horrible cast—" She banged on it, the sound a hollow thud. "I can't do schoolwork."

"Of course you can work. There's nothing wrong with your brain."

Ellie turned away and stared at the door, as if willing Emmet to appear. And he did—sauntered past as if he had other things on his mind, but Louisa knew he was checking to make sure Ellie was okay. He paused. "Things going well?"

"Daddy." Ellie's voice quivered in the saddest possible way.

"Things are just fine." Louisa grabbed a bit of chalk. "Let's do some arithmetic now. What is the answer to this?" She wrote "1 + 1=" on the blackboard.

Emmet hesitated, watched a moment longer then moved on, and the outside door whacked shut.

"Ellie?"

The child stared clear through Louisa. "I don't know."

"You aren't even looking." She tapped the blackboard.

Ellie glanced at the numbers. "Can't remember."

Louisa crossed her arms and faced the child squarely. "I don't think that's the truth. I know you know the answer to one plus one."

They did a stubborn silent duel.

"Two." Ellie was not happy about admitting it.

"Good. Now two plus two."

"Where's my daddy? I want my daddy."

"Do you need to go to the bathroom?"

"No. I want my daddy."

Louisa took two steps until she stood right next to the bed. "Your daddy is working, and you must too."

"I'm sick."

"No, you've got a broken leg."

The big gray cat Louisa had met the day before jumped on the bed and stared into Ellie's eyes.

Louisa laughed. "The cat is telling you to do your schoolwork."

Ellie shoved the cat to the floor. He landed with a thud and stalked away. "I want my daddy!" Ellie yelled loudly.

Emmet crashed into the house and strode into the room. "Did you call me?"

Ellie nodded, her eyes brimming with innocent tears. "I have to go to the bathroom and Miss Morgan won't let me."

Emmet shot Louisa a stinging look.

Louisa wisely refrained from rolling her eyes at the child's dramatics. Instead, she quietly headed for the door. "I'll step out while you tend to her needs."

She came face-to-face with Auntie May. "How long have you been here?"

"Just got in. Emmet and I were fixing the shingles."

Her eyes narrowed. "She been giving you grief?" She tipped her head toward the bedroom.

Louisa opened her mouth to answer, then realized it would be inappropriate to speak of her concerns. "We're getting a routine established." Heaven help her if this was the regular pattern she'd be forced to follow.

"The little one is a tad spoiled, though I suppose it's to be expected. There's just the two of them."

"And you."

Auntie May snorted. "The child barely knows me. Besides, I'm just an old spinster." She bent to pet the cats crowding around her ankles.

Louisa wanted to see her expression. She longed to see acceptance and peace in Auntie May's eyes. Needed to know being a spinster wasn't an unhappy fate.

Louisa straightened her spine. She would become a happy spinster doing things to help others and bringing joy to herself as well. She'd start by showing Ellie it was fun to learn. She'd help the child deal with the boredom of her body cast. It would take more wisdom than her limited experience offered, but she could ask Adele for help, and she could pray. After all, hadn't God said in James chapter one, verse five, "If any of you lack wisdom, let him ask of God, that giveth to all men liberally and upbraideth not; and it shall be given him." It was one of the verses Father had Louisa and her sisters memorize.

Emmet emerged from the room. "Miss Morgan, please call me if Ellie needs to go the bathroom again." His voice and expression clearly said what his words didn't. He judged her unkind and unreasonable to not allow his child such basics.

"Of course." She knew full well there was no point in saying she had asked and Ellie had denied such a need.

This battle was between Ellie and herself. With renewed determination, she returned to the child's bedside.

At noon, when she was done for the day, she'd made absolutely no progress with the planned lessons. Ellie insisted she didn't know or couldn't remember anything and refused to do any work.

Louisa emerged from the room, knowing her hair was mussed and her face likely flushed from frustration and fighting back tears. Why had she thought she could do this job? A bubble of self-pity whispered she was totally useless, but Louisa ignored it. Fought back. She wasn't useless. Not in every aspect. She could help this child if Ellie allowed it.

Emmet walked her out, waiting until they were out of earshot to speak his mind. "I sense you and Ellie are not getting along."

"Miss Ross said I might encounter resistance. After all, Ellie has lost her freedom. On top of that, everything is new. Familiar things are gone." Let him think the latter observation came from Adele as well, even though Louisa spoke her own thoughts. "Her only defense is—" she wanted to say defiance, but doubted Emmet would appreciate such a description "—is to exert what little independence she has left. I believe she will soon tire of it and find there are more enjoyable ways to pass the time."

He looked doubtful. Louisa feared he would tell her not to return. But after several seconds' consideration, he sighed heavily. "You're right about one thing. She's lost everything. She can hardly be blamed for feeling out of sorts."

"She hasn't lost everything, though." Her words were quiet, coming from a place full of certainty that Emmet was more than enough for this child. "She has you."

"She'll always have me."

She nodded, though words pushed at her lips, wanting to warn that he couldn't promise such.

"As long as I live." He clenched his fists. "And I fully intend to raise her in such a way that even if something happened to me—God forbid—she would never feel like I was gone. I'd be in her thoughts and in her actions every day."

Peace filled Louisa. "Exactly what my father did."

Their gazes connected, forged a single thought about fathers and daughters…how each needed the other. How sweet the relationship.

Louisa tipped her head away first. "I'll see you tomorrow." It was half a question, but he nodded.

"Until tomorrow then."

She climbed behind the wheel of their old, unreliable automobile and turned toward home. She admired Emmet's devotion to his child. It reminded her of the love her father had lavished on her and her sisters. Louisa smiled as fond memories of her father filled her thoughts. Ellie was a fortunate child to know such love.

Not until she reached the turnoff did she remember that the fortunate child was also a defiant, uncooperative child. Tension grabbed the muscles of her shoulders and loosened tears. She let the car coast as she struggled to gain control.

Blinking back the moisture in her eyes, she looked at her home. Father had dreamed of operating a farm, growing crops and raising cows. But after he died and the Depression hit, the family had been forced to make sacrifices. They'd let most of the land go to the bank in exchange for the house, the outbuildings and a few acres.

The Morgan family didn't have much—their home, a barn, a cow, a calf and a reluctant garden—but it was so much more than many had. Over and over Louisa had observed families—beaten and broke—load their meager possessions to the sides and roof of their vehicle and drive away. Many couldn't afford the gas for driving and left with bundles on their backs. She knew just how blessed she, her mother and her sisters were. *Thank you, God, for allowing us to keep our home and stay together.* Her illnesses brought further tightening of purse strings that were already pulled about as taut as they could go.

"I prayed for a job so I could help pay the bills. Lord, You provided one when there were none available. I am not going to accept defeat or complain that it's hard." She sent the car toward home at a faster pace.

Mother watched her approach from the window and came to the door as she stepped from the car. "You look exhausted. Come in and rest." She twisted her apron in worried hands. "I'm afraid you will make yourself sick again."

Louisa hugged her mother. "I'm fine. I have no intention of making myself sick. You can count on that." Never again, if she had anything to say or do about it. She wouldn't jeopardize her health. It was far too precious.

"How did your first day go?"

She longed to share her frustration with her mother, but she knew it would only worry her. "About as expected. We're learning to adjust to each other."

Sally stood in the kitchen doorway, her eyes watchful. Sally didn't say much, but she saw a lot. Louisa could duck her head and avoid her sister's keen gaze, or she could face her and let her try to guess what lay behind her words. She knew the latter was the easiest way to deal with Sally, so she smiled at her. "How was your day?"

"I've been busy. Clara and I went to the orphanage and put in a garden for them."

"Good for you." Ten to twelve children lived at the home on the hill. A barren spot without trees or flowers, but at least the children were housed and fed. They attended school and church and appeared happy enough.

Mother had lunch ready and they sat down to enjoy it. Afterward Mother went for a nap.

Sally waited until the bedroom door closed, then gave Louisa a demanding look. "Tell all. How did it really go?"

Louisa blew out a huge sigh. "Ellie refuses to learn." She described the morning to her sister, including the part when Ellie made it sound as if Louisa wouldn't let her go to the bathroom.

Sally drew back, looked shocked. "She sounds dreadful. Are you going back?"

"I'm not about to give up."

"You're stronger than I am. I wouldn't be able to face such a situation."

Louisa chuckled. "I'm not strong. You know that as well as I do." Her thoughts darkened, but she refused to be controlled by her disappointment.

"You're strong in a quiet way. Perhaps because you've had to fight to get over pneumonia and influenza."

The darkness drew closer. The pain beckoned. But Louisa saw it for what it was—self-pity. And refused to open the door and invite it in. "I'm going to take that as a compliment." She thought of Ellie. The child needed to learn how to make the best of her situation.

She'd return tomorrow and try again. She'd show Emmet she wasn't unkind to his precious little girl.

"The kids at the orphanage are sweet. I'm going back after school is out with cookies for them. Why don't you come with me?"

Louisa's heart flopped in protest. See kids? The idea mocked her barrenness. "I don't think—"

"I know what you're going to say. You don't want to be reminded you can't have children of your own. But these kids will likely help you. They know how to enjoy life despite their loss and disappointment."

Sally's words stung. "Are you saying I don't?"

Sally looked shocked. "I didn't mean it like that. I only thought seeing them would cheer you up. You know…after dealing with a child who is feeling sorry for herself."

"You might be right. I'll go with you. I'll even help you bake cookies." Maybe she'd learn a thing or two about working with children who had suffered unfortunate events in their life that would help her deal with Ellie.

Somehow she had to prove to herself she could handle the job God had placed in her lap. But she wondered if He had more faith in her abilities than she did.

Over lunch Emmet listened to a litany of complaints from Ellie. Louisa was too harsh. She didn't explain things well.

"I don't think she likes me."

Emmet chuckled. "What's not to like? You're a sweet, smart, funny little girl." He hoped Louisa was right, and this resistance was only an adjustment period. Strange that Louisa and Ellie hadn't struck it off right away. From his first look at Louisa, he'd thought her beautiful—not just in appearance but in a deeper way. Her beauty seemed to come from within.

He fisted the idea away. It didn't matter what he thought of her. Only that she was kind to his daughter. He would tolerate nothing less.

He carried the lunch plates and glasses to the kitchen and grabbed a cup of coffee. A stack of dirty dishes waited to be washed. "I'll sit with Ellie for a bit then clean up this mess."

Auntie May shooed him away. "I do believe I can manage to wash a few dishes. Or at least let the cats lick them clean."

"Leave them. I'll do them later." He did not want Ellie eating off cat-cleaned dishes.

Auntie May's teasing chuckle made him realize he'd been tricked. "You're joshing and I missed it."

"You sure did. There was a time I'd have never gotten that past you." She sobered. "I think you've grown far too serious."

"Sometimes life isn't a joking matter." He headed for Ellie's room.

"People should never forget to find and appreciate the good things God gives us."

He paused to consider her. "I sometimes find it hard to believe in such."

"And there lies your problem. Emmet, my dear boy, I'm not saying bad things don't happen. I'm only saying you don't need to let them steal away the good things too."

He studied the words a moment but could find no personal truth in them. Except for one thing. "I have something I appreciate…Ellie." He ducked into her room, a wide smile on his face as he planned to enjoy the afternoon with her. But her arms were flung above her head and she snored softly.

Suddenly the next few hours looked lonely and bleak. He returned to the kitchen.

Auntie May glanced over her shoulder where—he was relieved to see—she had a wash pan full of hot soapy water.

"She's asleep." He downed the lukewarm coffee Auntie May seemed to favor and yearned for a cup of strong, hot brew.

"Why don't you have a look around town and see how the place has changed since you left? I'll watch out for Ellie."

"She'll be bored."

"Seems to me I can manage a little girl for an hour or two. Now shoo."

So he "shooed," right out the back door and down the lane that had once been his playground. He didn't expect he would see any of the kids he'd grown up with. The girls would be married. And the boys who weren't also married would be looking for work, perhaps riding the trains back and forth across the land.

He cut down a side avenue and ventured toward the main street. The buildings were familiar, even if they needed paint and repair. He stopped and stared. Mr. Smith's fence had fallen down. Mr. Smith used to put a lot of stock in that fence. Emmet circled the corner of the lot and looked at the house. The door sagged. The windows were bare.

He saw a young man striding down the street and called out. "What happened to the Smith family?"

The man crossed to Emmet's side. "They used to live here, didn't they? They were gone before my time. But my wife said they lost everything in the crash and went to live with Mrs. Smith's mother. No one has lived here since. Lots of empty houses around. Mostly abandoned by the occupants who could no longer make a living. Many have been taken by the bank because the mortgage payments were in default."

The two had fallen into step and continued toward the heart of town. Emmet studied the businesses. "Sharp's General Store. I remember them. There was a girl many grades below me...can't remember her name."

"Joanie?"

"That's the one. I don't suppose she's still around? She'd be what? About nineteen or twenty."

"She's still around. I'm guessing you used to live here."

Emmet explained how Auntie May was his guardian growing up. "I moved away nine years ago. Got married and have a little girl."

"Welcome back home."

Home. It had been once, but now? Truth be told, he didn't know where home was anymore. Rather than try to answer the comment, he asked the man about himself. "Gather you're a newcomer."

"Recent. I've been here about a year. Judd Kirk. I married a pretty young gal from this area, and we bought a farm near town. It's also near her home. Perhaps you know it—the Cotton place."

"Sure, I know it. There were a couple kids in school

with me. They're gone, you say?" They'd arrived at the general store and trod indoors.

"Yup. Left the place lock, stock and barrel, which was handy for me." Judd glanced around. "Why, here are my two sisters-in-law. Come and meet them." Already Judd strode toward the young women.

Emmet stared. Louisa. He didn't want to see her outside the hours she tutored Ellie. Anything more felt as if he'd crossed a mental barrier he erected around his life. But of course, in a town the size of Golden Prairie, they would naturally run into each other, unless he stayed within the boundaries of Auntie May's house and yard. He'd done that for four days and found it stifling. Still, perhaps he could excuse himself on the pretext of urgent business. But too late. Judd led the young women toward Emmet. "My sisters-in-law, Louisa and Sally Morgan."

"Louisa and I have already met. She's tutoring my daughter." Did he see the same flicker of regret over this meeting as he'd felt? The idea stung. Why should she want to avoid him? He shifted his gaze to the other girl, Sally, and greeted her.

Judd laughed. "It's a small world. Or should I say it's a small town."

Louisa gave Judd a quick smile.

"Sally and I are preparing to make cookies to take to the orphanage. We needed raisins."

"A tea party?" No mistaking the curious tone of Judd's voice.

"Why don't you pick up Madge and join us?" Sally offered.

This was obviously a family event. Emmet edged away.

Judd stopped him. "Why don't you come along too?"

"I can't."

"Bring your daughter. She'll enjoy it."

Sally groaned. "Judd, the reason Louisa is tutoring his daughter is because Ellie is bedridden in a body cast. She can't join us."

Judd grabbed Emmet's shoulder. "Right. That would be who I made the tripod for. Oh, man, I am so sorry. That's tough on a little girl."

"Thanks."

"Good thing you have Louisa to tutor her. Couldn't ask for anyone better."

"Judd." Louisa tried to stop her brother-in-law, but he ignored her.

"She knows what it's like to have to stay in bed. I admire how she's handled her illnesses so well. I think I'd want to moan and groan and feel sorry for myself. But not Louisa—"

Judd leaned close to Emmet and chuckled. "Don't be fooled by her looks. She's a fighter."

Emmet watched the pair of sisters gather up their small parcel and head for the door.

Sally whispered something to Louisa and hung back. Louisa grabbed her arm and pushed her forward. Louisa paused before they exited and gave Judd a demanding look. "You'll let Madge know right away so she can get ready?"

Judd laughed. "I'll get on it immediately." The look he gave Emmet burgeoned with amusement, and he lowered his voice to a whisper. "I better say goodbye or face the wrath of three sisters, because if one is offended they're all offended. Sure you can't come along? You know—to give me a little moral support?"

"Judd, are you coming?" Louisa's voice was sweet

and inviting, but Emmet saw the way Judd jerked to attention and guessed that beneath the gentleness lay solid, unyielding bedrock.

"Sorry, I can't leave my daughter." He liked the man and wished they could spend more time together. He missed company beyond Auntie May and Ellie. "Why don't you drop by when you get a chance?"

Judd gave him a considering look. "I just might do that. Right now I better go find my wife and tell her of her sisters' plans." He hurried after Sally and Louisa.

The store felt empty when the trio left. Emmet gave himself a mental kick. He was used to being alone, out in the open, riding the range, working with cows. Company—and companionship—was sporadic and fleeting. So why should it bother him to be left behind? He must be getting befuddled.

He crossed to the candy selection, chose a red-and-white peppermint stick, paid for it and left the store. Ellie would be awake soon, and the candy would brighten her afternoon.

But later, as he sat beside his daughter, watching her suck the peppermint stick, the rest of the day stretched before him, as endless as the vast horizon. The only break in sight was Louisa's return in the morning.

For Ellie's sake only. The hours must be even longer for her.

Chapter Four

Louisa stopped at the last corner before the Hamilton home. She wasn't eager to start the session with Ellie.

Rather than dwell on her doubts and fears, she thought of the few hours she and her sisters had spent at the orphanage. Louisa had dreaded the event but was determined not to let her sisters know. However, from the first rowdy greeting to the last goodbye, she'd enjoyed every minute. The children were happy to see them. Several acted as if they especially liked Louisa, which was heartwarming. One of the older girls brought her some drawings she'd done and listened eagerly as Louisa showed her how to add shading and correct perspective to her rather appealing work. Another child, a girl close to Ellie's age, brought a book and begged Louisa to read it to her.

"What grade are you in, Leila?" she'd asked.

"Grade one. I'm six."

Louisa asked her to read aloud from her reader. The child read eagerly and clearly. Ellie was in second grade and should read even better.

Perhaps today, Louisa would discover Ellie's reading level. She turned the corner and headed toward the house. At the front gate, she parked, gathered up determination and courage and shoved them into place, then stepped forth to face the battle. *God, guide me, bless me with Your wisdom.* She took the awkward parcel from the backseat.

Emmet opened the door as she approached. He sent a questioning look at the bundle in her arms but didn't ask about it.

At the way he seemed to assess her, Louisa's cheeks burned. Judd should not have told him about Louisa's illnesses. Three bouts of pneumonia. Influenza that hit her so hard. She'd asked Madge to remind him no one outside the family must hear of Louisa's barrenness. She didn't want to be the recipient of pitying looks.

"Good morning." She kept her voice cool. Professional. She wasn't a teacher, but she would act like one. Emmet was a parent of a student. Nothing more. "How is Ellie this morning?"

"Okay. And you?"

She faltered the slightest. Why did he ask? Did he think she might get ill at the least little thing? She tilted her chin. She had no intention of getting ill. "I'm fine, thank you. Eager to start my day." Eager might be a slight exaggeration. But she would show no fear, no regret, no desperation. God was at her side. *The Lord is my shepherd. He leadeth me beside still waters.* Would the waters be still or troubled today?

Emmet kept pace at her side as she crossed the front room. "I'm glad you understand that Ellie is finding it difficult to adjust to her situation. It's a relief to know you'll be patient with her."

Did she detect a warning in his voice? She stopped and faced him. "Mr. Hamilton—"

"Please, call me Emmet."

Did teachers call parents by their first name? Would doing so cross a line she didn't wish to cross? She needed to keep things impersonal between them. Not one step further than her feelings had already transgressed.

"As you please. I am being paid to teach your child." The school board had hired her with specific expectations…keep the child up to speed with her classmates. Only, her position depended as much on Emmet's approval as the school board's expectations. Emmet had the right to say yes or no to her being Ellie's tutor. "I'll do my best to help her keep up with her class work."

"I care less about Ellie's schoolwork than about her happiness."

What more could anyone ask of a parent? But life wasn't always that simple. "I hope I can achieve the one without sacrificing the other." But it would take Ellie's cooperation. Something she suspected that would not come without a battle.

"That's all I ask."

Louisa stepped into Ellie's room and read instant defiance in the child's eyes. She was trapped between what Emmet believed was possible and what Ellie clearly would not allow—Louisa teaching her.

She considered putting aside the role of teacher and simply amusing the child, but her agreement with the board was quite specific and she couldn't, in good conscience, pretend she fulfilled the terms without doing so. If she couldn't teach Ellie she must quit. And that was something she would not do. Not with those medical bills stacked up on Mother's desk.

Adele had given her more advice. "Make it clear that there is a certain amount of work to be done each day. Be matter-of-fact about it. Then do it."

"But what if she doesn't cooperate?"

"That's where discipline comes in. You might try providing rewards, incentives, if you like."

Louisa crossed to the little table where she arranged her lesson plans that she and Adele had drawn up together, the books she intended to use and the odd-shaped parcel.

"What's that?"

"It's for you. You can have it when you complete today's lesson." She picked up the chalk and wrote on the blackboard: "Reading, Arithmetic and History." "Three subjects. We won't spend long on each, but they all have an assignment that must be completed."

Ellie eyed the package, her curiosity obvious.

Good. Louisa had already tried reading and arithmetic without success, so she went for history. "Grade twos are studying the history of Alberta. Today we are going to talk about the establishment of the North-West Mounted Police." She loved the drama of the march west and had a picture book illustrating it. She began with explaining the need for a police force to settle the troubles in the West. She showed a picture of the colorful troop ready to set out—noble and hopeful, unaware of the challenges they would face.

But Ellie stared at the present as Louisa continued reading. If Ellie cared to look at the pictures, they were there before her. Adele had assured Louisa that Ellie would soon be drawn into the lessons.

Louisa came to the end of what she planned to read for the day.

"Now I want you to choose a project. You can either draw a picture about the march west or write a story. You can pretend to be one of the young police officers or—"

"What is that?" Her gaze hadn't shifted from the parcel.

"If you want to open it, you have to do your lessons." She placed a bed tray before Ellie, tilted so the child could write, and put a sheet of paper on it. "Do you wish to draw a picture or write a story?"

"Neither." The girl certainly knew how to put on a pout. "Daddy won't like that you're teasing me. He lets me have anything I want."

"That makes for mighty poor character." Adele had prepared a list of questions should Ellie balk at working on her own initiative. "Here are questions about the North-West Mounted Police. You can do them." There were five very simple questions.

"I don't want to."

At least she wasn't insisting she didn't know or couldn't remember. Louisa wondered if this was progress. "If you want to see what's in the parcel, you must first do your work."

"No." Ellie swept the tray to the floor with a clattering racket. "Why are you being so mean to me? I don't have a mother, you know."

"Well, I don't have a father."

"You're a grown-up. You don't need a father."

"Even grown-ups need a father now and then." She picked up the tray and rescued the paper and pencil, replaced them on the bed and tapped the page. "Please answer these questions."

"I don't want to, and I generally do as I please."

Louisa sighed. "There's a name for children like that."

Ellie scowled. "What?"

Should she tell her? "Spoiled."

Ellie screeched and tried to push the tray off the bed again. But Louisa held it firmly in place. "Let's get this done so we can move on. We still have reading and arithmetic to do this morning."

Ellie screamed louder.

Emmet strode into the room. "What's going on here?"

Ellie sobbed and reached for Emmet. "She's being mean to me."

Emmet wrapped his arms about the child's trembling shoulders. "Hush now. You're okay. Daddy's here." His voice was warm and gentle, but the look he gave Louisa accused her of senseless cruelty.

Louisa sighed. She couldn't fight them both. But she wasn't about to admit defeat. She stiffened her spine and thought about how to deal with this.

Ellie snuggled into her father's shoulder and lifted her eyes to Louisa. There was no mistaking the glint of triumph.

Emmet extracted himself from his daughter's arms and faced Louisa, but she spoke before he could.

"We need to talk. I'll wait for you in the front room." Her stride was far steadier than her insides. She crossed the kitchen. Auntie May sat at the table with four cats on her lap and one draped over her shoulders.

"You're never beat until you quit," she murmured.

Louisa flashed a trembling smile. Exactly the words she needed to hear. She wasn't about to quit. Nor admit defeat.

Emmet backed out of Ellie's room, assuring his daughter he would be back in a few minutes, then he gave Louisa a curt nod and strode into the front room.

Louisa followed, and although she felt like being meek and apologetic, she kept her head high and her step firm.

"Miss Morgan, I fear you are most unsuited for this job." His eyes flashed with anger.

An answering flash burned her eyes. "I consider Miss Ross to be a fine teacher, with all the skill that experience and study can give."

"We aren't talking about Miss Ross."

"Indeed, we are. She recommended me for this job. She supervises the lessons. She also gives advice as to how to deal with a child who doesn't welcome having to keep up with her studies. I suggest if you have a problem with my methods, you consult her."

He looked askance. "I have no quarrel with Miss Ross. I'm sure she's a fine teacher."

"One of the best. We are fortunate to have her."

"That might well be the case, but she isn't the one in Ellie's room making her cry."

Louisa refrained from pointing out the tears were for Emmet's benefit to elicit his sympathy. And they worked very well. "Before you decide to dismiss me, you should consider I am the only one available to do this job, unless you intend to scoop up one of those hobos down by the tracks."

Emmet looked as if she'd suggested dipping his child in mud.

"I thought not. Then why don't we consult Miss Ross and get her help in sorting this out?"

"Sounds like a fine idea. After school today?"

"She's already expecting me." They had arranged to meet almost every day to discuss lessons. "I don't believe there is any point in me trying to continue this morning."

Louisa returned to the bedroom and gathered her things—including the wrapped gift—then paused to say goodbye to Ellie, not caring at all at the pleased look on the child's face. This wasn't over yet.

She could only hope Emmet would realize that if he let Ellie win this battle, she would be the loser, not the victor.

Later that afternoon, Louisa waited outside the classroom for Emmet. She'd arrived a few minutes before, but it didn't seem fair to go in without him. He might wonder if she was seeking to get Adele on her side. It had been tempting to do so, but in the intervening hours since she'd marched out of the Hamilton house, her resolve had grown. She would not fail.

Emmet approached, his strides firm, his jaw squared even more than she'd noticed before. He was a man determined to do what was best for his daughter.

Louisa mentally drew herself to rigid attention, as if readying for duel. How silly. A giggle tickled the back of her throat, but she wisely restrained it. They weren't adversaries. They both wanted the same thing—what was best for Ellie. Only problem was they obviously considered that to be two different things.

Her amusement died as quickly as it had come, and the prayer she had whispered all afternoon filled her thoughts. *Lord, show us a way of compromise that will enable me to teach Ellie.*

"I'm ready." Emmet paused at her side and indicated she should lead the way.

She proceeded down the hall to the room where Adele waited for her. They passed a closed door. "Before the Depression and drought drove so many people from the land, this room held the older grades. Now even the desks in one room aren't full, and there are no students above grade five." Why did she explain this to Emmet? He had attended classes here when he was younger, when both rooms held children. "I feel badly that many children will be deprived of an education because of their family circumstances." She had never before felt the need to fill silences with idle chatter.

"You hold learning in high regard, don't you?"

She cast a sideways glance at him. Was he mocking her? No, he looked serious. "I believe there is much value in learning."

"Reading, writing and arithmetic are handy skills."

"So are art, music, languages, history and so much more. The more we know about our world, the better equipped we are to live successfully in it. But learning also teaches us to think past the obvious, past our own experiences."

He chuckled softly, puckering the edges of her resistance to him. "I always thought experience was the best teacher."

"It is sometimes a cruel teacher."

They considered each other. She saw in his eyes a dark familiarity with the sort of pain she meant, and she understood something as clearly as if he had written it in bold letters across his forehead. He'd lost much and now protected Ellie, perhaps even indulged her, because she was all he had left, and he feared losing her.

Instinctively she touched his arm, signaling she understood. "There is no substitute for experience, but I believe a solid education can equip us to deal with life. Of course, our best help in life is to trust God. He promises to guide us through."

Emmet could have been frozen stiff, for all the indication he gave that he heard her or was aware of her touch. Yet she didn't withdraw her hand. She felt his troubled soul through her palm and wanted to soothe it. "You do believe in God's love and care, don't you?"

He shuddered. "I think I do. I like to think God brought me back to Golden Prairie for a reason, but I think He could have found a better way to do it than through Ellie's accident." By the time he finished, his voice grew harsh, uncertain. He shook his head. "I struggle to trust God when things are hard."

She crossed her arms about her waist, pressing tight, her palm still warm from where it had touched him. "I suppose that's what it means in Second Corinthians five, verse seven, when it says, 'We walk by faith, not by sight.' When we can't see why things are the way they are, we choose to trust God anyway."

"It's that easy, is it?"

She smiled widely. "No, it's that hard—but I prefer to trust God rather than my own assessment of the situation." It had been a struggle to come to the place of trusting God in her barrenness, but she had to believe He had something else in store for her—something that would bring her satisfaction.

Adele must have heard them outside her door as she swung it open. "Mr. Hamilton, Louisa. I didn't expect the two of you. Do come in." She glanced from one to the other. "Is there a problem?"

Emmet spoke before Louisa could answer, but it didn't matter. They'd come with a common purpose. "We agreed to seek your advice in Ellie's lessons."

"Very well." Adele waved them toward the front row of desks as she sat behind the big teacher's desk.

Louisa had no problem slipping into hers, but Emmet had to wedge into a desk designed for young children, not broad-chested men. Louisa ducked her head to hide her amusement and shifted her gaze toward Adele.

Adele Ross had become a friend when she learned of the collection of books Louisa had and begged to borrow a few. The woman pulled her hair into a severe knot at the back of her head, as if to prove her serious state of mind, as suited a teacher of young children. But Louisa knew she had the kindest heart and a long store of patience to accompany her cheery attitude. They had never discussed their respective ages, but Adele was probably nearing thirty. Closer to Emmet's age than Louisa's. She hadn't thought of that before and tried to assess if either of them showed a flicker of interest in the other. When she detected none, she relaxed. Though why she should be relieved made no sense. Emmet and Adele would make a good couple. Except it would mean Adele would have to give up her teaching position. Although some school boards now allowed married teachers, this one did not.

Adele looked at Louisa. "Perhaps you'd better explain."

Glad to be brought back from the useless side trail her thoughts had started down, Louisa nodded. "I have been unable to get Ellie interested in the lessons and Emmet—Mr. Hamilton—feels I am not suited for the job."

Adele blinked in surprise, then did her best to hide it. She turned to Emmet. "Is that correct, Mr. Hamilton?"

"Ellie is unhappy with Miss Morgan's lesson presentation. I thought you could suggest someone else. Someone who could get Ellie's cooperation without upsetting her."

Adele nodded slowly and considered his request several seconds before she replied. "I can think of no one I would consider more suitable than Louisa."

Louisa smiled her thanks and gave Emmet a pleased look. She'd told him much the same, but it was gratifying to have Adele verify it.

Adele leaned forward, her hands clasped together, and addressed Emmet. "Why do you think Ellie is upset about the lessons?"

Emmet shot Louisa a look that reminded her of his daughter—full of defiance. "She says Louisa is mean to her."

"I see. Precisely what does Louisa do that would fall into that category?"

Emmet opened and closed his mouth, then blinked twice. "I don't know exactly. But several times I have come into the room in response to Ellie's cries." He glared at Louisa. "You must be doing something."

Before Louisa could defend herself, Adele spoke. "I have been a teacher for a number of years and I know how serious a charge such as this is. But I need something more solid than the cries of your daughter."

Louisa tried to protest, but Adele lifted a hand to signal silence. Was Adele taking Emmet's side? Just because he was the parent? Adele smiled, taking the sting from her actions. "You'll get a chance to speak, but I must get to the bottom of this."

Louisa sat back and fumed. There was no bottom. No top. No sides. Because she'd never been mean. Not once.

"Now, Mr. Hamilton, please explain. Did you see Louisa strike your child?" She waited for Emmet's answer. "No. Did Ellie accuse her of doing so?" Another pause in which Emmet could only shake his head. "No.

Call her cruel names? No. Does she expect Ellie to do more work than she is capable of in her circumstances?"

Emmet shrugged.

Adele pressed him. "How much work has she done?"

"I've seen none."

"You've seen nothing that could be constituted as cruelty. And you've seen no work. Is that correct?"

Emmet refused to answer. "I've seen Ellie cry. Heard her accusations."

"I'm not discrediting that. But let's hear Louisa's explanation, shall we?"

Emmet sighed. His look said he'd like to see her get out of this.

"We have planned the lessons together. Nothing a grade-two student shouldn't be able to do. In fact, many of my grade-one students could do the work." Adele turned her gray-eyed gaze to Louisa. "How far have you come with the lessons?"

Louisa hung her head, a sense of complete failure swamping her. "I've accomplished nothing."

"And why is that?"

She shared her concerns with Adele, but hated to admit she had only failure to report. "I have been unable to gain Ellie's cooperation."

"Can you explain what you mean by that?"

Louisa brought her head up and spoke directly to Emmet, ignoring his defensive expression that indicated if there was a problem, it was not Ellie's fault. It couldn't be. "I am not a teacher, but I have a very good guide. I've followed her suggestions. She said to win the child. She said to give her time to accept the idea. I tried. Then she said Ellie must understand she has to continue her lessons. Again, I tried, but no matter what I do, Ellie says she doesn't know, doesn't remember or flatly refuses to do any of the work. When I read she does her best to ignore me. I even brought a present as an incentive, as Adele suggested. That brought on an outburst because I refused to give her the present until she did her work." She waved her hands in frustration. "I value learning. I know what it's like to fall behind. I want to help Ellie, but she won't let me." She hated to admit failure, but she couldn't continue to insist on being Ellie's tutor when Ellie resisted her. "Perhaps you're right. Ellie is falling behind because I can't reach her."

Adele held her palms toward them. "Let's not be hasty. Frankly, not only is Louisa the best person for this job, but she's the only person remotely qualified. We'd have to advertise across the province to find someone else, and let's be reasonable. How many applicants would we get for a two-month job that's only four hours a day?"

"Probably lots of unemployed teachers looking for work," Emmet muttered.

"I expect that's so. But I would think you'd want references. All that takes time." Adele let her comments hang in the air. "Emmet, what do you want for Ellie?"

"That's easy. I want her to be happy."

"Right. Is she happy with things the way they are?"

"I suppose not. She's restless, wishing she didn't have to be confined to bed in a body cast."

"So perhaps school lessons might prove a welcome distraction?"

"I had hoped so."

"Good." She turned to Louisa. "What do you want here?"

"To do the job I was hired to do. To help Ellie keep up."

"Why?"

Adele's question opened a whole vista of truth to Louisa. It was more than the money. She'd always felt a spectator on life. Never very useful. This was her chance to prove to her mother and sisters…and herself…that she could do something, make a difference. "I believe I can do this. I can help Ellie. I want to because I know how difficult it is to fall behind your classmates, to struggle to catch up and keep up. And because I firmly believe learning can and should be fun."

Adele's eyes gleamed with pleasure at Louisa's confession. "Mr. Hamilton, do you have any objections to Louisa's goals for your daughter?"

Louisa and Emmet studied each other. Wary adversaries? Or something more? Something that went beyond teaching, beyond Ellie's needs. She sensed in him a deep hurt that echoed her own. Of course he had pain—he'd lost his wife, and before that his parents, and now his child was injured. Perhaps by helping Ellie, she could help him. Ease some of his concerns. She'd told God she would serve Him in whatever job He provided. This was a job. Nothing more.

But she could not deny she hadn't expected a job to dig deep into her heart and open up longings she knew she must deny. Somewhere in the past two days, despite Ellie's cantankerous ways, Louisa had crossed a line. She'd begun to care about the Hamiltons. She wanted to help Ellie because she cared. She wanted to help Ellie because it mattered to her that Emmet, although he loved his daughter deeply, was allowing her to rule his life.

Adele broke into her thoughts, still addressing Emmet. "Do these goals contradict yours in any way?"

"I suppose not." His gaze held Louisa's, searching for what, she did not know. But she let him probe deep past the surface of their words and association until she felt as if his thoughts had reached deep into hers, found an anchor pin and secured a hook to it.

"Perhaps there is another way to address the problem. A compromise?"

Louisa forced her gaze toward Adele. Would it include her keeping the job? She darted a glance at Emmet. Did he look even vaguely interested?

He caught her looking and shrugged. "What do we have to lose?"

She turned back to Adele. "What do you suggest?"

"I think you two should become partners in this venture."

"Partners?" Louisa and Emmet echoed the word in unison. How could they possibly work together? Even being here and discussing Ellie's need had opened a window in Louisa's heart, revealed a hunger she must deny. She looked it squarely in the face. Yes, she longed to earn the love of a man such as Emmet—strong, committed, loving—but her barrenness made it impossible. Even if he knew…even if he said it didn't matter. It would be unfair to burden a man with the same limitations she must accept.

Her best plan would be to avoid him as much as possible. Whatever Adele meant by partnership, Louisa hoped it meant a simple shake of hands in shared concern.

Adele took their silence for agreement. "I think Ellie is feeling you two are in opposition. Either it threatens her, or she's taking advantage of it. Perhaps even both. I think by presenting a unified front, she will realize she has no alternative but to do the assigned work. She'll soon learn that lesson time can be fun and help her pass the long days. I have laid out the lesson plans and will continue to do so. I suggest the two of you work out how to deliver them. You're welcome to use any of the material I have." She waved a hand to indicate the books and objects in the shelves around the room.

Work together. Plan together. Louisa choked back a protest. How was she to stay professional when every time she turned around, she encountered feelings that were decidedly not professional? And now to consider spending more time in his presence…how was she ever going to keep her feelings locked away?

Chapter Five

Emmet pried himself from the too-small desk and followed Louisa out of the classroom. With a murmured goodbye and thank-you to Miss Ross, he closed the door and sucked air into lungs too stunned this past half hour to function properly.

Partners? Work together? A unified front? Shoot. He didn't want to be united with Louisa on anything. Just sitting next to her in the classroom, feeling her fragile resistance—he was wrong on that score too. She was about as fragile as the first spring crocus that fought its way up through the snow and waved its head cheerfully through the winds and storms of the season. What had possessed him to agree?

One thing only. And it was all that mattered. It was best for Ellie.

Louisa too, appeared to need time to pull herself together after Miss Ross's surprise suggestion.

He'd been awed by Louisa's passion that Ellie keep up with her classmates. And more than a little moved by it. If he were honest, he'd felt just a tiny bit guilty that he was concerned solely with her happiness. For a fleeting moment, it seemed almost irresponsible.

But he had his head back where it belonged after the brief period of confusion. Squarely on his shoulders. He would not let anything Louisa said or did confound him again. "Looks like we're stuck working together." He excused the roughness of his words and his voice on the need to keep boundaries firmly in place. He wanted only one thing from Louisa—help teaching Ellie, because he now realized how important it was for her to keep up with her studies. "So let's figure out a way to make this work." He headed for the outside door, Louisa at his side.

"How do you suggest we do that?"

"I suppose we need to plan our approach, as Miss Ross suggested." But when and where? "I don't like leaving Auntie May to watch Ellie too long." Ellie clearly didn't appreciate it either, but he refrained from saying so, still feeling as if he was somehow lax in wanting to keep her happy. "It's too big a chore. Besides, Auntie May has enough to do."

"What with feeding her cats and all." Her dry tone informed him that Louisa teased, and he chuckled. His tension dissipated in his amusement.

"I fear she will fall over one of them and injure herself." He'd meant to be teasing too, but realized it was a deep-seated worry. He didn't care to lose any more of his family due to an accident.

"I don't think you need to fear for her safety. She seems to know how to avoid them when she's walking. You know, I've always admired how sure-footed she was."

"Comes from dancing around cats. Keeps her nimble." He did a little side jump to illustrate, bringing a merry laugh to Louisa's lips. He tucked a smile into the corner of his mind, pleased to have amused her.

Shoot. How did he get so far off track? If this was a sample of how it would be to work with her, it did not bode well for keeping it businesslike. And yet, somehow, he couldn't honestly object. But back to the task at hand. "If we wait until after Ellie goes to sleep..." Then what? Auntie May liked to curl up with her cats and a book in the evening. He didn't want to take advantage of his aunt by asking that she be alert to Ellie's call.

"I could come back into town later. I'm sure it won't take long to deal with this."

In fact, they might be able to stand on the step and sort it out in a matter of minutes before she left. Yet somehow he didn't suggest it. "If you don't mind. That way I could be available without expecting Auntie May to cover for me."

"I don't mind. Like I say, I'm sure it will only be a short while. Then I can visit a friend."

"Good." They stood before her battered car. "I'll see you later then." He planted his hat on his head, nodded goodbye and strolled away. Not until he heard her car start and breathed in the gas fumes and dust of her departure did he wonder if spending more time with Louisa was a wise idea. But it was too late to change his mind, and because it was for Ellie he had no intention of doing so.

Emmet explained to Auntie May that Louisa would be coming because they were going to work on Ellie's lessons together.

"Excellent idea, my boy. You'll soon discover what a

fine woman she is. You know, you could do worse than think about asking her—"

He cut her off right there, knowing she was about to suggest he ask Louisa out. "I have no interest in such things. Not now. Not ever."

She looked at him, her face awash with concern. "Emmet, you are a young man. You can't carry your hurt like a shield all your life."

He intended to do exactly that, though it was caution he carried, not hurt. He was long past hurt. "My life is busy enough with the ranch and a child to raise."

"Troubles shared are troubles halved."

"We'll use the front room so as not to disturb Ellie, if that's okay with you."

She studied him, letting him know she understood he ignored her suggestion of sharing troubles. "I prefer the rocking chair in the kitchen, as you are well aware. Does Ellie know about your new plan?"

Ellie slept in the next room, exhausted by another crying spell. She missed her pony. Her friends. Even Betsy. "I haven't said anything." Seems the least little thing set her into a bout of tears. Hopefully she wasn't going to end up like her mother. Jane had resorted to tears to get her own way so often that Emmet had learned to ignore them. Or had tried to, but they never failed to make him feel guilty.

"It's something Louisa and I will plan together."

A gentle knock sounded at the door.

"I expect that is her now."

"'Spect so. You better let her in. And don't worry about me. The cats and I will be quite happy in the kitchen." She sat in a rocking chair so well used that the rockers had a ridge where she changed direction. "Run along now." She shooed him away.

He crossed the room and opened the door. The sun had settled toward the horizon and slanted rays into his eyes, so he didn't see her face clearly. For some unfathomable reason, that bothered him. He wanted to see her expression, know what she really thought about this arrangement. Perhaps if he did, he could understand how he felt. Because this did not feel like business. It felt like a social call. He had struggled the past hour to try to drive that thought away, but it refused to leave.

"Come in. Have a seat." He waved toward a little table he'd cleared off and against which he had shoved two chairs, assuming she would want to show him material.

"Thanks." She sat and waited for him to sit opposite her, then she opened a notebook. "These are the lesson plans Adele helped me prepare." She pointed to the outlined notes. "As you can see, we aren't aiming to do more than basics. Her assignments have also been adjusted so she can do them without too much effort. We realize it's difficult for her to do much while flat on her back."

He glanced over the material. "These seem fairly straightforward."

"You're still thinking I'm the problem here." She sucked in air. "You might be right. I get the feeling she resents my presence. Perhaps by having you in the room and presenting part of the lesson, she can see I only want to help her."

"I agreed to do so. I'm just uncertain of my role. What do you want me to do?"

"I guess it depends on what you want."

"What I want has nothing to do with lessons. I want

her to not be injured in the first place. I want—" *I want her mother to still be alive. I want my parents to be alive.*

"I'm sorry. It can't be easy raising a child on your own."

"It has its challenges for sure, but I wouldn't trade it for anything. My only regret is not having more children." He leaned forward. "I envy you your sisters. I longed for brothers or sisters when I was growing up. And when I married, I vowed I would not have an only child. But life did not follow my plan."

Louisa kept her head downturned. "Nor did mine," she murmured.

The pain in her voice seared his heart. He knew such pain. "What happened?"

She lifted her head. Her expression silently wept. His breath caught in the back of his throat at such raw pain. She drew a shuddering breath and then smiled, driving away the darkness, replacing it with sunshine as bright as what he'd faced when he opened the door. "We all have troubles, but I've learned that when we need God most, He is the closest. Knowing how much He cares for me is a gift beyond measure."

He wanted to know the size and shape and extent of her troubles. Wanted to take them from her. Just as he longed to take every trouble falling into Ellie's life and carry it himself.

She turned her attention back to the papers before them. "I've prepared the history lesson so I can teach that. The arithmetic is straightforward. You could teach it if you like. Reading…well let's work together on that."

He pushed his thoughts back to the task at hand—the only thing that mattered—getting Ellie to do her schoolwork. Soon they had settled the lessons. The evening ahead stretched long and empty. He ached for someone to talk to. Sure, he had Auntie May and Ellie, but that wasn't what he meant.

"Would you like to go for a little walk before you leave? Watch the sunset?"

She tucked the lesson material into her satchel without answering.

Obviously she expected their relationship to be based solely on the task at hand. As did he. He shouldn't have asked. But how could he withdraw the offer now without sounding rude?

Before he could think of a way, she turned her face upward and smiled, sending rays of golden light into his heart.

"I think that would be nice."

The woman had a beautiful smile. He couldn't imagine why she didn't have a dozen young men at her beck and call. Except most young men were struggling to keep body and boots together.

Emmet pretended he wasn't relieved it was too late to change his mind. He told Auntie May his plans, ignoring her triumphant grin. They left the house, paused as Louisa put her satchel in the car, then turned their steps away from the heart of town. "I used to play scrub ball in that lot." He pointed to the empty bit of land. "Can't imagine I was once so carefree. Seems like a lifetime ago."

"Tell me about your ranch."

He gratefully accepted her attempt to pull the conversation to safer channels. "It's small. Tucked away in the foothills to the west. The land is beautiful. You can see the mountains simply by lifting your head and looking."

She sighed. "I'd love to see them up close. I've had glimpses when we went to Calgary. That's all."

"They're a sight to behold, that's for sure."

"I suppose you're anxious to get back there."

He considered the question. "Seems I should be, but I'm not."

She stopped to study him.

He grinned but knew it was crooked and uncertain. "I guess I can't think of the place without associating it with bad things."

She nodded, her eyes brimming with sympathy. "Your wife died out there."

He couldn't maintain even a shaky smile.

"I'm sorry." She touched his arm, then withdrew her hand. But just as when she'd pressed her palm to his arm in the hallway of the school, a feeling of comfort raced through his heart. How did she do that? Give a healing balm simply with a touch? "She didn't die at the ranch, for which I am grateful. We were in town buying supplies, and a team was frightened by a strange dog barking at their heels. They bolted. Before anyone could stop them, they ran over Jane."

She shuddered. "How dreadful. Where was Ellie?"

"I had her in my arms. I pressed her face to my shoulder so she couldn't see." He'd protected her then. He'd protect her now.

"How old was Ellie?"

"Four."

"And you've managed on your own since?"

"I had an older woman as a housekeeper for almost two years, but her daughter needed her so she left. Then I got Betsy, a neighbor. She came after school and stayed until I was back for supper. But I discovered she spent as much time elsewhere as she did with Ellie. That's how Ellie came to be alone when she broke her leg."

"Poor Ellie. She must have been very frightened."

"Indeed." He didn't want to think about it. Or talk about it. If something happened to Ellie… He shifted back to a safer topic. "The town has gone downhill since I left. So many places vacant."

"I know. It's sad." She sighed, and he felt guilty at having brought up nothing but depressing topics.

"What do people do for fun around here? Sorry, I didn't mean that to sound critical. I'm just wondering."

She chuckled softly. A man could grow to appreciate amusing her.

"I enjoy weeding the garden."

That was her idea of fun?

She giggled. "Guess that's not what you meant."

He glanced at her then. He'd admired her beauty before, assessed it as more than skin-deep, but at the way happiness and joy bubbled from her sparkling eyes, he almost tripped. A man could forget all his carefully constructed fences, find them blown over and useless in the face of such deep-rooted beauty. "I can't believe it's your idea of fun." His voice deepened, revealing just how much he'd been touched. Hopefully she would assume it was only because he teased her.

"No, really, I consider it a blessing to be able to do physical work. There was a time I couldn't. A person learns to appreciate ordinary things when they've been deprived of them."

"I know you were ill enough to be confined to bed. What was wrong?"

"Pneumonia. Three winters in a row. Seems my lungs never got completely better before the next winter would start it all over." The joy in her eyes abated, as if the memory of those days hurt.

He cupped her shoulder, wanting to share her sorrow as she had shared his. He wanted to restore the bubbling happiness. "You're better now though?" She seemed fragile in appearance, but he had discovered she was actually about as fragile as steel. He didn't want to think her health was precarious.

She laughed. "I'm better. Ready to tackle life and enjoy it to the fullest. No more sitting on the sidelines idly watching. Which is why even weeding the garden is pleasant."

"But seriously, what do you do for pure enjoyment?" He wanted to know, though why he should care... He wasn't about to examine his reasons, and declared his question to be an attempt at pleasant conversation.

"I bake—"

"Like the cookies you took to the orphanage?"

"Yes. We took oatmeal raisin and also molasses cookies because they are our favorites. They were Father's favorites." Her expression filled with sadness. He wanted to bring back the sunshine.

"How did the visit to the orphanage go?"

"Good." She told him about the children. "They appreciate the least little kindness. Poor little waifs."

"Okay, you weed the garden and bake cookies. What else?"

"I read. I draw. I sang in the church choir for Easter. I generally keep busy. But maybe you mean what is there for a single man to do in the community." They walked along a dusty trail that paralleled the railway tracks. She slowed and considered him. "Are you looking for a way to meet young ladies?"

Heaven forbid. He never wanted to marry again. But

he wanted to see her reaction if he suggested otherwise. "Are there lots of young ladies around?"

She ducked her head, but not before he thought he caught a flash of disapproval—or was it disappointment? Was she even faintly interested in him as a man?

"Of course, I've already met three charming young ladies."

Her head jerked up, and she considered him with wide-eyed surprise. "You have?"

It pleased him to no end to see her interest. "Miss Ross seems like a good person."

"Yes, of course she is."

"Then there are those two young ladies I met in the store."

Her eyebrows shot up in silent question.

"You know. Miss Sally Morgan and her very charming sister, Louisa." He laughed at the confusion in her face and admired the way her cheeks bloomed pink.

"Oh, you're teasing me."

He was more than half-serious, but why was he enjoying teasing her? Their relationship was to be nothing more than business, even though they were partners now. He liked the idea more and more.

She continued down the trail, every step raising a puff of dirt. "Look." Her voice filled with wonder.

He'd forgotten they were supposed to be admiring the sunset and followed her gaze to the west.

They stood side by side and watched colors shift from pink to orange to deep red. Gold tinted the scattered, empty clouds.

She sighed. "Times like this I wish I could really paint, instead of just puttering." She continued to stare at the sky.

He angled sideways so he could watch her expression as much as he watched the sky. A chain of emotions crossed her face. Awe, a restlessness he supposed came from a desire to be able to paint, a look of determination—he wanted to ask what it meant—and then peace swept over her face so completely that he ached inside. Why couldn't he feel the same peace?

"I have only to look about to see the hand of God in the sky, the trees and the flowers. 'The heavens declare the glory of God; and the firmament showeth his handiwork.'"

"The nineteenth Psalm. I memorized it in Sunday school. I learned a hundred verses and won a Bible." He still had it, tucked away in his things. It had been a long time since he'd opened it. To his shame.

"My father had us memorize verses. He also taught us to read our Bible every night. I promised him I would make a habit of it, so I try not to miss a night."

"Seems your father was a good man."

"Yes, he was." She shifted to look at him more closely. "I'm sorry you lost your father so early. Like I told Ellie the other day, we all need a father."

"He was a brave man. Wasn't a thing that could stop him if he decided to do something." Except he had been stopped. "Of course, we all discover sooner or later that there are things we can't change, can't move, can't correct."

"Too true." She stared again at the sky, her expression clouded. Then she smiled, and that incredible look of peace returned. "But nothing is too hard for God. Where He leads, He makes a way. All I have to do is trust and obey." Softly she sang the hymn.

He couldn't stop watching her, his heart pounding

against his rib cage in hungry insistence. He'd forgotten how sweet it was to trust. "It's hard to trust when things go so wrong."

"The hymn 'Trust and Obey' was written for D. L. Moody to use in his preaching. He once said, 'The Word of God alone makes us sure. Obedience to God makes us happy.' If we want to be happy, sure and safe, seems we have to turn things over to God and let Him take care of them. He has promised to meet our every need."

Did he detect a catch in her words? "Don't you struggle to believe that?"

"Every day. But I constantly choose to trust and obey to the best of my ability. Of course, I fail badly and often, but that's my human frailness."

He laughed. "I'm beginning to think you are anything but frail."

She tilted her head and considered him. "Why do you say that?"

"Because I've seen you in action. Once you take up a cause, I think you will fight for it until the end."

She grinned. "I do believe you're right. Sally says it's because I had to fight to get well."

"It's made you—*tough* isn't the right word." He tapped his finger against his chin. "Steel disguised as china."

Her mouth dropped open. Her eyes grew dark. And she stared.

"Don't look so surprised."

"But I am. And I'm trying to decide if I'm flattered or not."

"It's not an idle compliment. It's simply an observation."

They turned back toward town.

"I will try and live up to your evaluation of me." She lifted her chin and squared her shoulders.

"It wasn't meant as a challenge, you know. You aren't going to do something foolish, are you?" He'd seen how stubborn foolishness could lead to disaster. He'd seen the runaway wagon coming. Called Jane. Warned her to get out of the road. But Jane waved away his warning. She had her mind set on getting something from their own wagon and would not move until she was done. Jane was like that. "I don't want my words to influence you to take silly chances."

She grinned. "Emmet, I value my life and my health too much to do anything to jeopardize it. However, there are other challenges I can face that don't carry any risk."

He caught her by the shoulder. "Are you talking about Ellie? Because if you think this is a battle you must win—"

She shook her head and patted his shoulder. "Emmet, I am far more interested in winning her favor and helping her than I am in proving I am more stubborn." She grinned. "Though I probably am. But I like to think I am wise enough to pick my battles." She sucked in air as if readying herself to face a challenge. "No, the battle I am prepared to win is one with myself."

She marched onward.

He stared after her.

She called over her shoulder. "Aren't you coming?"

He rushed to catch up. "You can be very unsettling at times. Just when I think we understand each other, you shift gears."

Her chuckle rang out. "Don't worry about it, Emmet.

It doesn't concern you. We have a job to do—get Ellie to learn her lessons."

Emmet faced straight ahead and wished they hadn't gone so far from town. She might as well have slapped him in the face and stomped on his toe, her message was so clear. Her only interest in Emmet was teaching his daughter.

Well, wasn't that all he wanted too?

Of course it was. He'd let the warm air and the nice sunset sidetrack his thoughts only momentarily. He ought to thank her for her timely reminder. Instead he pointed toward a robin singing on the branch of a thin poplar tree.

She paused to listen. "You ever notice how birds sing no matter what their circumstances? If it's windy, they hang on and sing. If it's hot, they chirp more merrily. If it rains—and don't we wish it would?—they ignore it and sing anyway. I think God created them as a lesson for us."

"Sing anyway?"

"Yes. Don't you think that's a good plan?" She smiled at him, oblivious to the fact he had pulled his emotions back behind bars, where they belonged.

"I guess it's a good idea. But for me, I have an even better one—take care of Ellie no matter what."

She studied him. "I think you can do both at the same time. And what better thing to teach Ellie? Sing anyway."

They reached town where, in front of three houses, the residents sat on their porches. They called a greeting, and Emmet and Louisa returned with their own.

Then they made their way back home and stood by

Louisa's car. "Thanks for coming," Emmet said. It had been an interesting evening.

"Thanks for the walk. It was nice." She climbed into the car and, ignoring the banging and coughing, waved goodbye. "See you in the morning."

He watched until the cloud of dust blocked her from view. "Tomorrow," he whispered. "When we make learning fun for Ellie."

Ellie. She was his only concern.

Then why, as he prepared for bed, were the things Louisa said filling his thoughts? Along with the way her face had glowed with serenity. But of course, it was easy for her to be content with life. She'd overcome her illnesses and was now as healthy as anyone. No wonder she could sing so readily.

Life was not so simple for him.

But he dug through his belongings and found his award Bible. He had neglected it far too long. Had let his faith grow dim. It was time to look for the peace Louisa revealed.

Chapter Six

Louisa banged her hand against the steering wheel. She shouldn't have agreed to go out walking with Emmet. But it seemed he was as lonely as she. Then she had asked personal questions. Given personal information. "Professional," she muttered. "A job." But every minute spent anywhere near him made her acutely aware of emptiness in her heart that ached for—

"Enough." She could have none of the things she ached for. "Sing anyway." Silly thing to say. No wonder he looked as if she'd gone crazy. But she'd only wanted him to understand the peace and contentment that was found in trusting God despite difficult things. He could experience it too if he chose. And even more important—she determinedly pulled her thoughts back to the only thing that mattered…helping Ellie. Emmet could teach her to be happy in her present circumstances. A lesson that would be invaluable as she grew older.

Mother waited for her. Beyond her, Sally roamed about the kitchen.

"Sorry I'm so late."

"I don't like you going out in the evening. You must take care of yourself." Mother's face twisted with concern.

Louisa hugged her mother. "I didn't do anything that would cause me a problem." Though she'd come perilously close to letting her heart consider Emmet as more than the parent of a child she was tutoring.

Sally waited until Mother went to her room. "Were you planning lessons all this time?"

"We went for a walk."

Sally squealed. "I'm so glad to hear that."

"No reason you should be."

"I like to think my big sister is finally allowing herself to look at a man in that way." She batted her eyelashes and looked dreamy.

"I am not. I cannot. I will not."

"Oh, Louisa, there's absolutely no reason you can't."

"Sally, it would not be fair."

"Not all men want—"

"Emmet has already said he regrets not having more children. Says he hated being an only child growing up." She didn't say anything more. She admired him for his devoted love to Ellie, reminding her as it did of her father. But her only association with him would be as Ellie's tutor. She must guard her heart. Otherwise...

But as she lay on her bed, recounting the little walk and the things he said, she recalled he asked what there was to do. Poor man. He must feel housebound. Someone should invite him out. Seems he could leave Ellie with Auntie May in the evenings after she'd gone to sleep.

Perhaps the Morgan girls could do something. She'd noticed that Judd and Emmet were already acquainted. She'd talk to Madge and see what—

Stop. It was not her responsibility to plan a social life

for him. Her job was to be his child's tutor. She'd do well to brand that on a slab of wood and nail it across her wayward thoughts.

The next morning Louisa had her resolve firmly in place as she stepped into the Hamilton home. She tucked the satchel under her arm and held it tight to her body. The sound of Emmet's voice came from Ellie's room, and Louisa headed across the floor.

Auntie May sat at the table mixing up a dreadful-looking concoction. Louisa tried not to look disturbed by the glutinous brown mixture.

Auntie May laughed. "It's for old Stormy. She can't eat regular food anymore, poor thing. But she is so sweet and gentle, I don't mind fixing her something special. Yes, you are a regular sweetheart, you are." She crooned to the ragged black cat on her lap then grinned at Louisa. "Just an old woman with old friends. They're waiting for you." She tipped her head toward the doorway, and Louisa understood she meant Emmet and Ellie, not the friends of Louisa's future—old cats.

Louisa closed her eyes to shut out the sight of Auntie May, and vowed she would find some other way to fill the lonely hours of her life. She would not become reclusive and odd.

"You're just what that pair in there needs."

Louisa jerked her eyes open and stared at the older woman. "Me? What on earth do you mean?" She wasn't what any man needed, and it seemed she couldn't even tutor a child.

"They're stuck in a narrow place without realizing it. They need rescuing more than they know."

"I'm prepared to do my best to help Ellie with her

lessons." She didn't know if that was what Auntie May meant or not. Moreover, she didn't care to find out, so she hurried into Ellie's room.

Emmet stood at her entrance. He smiled. Her heart lifted in response, and her answering smile was so wide it stretched the skin of her cheeks. His eyes flashed pure blue. She knew that meant he was pleased. Pleased to see her? More likely, pleased to think of getting Ellie on track with her lessons. This was only a job for both of them. She knew that.

She shifted her gaze toward Ellie and caught a flash of defiance. The child was as unwelcoming as Emmet was welcoming. It promised to be another challenging day. Steel disguised as china, Emmet had said. She'd assured him she chose her battles carefully and vowed this would not be a battle zone.

"Good morning," she said. "Did you notice how loudly the birds are singing this morning?"

"Sing anyway?" Emmet's quiet voice reminded her of their conversation last night and reignited all the feelings she had firmly squelched. She battled them back into submission.

"Shall we begin?"

Emmet nodded, and as they had discussed, he spoke to Ellie. "El, I don't want you to fall behind in your schoolwork, so I'm going to assist Miss Morgan with your studies."

"How you gonna do that?"

"I'm going to help her teach."

"You're not a teacher. You're my dad." With each word, resistance grew clearer.

"Moms and dads help with homework, don't they?"

She nodded reluctantly.

"That's what I'm going to do. Help you."

"What about her?" Ellie clearly thought Louisa wasn't needed.

For a moment, Louisa thought the same thing. Emmet could do this on his own. But she'd been hired to do a job, and she would do it if at all possible.

Emmet chuckled. "I don't think I'd be a very good teacher on my own." The way he looked at Louisa—his eyes blue and smiling, his gaze shining with approval—threatened to destroy the locks on her heart.

She sucked in a steadying breath. "Your father and I are going to work together."

The look Ellie gave Louisa was far from welcoming, but it disappeared instantly as she favored her father with a wide smile. "I guess that means you're going to stay here."

"For now."

Louisa caught the tiny note of caution. Did he sense that Ellie had manipulated him into this? Not that she could have guessed it would turn out this way.

Ellie sent a look at Louisa that warned she would be happy when Louisa was gone and she had her father to herself.

Louisa returned the look, silently informing the child she could not drive Louisa away against her will. She was discovering more steel in her core than she had ever been aware of.

She and Emmet had decided to start by repeating the failed history lesson, so while she opened the picture book of the history of the North-West Mounted Police, Emmet edged his chair closer to the bed so he could study along with Ellie.

Louisa opened the book and began her story.

Ellie interrupted. "You did that yesterday."

"Do you remember it then?" She would be surprised if Ellie heard more than a word or two.

"Of course I do."

"Then here is your assignment." She repeated the instructions as Emmet adjusted the bed tray.

His attention on his task, he likely did not see the look of raw defiance on Ellie's face. Louisa understood the child's quandary. She didn't want to cooperate with Louisa but also didn't want her father to guess at the little game she'd been playing. As soon as Emmet finished, Ellie smiled sweetly. "Will you help me, Daddy?"

"Of course."

Louisa considered it a victory—at least Ellie was doing schoolwork, even if she was getting Emmet to write the answers for her. Ellie's knowledge of the subject surprised her. The child had taken in far more than she would have guessed possible.

"Do you want to draw a picture too?" Emmet asked.

"I can't draw."

"I expect you can draw as well as I can. Look." He scratched away on the paper.

Ellie giggled. "What is that?"

"Horses. I can't believe you had to ask." He turned the picture toward Louisa. "It's pretty obvious, wouldn't you say?"

Louisa pressed her lips together to stop a burst of laughter and tried to give the drawing serious consideration. But it was impossible. She'd never seen such awkward-looking animals. "They have such short legs… and long square bodies."

Ellie rolled her eyes. "They look like boxes on sticks."

Louisa couldn't contain her amusement any longer and laughed aloud.

"I did my best." Emmet tried to sound offended, but he laughed too.

Ellie stared from her father to Louisa, fought a battle with her resistance but a giggle escaped. She giggled until tears rolled down her face.

Emmet stared at her and pretended concern. "Don't cry, Button. It's only a picture."

Ellie giggled harder.

Auntie May appeared in the doorway. "Now that's a sound I can live with."

Louisa sucked in air that went deep into her lungs, refreshing, renewing. "That felt great. Like the Bible says, 'A merry heart doeth good like a medicine.'"

Emmet sobered, though his eyes continued to brim with laughter. He grabbed a hankie and wiped Ellie's eyes. "Are you going to be okay? Should I call the doctor?" He donned a serious expression. "'Miss Polly had a dolly that was sick, sick, sick, so she called for the doctor to come quick, quick, quick.'" He sang the words in a gruff voice.

Ellie giggled. "Daddy, you're silly."

Louisa's knees felt like strings of unbaked bread dough. She gripped the blackboard easel, hoping it was strong enough to bear her weight. The sounds of a child giggling and a father singing as the warmth of the sun puddled across the quilt on the bed were heartbreaking to her. The only thing in the scene she could look forward to in the future was the quilt. Perhaps she would make quilts to distribute to the less fortunate. But the ache inside her screamed against making them for others. She wanted to make them for her own family. Her own children.

She struggled for control. *Please God, hold me up.* And she meant more than her weak knees. She meant the future, the present, this moment of watching father and child.

When she could speak without revealing her tyrant emotions, she suggested Emmet should do the arithmetic lesson.

Looking uncertain, he wrote half a dozen simple problems on the board. Louisa stood to one side, although she longed to sink to the chair at Ellie's bedside.

Emmet read the first problem. "One plus one? This is way too easy. Ellie knew this before she started school."

"Two." Ellie's answer was brisk.

Emmet grinned. "One plus two?"

On and on they went, Ellie suddenly remembering things that only yesterday she couldn't.

"Do I get recess?" Ellie asked when Emmet declared arithmetic over.

"I think you deserve it."

She eyed the parcel on the table. "Can I open it?"

Louisa shook her head. "Not until we're done."

Ellie screwed up her face, ready to protest.

Emmet opened his mouth. But Louisa didn't give him a chance to voice his objection.

"I remember you said you like playing hide-and-seek. Do you want to play the game during your recess?"

Ellie snorted. "I can't hide."

"You could if you were no bigger than a button."

Ellie looked intrigued, as did Emmet, although Louisa did her best to avoid looking directly at him. Still it was hard to ignore his presence in the room. The place was so crowded, he couldn't return to the chair without brushing her shoulder in passing. Her heart clamored to her ribs and hung on as if drowning. Which perfectly described how she felt—drowning in her own foolish emotions.

She forced her mind back to explaining the game. "You pretend you are the size of a button. You can hide anywhere in this room, and we have to find you. You can give clues by saying warmer or colder. I'll go first to show you." She glanced around the room, being careful not to pause in any one spot and give away her hiding place. "Okay, I'm ready. Come find me."

"Are you in that jug?"

"Cold as ice."

Soon both Emmet and Ellie were guessing.

"Warm. Warmer." They drew close to her hiding place, which was on the tray over the bed.

Emmet glanced about, looked down at his shirt. "In my pocket?" His gaze grabbed her and held her in an invisible grasp.

She could not stop a jolt of something powerful and demanding from rushing through her like hot wind off the prairie, bringing both pleasure and pain. Close to his heart. Oh, if only it could be. But she must concentrate on what she could have. Not what was impossible. Find contentment. Trust God. "Colder," she managed, though her voice felt distant.

"On the tray." Ellie tapped it.

"You found me. So now you can hide."

They played the game for a few more minutes. Time Louisa used to pull herself back to reality. When she felt she could face Emmet and speak without her heart exploding with empty, impossible dreams, she suggested they try reading.

"I don't want to." Ellie switched from happy to angry so fast, Louisa almost lost her balance.

Emmet looked as surprised. "This is your last lesson, then you can see what Louisa has in her peculiarly shaped parcel."

"I don't care."

Louisa and Emmet stared at the child. They both knew she wanted very much to open the present.

Louisa handed the reader to Emmet. "Maybe for you?"

He opened to page one. "Would you read to me?"

Ellie shook her head.

"Tell you what. I'll read a line then you read a line." He read aloud, then paused for Ellie to continue.

She gave him a defiant stare.

Louisa found the earlier reader and handed it to Emmet. The same thing happened. Could Ellie not read, or was she being stubborn?

But all three of them were getting frustrated, and there seemed no point in trying to continue.

Louisa retrieved the storybook she'd begun two days ago. "I think that's enough reading. Instead, I'll read you some more of my story." It was one of the Winnie the Pooh books. "I loved these stories. My father would read them with different voices for all the characters. Do you know how the stories came to be?"

Two blond heads shook in unison.

"Winnie was a real bear. During the Great War, a soldier from Winnipeg bought the bear cub from a hunter for twenty dollars. He took the bear with him to Britain, but when his troop was posted to France, he turned the bear over to the London Zoo. Christopher Robin was a real little boy. His father wrote these stories for him, making Christopher's stuffed animals characters in them."

Emmet and Ellie seemed mesmerized by the story.

Satisfaction slipped through Louisa like a sweet drink, and she read a chapter to the pair, wondering which one enjoyed it most. Emmet laughed as much as Ellie as Louisa made each character come alive.

She closed the book.

"Aw." A duet of protest.

She grinned. "I never get tired of the stories." She'd always thought how much fun it would be to read them to her own children, but reading them to Emmet and Ellie would have to be pleasure enough. She pushed away every trace of regret and reached for the parcel. "I think you earned this today." She set the parcel on the tray.

Ellie gave Louisa a fleeting smile and Louisa let satisfaction sift through her.

With Emmet hanging over Ellie, as curious as his daughter, Ellie ripped the brown paper away to reveal a box. "What is it?"

"Open this." She showed her how to pull open the front to reveal—

"Ooh." Ellie stared.

Louisa grinned, pleased at the reaction. "It's a dollhouse."

"In complete detail," Emmet said. "Where did you get this?"

"I made it one winter when I couldn't do much else." She handed a fat envelope to Ellie, who opened it to reveal a family of paper dolls with every imaginable outfit, from ball gowns to nightgowns to winter hats and muffs.

"What do you say, Ellie?" Emmet prompted.

"Thank you." She flashed the first genuine smile

Louisa had received, and it settled somewhere deep in her heart with the doggedness of a summer drought.

Louisa told herself she was happy simply to give the child a bit of pleasure during the weeks she must remain in bed. But she could not deny the ache that echoed in her thoughts. This was as close as she'd ever get to the dream she'd cherished as long as she could remember. It was that dream—of a husband and children of her own—that made her keep her old readers, made her spend countless hours creating a dollhouse. "You're welcome. I hope you get lots of enjoyment out of it."

Ellie was already outfitting dolls and placing them in various rooms of the house. Emmet bent close, his head touching Ellie's as they arranged things.

"It's time for me to leave." Seeing them like this, the perfect father-daughter pair, triggered a thousand errant emotions in Louisa's heart. Longing for things she could never have. Sorrow over dead dreams. And, she insisted, happiness that she had a hand in creating this sweet moment. "I'll see you both again tomorrow." She gathered up her belongings and tried to slip away before her emotions completely escaped her control.

But Emmet followed her out of the room, catching her elbow in his cupped hand as if she needed his gentle assistance. She told herself she was capable of navigating the kitchen and front room without help, but she couldn't convince herself to pull away. Because her traitorous heart rejoiced in the touch.

He escorted her to her car, but rather than open the door as she expected, he turned her to face him. He brushed his fingers along her cheek and smiled. "It was incredibly generous of you to give that dollhouse and dolls to Ellie. I would think you'd want to keep it to give to your own children."

The words sliced through her, leaving her insides torn and bleeding. She had made it for that precise purpose. But it was not to be.

She grabbed the door handle and wrenched it open. "I must go." She blinked back the moisture in her eyes. She would not cry. What was the use? What could she do but throw herself upon God's love and let Him carry her?

She turned and headed out of town, but she paused before the turnoff to cry out her pain to God and seek His strength. By the time she reached the house, she was smiling. No one must ever know the way her insides wept.

Chapter Seven

Emmet stared after Louisa long after she disappeared from sight. What had sent her scurrying away so suddenly? He'd been about to ask her to come back in the evening so they could discuss tomorrow's plans. Now he didn't know what to expect.

The generosity of her gift to Ellie filled him with awe and appreciation. She must have spent hours creating the dollhouse. Was she now regretting giving it away? Did that explain why she had suddenly turned tail and left in a rush? Didn't seem she could be in a hurry for some other appointment. He retraced the conversation. *Save it for your own children.* Had those words sent her fleeing? Was she afraid to have children? Was her health too uncertain? Though he saw no evidence of poor constitution.

Perhaps she would explain later.

Whistling under his breath, he hurried back to check on Ellie. Apart from the reading lesson, it had been a good day. Thanks to Louisa. She would make a wonderful mother.

He told himself repeatedly he wasn't interested in her, especially in that way, but he found it harder to believe.

Ellie grinned at him. "This is fun." She had to be persuaded to set the dolls aside for lunch.

An hour later, the dishes were done and Ellie played happily with the dolls and dollhouse. Emmet sighed. He wasn't used to idly passing time around the house. He needed open air. Hard physical work.

Auntie May glanced up from mending a shirt. "Why don't you go do something useful? You're bothering me with your pacing and sighing."

"I wasn't—" Only he was. "I need some hard work."

"Then go find some. Me and Ellie will be okay by ourselves." She raised her voice. "Won't we, Ellie?"

"You'll come back for supper, won't you?" Ellie asked.

"Of course." He meant to be back in case Louisa came by to discuss lessons. And to put Ellie to bed as well.

"I met Judd Kirk. He owns the Cotton place now. I'll go out there and see if I can do something useful."

He found Judd fixing fences and lent a hand.

"It's a steady job," Judd complained. "The wind blows tumbleweeds and Russian thistle that piles up along the fences then fills with dirt. Next thing I know, the fences are buried or blown down."

As they worked, Judd talked. Emmet learned how his wife, Madge, had saved the family home from bank foreclosure. He told an amusing story about posing as a teacher and tutoring Louisa so he could spy on a man who had taken Judd's mother's money and lost it in some scheme.

"You must have enjoyed your little game." His jaw hurt at the thought of Judd and Louisa poring over books and sharing secrets.

"Not at all. I wanted to be honest. I wanted to be Judd,

an outdoorsman. I wanted to openly show my growing love for Madge."

"So what happened?"

Judd leaned back to stretch his muscles. "First, Madge discovered my true identity. Then she discovered who I was watching and forced me to confront my reasons. In the end, I admitted I was trying to make things right in my own wisdom. Madge taught me to trust God for both justice and the future."

Emmet leaned back too. Extracting the wire fence from the burden of weeds and dirt was hard work. He thought of Louisa singing "Trust and Obey." "Seems the Morgan girls have a passion about trust."

"I suppose they do. But so far as I can see, they're right. God can run things much better than I can." He returned to rescuing his fence.

Emmet threw his efforts into the work as well. He trusted. Of course he did. But not like Louisa. Her trust was like a sweet nectar permeating her thoughts, her actions and her attitudes. But unlike him, she hadn't watched everything she valued get snatched away. Well, not quite everything, thank the good Lord. He had Ellie. And his determination to protect her. He'd failed in the past. And Ellie was paying. Poor little Button. But he'd be more diligent in the future.

Several hours later, he returned home sweaty but happy. Nothing like hard work to make a man appreciate life.

Ellie still played happily with the dolls and dollhouse and smiled at him as he stepped into the room to check on her. "Do you need to go to the bathroom?"

"Auntie May helped me."

That was a first. Emmet felt a mixture of relief that

she had let someone else assist her, and a twinge of guilt because he hadn't been available. It wasn't as though he needed to do everything for her, only make sure it was done. Yet he couldn't dismiss a tiny thread of regret.

He and Auntie May ate their supper at Ellie's bedside to give her company. He let her play for a while after they finished. "It's time to get you ready for bed." He put the dolls and house away. "I'm afraid you will have to leave it until after your lessons are done tomorrow."

Ellie protested, but already her eyes were drooping. By the time he'd sponged her and helped her brush her teeth, she could barely stay awake. One of Auntie May's cats jumped up and curled up next to Ellie. Before he cleaned up the basin of water, both were asleep.

Auntie May sat in her rocker, her Bible on her lap… well, almost on her lap. Two cats lay between her knees and the book.

Emmet stared at the clock and then out the window. Would Louisa come tonight? But he saw no automobile approaching and sighed.

Auntie May tsked. "Go on outside and wait. I need some peace and quiet."

Good idea. He flung open the door, and his heart grabbed at his throat. Louisa stood before him, her hand raised as if to knock. "Where did you come from? I almost ran over you." His heart still bounced erratically. He stared past her. "Did your car break down?"

"I walked."

"Walked? Why? Isn't that a bit far?"

"Are you my mother?" Her voice was as soft as butterfly wings, but he didn't miss the note of warning. And it triggered unreasonable emotions. Anger. Longing. A thousand fleeting things.

"Do I look like anyone's mother?"

She giggled, and his anger evaporated. "Not like any I've seen, I must confess." She tipped her head toward the empty street. "I walked to save gas."

He wanted to say forget about saving gas. If something happened to her... But she was right. He wasn't her mother, but he'd make sure she got home safely.

"I went to see Adele and get some more work for Ellie." Louisa indicated her satchel.

"Come in." They sat as before, but Louisa didn't pull out any lesson plans.

"I asked if it's possible Ellie doesn't know how to read. She said the teacher should have informed you or dealt with it, if that were so. She gave me suggestions on how to present the work in a different way."

"I assumed—" He tried to think if Ellie had ever read anything aloud to him. "Would she be able to do her written work if she can't read?"

"I noticed she got you to write down her answers."

"But at school? How could it be possible?" How could he have missed it? Wasn't it his responsibility as her parent to know, rather than trusting someone else to take care of it?

Her eyes filled with distress. "I know. But none of that matters. If she can't read, it's up to us to help her catch up."

Her assurance smoothed his insides. "What's the plan?"

She opened her satchel then and pulled out papers. "I have a few ideas on how to turn reading into a game. I'll work on that tonight." She handed him arithmetic sheets. "In the meantime, she can go as fast as she wants in other areas. Shall we follow the same system we used this morning?"

"Sounds fine to me."

"Good." They reviewed the planned work, then she shoved everything except the arithmetic sheets into the satchel and pushed the chair back. "I must get home and do some preparation for tomorrow."

"I'll walk you home."

"It's not necessary."

"I won't let you walk home alone." He poked his head into the kitchen to tell Auntie May.

"Run along and have fun." She winked.

Emmet opened his mouth to protest, explain he was only acting responsibly, then changed his mind. What was the point in arguing when a large portion of his brain cherished the same idea? Despite all his arguments to the contrary, he meant to enjoy her company.

They sauntered down the street, waving to a neighbor in a front yard and another on his porch. The voices of children at play carried on the air, as did the grit of dust in the dry wind. Yet he didn't mind. The evening was soft with warmth, contentment and a pretty woman at his side. "I went out and helped Judd this afternoon."

She missed a step. "You did? Why?"

"I got tired of hanging about the house. Ellie was so happy with the dollhouse, she didn't care if I was there or not."

Her cheery laugh broke forth. "I didn't mean to replace you."

"It was a very generous gift."

"I have no need of it." Again that sad note in her voice. Again he wondered at its cause. Tried not to think his explanation was correct. Louisa didn't seem the kind to shy from physical challenges, but last time the words had sent her fleeing out the door. No door to use this time, but he didn't want her retreating mentally. So he quickly sought another topic.

"Judd has some mighty big dreams for his farm."

Another burst of laughter. "When the drought ends, he's going to be a rich cattleman."

"I think that hope keeps him busy mending fences."

"He's a hard worker." She obviously adored her brother-in-law. "With big dreams."

They walked in companionable silence for a few yards. "A person needs dreams."

"Especially when circumstances offer nothing but defeat and disappointment."

"The drought will end. So will the Depression." He assumed that's what she meant. "In the meantime, sing anyway. Right?"

She studied him, her look full of teasing regret. "You aren't going to let me forget that, are you?"

"I hope you aren't trying to."

"Why?"

"Because if everyone gets down in the dumps, we are a doomed country. We need people who can still find joy and hope, despite everything."

"You think that's me? I believe that's the nicest thing anyone has ever said of me."

"Why are you so surprised? Isn't that exactly what you said you intend to do—sing anyway?"

"I said it. I meant it at the time, but sometimes I forget and let discouragement gain the upper hand."

A shudder raked her shoulders. They had stopped walking to face each other, and he cupped her upper arm. "Louisa, don't ever stop singing."

She looked deep into his eyes, exploring, examining. He almost unlocked doors to her search, but he could not. There were some things that could not be shared, the pain too deep. These were burdens he must carry alone. For a fleeting second he remembered his mother and father, tried to recall their last day. Though if he'd known it was their last day…

A person knew some things too late.

A look of utmost peace and contentment filled her face. The look he'd come to expect and hope for. "Sing anyway," she whispered.

"That's right." He tucked her hand around his elbow and they continued down the road. "So what big dreams do you have?"

"Sorry?"

"Didn't we just decide a person needs big dreams? I wondered what yours are."

If her hand hadn't rested on his forearm, he might not have known she stiffened. "No big dreams, I guess. Seems every dream ends in a closed door."

He looked down on her dark curls. Wished he could see her face. "Tell me about your shattered dreams."

She made a little sound of protest. "They aren't important. I hoped I could go to university. That's not possible with money being in such short supply. In the meantime I am trying to take one day at a time, follow the Lord's leading and not run ahead with plans of my own."

He wanted to pull her to a stop, tip her face upward and demand she explain the tightness in her voice. But she strode onward, insistently.

"Now tell me about your big dreams."

Oh, he had walked into that one blindly. "I no longer dream. Tried that and look how it worked out."

She looked at him then. Now, though, he didn't want her to, because he feared she would see what he couldn't disguise—his disappointment, his failure, his determination to protect what little he had left. "But you have Ellie. You have your ranch. You have your faith. Surely you still have dreams."

He gave what he hoped was a teasing smile. "Nope. About all I can do is sing anyway. Or at least try."

She looked about to argue, then sighed. "Sometimes it's the best we can do."

It didn't seem right that she should accept defeat so easily. Made him want to grab the future and pull it down like a big, fat, red balloon and offer it to her. It made him want to throw aside all his own disappointments and promise to dance and sing with her into the unknown.

But he couldn't. The future was not his to offer. And he had little faith he could walk boldly into the unknown.

She laughed.

He blinked. "What's so funny?"

"Me. 'Why are thou cast down, O my soul? Hope thou in God; for I shall yet praise him for the help of his countenance.' I have no need to feel sorry for myself with God's promise to guide me."

He wished he could find the same confidence in life.

"I turn off here." She stopped and pointed toward the house up the lane. "Do you want to come in and meet my mother and say hello to Sally?"

"I'd like to." He wanted to see her family, see her home, see the things that had shaped her into such a strong woman.

As they neared the house, she pointed to the garden. "Where I go to have fun." She grinned at him, and they shared a laugh.

"I want to warn you that my mother is overprotective of me, so don't be alarmed if she acts like I committed some horrible crime by walking to town."

"I expect she's only trying to protect you. I know how it is." He would never let Ellie do anything remotely dangerous in the future.

"Sometimes it is stifling."

They reached the door and Louisa opened it to call, "Hello. I'm home." A little black-and-white dog ran forward, wiggling as though he would turn inside out.

Louisa laughed and patted the dog. "This is my dear friend, Mouse. I've had him since we moved here."

An older woman stepped into the room. She had a mop of curly hair like Louisa's, only it had faded to gray. She fixed Louisa with a concerned look.

"Mother, this is Emmet Hamilton. It's his little girl I'm tutoring."

The woman smiled sweetly. "Delighted to meet you, Mr. Hamilton. Please, come in and have tea."

Emmet gladly accepted her invitation. He wanted to meet her family and see where she lived.

Louisa had fought a conflicting set of emotions all the way home from town. She didn't want to spend more time with Emmet, be constantly reminded of things she couldn't have. She'd freely released that dollhouse to Ellie, a sort of sacrifice. In the back of her mind, she had whispered, *Okay, Lord, I know I will never be able to give this to a child of my own. So I choose to give it to a child who has no mother.* It seemed fitting. But it had been a wrench. She'd spent months on that project when she was fifteen. Long past playing with dolls herself. She had made it for only one reason, and to have Emmet remind her over and over that she might have kept it for her own child was like hot coals to her heart.

But when he announced he would see her home... As if there was no question. As if he considered it his duty. And then acted as if it was more than duty. Well, suffice it to say she tended to ignore the reasons why she didn't want to spend time with him.

Seeing the speculative look in Mother's eyes warned Louisa she should have listened to reason rather than give herself excuses. Mother saw a marriageable man—handsome, strong, with a child, providing a ready-made family for Louisa. What she didn't see was Emmet's clearly stated desire to have more children.

Louisa would be forced to explain it again after Emmet left. For now, Mother greeted him warmly. "Won't you come in and have tea with us? Sally just made some cookies. They're fresh from the oven."

"I'd be happy to. Smells like molasses cookies. Yum." He glanced at Louisa, held her gaze a beat, not long enough to attract Sally or Mother's attention, but long enough to signal that he remembered Louisa had said they were Father's favorites. Knowing he remembered made it even more difficult to keep her heart from tripping happily down the trail of possibilities.

There were no possibilities, she reminded herself.

Mother waved Sally forward. "This is my youngest daughter, Sally."

Emmet nodded. "We've already met."

Mother blinked. "Really?"

"Yes, at the store."

"Oh, I'd forgotten."

Sally rolled her eyes behind Mother's back. Louisa wanted to groan but feared it would only bring demanding questions from Emmet, so she indicated he should sit across from her as Mother presided over tea.

As soon as everyone was settled, and not a moment longer than courtesy required, Mother addressed Emmet. "So tell me about yourself. I know you lived with your aunt, but where were you before that? What have you done since you left here?"

Louisa did groan aloud now. "Mother, how much do you need to know?"

Mother gave a gentle smile, but Louisa knew she hadn't relented one speck. "I probably should have made inquiries before. After all, you are in his company every day. It's my duty."

Sally chuckled, but wisely didn't encourage Mother.

"Mother, I am with his child." No need to give Mother any more hope that there might be more interest to nurture by admitting she and Emmet had agreed to work together teaching Ellie. "And Auntie May is in the next room."

Mother slid her gaze past Louisa and Sally and landed it squarely back on Emmet. "I'm sure you don't mind talking about yourself."

Emmet chuckled, sent Louisa a teasing look. "I don't mind in the least. After I left here and after working at various ranches, I found a bit of land to the west. I met and married Jane. Sad to say she died three years ago. I've been on my own since then, but when Ellie broke her leg and had to be in a body cast, I knew I couldn't stay on the ranch. So here I am."

Louisa noticed he hadn't mentioned his parents.

Seems he never did. Why was that? It wasn't as if he'd forgotten them. Hadn't he told her he still missed them?

"Yes," Mother said, her voice sweet with satisfaction. "Here you are." The look she gave Louisa said as plainly as words "Here he is indeed. Just what you need."

Louisa grabbed a cookie and took a bite big enough to choke on, but she stubbornly chewed it and downed it with a gulp of tea.

Emmet grinned at her, as if knowing what wasn't being said. "Mrs. Morgan, tell me what it was like to have three little girls running around." His grin remained, but his eyes grew shadowed. "I always wanted a passel of young ones scampering about."

Louisa couldn't meet his look, couldn't let Sally or Mother see how much the idea hurt, and kept her attention on picking the tiny cookie crumbs from her plate.

Mother sighed. "It was a lot of fun. My husband adored the girls and spent a lot of time with them. And they played together well. Girls, remember the tea parties you used to have?"

Louisa lifted her head as sweet memories swept through her. She grinned at Sally. "We had a whole crowd of stuffed animals and dolls."

Sally nodded. "I remember you used to make dolls out of almost anything. Remember the one you made from corn husks?"

"I read the Indians did that, so I had to try."

"And you made one out of a potato that had eyes looking like a face."

Louisa laughed. "You couldn't stop staring at it. I think you wondered if it would open its mouth and talk."

Sally laughed. "We had a lot of fun."

Emmet's expression was hungry, full of longing. "It sounds like it."

Louisa wanted to erase that look from his face. "You had lots of playmates. What did you do besides play scrub ball in the vacant lot?"

The look he gave her said he understood she meant to make him see beyond being an only child. But she couldn't say if he appreciated it or not. At least, not until his eyes flashed blue and he smiled. "Depended on who I was playing with. The Crates family had half a dozen boys. Two were older than me, one my age and two younger, but they seemed to always do things in a group. And the things they did made people sit up and notice. They tore down an old abandoned shack and turned it into a fort down by the tracks."

Louisa and Sally glanced at each other in surprise. "I wonder if that's the same shack the hobos still use," Louisa said.

"It might be." He laughed. "We used enough nails to hold it together for a long time."

After that, they talked about people in the community—who still lived there, who had moved out, who had moved in—until Emmet pushed his chair back. "I must be on my way."

Mother sent Louisa a glance that said as loud as a ringing bell "Walk the man to the door and show a little interest."

Louisa knew it was best to follow her mother's silent instructions, so she accompanied Emmet to the door.

"I enjoyed the visit. Thanks for inviting me."

Let's not make a habit of this. Mother will start making wedding plans. And whether or not you know it, it isn't something either of us want. "Anytime. I'll see you tomorrow."

He reached out to touch his hat, realized he didn't wear it and settled for a sketchy salute instead. "Until tomorrow." He walked away.

She caught the sound of his whistle as he headed down the lane.

Sing anyway.

She needed the reminder, especially as she turned to face her mother's inquiring look.

"You didn't tell me he was so handsome. And a Christian."

"Mother, what difference does it make?" She sought strength in Sally's sympathy but Sally offered none, either by her look or in words. Of course. She was sure any man would be willing to overlook Louisa's barrenness if he loved her.

"I suppose it doesn't matter if he's handsome—though it helps—but being a Christian is the number-one requirement."

She knew her mother had purposely misunderstood Louisa's protest. "I believe in my case, there's an even more important consideration, which you well know. You both heard him. He longs for a big family. Now I really must do some work for the lesson I want to present tomorrow." She wrapped dignity about her like a shroud and climbed the stairs to her room, little Mouse trotting at her heels.

In her room, she scooped up the dog and sank to the edge of the bed. Her heart ached with unshed tears and futile dreams of living on a ranch, listening to a child's laughter and play, sharing the moment with a man with flashing blue eyes.

It would never be for her. But she didn't have time to mope. She gathered together paper and pencils and began to fashion illustrations for the lesson. But drawing pictures she hoped would help Ellie learn to read only made her insides hurt more, and she dashed a tear from her eye before it could drop to the paper and ruin her work.

Sometimes it was extremely difficult to find a song to sing.

Chapter Eight

Emmet had never got this much pleasure from lessons when he went to school. Back then he hadn't enjoyed watching the teacher's eyes flash with humor as she reminded him of how he whistled as he left the Morgan home. "Sing Anyway is my motto. Maybe yours is Whistle Anyway."

Nor had he noticed a teacher's eyes darken with emotion as she talked about the hardships of the Mounties' march west. Not only did he notice, but his heart had been tugged to join in the same sadness. He knew relief when they moved on to the next subject, which was arithmetic. At least Ellie did well in that subject.

Louisa had driven her car this morning. He felt a twinge of regret. If she'd walked, he'd be duty bound to see her home. She returned to her car when they took a short break before they tackled reading. When she came back, she carried a brown folder. "For our reading class," she explained. She must have seen his worry, though he'd tried to deny it all morning. "Don't look so concerned. We're going to play a game. Ellie will learn to read because it will be fun."

Louisa set the blackboard where Ellie could see it.

Emmet sat at Ellie's side, ready to assist and encourage in any way he could. His insides twisted and coiled. He should know if Ellie couldn't read and needed extra help. What kind of father wouldn't know?

Louisa placed a picture on the easel—a drawing of a ball with the word below. "Ellie, I'm going to show you a game. First, we have to name all the objects. What's this?"

"A ball." Ellie sounded cautious.

"Too easy, I know, but that's okay. So the word says, 'ball.' Look at it and remember."

Ellie nodded.

Louisa put up more pictures with words below—half a dozen in all. Cat. Dog. Doll. Sun. Run.

All this work for a child who wasn't her own. Louisa would make a wonderful mother. He'd often wished Jane had given Ellie more attention, but Jane was happy if Ellie played alone without interfering with Jane's chores.

He jerked his thoughts away from making a comparison between the two. It wasn't fair.

Louisa took a big pair of scissors from her bag and cut each picture in half. The top half had the picture, the bottom half the word. She shuffled them like cards, passed six to Ellie and kept six for herself. "Now let's play. As soon as either of us gets a match between the picture and the word, we put them down. For every match, you get to take a card from the other player. You go first. Do you have any matching pairs?"

Emmet glanced at the cards Ellie held and saw two pairs. He let Ellie study them. When she matched "cat" with the picture, he wanted to cheer.

Louisa let Ellie take a card from her hand.

Emmet waited as Ellie looked at the pictures. He could almost feel her intense concentration. When she matched "run" and the picture, he clapped and she beamed with victory.

She got four out of the six matches.

Louisa beamed. "Do you want to play again?"

"Yes."

They played until Auntie May stuck her head in and said, "Lunch in fifteen minutes."

Ellie didn't want to stop.

Louisa placed the cards facedown on the bed. "You can play a game on your own. Pick up two cards."

Ellie did.

"Do they match?"

She studied them a moment, then shook her head.

"Then put one back and try another. When you find a match, put it aside and keep playing until you get them all."

Ellie's attention was on her game as Louisa prepared to leave. "I'll make some more cards for tomorrow if you like."

Ellie glanced up and nodded.

Emmet walked her out. "You could stay for lunch."

"Mother expects me home."

He didn't want her to leave. In fact, he wanted to hug her tight and thank her for all the work she'd done for Ellie. "She can read, can't she?"

"She's uncertain, but she learned those six words easily enough."

"You did so much work on this. How did you think of the games?"

Louisa's smile was sweet enough to stop the birds from singing. "Adele suggested I make it a game. I couldn't think what might work, so I prayed. And this idea came."

Emmet couldn't get his thoughts around how much she put into teaching his child. It amazed and awed him. "I truly appreciate how you're helping."

Their gazes caught and held in a powerful sense of oneness and belonging, of wanting and needing. The look went on and on, her dark eyes searching for truth and so much more. More than he could give. He closed his thoughts to her. Regretted it the moment she blinked and shutters closed her off. Then he half convinced himself there was nothing he could do differently.

"I'll see you tomorrow then." She made for the car.

"What about preparing the lessons tonight?" Just the idea she might not come back made him forget all his good intentions.

She didn't turn right away. Long enough for his mouth to go dry and a thousand arguments to change her mind crowding his own.

Then she slowly faced him, her face a mask, her eyes veiled. "Are you sure you want to do this? You must have other things you'd like to do."

He had nothing that interested him more. That thought seemed at odds with earlier promises he had made for himself, but he dismissed the idea. "We need to make sure we are doing what Ellie needs."

The mask grew more wooden. "Then I'll come back after supper."

He wanted to tell her to leave the car at home. Give him an excuse to escort her back. But how could he? He had to confine his interest to what was best for Ellie. Never again dare he put anything before her needs.

* * *

Rather than make a trip back to town when school was out, Louisa stopped to speak to Adele during the noon break and get work for the next day.

Adele asked about the reading lesson, and Louisa told her what happened. "Good for you. You've got the instincts of a natural teacher. Have you ever considered going to Normal school?"

Louisa looked around the schoolyard where Adele was supervising. Children played and swung. Girls huddled together near the garagana hedge. Boys ran after a ball.

She loved helping Ellie, working with Emmet to help his little girl with her studies, but she didn't know how she could see a whole classroom of children every day, face the fact she would not have her own. "I can't afford it." It was a convenient, and true, excuse.

"I borrowed the money to attend."

Louisa nodded, as if giving the idea some thought. But even if she found Normal school appealing, she didn't know anyone who would lend her money. What about Uncle Peter? No. She'd never consider asking. Peter was her father's brother. He had never married. At Father's funeral he had said several times, "If there is anything I can do… If you need anything… I can help with expenses." Mother had been offended.

"Your father took care of us very well," she told the girls privately. "We aren't charity cases for your uncle."

Mother would never allow any of them to ask him for anything.

Louisa left Adele a few minutes later and drove home. She dreaded facing her mother. She'd likely demand a full description of the morning. If only she could tiptoe inside and find sanctuary in her room. But as she stopped before the door, she heard Mouse barking a frenzied greeting. Everyone in the house would know Louisa had returned.

The door opened and Sally waved at her. "The coast is clear. Mother has gone to visit Mrs. Roberts. She'll be gone all day. I think Mrs. Roberts is about to have her baby."

They shook their heads. "Poor Clara," Louisa murmured. Sally's friend was the eldest of six, now about to be seven, and carried a full load of responsibility— but secretly Louisa envied the girl all those little ones to care for.

Sally laughed. "Clara considers it a blessing. She can hardly wait for this baby. She said it had been too long." Clara's youngest brother was six, almost seven. "Are you hungry?"

"Starving. What are we eating? Or did you eat already?"

"Soup and sandwiches, and I've been waiting for you." They sat at the table and bowed their heads.

"It's your turn," Sally murmured, so Louisa said grace.

She'd barely said "amen" before Sally leaned forward like a coconspirator. "Did you have fun this morning?"

The pain she'd been holding back all morning burst from its restraints and ran wild, spreading through her body like a raging prairie fire. "Oh, Sally, it's so hard. I gave her the dollhouse I made. I make up little games for her. I stand and watch how much Emmet loves his daughter, and I try to be grateful for what I have. But inside I die a little every day, knowing I can never have a part in it."

Sally sat back, her lunch forgotten. "I didn't realize it was so hard. Maybe you should quit."

"No. I intend to prove I can do this. I'm tired of being weak and fragile." She ignored Sally's mocking laugh. "I am holding on to the promise of that paycheck at the end of the two months. I'll give it to Mother to pay the bills and feel like I've done something useful for the first time in my life."

"Oh, Louie. You have contributed so much to our family. How can you think you have to prove anything?"

"I have contributed nothing but anxiety and medical bills."

Sally reached across the table and took Louisa's hands. "Oh, my dear, dear sister. No one cares about that. What we care about is your sweetness, which hasn't been affected by illness. We appreciate how patient you are no matter what you must endure. Do you know how many times I fell asleep listening to you sing? Or play the piano? I always knew things weren't all that bad so long as you could sing. That's worth more than anything money can buy."

Sing anyway. Sometimes it was hard, but knowing it encouraged others, Louisa renewed her vow to do so.

"Sally, you are far too generous, but I thank you. Now eat your soup before it gets cold."

They ate in companionable silence for a few moments, then Sally put her spoon down and stared at Louisa. "You gave your dollhouse away? I can't believe it."

Louisa shrugged. "I thought of keeping it to give to a niece, but I can always make another if you or Madge have a little girl. Ellie has no mother, so I thought appropriate."

Sally looked as if she meant to say something, then

changed her mind. Had she been about to point out that Louisa couldn't have children and Ellie needed a mother? If that was her intention she had, thankfully, thought better of it. If Emmet married again, he would want more children. He was very clear on that matter.

They had almost finished when Sally jerked her head up. Louisa smiled, knowing she was about to hear one of Sally's sudden brainstorms.

"I know what will cheer you up. Let's go to the orphanage. We can play with the babies when they wake up. And when the older kids come home from school, we can do things with them. You know, like play games, read and sing to them, help them with homework. Let's go."

Louisa wanted to say no. She wanted to retreat to her bedroom, wrap her arms around little Mouse and wallow in her sorrow. But there was no value in that. She would be cheerful despite her sadness. And making the children laugh would surely ease her own misery.

The afternoon passed quickly and pleasantly with the children and staff at the orphanage. By the time they returned home it was past supper time, but Mother was still away so the girls scrambled eggs and had them on toast for their meal.

They finished and sat back, relaying stories of the children when a knock sounded on the door.

Mouse leaped from Louisa's lap in a frenzy of barking.

Louisa laughed. "Some guard dog you are. We already know someone is there. Silly dog." She and Sally exchanged looks full of curiosity. Who could it be? Did it signal bad news? Perhaps Mrs. Roberts—she wouldn't consider all the things that could go wrong. "I'll get it."

She crossed to the door, took in a deep breath before opening it. "Emmet? Is something wrong?" She cupped her hand to her throat in alarm. "Ellie? Auntie May?"

He reached for her, caught her elbow. "Everything is fine."

Relief made her legs wobbly. She welcomed his steadying touch. Almost immediately, a new kind of weakness claimed her heart and body as his touch reached into her inner being, uncovering wants she thought she had successfully buried, and laying claim to them.

"I thought I'd come here to do lesson preparation. Save you the trip to town."

She needed to step away from his touch. She needed to answer the man. She needed to bury her feelings. But she couldn't move, couldn't speak and, heaven help her, couldn't find the will to deny the longing in her heart... longing for love, home, family. A groan escaped her heart and pressed against her teeth as she fought against disappointment.

"I'm sorry." Emmet gripped her elbow more firmly. "Is my being here a problem?"

Sally had moved to the doorway. "You surprised her, I think. Come on in."

Emmet dropped his hand to his side and waited.

Feeling as if she had been set adrift in a vast ocean with no horizon in sight, Louisa blindly followed her sister, Emmet at her heels.

"We just finished supper." Sally scooped up the dirty dishes, carried them to the basin then wiped the table clean. "There you go. You can go over lessons here."

Emmet hovered behind a chair.

Louisa realized he waited for her to sit, or show any

degree of civility. "Have a chair while I get my satchel."
She scurried from the room, didn't slow her steps until
she reached her room. She sank to her bed. *Oh, Lord
God, I am trying to trust You but sometimes it is so hard.*
Impossible. *With men this is impossible; but with God
all things are possible.* Matthew nineteen, verse twenty-
six. A verse Father had taught her, had repeated to her
when she struggled to breathe through the worst of her
pneumonia. She'd clung to the comfort of that assurance. *Thank You, Lord. I will trust You.* She rose from
her bed, squared her shoulders, grabbed the satchel from
the chair where she had tossed it and marched down
the stairs to face Emmet. She faltered at the last step.
Gird yourself in God's strength, she reminded herself
briskly and lifted her chin a little higher as she entered
the kitchen, where Emmet watched her, a worried look in
his eyes. He'd guessed something upset her. She vowed
he would never know what or why.

"I have the materials here." She sat across from him
and pulled out the lessons. "Adele suggests we go as
quickly with arithmetic as Ellie can handle. Success in
this area will help her tackle the more challenging subject of reading." There were several sheets of equations
then some problems, which would require Ellie to apply
her knowledge of addition.

None of this required more than a few minutes. They
could easily discuss everything before they began in the
morning. So why did he insist on this preparation time?
Why did he come out to the farm?

She answered the question herself. No doubt he was
lonely.

I suppose the least we can do is make his visit more

enjoyable. Surely that was their Christian duty. Grateful for the excuse, she relaxed.

"Would you like tea?" she asked.

"I don't want to be a nuisance, but I have to confess I get bored in town. Would you mind—" He ducked his head without finishing.

Louisa and Sally exchanged glances. Sally tilted her head toward Emmet, signaling that Louisa should help him.

"Please feel free to ask anything."

He raised his head, gave her a piercing look, and she smiled, knowing her assurance eased his tension. "Very well. I miss the ranch. I thought if you showed me the barn and we could walk around a field… Well, I would enjoy it immensely."

"Very well." Louisa refused to look at Sally, knew she'd see a gleam of encouragement. But Louisa's wayward heart needed no encouragement. It needed a good stiff dose of reality. However, she didn't mind showing him around the farm. Even if most of it belonged to another now. He deserved kindness and friendship. That was why she would do it. No other reason.

She only wished her heart would obey her mind. Instead it sang a secret song of something beyond friendship. And beyond possibility.

"We can have tea when you get back." Sally tried to sound matter-of-fact, but Louisa heard the little note of happiness that her sister was stepping out.

"Shall we go?" Louisa headed for the door, paused to murmur for Sally's ears only. "It's only a tour of the farm. Nothing more. Remember, it can be nothing more."

Sally shrugged, totally unrepentant.

Emmet waited on the step and Louisa joined him.

"What would you like to see?"

"Everything. Do you still farm any land?"

"We kept only enough for a bit of pasture. We keep a milk cow and calf."

"What about winter feed?"

"We buy it. Or more likely, trade for it. Judd helped us find feed last winter." Such mundane conversation, but she welcomed it. A safe topic.

They went to the garden. The only thing visible was rhubarb. "There should be tiny plants poking through soon. We water it faithfully. Once they're up we'll have to fight off the hordes of grasshoppers." The insects were already beginning to hatch. Soon there would be thousands of them, eating anything that survived the winds and drought.

She led him to the barn. "Father had dreams of several cows and horses here."

Mice rustled across the floor overhead.

Emmet breathed deeply. "I love the smell of hay."

Curious about his life, she faced him. "Tell me about your ranch." It was only natural to want to know a little more about him. After all, she taught his little girl and spent several hours a day with him. Only she didn't want to know because of Ellie. She wanted to know Emmet. And no amount of reasoning and mental argument erased that truth. She wanted to know what he liked first thing in the morning, what his favorite time of day was, what tiny things gave him pleasure... She must stop this foolish meandering of her thoughts.

"My house is on a little hill. A creek flows by on the west side. In the spring the creek is full and noisy. Later in the summer it is slow and quiet. When I need to think, I have a place by the creek in a little grove of trees where I sit and watch the water. Deer often come to water at the creek."

"It sounds wonderful." She couldn't remember moving to the empty manger and perching on its edge, Emmet beside her, but that's where they were.

"It's nice all right."

"Tell me about your house."

He slanted her a teasing look. "I don't think you'd be impressed with it right now."

"Why not?"

"A widower and seven-year-old don't make good housekeepers." His eyes were so blue she thought the sky must be reflected in them. "What it really needs is a woman's touch."

"And more children running through the rooms?"

"That would be nice."

She pushed to her feet. "Let's look at the fields. Mr. Emerson planted the closest one last week, but we need rain to make it germinate."

He followed her. "The original house was log. But it was small so I added on—frame structure. It turned out rather nice, I think. The original is the kitchen and living room with a loft above. The addition is four bedrooms and a storeroom."

They reached the field, and Louisa scooped up a handful of dirt. It was so dry it sifted through her fingers. She shook her hand. "We need rain." She didn't want to hear about the four bedrooms that longed to be filled with children. She didn't want to hear about the house on the hill, the creek and the private spot in the trees.

But Emmet continued on as if she'd asked him to describe every detail.

And despite her denial, she wanted him to.

"Like I say, the house has been neglected since—well, since Jane died."

Tell me more, her heart begged. *Talk about something else,* her brain insisted. "What did you do with your animals when you left?"

"In the summer they graze the high pastures. They need little supervision, but I asked a neighbor to check on them. I'll have to bring them down to home pasture before the snow comes."

He'd have to leave by fall. That would be a relief to her mental wrangling. Only, she counted off the months with a sick feeling. It was mid-May. When would he head back? September? Earlier if Ellie was ready to travel? It took all her inner strength to push her regret into submission and turn the conversation to something else.

"I visited the orphanage this afternoon. And it gave me an idea. There's one little girl there who is a little younger than Ellie and seems pleasant. I thought if you asked her to visit, it would provide Ellie with some company her own age."

Emmet faced her, surprise in his blue eyes. "I think that's a great idea, especially if you think this child is appropriate."

"Appropriate?" When did children have to pass inspection?

"I'm sure you realize I wouldn't want Ellie associating with a child who, for instance, had a foul mouth."

She chuckled at his expression. "You look ready to fight off any danger she might encounter."

"I am. If I'd been more vigilant, she wouldn't be where she is now."

"Emmet, accidents happen and sometimes illnesses. We do our best and leave the rest in God's hands."

"I try." He seemed to struggle with his conflicting need to be in control and desire to trust God. "By all means, invite this child to visit if you think it's appropriate."

She wanted to say something to ease his mind. Perhaps offer comfort, but she dare not let herself say all that was in her heart—a longing to stand at his side through accidents and trials, an ache to put a woman's touch to his neglected home.

Instead she steeled herself to speak calmly, as if nothing mattered but inviting a child to play. "I'll see to the arrangements."

Helping Ellie was the best she could do to satisfy her desire to help him.

Chapter Nine

Emmet left after he shared tea and cookies with Louisa and Sally. He walked back to town. He could have driven his truck, but he preferred to walk the three miles. It gave him time to think.

Trouble was, his thoughts made no sense. Why had he come out here? Lesson preparation wasn't the answer. Why had he told her all about the ranch? How the house sat on a hill? As he told about the rooms he'd added to the house, he imagined her in the house, filling it with love and laughter, faith and—dare he admit it? Yes, children. After Jane's death, or maybe even before it, he had vowed he would no longer dream such dreams. Jane had given him only one child, and although he loved Ellie, it was a disappointment. He longed for a large family. In part, he wanted to fill the hollowness in his heart he'd known since his parents died so suddenly.

Not a hint. Not a moment of warning. Here one minute, gone the next.

He had been alone. So alone.

The feeling had never quite left him. Not when Auntie May gave him a home—a perfectly acceptable home.

He had no doubt Auntie May loved him. His marriage had not robbed him of the feeling. Not that it was Jane's fault. She loved him decently enough. Having Ellie was the closest he'd come to satisfying the emptiness within himself. It was the best he could expect.

But in his mind he saw Louisa at the stove in the ranch house. Saw her bending over a child's bed. Saw her standing on the veranda, watching for him to return for supper.

He kicked a lump of dirt that poofed into a cloud of dust. All she'd done was help with Ellie's lessons. Yes, she was good with Ellie, but she'd given no indication that her interest in either of them went beyond her job as a tutor. And he would do well to keep that in mind. For the time being, this was best for Ellie. He would do nothing to change that. And when they left again, just the two of them, he would continue to do what was best for her.

And safest for him, a faint voice insisted.

Yes, what was best for him was keeping his heart's desires under lock and key. He'd already learned his dreams were empty. Led only to more hurt—watching Jane die and having to bury her was the second-hardest thing he'd ever faced.

Somehow he managed to guard his heart throughout the lessons of the next day, and then two days later, Louisa brought Leila to visit. He'd asked her to be present.

"After all, we're strangers to her. She'll feel better if you stay."

So Louisa had agreed. He couldn't tell if she welcomed the idea or not.

Leila edged forward when she saw Ellie. "You broke your leg?"

"Fell out of a tree."

Leila's blue eyes were wide with disbelief. "Your mommy let you climb trees?"

"Ain't got no mommy."

"Me too. I got no daddy either." She slid her gaze to Emmet and studied him long and hard, her eyes practically eating him up. She had long, blond, baby-fine hair tied back with a limp bow. Her fair skin was a marked contrast to Ellie's darker skin. In fact, compared with Ellie with her dark blond hair and brown eyes, she looked ethereal.

"You got any brothers or sisters?" Ellie asked.

He heard the hungry note in her voice and understood Ellie ached for siblings just as he had.

"I had a sister, Emmy. She died along with Mama and Papa."

Emmet shot a glance at Louisa, saw an echo of his shock and pain. Children should be spared such sorrows. But he knew they weren't. He wasn't much older than Leila when his parents had died. He leaned down toward Leila. "Honey, what happened to your family?"

She clung to his gaze, sucking up strength and demanding something more from him.

He only wished he knew what it was she wanted. He would gladly give it if it lay within his power. "They got sick and died. All except me."

"You don't have any relatives you can live with?"

"Only my grandma, and she is very old and lives across the ocean."

Ellie shifted in the bed, as if trying to move over. "You want to play dolls with me? Miss Morgan gave me this dollhouse."

Leila instantly brightened. "That's a nice dollhouse."

She climbed up on the chair beside Ellie, and soon the girls were playing happily.

Louisa signaled Emmet to leave the room.

A minute later they stood in the kitchen, staring at the table.

"Poor child," Emmet murmured.

"I know. It seems so unfair they've lost their parents and I—" Her voice broke and she stopped speaking. "Sometimes," she whispered, "it's hard to remember to sing."

He clasped her hand, wanting more than anything to bring the music back to her voice. "Louisa, don't ever stop singing. What would happen to our world if all the songbirds grew silent?"

She gave him a look of pure disbelief. "I'm no song-bird."

"Ah. But you are. Nicely disguised as a beautiful woman, but still a songbird underneath."

Her cheeks blossomed like June roses. Her gaze darted away and then returned, almost as hungry as the look in Leila's eyes. "I am not."

He didn't know if she meant she wasn't a beautiful woman or a songbird. Maybe both, which is exactly what he meant when he said, "You are indeed."

She eased her hand from his. When she pressed it to her waist as if she cherished the feel of his palm, he grinned. "The girls are enjoying each other." Their happy voices came from the other room.

"I thought they might."

He didn't want Louisa saddened again by thinking of orphaned children. Besides, he wanted to enjoy her company without the excuse of schoolwork. Just this once. Auntie May was outside puttering about her garden. "Do you want to see an old photo album?"

"Of you?" Did she sound eager?

"Maybe."

Emmet led her into the front room, waited for her to settle on the old sofa that had likely made the trek west with Auntie May's grandparents. His father's grandparents. He seldom thought that far back in his family tree.

He put a black photo album on her lap and sat close to explain the pictures. "My great-grandparents, before they moved west."

She bent over the picture to examine it closer, giving him plenty of time to study her—the tumble of dark curls, a profile that would be suitable for a cameo. She glanced up and caught his interest, and the pink returned to her cheeks. "You look like your great-grandfather."

He turned the page to pictures of the house they'd built in the British Territories, now Alberta. There were more pictures of his grandparents and great-aunts and uncles. Cousins back east he had never seen. He flipped the page, and his heart stalled. He'd forgotten this page.

She waited. Then prompted him. "Who are these?"

"My parents." His voice sounded distant and hoarse.

"And that would be you in your mother's arms?"

It was. He could only nod. She turned to the next picture. A little boy in a pair of knee pants, holding a cap. "You?"

"I was five. Still in short pants."

On the next page would be the picture Auntie May had insisted on taking. The two fresh graves.

Emmet took the photo album and closed it. He did not want to be reminded. That portion of his life was forbidden territory.

Louisa shifted, considered him long and hard. "Emmet, what happened to your parents?"

"They died."

"How?"

He shook his head. "It doesn't matter how, does it?"

"I think it does."

"I don't wish to talk about it." He stared at her, silently daring her to take this any further, informing her the subject was closed.

"As you wish." But her gaze remained demanding, sorrowful at the same time.

He didn't need sympathy any more than he needed reminders. "I better check on the girls."

She rose to follow him and laughed as they stepped into the room.

Leila had found an old red hat on the shelf and wore it. She had been twirling about and skidded to a halt at the sight of two adults. She yanked the hat off and returned it to the shelf. "I was only showing Ellie a little dance."

Emmet chuckled. "It's okay. Auntie May won't mind, so long as you don't damage anything."

Leila stared at the floor. A shudder raked her shoulders.

Emmet gave Louisa a help-me look. Why was Leila upset?

Louisa lifted one shoulder, then knelt beside the child. "Leila, what's wrong?"

"Nothing," she murmured.

"She likes that cup." Ellie pointed toward a chipped cup on the top shelf of the china cupboard.

"Is there something special about it?" Louisa asked.

"It reminds me of Mama."

Emmet could not take the way the child's voice cracked with emotion. "Would you like to have it?"

Leila's eyes threatened to consume her face. "It's not mine."

"I'll give it to you." He removed it from the shelf and handed it to her.

Leila shook her head. "Matron will be angry that I made you want to give me something. We aren't supposed to beg."

"You didn't—" He turned to Louisa for guidance.

"Maybe you can leave it here for now. But it's yours."

Leila took the cup and held it between her palms.

Emmet wondered if she even breathed as she studied the purple flowers on it. "Thank you. Very, very much. Mama would have loved this cup. She had a saucer with a crack that had these same flowers on it. She said her mama had given the cup and saucer to her, but all she had left was the saucer."

"What happened to it?"

The child's eyes filled with liquid, but she did not let a tear escape. "I don't know. I only brought my clothes with me and my doll."

"You still got your doll?" Ellie asked.

Leila nodded, her eyes flashing mischief. "I keep her hidden under my underwear so no one will touch her."

Ellie wrinkled her nose. "Phew." Both girls laughed.

Louisa chuckled too, her eyes sparkling as much as the little girls'. She met Emmet's gaze. "No better place to hide something, you know."

He shook his head. "Makes no sense to me."

Still chuckling, Louisa waved at him to follow her from the room. She put the kettle to boil. Her shoulders quivered.

"You're laughing at me." He tried to sound regretful.

She faced him. It was plain as could be that she struggled to contain her amusement. "I'm laughing at the situation. I never realized how different boys and girls were."

"It's amazing. Surprising and interesting. Who'd think a chipped bit of china could bring so much happiness to a child?"

"Because it reminded her of her parents." Her eyes darkened. Delved into his heart, searching…for what? She opened her mouth. Seemed to reconsider. Closed it again. "I think it's good for her to have something that reminds her of them."

He knew then what she'd wanted to say and was grateful she had changed her mind. She'd considered saying something about the way he refused to talk about his parents. How could he possibly explain he didn't want to remember them? It brought only pain.

They sat at the table and had tea, listening to the giggles and whispers of the girls in the other room.

"It was a good idea to suggest Leila visit." He leaned across the table, as if about to share a secret. "You are very good with children."

She blinked. Seemed to pull back into herself. "I guess I remember my own childhood well."

He saw the silent challenge in her eyes and changed the subject before she could voice it. "Have you considered becoming a teacher?" Though she surely belonged in a home, with her own children. The thought tugged at his heart. But he wouldn't again picture her in his house. This afternoon's reminder of his parents and the pain of their death made him more determined to guard his heart.

"I can't afford to attend Normal school."

"I'm sure there's a way—"

"I don't wish to discuss it." Silent determination made her expression brittle.

Likely holding out for marriage. He wondered if he preferred to picture her married to someone, raising his kids, or unmarried and teaching. Neither sat very comfortably. But he would not follow his line of thought, knowing it went to places he must deny himself.

"It's time to take Leila back." She called Leila.

The girls whispered something and cast furtive looks at Louisa and Emmet.

"What are they up to?"

Louisa shrugged. "Secrets are very important to girls. Boys too, it seems."

It was a little dig about him closing the photo album, refusing to talk about his parents. "Entirely different reasons, I expect."

"If you say so."

Leila took Louisa's hand. "Thank you for having me, Mr. Hamilton."

"Thank you for coming."

"Bye," Ellie called.

Emmet escorted Louisa and Leila to the door. He couldn't bear the thought of them leaving with constraint between himself and Louisa. "I have secrets for a very good reason."

She nodded. "I'm sure you do." She paused on the step, let Leila run to the car alone then turned to face him, her expression full of something far beyond curiosity. "Emmet, I don't mean to pry. But—" She shrugged.

"But what?"

"It's none of my business, is it?"

He wanted to say no, it wasn't. It wasn't anyone's business. But he couldn't deny her concern any more than he could deny the ache in his heart at keeping doors closed to her. It simply had to be that way. "What if I say I want it to be your business?"

"Okay. I don't know if I can explain it well, but I feel like whenever your parents are mentioned a huge lump of something chokes you. I guess I wonder why you don't want to get rid of that lump." She shrugged. "That's all."

That's all? That was like saying the sky was a little blue, the horizon was only a tiny distance away, the wind barely stirred the air. It wasn't little at all. The lump—as she described it—filled his insides. He couldn't pretend it wasn't there. He could only try to ignore it. He'd been trying for eighteen years, mostly with success—until he'd opened that silly photo album.

She touched his elbow. A thousand shivers raced up his veins, threatening to break the locks on a solid door. He feared what would happen should the door ever fling open.

"I can't. I simply can't." Did his voice sound as anguished as he felt? He hoped not.

"I'm sorry," she whispered. "The last thing I want is to upset you."

He nodded. Tried to say he wasn't upset. Failed. Feared his eyes betrayed his pain.

"Miss Morgan?" Leila called from the car.

"I have to go." Louisa sounded as if the idea hurt her deeply.

Louisa listened to Leila's happy chatter with only a tiny portion of her brain. The rest thought of Emmet. Why had she said what she did? Pushed him into a corner, forced emotions from him that obviously caused him such anguish. What made her think she had the right to probe at his wounds?

She wouldn't have thanked him for probing at hers.

Thankfully he didn't know her deepest wound. Nor would he ever.

She delivered Leila at the orphanage and spoke to the matron, assuring the good, solid lady that her little charge had been a perfect guest.

But she didn't immediately go home. She needed time to think. At first she thought of going to see Madge, but this was too deep, too personal to discuss with either of her sisters. Or her mother. There was only one source of wisdom and comfort for the confusion she felt, and she pulled the car off the road at a dusty approach and leaned back. *Oh, God. Help me. I feel like I'm caught in a whirlwind. I don't want to cause Emmet pain, and yet I know his past is really eating him up. Help him find his own song. And Lord, while I'm asking, please, please guard my heart.*

She sat for a few minutes, letting God's peace envelop her, then turned the car toward home.

The next morning she returned to the Hamilton house, her emotions firmly under control, and she was determined to keep them there. Emmet seemed relieved that she was a little distant—a fact that bothered her only slightly. She reminded herself it was far better to be interested only in doing a good job. And expecting nothing from him, apart from helping her teach Ellie.

They slipped into a routine. He spent less and less time in Ellie's room helping with the lessons. That was good, Louisa told herself repeatedly. Ellie was progressing nicely. Flying through arithmetic and now able to read at the beginning of her grade-two books. Louisa's

goal was to see her able to read at the level of her classmates before she finished her contract. She had four
weeks left. Once Ellie's cast came off, Louisa would no
longer be needed.

It wasn't a thought she allowed herself to dwell on.

"I wish Leila could come again." Ellie's words
brought Louisa back from her mental wandering.

"Ask your father. I'm sure he would approve."

"Daddy!" she yelled.

"I didn't mean this very minute." She had trouble fo-
cusing on anything but her trembling heart when Emmet
was in the room. But it was impossible to take back Ellie's call. Emmet bound through the door.

"Did you need me, Button?"

"Louisa said to ask you if I could invite Leila to come
and play with me again. Can she?"

Emmet considered his daughter a moment, then
shifted his gaze to Louisa.

She forgot to breathe when she saw the darkness in
his eyes. What did he want from her? Whatever it was,
she feared she could not give it.

"Would you be willing to bring her?"

Louisa couldn't for the life of her remember what they
had been talking about and scrambled to think what he
meant. Oh, right. Leila. "I think I could make arrangements for her to come after school."

"That would be nice."

Still he watched her. She gripped her hands together,
determined she wouldn't touch him, ask what bothered
him, offer to help in any way she could. Instead, she
forced her thoughts to center on arrangements for Leila's
visit. "Would tomorrow be good?"

"It would be fine."

Ellie cheered, freeing Louisa from the intense, demanding look in Emmet's eyes.

Ellie enjoyed the visit so much they arranged for Leila to come over a couple of times a week. Louisa liked seeing the friendship develop between them. It reminded her of the fun she and her sisters had shared growing up. But there was one big difference. The girls weren't sisters and would have to part in a few weeks. What would happen to the friendship when Emmet and Ellie left? Would both little girls be hurt?

She expected Leila would be as heartsore as Louisa.

She renewed her vow to continue the work without breaching any more barriers. The lesson preparation did not require she and Emmet meet every evening, but they still needed to get together for planning a couple of times a week.

Emmet insisted on coming to the farm. A form of sweet torture. She couldn't—wouldn't fall in love. She told herself this every day.

Even so, she could not imagine the pain she must endure when they left. Knew it would rival the pain of learning she would never bear children.

Lord, I'm trying to trust You. But my emotions get in the way. Help me. Hold me up lest I fall.

She feared she would soon test the truth of those words.

Chapter Ten

"**M**ay I sit with you?" At Emmet's voice behind her as she edged into the pew after Sally, Louisa jerked about, her heart in her throat.

"What are you doing here?" she whispered. He never came to church, because he had to stay with Ellie.

"Auntie May said I would turn into a heathen if I missed church another Sunday. She volunteered to stay with Ellie. They had some scheme cooked up. I believe I heard something about a bed picnic. I was warned not to return before supper time, so I'm at loose ends. Any suggestions as to how I should spend the afternoon?"

Sally overheard. "Join us. Madge and Judd are coming. It will be fun."

"I'd like that."

Louisa kept her head down, giving a great deal of attention to settling herself, arranging her purse and Bible on her lap, all the time resisting an urge to check and see that her hat was still on straight. And not looking at Emmet as she fought a battle in her heart.

Having him sit beside her in church crossed some kind of barrier. She hadn't expected she would be so blindsided by his presence. Her defenses weren't constructed.

Sally nudged her, and she realized the pastor had announced the first hymn. Her beloved sister took the hymnal before them and turned to share it with Mother. That left Louisa no choice but to share Emmet's hymnal. She barely touched the edge of the book, and yet every cell in her body tingled with awareness as she tried hopelessly to remain indifferent.

And then he began to sing. A hoarse, gravelly sound. Not unpleasant any more than the sound of water bubbling over rocks in a sun-warmed stream was unpleasant. She'd heard him sing silly songs to Ellie. Heard him whistle while he worked, or walked away from her house. But hearing him sing in church, while sitting next to her, joined by a narrow eight inches of book...

Her throat tightened, and she couldn't get out the words of the hymn. She coughed discreetly. Let the others think a tickle in her throat had choked her voice.

Throughout the service she was acutely aware of Emmet. His solidness. The warmth of his almost-touching body. The silent in and out of his breath. Her own twitching nerves.

She forced her attention to the sermon. Heard every word, but for the life of her couldn't have repeated a one of them.

By the time the last "amen" had been uttered, the final benediction offered, the last relaxed sigh of the congregation released, Louisa felt ready to explode from her skin. But she calmly rose when the others did. Nodded and smiled at Emmet as if he were one of their old, familiar neighbors sharing the pew, and made her way demurely after him to the aisle.

He stepped aside to let the Morgan ladies go ahead of him.

Sally paused, turned. "You'll be out right away? Or do you want a ride with us?"

"I'll be out in a few minutes. I need to let Auntie May know where I'm going. Just in case she needs me." He shifted his gaze between Sally and Louisa.

Louisa told herself she didn't see a flicker of hesitation. As if he'd guessed at her uncertainty and hoped she'd echo Sally's invitation. But she couldn't. She dare not admit to anyone, including herself, how much she wished she could put her arm through his and draw him into her family circle.

"We'll see you in a little while then?"

Emmet nodded agreement to Sally's question. Outside he strode down the street without a backward look.

Sally pulled Louisa toward the car. Mother lingered, talking to Mr. Roberts. No doubt asking after his wife and the new baby.

"I've never known you to be so rude."

Louisa stared at her sister. "I was not rude."

"Would it have hurt you to extend just a hint of welcome to the man?"

Louisa pursed her lips. "Did you ever think I might not want him spending Sunday afternoon with us? Do you know how hard it is to see him every day, be constantly reminded that I can never have—" She wouldn't say she could never have him. "What he represents."

"That's your choice. No one said you had to turn into a prune-faced spinster. Why you've closed your heart to the possibility of love without once giving a man the chance to decide if he is willing to accept you as you are is beyond me."

Pain sliced through Louisa's insides, leaving a trail of tears. "Sally, I've never known you to be cruel like this."

Sally sighed. "Louisa, I am not being cruel. Only pointing out that you might have closed the door prematurely."

"You've heard him yourself." She could manage only a tight whisper. "You know he wants more children."

"You don't have to fall in love with him. But it doesn't mean you have to shut yourself up in a cold casket either."

Louisa could not speak. Could barely remember how to breathe. No, she didn't have to fall in love with him.

How she wished she hadn't.

Sally grabbed her arm. "Mother is coming. Put on a happy face. We're going to go home and enjoy the afternoon with friends and family. You think you can manage that?"

"Of course." Friends and family. She had to remember it was nothing more.

Emmet changed his mind about going to the Morgans a dozen times after he left the church. For days he'd been aware of constraint between himself and Louisa. It was his fault. No doubt she felt he'd put her off by refusing to talk about his parents. But he finally concluded it would be rude not to show up.

So he told Auntie May and Ellie where he'd be. Laughed at the way they obviously wanted him to hurry and leave. He caught a glimpse of dandelions, cats and something red and furry on the bed. They expected Leila to appear soon. "I'd have brought her from church if you told me."

Ellie shook her head. "You weren't supposed to come back until supper time. It's your day off."

Emmet couldn't decide if he appreciated that the pair had schemed to allow him to be away for the afternoon, or if he felt suddenly useless.

But at least he could join the Morgans and Kirks without feeling he neglected his duties. He decided to walk, hoping the time and activity would enable him to discipline his thoughts into submission.

His stride ate up the miles, but when he headed up the lane toward the house, his steps slowed. An afternoon of adult company sounded fine, though he thought only of one person—Louisa. But—he threw back his shoulders—he could spend a relaxing afternoon without forgetting all his hard-learned life lessons.

Mrs. Morgan waited in the open doorway as he approached. "We're always glad to have another young man join us. Poor Judd is sadly outnumbered, I fear."

"Not a problem for me." Judd stepped from the kitchen. "Though I admit I am sometimes baffled by the reasoning of the female mind."

Remembering Louisa, Leila and Ellie hiding something in an underwear drawer, Emmet laughed. "I've known the same confusion from time to time." He glanced past Judd's shoulder. Saw Louisa watching him. Caught a flash of awareness in her eyes before she ducked away to put a dish on the table. Dare he hope that somewhere inside, she allowed a tender feeling toward him?

"Come in. Dinner is ready."

He knew a jolt of gratitude that Sally's words prevented him from following that errant thought any further.

Sally waved him to a chair. The others took their

places. Sally at one end of the table, Mrs. Morgan at the other. Judd and Madge side by side across from him. And to his left, Louisa. He wanted to glance at her, watch her face for hints as to how she felt.

He'd been so aware of her at his side during the church service that it was downright annoying. He could barely get his lungs to work for the tension of each moment.

So what, his brain mocked, are you doing here? Hoping to become immune to her?

Mrs. Morgan asked Judd to say the blessing. The food was passed. Simple, plain food, but more than adequate. Many survived—existed—on far less. The other day in the store, he'd heard terrible stories of people eating unusual things to keep themselves alive. One family had nothing but turnips to see them through the winter.

"Clara didn't come to church." Sally passed mashed potatoes to Emmet. "I wonder if her mother is doing poorly."

Mrs. Morgan answered her. "Mrs. Roberts is feeling better, according to her husband, and the baby is doing well."

"I suppose Clara is simply busy." Sally seemed content with the observation and the conversation shifted to other things, like who had moved on and what people were doing to cope.

Emmet hated to think of Louisa and her family struggling against the challenges of the drought and depression, and yet they didn't complain, only expressed concern for others.

"I bought four cows and calves." Judd was obviously pleased with his acquisition. "The man said he'd had enough of trying to eke out a living in this country and was headed west. Figured he could find work at the coast."

Emmet couldn't help but wonder how he would feed the critters, so he asked. Judd went into a very detailed account of his plans.

Madge sighed. "You should have never asked him. Honey, tell Emmet about how you worked on a ranch in the foothills." She grinned at Louisa, and the girls shared a moment of amusement.

Judd rattled his lips. "You're mocking me." His expression, though, said he considered it a privilege that his wife would tease him. He shifted his attention to Emmet. "I'll tell you later if you're interested. Madge, tell them about your baby chicks."

She leaned forward and explained in great detail how she'd put fourteen eggs to set and had ten healthy chicks.

Judd chuckled and whispered across the table, "If you think that's a lot of information, then don't ask about her garden."

Madge broke off midsentence. "Now who is mocking who?"

"Whom." Louisa corrected, and everyone but Emmet laughed.

Louisa broke off. "Sorry. I guess it's silly to a spectator, but we play these little games with each other."

"Speaking of games." Judd glanced around the table. "How about croquet after the dishes are done?"

"You're on." The three girls leaped to their feet and began gathering up the dishes.

Mrs. Morgan started putting things away, but Louisa caught her about the waist. "Mother, we have lots of help. You go nap and read your book."

Mrs. Morgan smiled at each of them. "I don't mind if I do."

Before she made it to her room, Madge whipped a tea towel around Judd's waist and secured it in his waistband. "You're the chief bottle washer."

Louisa tossed Emmet a towel. "Why don't you be the chief drier?"

Judd rolled his eyes. "They think they can soften us up so we'll be nice to them."

Madge planted her hands on her hips. "I believe you are my partner. Wasn't that part of our wedding vows?"

Another burst of shared laughter. This time Emmet joined in. He glanced at Louisa to gauge her reaction. Their eyes met. The air between them seemed to shift and buckle like shimmering heat waves. He forgot all his good intentions. He forgot to check the locks on his heart. He—

"Hey, Emmet. You going to dry this?" Judd nudged him, bringing him back to his senses. He carefully checked to make certain all the bolts were in place on those invisible doors as he turned away from Louisa's dark eyes and concentrated on drying dishes.

They finished up and carried a croquet set outside. Sally handed mallets to everyone. "Judd and Madge can challenge Louisa and Emmet. I'll be the referee."

"Referee? What kind of rules do you follow?" He'd played croquet a few times. One of the neighbors at his ranch liked the game and often invited others to join. It seemed like a gentle game to him.

"You haven't seen Judd play yet."

"Me?" Judd clutched at his chest. "I am a superb player."

The girls chortled.

Louisa fell in at Emmet's side. "I better warn you, Judd always has to win."

"Judd thinks he's superior because he's a man." Madge sounded as if it was a dreadful fate.

"I'm just a better player." Judd gloated, bringing another burst of denial from the girls.

Louisa leaned closer to Emmet to whisper, "Sounds like someone needs a little competition."

Emmet shifted so his mouth was close to her ears. So he could breathe in the sweetness of her. "We might just give him what he needs." And who—a distant voice demanded—would give *him* what he needed? He straightened. Forced the traitorous question into the back regions of his mind.

She laughed and took her place at the start. "Let the game begin."

Within minutes, it was obvious Judd had only one goal in mind—win by any means. Emmet was equally intent on proving his worth as an opponent. Sally was kept busy calling fair or foul and admonishing Judd to play by the rules.

After each turn Louisa and Madge stood back to watch Judd go after Emmet's ball, roqueting it out of the play area.

Emmet retrieved his ball and returned it to the imaginary yard line. "I hope you never decide I'm an enemy. You would stop at nothing to destroy me."

Sally warned Judd to stay within the boundaries.

Judd snorted. "I don't need to bend the rules to win. I'm just a better player." He swung his mallet with enough force to make Louisa shudder.

Emmet almost grabbed her to keep her safe from this attack. But the violence was restricted to the ball.

Judd leaned back, gloating.

"You've obviously had more practice, which doesn't equate to being better." Emmet lined up his shot and returned his ball to the playing area with precision. Only it encountered a lump in the rough yard and veered off course.

"Too bad," Louisa said. "But we'll still win."

Judd scoffed. "Not likely. Hurry up, Madge."

Madge sighed. "Louisa, I don't know why we're even playing. If these two want to go at each other, let them." She backed away, indicating she withdrew.

Louisa hesitated. Emmet wanted her to continue playing as his partner. He liked the sense that they fought a common enemy. Did she enjoy working together as much as he did? But Judd grinned at him—though it would better be described as a mocking sneer.

Louisa retreated to Madge's side. "This ought to be fun. I can't wait to see Judd defeated."

Emmet's chest seemed to grow several inches at her support of him.

"I wouldn't be counting my chickens before they hatch," Madge warned, which brought a burst of laughter from her sisters.

"You know a lot about hatching chickens, after all," Sally teased.

Louisa watched Emmet, her silent encouragement filling him with determination. She cheered as he played, sending his ball through a wicket.

Judd followed with a nasty hit. Emmet shook his head in mock sadness. "Where did you learn to be so competitive?"

"From my brothers."

As the pair continued to play, Judd explained. "Brothers teach you to play a game well. Then they teach you how to defend yourself." Wham—on Emmet's ball. "Then they teach you how to defeat your opponent."

Emmet knocked his ball back in. "You don't need brothers to learn how to play hard and fair."

"Nope." Wham again. "But without brothers, it seems to me you have a choice about how you play a game. With brothers, you don't."

"Don't we always have a choice about our actions?" He felt as if he was parroting something Louisa said, and he glanced in her direction.

Her eyes said she recognized the echo of her beliefs. For a moment their gazes held in an invisible bond, then Louisa turned away and wrapped her arm about Madge's waist. "I can see it's much better to have sisters. We are always so kind and helpful to each other."

"Yes, indeed." Madge placed her arm around Louisa's waist and giggled.

"I'm certainly glad for a family of girls." Judd came over and gave Madge a quick kiss. "Especially the middle sister." He returned to the game.

In the end, Judd won…by sheer determination, Emmet figured.

"I'll give you a chance to win the next round." Judd seemed eager to have another go.

Emmet handed the mallet to Sally and held his hands up in mock defeat. "I concede."

Judd did a victory dance and shook his hands together over his head.

Madge groaned. "It wouldn't hurt you to be a little humble about it."

He pulled her into his arms and kissed her.

Emmet turned away. Their love was so apparent. He'd

tried love once. But he'd failed as a husband. He hadn't been able to protect Jane, keep her safe. Part of him wanted to yell a warning to these people. Love hurts. But perhaps they would be spared the grief he'd known.

Judd grabbed Madge's hand. "Mrs. Kirk, let's you and I walk home across the fields. What do you think of that idea?" The adoring smile blessed Madge with his love and devotion and left Emmet feeling alone and cranky.

Madge beamed her love back at Judd. "Whatever you say, Mr. Kirk." She ducked her head in mock submission, then laughed as they raced toward home.

Sally yawned. "I have a book to read."

That left Louisa and Emmet stranded in the yard. "Shall we go for a walk?" He half expected her to demur, but instead she turned toward the trail that led past the barn and he readily fell in at her side.

The sun shone brightly. The sky spread out from horizon to horizon like an unbroken blue canvas. All in all, a beautiful afternoon. He didn't mind in the least sharing it with a beautiful woman.

"I've enjoyed the afternoon."

"I'm glad. I was afraid you might find my family overwhelming."

"Not at all." They paused to lean on a wooden gate. "You have what I've always wanted."

She looked as surprised as if he'd announced he carried rain in his back pocket. "Really? I can't imagine."

"Family. Siblings." His voice had thickened, but he couldn't help it. "I always felt lonely growing up alone." Abandoned.

She looked away, her gaze seeking the far edge of the field. "You know what I want?"

"No. What?" Whatever it was, he wished he could give it to her.

She paused for a beat. Two. Shuddered as if a chill had raced across her shoulders. She tried to speak, but her voice caught.

It obviously meant a lot to her. And his heart softened with such a protective urge that it was all he could do not to pull her into his arms and hold her close, keep her safe.

"For it to rain." Her voice rang with determination. "I pray for it every single day."

He knew without a doubt that wasn't what she'd started to say. Disappointment stained his insides. What was she afraid to admit she needed? For that matter, what made him think he could do anything about it? Keep her safe? What a bitter thought. He couldn't keep anyone safe.

She faced him squarely with a look of such fierce determination that he blinked. "We have no choice but to trust God. He will supply all our needs."

He wondered if she meant simply rain—or the lack of it—but her faith blared through him, seared away doubts.

"I do believe that." As he had never before believed.

Chapter Eleven

Louisa managed to walk back to the house with Emmet. Somehow bid him goodbye. Her lungs felt as tight as when she'd had pneumonia. Only she knew it was shock and sorrow, and her struggle to contain them, that caused her distress. She tiptoed into the house, not wanting anyone to see her. Her sister and mother knew her too well not to notice how stiff her face was as she held back her emotions. But the house was quiet. Mother must still be in her room, and Sally was likely reading in her room as well. She'd do the same, and she stumbled upstairs, Mouse whining at her heels.

The dog jumped to the bed, but Louisa's limbs were too stiff to be able to sit, let alone lie down. She stood in the middle of the room, as lost as if she had somehow landed in a foreign country. Nothing in her room seemed familiar. Maybe looking out the window would help. But she couldn't move.

Her insides groaned, but no sound escaped her lips. She couldn't find a word or sound to express the gut-wrenching way she felt.

He wanted more children. She'd almost confessed

how much she wanted them too. How it was impossible. Caught herself just in time. She couldn't confess it to him. He would despise her inability if he knew.

She'd substituted her desire for rain at the last minute. But as she vowed she trusted God, tension had eased from her insides. Unfortunately the release had lasted only until Emmet said goodbye. Then it returned with wicked insistence. She counted the number of weeks until Ellie would have her cast off and this torture would end. It seemed an eternity away.

I must trust God. He would not send me more than I can bear.

Oh, but how much did He think she could take?

Strength slowly returned to her limbs. Overwhelming exhaustion followed. She sank to her bed, cradled Mouse in her arms and fell asleep.

The next day, still feeling as if she needed to sleep a week or longer, she returned to tutoring Ellie.

"My daddy had to take care of some business," Ellie said by way of greeting. "He won't be here today."

A reprieve. *Thank You, Lord.* Only, regret twisted with gratitude. She missed him.

She better get used to it.

The morning passed slowly. Although Ellie did her lessons well, Louisa found it difficult to concentrate until Ellie crossed her arms over her chest and glared at her.

"What's wrong with you?"

Louisa snapped to attention. "Nothing. Why?"

"Did I do something wrong?"

"Not that I know of. Why do you ask?"

Ellie's face crumpled, and tears flowed. "Why are you mad at me?"

"But I'm not. Why would you think that?"

"'Cause you act like it."

Louisa shook her head. "But I haven't said one cross word."

"You pretend you don't hear me."

"Oh, honey. I've been distracted is all. My mind has been on other things. I'm sorry. It's not your fault. Not for a minute."

"You sure?" Ellie's voice still carried her tears.

"Of course I'm sure." After that she devoted her attention to the child and, to her relief, found it helped her forget her problems.

As the days passed, she continued to find solace in teaching Ellie. But it only partially relieved the ache that grew like lengthening evening shadows inside her soul.

One afternoon, after a morning with Ellie, she made her way home but paused at the turnoff to Madge and Judd's house. Madge was the practical one. Perhaps she could help Louisa find a solution to her growing restlessness. She turned down the drive.

Madge saw her coming and hurried to meet her. "It's been a long time since you've been here."

Louisa laughed. "Not much more than a week. We all came last Friday."

"But you haven't paid me a visit." She drew Louisa's arm through hers. "Never mind, I know you're busy. Come see my garden." Plants were poking through. Madge glanced skyward. "Oh, for some rain."

The remark echoed Louisa's comment to Emmet. The darkness inside overwhelmed her. She sank to the grass beside the garden and buried her face in her hands. "Oh, Madge. What am I going to do?"

Madge sat beside her. "What's wrong?"

"Everything." She sounded like a spoiled child, but she didn't care.

"Maybe you'd like to be a little more specific."

She flashed Madge a trembling smile. "I don't know if I can be." Or perhaps she simply didn't want to confess the truth.

"It's about Emmet, isn't it?"

Louisa stared across the garden.

"I see how he looks at you. How you look at him."

She flinched. "I try not to—"

"What? Feel something for him? Louie, why not let yourself care?"

Louisa pressed her lips together and held back the pain. She didn't speak for a moment. When she did, her voice trembled like the last leaf of summer in a winter wind. "You heard him. He's always wanted a large family. I can't give him that."

"Judd wanted to go back to the mountains until he fell in love with me. He says after that, his priorities changed. He wanted a secure home. He wanted to be near family. Maybe Emmet is the same."

Louisa shook her head. "I would never be able to give him what he wants."

"On the other hand, maybe you can give him what he needs."

The idea scratched across her thoughts. If only she could believe it.

Madge went on. "Maybe what he's looking for is something that family represents."

"Like what?" What was there besides lots of joy as children ran about? Pleasure in watching them grow and develop? Sharing around a crowded table or in a circle in a front room? She didn't even have to close her eyes to imagine herself in a big living room made of logs, the windows overlooking a stream. It was winter. The stream was frozen and children skated on it. A baby cooed in its cradle. And Emmet played with a toddler. Her insides felt bitter at her foolish dreams.

"I would think that happiness, love, security, partnership are all things that don't require having children."

Madge's words were but meaningless letters of the alphabet. Louisa knew they held no answer for her. Emmet—if he ever thought of marrying again—wanted children. Lots of children.

Louisa sighed deeply. "I seem to have a natural aptitude for teaching, or so Adele tells me. I would go to Normal school if I had the money."

Madge didn't say anything. Louisa gave her time to digest the information, and when she still didn't venture an opinion, she turned to study her face. Madge wore a careful expression.

"What?" Louisa asked, knowing Madge wanted to say something.

"It's your life. And although I agree you would make a dandy teacher, I don't think you should choose to become one simply to avoid facing life."

Madge's evaluation of Louisa stung. "I am not trying to escape life. I have no intention of avoiding it. I spent enough years on the sidelines. But I think I would get a lot of satisfaction out of teaching children."

"I think what you mean is you would find it a substitute for having your own family."

Louisa shifted so she could lean very close to Madge. "I can never have my own family. You know that."

Madge stuck out her chin. Their faces almost touched. "No. You cannot have children. It isn't the same thing."

"I thought you might offer some words of comfort or wisdom. After all, you're the one who always knows how to solve a problem. Instead you mock me."

Madge chuckled. "I gave you answers. You just aren't willing to consider them." She tucked her hand around Louisa's elbow. "Now forget about it and come see what I've done in the house."

Louisa allowed Madge to drag her along. By the time they reached the kitchen her anger had evaporated. After all, she could hardly blame Madge for not understanding what it meant to never be able to have children. And despite Madge's argument that love would be enough, Louisa would never force a man she loved to make such a choice.

Madge pointed out the new curtains she'd made. "From an old dress Judd's mother gave me." Louisa noticed the vase full of wild buffalo beans and pussy willows.

"Now sit and we'll have lemonade."

Boots thudded on the step.

"Oh, good. Judd is going to join us." Madge looked toward the door, a look of such sweet expectation on her face that Louisa had to turn away. She would never be able to experience that emotion. *Lord God, help me be strong.*

"Hon, I brought company." Judd stepped into the room, Emmet at his heels.

Dismay jolted through Louisa. She half rose, intent on escape, but the men blocked the doorway.

Madge glanced at Louisa, silently signaling her to stay put.

Louisa sank back, her chest pressing toward her backbone.

Emmet saw her. Nodded a greeting. Hung his hat beside Judd's as Judd explained he and Emmet were taking down an abandoned building and using it to build a bigger chicken house. "The way my wife successfully raises chickens, the little shed she's been using is not going to be good enough." He pulled Madge close and kissed her nose.

Louisa couldn't tear her gaze from Emmet's. His look went on and on, silently laying claim to her thoughts even as she scrambled to put up barriers, to block the emotions that she feared tumbled from her eyes.

Then Judd pulled out a chair and indicated Emmet should sit.

Louisa sucked in air and shifted her gaze to the center of the table, where the vase of flowers stood on a lacy doily.

Conversation winged back and forth past Louisa. She nodded, smiled and made an occasional comment, but it wasn't until Judd and Emmet left to return to their work, until Louisa said goodbye to Madge and hastened homeward, that she could breathe without her eyes stinging. *Oh, God, help me.*

He wouldn't be here much longer. Somehow the idea offered no comfort, only an ache drawn out down a long empty road. She must make plans. Find escape from her memories. More and more she considered the possibility of attending Normal school. If only she had the finances.

Emmet did his best to be out of the way when Louisa came to the house. He sensed she didn't welcome his presence and the knowledge sliced through him, even as he assured himself it suited him. He didn't want to feel anything for her except appreciation for her work with Ellie.

Tomorrow he was scheduled to take Ellie to the doctor to see if her body cast could come off.

"I'm going to run and run and run as soon as it's off," Ellie said.

"You might have to take it easy for a little while and be content to walk."

"Nope. I'm gonna run."

Emmet knew there was a chance her leg wouldn't be better. She might have to wear the body cast longer. But he didn't have the heart to tell her so. If only he could make things work out the way Ellie wanted. He waited until Ellie fell asleep.

"Auntie May, I'm going out for a while." Waiting for tomorrow and the verdict filled his brain with sharp fragments of something.

He turned his steps down a familiar road. The one that led to Judd's. And past that, to the Morgan farm. But he wouldn't stop at either place. He just needed to walk off his tension.

He passed the Kirk farm. Saw Madge in the garden. She glanced up and waved. He waved back and continued on his way.

Despite his resolve, his steps slowed as he approached the turnoff to the Morgan home. He'd have a quick glance and see if anyone was outside. Yes—a figure in the garden. Louisa. He would recognize her anywhere. Doing what she enjoyed. He grinned as he remembered her saying that's what she did for fun.

She straightened—her back to him—and stretched, then returned to her task.

It would be unseemly to pass without speaking to her.

He allowed himself the convenient excuse as he headed her direction.

She heard his approach and turned. A flash of welcome lit her eyes, then she shuttered it.

But it was enough to make him feel welcomed, if only temporarily. It was enough that he knew he was right in coming here.

She waited for him to cross the last three feet. "I suppose you're excited about Ellie getting her cast off."

"Nervous, if you want the truth."

"Really? Why?"

"She's so eager. How will she deal with it if the doctor says she must wear it another month?"

"That's possible? I didn't know."

They perched on two of the five rocks at the end of the garden. Louisa smiled. "Not comfortable chairs, but Father put them here shortly after we moved. He said a person needed to take a break once in a while, but he didn't think we should get too comfortable." She studied him. "I know it sounds trite to say God is in control. But He is." She looked so serene. So positive.

"Aren't there times when you find that hard to believe?"

Something dark flickered through her eyes, and she nodded. "I'm grateful He doesn't change like we do. He's the same yesterday, today and forever."

He clung to the words and held her gaze. "Thank you."

Her smile flashed. "I only repeated God's word."

"I know, but I needed the reminder. Would you—" He hesitated. Would she think his request odd? Or too personal? "Would you pray with me?"

"Of course." She reached for his hands, stopped, but

before she could pull them back to her lap, he took them and bowed his head. "God, I ask You to make things go well for Ellie tomorrow. Help me trust You more." It wasn't elegant, but he spoke what he meant. He continued to hold her hands, enjoying the strength and oneness the contact provided.

"Lord," she whispered. "I ask the same thing. Help Ellie's leg be healed. Help me trust You more."

He raised his head. Watched her slowly lift her face to him. Their gazes locked, searched—hers a little guarded, his anxious. Dare he dream that somewhere inside her heart lurked a tenderness toward him?

He would not dream such dreams. Allow such hopes. But he couldn't help himself. So he sat smiling at her, their hands still clasped.

"Would you come with us tomorrow?"

She blinked, sat up straighter, pulled her hands to her lap. "I don't know."

"Ellie would like it." He cracked a door inside him ajar and allowed a deep-throated admission out. "I'd appreciate it."

"Okay." She nodded slowly.

Her agreement eased his tension. He could face whatever happened with her at his side, knowing her faith would never waver. More than that, he was certain she shared his concerns, his—

He could not allow himself to take the thought to a conclusion. He would not think about what it would be like to have someone to share the ups and downs of every day.

"I'll see you tomorrow."

Doc came to the waiting room. When he saw Louisa he looked startled, then gave a flash of a smile before he turned to Ellie. "Well, young lady, I suppose you'd like to keep that cast a little longer."

"No, I don't. I want to get rid of it."

He chuckled. "Then let's see what we can do. We'll take some pictures of your leg. As soon as the films are developed, we'll know if the cast comes off or not. Emmet and Louisa, you can wait here." He called his nurse and they wheeled Ellie to the X-ray room.

Emmet leaned over his knees, his heels bouncing up and down in a frantic rhythm.

Louisa realized how nervous he was about Ellie. She could offer him no assurances about the leg. "She's in good hands. Doc has cared for me a number of times, and he is the most gentle, kind person one could ask for."

Emmet nodded. "I hope she's not scared in there."

Louisa touched his shoulder and got his attention. "We are talking about your daughter, aren't we? Ellie, the girl who climbs trees, rides horses and confronts challenges with a jutted chin?"

His gaze claimed hers. He read her encouragement, her comfort and perhaps a whole lot more that she didn't intend he should see. Then he chuckled. "Right."

She retreated back into the protection of her guarded heart.

He blew out a long breath. "It's me who's worried. What if her leg isn't better?"

"Then you take her back to Auntie May's house and continue to care for her as you have."

"It's that simple, isn't it?" He didn't seem relieved.

She touched his arm, feeling his tension beneath her fingers. "I'm not saying it's simple, only that if it's necessary you will do it. You will always do what is best for her."

He nodded and settled back, as if he had found his direction on a compass. "You're right."

Over the waiting room door hung a big clock that ticked the minutes off in merciless reluctance.

Emmet sprang to his feet and strode over to look down the hall. "What's taking so long?"

She wished she had words of comfort, but it did seem Ellie had been gone a long time. She hurried to Emmet's side to stare down the hallway.

He reached for her hand and squeezed. She squeezed back, as tense as he. What if something was wrong?

Without giving herself a chance to consider her actions, she pressed her shoulder to his, finding and receiving comfort from the touch.

A door opened. The nurse wheeled Ellie toward them. Emmet rushed to Ellie's side.

Louisa wisely went to Ellie's other side. She must remember who she was and her role here, and not cling to Emmet so blatantly.

"What did the doctor say?" Emmet demanded of the nurse.

"He's reading the X-rays right now. He'll be with you soon."

"I'm tired of waiting," Ellie whined.

Louisa took Ellie's hand on her side, Emmet the hand on his side, and they leaned over the child.

"We'll know soon." Louisa tried to sound cheerful, but she was as anxious as the other two. She thought her muscles would snap like an overstretched rubber band by the time Doc strode back into the room.

"Good news."

The air whooshed from three sets of lungs.

"Her leg looks fine. However, she will have to be

careful for a while. Now let's get that cast off and get her on crutches. She'll have to use them until I say otherwise. I'll have my nurse instruct her."

Emmet grabbed two hands—Louisa's and Ellie's—and raised them in a victory salute, then shook the doctor's hand.

Louisa couldn't stop smiling. Neither, she guessed, could Emmet and Ellie. It was good to celebrate such a wonderful occasion with them.

Doc and his nurse took them to a little room where they endured the nerve-racking ordeal of watching the cast being cut away.

When it was off, Ellie sat up for the first time in weeks. She swayed a little.

"Take your time," Doc advised.

But Ellie wasn't about to waste a minute of her first hours of being free. She made to spring from the bed, but Doc caught her.

"You have to use crutches for now."

The nurse helped her to the floor and showed her how to use the crutches. Ellie balanced on her crutches, her eyes bright.

"You are to use these at all times, young lady," the doctor warned. He stood to speak to Emmet. "She'll need time to build up the muscles to support that bone."

"She'll be careful." Emmet meant he'd make sure she was.

Louisa couldn't stop smiling. She'd never seen Ellie standing. Never seen her without the bulky cast. Something inside Louisa glowed with an emotion she wouldn't admit to. She looked at the thick mane of dark blond hair and thought how she'd like to brush it and fasten it back with a bow.

A troubling thought pushed at her joy, but she refused to give it any attention. Today was a day for celebrating.

Emmet guarded Ellie as she swung from the room. "Slow down."

Ellie sighed and rolled her eyes, which brought a tickle of laughter to Louisa's throat.

Emmet glowered at them both. "It's my job to take care of you."

"I'm being careful." Ellie slowed down measurably. "Can we go to the store and get a piece of candy? I want to go inside and pick my own."

"Seems reasonable." Emmet helped Ellie into the truck, held the door for Louisa then ran around and climbed in behind the wheel.

Louisa allowed her happiness at sharing this moment with them to balloon until it obliterated every other thought. This was a day to remember only with joy.

She and Emmet stayed on each side of Ellie as she negotiated the steps into the store. Joanie stood behind the counter.

"Hello, Louisa. Hi, Emmet. Guess you don't remember me?"

Emmet spared her a quick smile. "Last time I saw you, you had pigtails and a muddy face."

Joanie wrinkled her nose. "I was a tomboy, wasn't I? This is your little girl. I heard about her."

"Ellie, this is Miss Sharp."

Joanie snorted. "It's just plain Joanie. Nice to see you out of your cast, Ellie. How about a candy stick to celebrate? A treat."

"Thank you." Ellie hobbled to the display of candy.

Emmet angled against the counter, standing close to

his daughter to guard her. Joanie stood by Louisa. "Tell Madge to come and see me. I've got some good news."

"Conrad has asked you to marry him? Finally?"

Joanie shook her head. "Not so far. He's a stubborn, stubborn man. I hope he doesn't expect me to wait forever. One of these days I'm going to find me someone else." She eyed Emmet up and down. "You looking for a wife, Emmet?"

Poor Emmet. He glanced toward the door. Louisa figured the only thing that kept him from running was his concern for Ellie.

Louisa chuckled. "She's teasing. She's only interested in one man. Conrad Burns. Only, his parents are both dead, and he's raising four younger siblings."

Joanie snorted. "You think he'd be glad of my help, but no. The man says he doesn't want to burden me with his responsibilities." She huffed around the counter. "No, sir. He'd far rather burden me with loneliness and impatience." She bent her head so low, it almost touched Ellie's. "This is a new flavor—green apple. I like it. Want to try it?" She held it up and popped it in when Ellie opened her mouth. "Good, isn't it?"

Ellie's eyes widened, and she nodded. "Can I have a licorice too?" She gave her father an appealing look. When he nodded, Joanie put one in a paper bag and handed it to Ellie.

A few minutes later they departed.

"I don't want to go home," Ellie said, craning her head from side to side to see everything. "Can we go by the school and pick up Leila?" School was almost over for the day.

Emmet hesitated. "I don't want you overdoing it."

"Please, Daddy, please."

Louisa turned to look out the side window to hide her amusement.

"Can we take her on a picnic? It would be so much fun to celebrate. After all, this is a very special occasion for me." Ellie's voice grew shrill with excitement.

Emmet groaned. "I don't suppose I could say no?"

Ellie quieted. "I suppose you could, but do you think it's necessary?"

Louisa grinned at Emmet across the child's blond head.

He shook his head in mock resignation, but his eyes glowed with joy. "Only if Louisa will join us."

"I'd love to." How could she refuse a part in this joy? "If we go by the farm I'll prepare food." There was bread enough for sandwiches, and no doubt Sally would have made more cookies. Simple but adequate. After all, it wasn't the food that was important, it was sharing this special occasion.

So they went to the school, where Ellie insisted on getting out and standing by the car. Several children raced by her and waved, then Miss Ross spotted them and hurried over. "You are back on your feet. What good news. This means—"

Leila saw Ellie and screeched, "You're all better!" She danced around Ellie, sending them both into a fit of giggles.

Adele stepped back. "You have two very happy little girls. Leila hasn't stopped talking all day about the possibility of Ellie getting her cast off." She beamed at both of them, then turned to Louisa. "Come by in the next day or two."

Louisa's balloon deflated. She had been pushing away what this meant…she'd no longer need to tutor Ellie. The child could go to school. Emmet and Ellie would likely return to their ranch. Her temporary happiness had come to an end. Now was the time she had dreaded. Had tried to prepare for. Somehow she would hold her head high and make it through. If only she hadn't agreed to accompany them on the picnic. But she had, and she wouldn't disappoint Ellie by retracting her promise.

Leila squeezed in beside Ellie in the truck and hugged her. "Now we can make a playhouse in the bushes like we talked about."

Louisa wanted to warn Leila that her days of enjoying Ellie's company would soon end, when Emmet took his daughter back to the ranch. However, the facts would have to be faced soon enough. In the meantime, let the girls enjoy each other.

The pair chattered away as they drove to the orphanage and received permission to take Leila for a few hours. Then they swung by the Morgan place so Louisa could pack a lunch.

Emmet and the girls waited outside so they could play with Mouse.

Mother was away visiting a friend, but Sally was home and helped Louisa prepare the food.

"It's nice to see Ellie up and about," Sally said. "How do you feel about it?"

"It's a joyous occasion. That's why we're celebrating with a picnic."

Sally nudged her, forcing her to meet her look. "I asked how you feel."

She met her sister's eyes without flinching. "Why, I'm happy, of course."

"You will be out of a job. More important, you will

no longer have an excuse to see Emmet. Or Ellie, for that matter."

Louisa blinked away the sting in her eyes. "I've known from the beginning it was temporary."

"Does it have to be?" Although Sally's voice was soft, it was also prodding.

"You know it does." She stubbornly concentrated on packing cookies into a basket.

"Oh, Louisa. Stop running away."

"I have no intention of running anywhere."

"Except from your heart."

Let Sally think love could be enough. Let her believe other things didn't matter. May she never experience the pain of knowing otherwise. "I will celebrate the good news with Emmet and the girls. Then I will say good-bye as I planned." She grabbed the basket and marched for the door.

Sally called after her. "I will pray you get over your stubborn denial."

Louisa ignored her words and handed the basket to Emmet, who stowed it in the back and called the girls to climb in the truck. They bounced forward on the edge of the seat.

"Where are we going?" Leila demanded.

"A long, long ways," Ellie said. "I don't want this day to ever end."

Louisa tried to keep her attention on the familiar scene out the front window, but when Emmet groaned, she couldn't stop herself from turning toward him. His gaze caught hers and held it in a warm smile.

"I think we'll stay close to home. Don't you think that's wise, Louisa?"

Two little girls turned to her, silently imploring. She

forced herself to turn from Emmet's gaze and consider the children. "I think Ellie should take it easy for a day or two. Wouldn't you agree?"

Ellie looked ready to deny the need, but Leila nodded. "I wouldn't want anything to happen to her. We'll be happy anywhere." She turned to Ellie and took her hand. "Won't we?"

Ellie studied the younger girl, and her expression softened. "Uh-huh."

Startled by how connected the two seemed, Louisa shifted her attention to Emmet. Was he aware of how close the girls had grown? From the speculative way he considered them, she thought he was starting to notice. She turned away. How could any of them escape this situation without pain? She could tolerate it, but the girls? It didn't seem fair. But hadn't she learned life wasn't always fair, if one judged it from an earthly view? She could only pray they would all be better and stronger for the experience.

In the meantime, she meant to do everything in her power to help the girls have an afternoon they would not forget.

"There." She pointed toward a little grove of trees. "That's a nice place for a picnic."

Emmet pulled to the side of the road and came around to help Louisa out. Her heart burst with longing as he took her hand and waited for her to gain her feet. Thankfully he didn't seem inclined to prolong the moment, and turned to lift Leila down then edged Ellie out. But he kept her in his arms.

"I think I better carry you across the field."

"I'll take her crutches." Leila gladly carried the burden. Louisa grabbed the picnic basket and followed them.

Ellie proudly clung to her father, while Leila bounced happily at his side.

"Stop. Shh." Emmet halted and held his finger to his lips.

"What?" Ellie whispered.

"A baby antelope. See it?" He pointed.

Louisa followed the direction he indicated and saw nothing but yellowed grass and gray rocks, then she noticed the shape of a tawny-colored rock. A little animal no bigger than a jackrabbit curled into a ball.

"Where? I can't see it." Leila wavered on tiptoes.

"You aren't tall enough." Emmet scooped her up in his free arm. Two little heads pressed to each side of Emmet's face.

At the sight, Louisa's mouth went dry as the grass at her feet. He deserved to have his arms…his home…his heart full of children.

Leila saw the baby antelope at last. "Ohh. Can we touch it?"

"Best we leave it be."

"But he's all alone. I bet he's afraid."

Louisa heard a note of longing that ached clear through her. This child knew about being alone.

Emmet's arms tightened around both girls, and she guessed he'd felt the same tug of loneliness in Leila's words. "The mommy will come back and get him after she's found her lunch."

Leila touched his cheek and turned his face so she could stare into his eyes. "You sure?"

He grew very sober. "I promise."

The two considered each other for several seconds. Then Emmet drew in a shuddering breath.

Louisa couldn't begin to understand what he felt. Disappointment that he had only one child when he ached for more? Pain that Leila had lost her family? She wasn't sure she even wanted to know, but she did want to help him and moved to his side. "Who's hungry?"

"I am," three voices chorused.

Leila did not ask to be put down, nor did Emmet make any indication he wanted to release her, so Louisa scooped up the crutches and followed them to the trees. They sat on the patch of green grass in the shade. Leila scampered to Ellie's side, and they were soon engaged in play that involved creating a family and a home from twigs and leaves.

Emmet kept his gaze on the distant horizon. Louisa wondered what he thought but was content to give her attention to the girls. She passed around the sandwiches and settled back with a sigh of contentment. Yet this would soon be over. She would not be spending quiet afternoons with Emmet and the girls. But for today, for this moment, she would not let the future steal from her joy.

Emmet chewed thoughtfully. "Good sandwiches. Thanks."

She chuckled. "They're only peanut butter and syrup."

His grin teased. "Maybe so, but the situation makes them special."

She nodded. "It's so good to see Ellie up and about."

"It's a huge weight off my shoulders, I can tell you." He grew somber as he watched the girls, and again she wondered what he thought. She squelched her curiosity. Before long, before she was ready to accept it, she would no longer be aware of his shifting expressions, have cause to wonder about his reactions or be aware of him watching her as he was now. She tried to keep her attention on rearranging the contents of the picnic basket, but forbidden, her gaze went to his. And her heart stalled at the insistent way he studied her.

"Louisa—"

Whatever he'd meant to say was cut off by Ellie's shriek. "Ants! Everywhere!" She flapped her hands over her legs and chest.

Leila sobbed quietly and stared at them crawling up her legs.

Emmet bolted to his feet, grabbed both girls and swiped his hands over their bodies until he was certain all the ants were gone. "You were sitting practically on top of an anthill. Why didn't I notice? You could have been bitten." He pressed both girls to his sides and hugged them.

Louisa wasn't sure who was more upset—the girls or Emmet. He blamed himself for being careless. She gathered up the rest of the picnic. "Seems you can't have a picnic without uninvited guests showing up."

Leila giggled. "Ants like picnics too."

Ellie sniffled, then seeing Leila's reaction, she straightened. "I'd say they do. Here's your old picnic." She tossed a bread crust at the ants. The girls laughed as ants clamored over it.

Emmet straightened. Seeing the harshness in his expression, Louisa touched his arm. "No harm done."

"I should have been watching more carefully." He scooped up both girls. "Let's get out of here." He glanced over his shoulder. "Can you manage?"

She nodded. Yes, she would manage. Somehow.

Ellie glanced back over her dad's shoulder. "I thought there were cookies."

Emmet chuckled. "I guess even ants can't dim your appetite."

"Nope."

Louisa's tension released. "We'll share them in the truck."

They ate cookies then drove back toward the Morgan place. Emmet stopped at the house. Louisa hopped out before he could climb from the truck and open the door. She hugged each of the little girls. Let her glance breeze by Emmet without meeting his eyes, then headed for the house.

"See you tomorrow." Emmet stood with one foot on the ground, the other still in the truck.

"Yes." Would she be saying her final goodbye then?

Her legs feeling much too long and decidedly wooden, she walked calmly indoors. Sally must have understood how fragile Louisa felt, for she squeezed her shoulder but kept her comments to herself. Somehow she made it through supper, helped with the dishes, carried water to the garden—said normal things, did normal things. But inside she was as lifeless as last year's brown, crackly grass.

She finally retreated to bed. Opened her Bible and read a few verses, as she had promised Father she would do. But nothing reached her soul. She had fallen in love with a man against her better judgment—and his little girl.

She must hold herself together until it was over.

The morning sun seemed weak. Or was it too bright? Louisa wanted to pull the covers over her head and ignore it. Ignore life. But she knew if she didn't show up at the breakfast table Mother would fret. *Are you sick? Should I call the doctor? I was afraid this would happen. I told you not to try and work.*

And if she let any of her emotions show, Sally would comment. *I told you it was impossible to lock your feelings up. Why don't you tell him how you feel? Once he knows the truth he won't care. Love is more than enough.* Sally was such a romantic.

So she rose, dressed, put on her happy face and went downstairs. Her smile was still firmly in place when she drove up to the Hamilton house. It faltered only slightly when she entered the house and heard voices in the kitchen.

"Come join us," Auntie May called.

Louisa trudged across the crowded living room to the kitchen. The three of them sat around the table. As usual, cats sat on the unoccupied chairs and crowded around Louisa's ankles.

"No more eating in bed," Ellie crowed.

"Coffee?" Auntie May asked.

Louisa politely refused.

"Have a chair." Emmet shooed a cat off the chair next to him and swept aside the hairs.

Louisa sat. How was she to say goodbye when everything in her called to say "I want to stay"?

Ellie rambled on about Leila and the games they could play now that she wasn't in a cast. Auntie May scolded a couple of cats for being too inquisitive about what was on the table. More than once, Louisa had wondered if she let them eat off the table like guests when she was alone. The clock over the table ticked loudly. Across the street a child called goodbye as he headed off to school.

Emmet looked at the clock. "I suppose it's time to start lessons."

"Aw. Do I have to?"

Louisa sucked in air. Now was the time. "I won't be tutoring you anymore, now that you can go to school."

Her announcement landed with a plop and lay silent and quivering as everyone stared at her.

Ellie let out a wail that sent half the cats scurrying into the other room. "I don't want to go to school. I want you to teach me."

Louisa widened her eyes to keep back the tears. "I'm going to miss teaching you." She reached for Ellie, wanting to hug and console her.

Ellie pushed her away. "You don't care about me. You were just being nice because you had to be."

"No, Ellie. That isn't true. You know it isn't."

"I hate you." Ellie struggled to her feet. Pushed away her father's helping hand. She staggered as one crutch went too wide.

Emmet scrambled to her side. "Take it easy, Button."

She shrugged away from him, made it to her room and slammed the door.

Incredible silence followed her departure, the only sound her muffled sobs.

Louisa pushed to her feet, backed from the room. "I'm sorry. So sorry." Then she fled.

Where could she hide? Where could she escape her feelings? She should find comfort in knowing that God was with her in this private torture. She had no choice but to seek His consolation.

She walked until she reached a dry, dusty slough. The willows surrounding it were verdant with new growth, and she turned aside into their shelter. She found a spot where the grass was flattened and sank down, buried her head in her hands and wept. *Oh, God, help me through this.*

Her tears were enough to water the drought-stricken land, but eventually they ended, leaving her drained but ready to march forward. Somehow she would get through this, and she would do so with grace and dignity because she trusted God to provide both.

Chapter Twelve

The next day, Emmet took Ellie to school, making sure Adele understood she was not to be too active.

"I'll keep her and Leila inside where they can play quietly."

He ached to stay. Ellie was his responsibility. It was hard to leave her in someone else's care. But he had no choice.

Just as he had no choice but to let Louisa go. She deserved more than a broken-down man with a seven-year-old child.

He strode out of town, the opposite direction he normally took. His steps pounded the truth from him. It wasn't what she deserved—although she surely deserved more than he had to offer—that made him let her walk away. Auntie May had lots to say about that. *Your child needs a mother. You need a wife. You can't pretend you're dead. You're a young man yet. What about your dream for a large family? Think what beautiful children Louisa would give you.*

He growled as he thought of the beautiful children.

Dare he allow himself to love again? Was it worth the risk?

He couldn't answer and scuffled his way back home, where he set about fixing the back fence. A job he shouldn't have neglected so long.

Auntie May came out at noon. "Lunch is ready."

He went indoors and sat at the table.

She eyed him as he ate. "Emmet—"

"No more. You've said all I care to hear. We'll be heading home any day now." Just as soon as the doctor gave his final okay on Ellie's leg. "I'm just waiting for her to manage without crutches."

In the meantime, he would make sure Auntie May's place was in good shape. He cleaned out the cellar. He organized the storage shed in the back corner. He pruned trees. He found some discarded cans of paint in the cellar, mixed them together to produce a puce green and painted the front door, the outside window trim and the back gate.

Ellie looked at it and gagged.

"Beggars can't be choosers," he grumbled, but he didn't know who was begging. Or for what.

Several days passed. Ellie sat one evening, her head hanging almost to her chest. He studied her with a watchful eye. Had she done too much? Had he neglected her again? So buried in his own misery and regrets that he didn't notice his own child's needs? Some father he was. He'd make a mighty poor husband, as he'd already proved. "What's ailing you?"

"I miss Louisa." Deep sigh. So dramatic. "Do you suppose she's mad at me 'cause of the mean things I said?"

"I don't know. A person should learn to guard their tongue."

Auntie May came into the room in time to hear Ellie's question and Emmet's reply. "Child, you could say you're sorry. Louisa doesn't strike me as the kind of person who would refuse to forgive."

Ellie perked up. "I will. Daddy, can you take me to see her?"

"Can't. I'm busy."

Auntie May snorted. "You're going to busy yourself right out of a life, if you aren't careful."

He shrugged.

Ellie knelt before him. "Please, Daddy. Please. I have to tell Louisa I don't hate her."

Emmet sighed. "You can be very persistent."

"It's important," she said with the dignity of being right. "Come on. Let's go."

"Now?" He kind of hoped he could put it off until she forgot.

"No time like the present," Auntie May said.

Yeah. Thanks, Auntie May. You're a great help. "Fine. Get your jacket."

"Daddy, it's warm out."

"Jacket or we don't go. You never know when it might rain." He didn't miss the way Ellie rolled her eyes, but he chose to ignore it.

They took the vehicle. No way could Ellie hobble that far. At least he was a good enough father to realize that. He kept his thoughts in negative territory in the hopes it would provide him an insurmountable barrier.

Ellie bounced forward on the seat as they turned toward the Morgan house.

"Their car is gone." His relief was bitter with regret.

"I guess they're not home." But no. Louisa stood in the garden watching their approach. He told himself he wished she was gone. But his heart pressed against his ribs, urging him to hurry forward.

"I see her." Ellie had the door half-open.

He grabbed her arm. "Wait until I stop. And use your crutches."

Mouse saw the unfamiliar girl and bounced on her four paws, barking.

"Mouse, cease and desist."

Ellie giggled as the dog obeyed the order. It even brought a reluctant smile to Emmet's lips. Trust Louisa to teach her dog fancy words.

Louisa dusted her hands and brushed her skirt before she crossed to the edge of the garden. She looked as if she wanted to turn into a bird and fly away. He could hardly blame her.

Did she still sing anyway?

Ellie didn't stop until she stood facing Louisa. "I'm sorry. I didn't mean those awful words. I don't hate you."

Louisa pulled the child into her arms. "I know that. I forgave you as soon as you said it." She held Ellie. And if Emmet didn't miss his guess, those were tears glistening on her lashes. "I care about you. Very much. Never forget it."

Ellie nodded, her face awash. "I don't want you to leave."

"I'm here, aren't I? Any time you want to see me, I'm here." She lifted her face to the sky, seemingly unmindful of the tears dripping from her jaw. She swallowed hard. "Ellie, I love you. I will never forget you."

They clung to each other for another moment, and Emmet's eyes glassed with wetness. Not tears, he informed himself. Not tears. He wouldn't get emotional about this. But she loved his child. It felt like a kiss from heaven.

Ellie broke away. "Is this your dog? I saw her when we went on the picnic."

"She is. This is Mouse. Mouse, meet Ellie." Mouse held up a paw for Ellie to shake, bringing a burst of giggles from her.

"I've never seen your place before, except the front of the house."

"Would you like to look around?"

"Yes, please."

Louisa looked at Emmet for his approval. He nodded.

They had a long, detailed look at the garden. Stopped to inspect Sally's chickens behind the wire fence. Moseyed toward the barn. Inspected the empty stalls. Talked about the mice that made homes overhead. Ventured to the house, where Ellie had to hear stories about every room, every piece of furniture on the ground floor. Then, leaving Emmet in the kitchen, they climbed the steps. He supposed she received the same detailed information of the rooms up there.

Mouse sat watching him. Emmet scowled at the dog. "Why aren't you with your mistress?"

Mouse seemed to grin, Emmet thought, then snorted at his foolishness. *Well,* he excused himself, *what would you call it when the dog hung out his tongue and pulled his mouth back like a happy clown?* "Of course you're happy. You get to live with Louisa."

He jerked from his chair and stared out the window.

Finally the truth could not be denied. He wanted to share his life with Louisa. She cared for his child. No doubt of that. Did she have similar feelings for Ellie's father?

Dare he ask? Dare he risk letting himself love again?

He heard Auntie May's mocking voice. *Love isn't a risk. Love is an opportunity.*

Ellie and Louisa descended the stairs. He rushed forward, ready to catch Ellie should she stumble, but she had grown very agile on her crutches.

Ellie held out a sheet of paper. "Louisa gave me this."

It was a pencil sketch—a likeness of Ellie. "It's very nice."

"I'm going to keep it forever."

"We need to go now."

Ellie nodded. She and Louisa exchanged some secret understanding. "Thank you."

Louisa walked them to the vehicle. He paused with his hand on the door. "Thank you for easing her mind."

"My pleasure."

He searched her gaze. Was there a flicker of affection in those brown depths? He considered suggesting an outing. But he stalled. Couldn't find the words.

"Thanks again." As they drove away, he mentally kicked himself.

Later, he tucked Ellie into bed. "You're much happier now. I'm glad."

"Did you hear? Louisa said she loved me. Did my mommy love me?"

"Of course she did."

"I can't remember her."

"You weren't very old when she died."

"Daddy, why don't you marry Louisa? She'd make a good mommy. And she'd be nice to you."

Emmet chuckled. "You have it all figured out, don't you?"

"Yup." She rolled over, cuddling her doll in her arms. "You'll ask her, won't you?" Little cupid might be tired, but not too tired to press her point.

"I'll take it under consideration."

Auntie May sat in her rocker in the kitchen. How much had she heard? He wasn't going to ask. Nor was he going to give her a chance to say anything. "I'll be out for a little while." With no destination in mind, he hurried down the back lane and across the dusty prairie. But it didn't take long to realize he couldn't outrun his thoughts. For the first time in three years, he allowed himself to think of sharing his life with someone other than Ellie. Sharing with an equal, a woman, someone to love.

The idea excited him.

The idea scared him.

It hurt to love. No, it hurt to lose, and loving came with that built-in risk.

He sucked in air—dry, dusty. Just as his life would be if he continued alone. Without Louisa.

He made up his mind. He would speak to her. Ask if she had a little tenderness in her heart for him. Enough to consider marrying him.

It took him three days to get his courage in place.

Three days of facing his inner demons. Three days of dark looks from Auntie May. Three days of persistent prodding from Ellie.

Finally he could take the tension no longer and headed to the Morgan place. He hoped they'd all be away. He hoped they'd all be home. No. He only wanted Louisa to be there. He hoped he would be able to speak when he saw her.

He turned into the laneway. Three women in the garden turned to face him. Great. All of them. He didn't want to see anyone but Louisa.

They seemed to hold a brisk discussion, then Louisa crossed toward him. "Hi," she murmured when she was five feet away.

"Hi." That was it. He could think of nothing more. Not one word.

"Is Ellie okay?"

"Yup." Absolutely brilliant.

"Is she liking school?"

"Think so."

Louisa nodded encouragingly. No doubt wondering why he had driven all this way to say four words.

He looked away. Perhaps he could think more clearly if he studied the windows on the house. Two beats. Nothing. Three tea towels whipped about on the line. He stared at them. His thoughts flapped about as uselessly. Time to act. "Louisa, would you like to come for a drive?"

"Now?"

Of course she was confused. Suddenly he knew what he wanted to do, where he wanted to take her. "Want to see if water is running over the dam?" The railway had a dam to the north to catch and hold water for the water tower. In good years, it ran over the spillway each spring.

Her eyes sparked with interest. "Okay." She called over her shoulder, informing her mother and Sally of her plans.

He jumped from the truck and escorted her around

to the passenger door, made sure she was safely seated before he clamored back behind the wheel.

"When was the last time you saw the dam?" he asked.

"A couple of years ago. The last time I saw it overflowing was three years ago."

They turned off the road on a sandy trail. The dam was five miles from the road. The trail was rough, at places only two parallel tracks running through the grass. "Doesn't look like it's used very often. It used to be a favorite picnic spot when I was a kid."

"I keep forgetting you grew up here."

"Look. Crocuses." He pulled to a halt and looked at the field dotted with them. The flowers had faded on many, leaving only feathery plumes that caught the sun in silvery threads. But there was still a scattering of purple flowers. "It must have been a purple carpet a few weeks ago."

"I wish I'd brought paper and pencil. Can I get out and look at them?"

"Certainly." He pushed his door open, intent on helping her, but she was already out of the truck and running across the field. She paused often to bend and examine a plant.

He stood at the verge of the field and watched. She was so full of life.

She straightened, grew very still. Signaled him to be quiet then pointed. He followed the direction she indicated and spotted a burrowing owl, standing on spindly legs beside a hole in the ground, watching with big-eyed caution and curiosity.

Louisa backed up slowly, quietly until she reached Emmet's side. "I don't want to disturb her. She probably has babies."

"Let's go then." He reached for her hand. Changed his mind. He would wait until he spoke to her before he could feel free to touch her.

They arrived at the dam a few minutes later.

"The water is very low." She sounded so regretful, he wanted to paint clouds in the sky then pull them down and empty them in the dam.

They got out and walked around.

"We used to row a raft across here." Now it was dry, hard clumps of clay. Very real evidence of the drought. As if he needed anything to prove it. The drifting soil, the parched grass were sufficient. "Come on. Let's go to the top of the dam." A road ran along the top, but they walked.

She breathed deeply. "I love the view from here. It's like you can see forever. Funny how everything looks different when you can see it like this. The colors fade to pastels, the shapes soften. Nothing looks as bad as it does close up."

"I guess that's so." He indicated they should sit. It was a perfect place to voice his question.

"A little like life, wouldn't you say?" She sat with her legs curled under her.

"Sorry?"

"Everything—even the bad stuff—will be part of the beautiful picture when viewed from a distance."

"It's nice to think that is so."

"I believe it. Because of Romans eight, twenty-eight. 'We know—'"

He joined her. "'—all things work together for good to them that love God.'"

She turned to him as he repeated the words and smiled. Her eyes darkened with what he knew to be joy.

Now was the perfect time. He shifted so they faced each other. He held her hands. Drew her close. Watched her expression grow cautiously interested. He admired the perfect shape of her face, her porcelain clear skin, her dark brown eyes framed with thick lashes. Her mouth, so pink and kissable.

He bent his head and caught her mouth with his own. Felt her quick indrawn breath, felt her kiss him back.

And then she jerked away, her head down, hiding her face.

"Louisa, I'm hoping you have some idea of my feelings for you so you won't be surprised when I ask, will you marry me?"

She jerked her hand away. Put both behind her back. Stared at him. Emotions chased across her face in rapid succession. He tried to catch and analyze all of them. Certainly surprise. He understood that. Then was it shock? Was his confession of having regard for her that unexpected? Then confusion mixed with…pain? Why pain? Had he properly voiced his feelings?

"Louisa, I love you. I want to marry you."

She bolted to her feet. "No. You can't love me. You can't want to marry me. I can't marry you." She rushed down the trail toward the truck.

He hurried after her. "I can certainly love you. And marry you, if I so desire."

"I can't marry you." She flung the words over her shoulder. Reached the truck and planted herself on the seat, facing straight ahead, her expression stony.

He climbed in beside her. "Louisa."

She held out her hands. "Stop. Say no more. Take me home."

He didn't make any move to start the truck. "Can you at least tell me why?"

"I will never marry. You hear me? Never."

"But—"

"Please take me home."

He started the truck, drove toward town. But her rejection twisted and turned, flapping against his thoughts. "Never marry? I can't see it. You're a beautiful woman with a beautiful heart. Okay, I understand if you don't care for me." No, he didn't. What about all those fun times they'd shared? The special moments? The quick exchange of smiles at something Ellie said or did? Had he read more into it than he should have? He couldn't believe that.

She didn't reply.

"Louisa, what's wrong?" It had to be something more than lack of feelings for him. Didn't it? Besides— a fledgling hope—she hadn't said she didn't care for him. Only that she would never marry.

"There is nothing wrong." Her voice was so tight, he figured the words had to edge out sideways. "Except I've decided I like teaching and want to make it a career."

He tried to shift his thoughts of her to include this bit of information. Yeah, she'd make a good teacher. But a better wife. However, her interests obviously didn't include marriage and motherhood. He had misinterpreted her kindness for something more than interest in teaching Ellie. He'd deceived himself in believing she had some regard for him. Worse even, he'd opened doors he'd vowed would remain forever locked.

He dropped her at the house, muttered goodbye and drove away. How many times did life have to up and smack him in the face for him to learn his lesson?

Three years ago he vowed he would never love again. He should have listened to himself. Instead his pride had been kicked about. His love had been tossed aside as if worthless.

By the time he reached home, he had made up his mind. As soon as the doctor okayed it, he was returning to the ranch. And he would never open his heart again.

Now all he had to do was face Ellie and Auntie May.

The latter was easy. She took one look at his face. "Oh, you poor boy." She hugged him and patted his back.

He allowed it, but his hands hung at his sides. He couldn't remember how to lift them. How to hug her back.

He simply did not have the emotional strength to do so. Feared he would break in half if he let himself feel anything.

Explaining to Ellie was much harder.

"She said she didn't want to marry me."

"You must have asked her wrong."

His smile struggled to his lips. "I did the best I know how."

"Maybe if I ask her?"

"No, Button. She was pretty clear that she doesn't intend to marry. We have to accept it."

Ellie went to bed without being asked and turned on her side, refusing a good-night kiss when he went to tuck her in.

He couldn't blame her. He'd do the same if he could. Turn his back to life, curl up in a ball and refuse to let anyone near him.

But he didn't have that choice. He loved Ellie and would devote his life to making her happy and keeping her safe.

Chapter Thirteen

"Something is ailing you," Mother said, worried lines creasing her forehead. "I think it's time to call the doctor."

"No, Mother." Louisa forced firmness into her voice. "I have no need of a doctor. I'm just a little blue at not having my teaching job anymore."

"If you say so. But you don't look well. Does she, Sally?"

Sally shook her head. "You really don't. Are you sure you're okay?"

"I'm fine." The doctor could offer no cure for how she felt. "I think I'll go talk to Madge."

"You do that. But don't overexert yourself."

With Mother's needless warning echoing in her ears, she tromped across the dusty trail to Madge's place. She wasn't ill. She was heartbroken and she knew of no cure. By the time she reached the doorway, tears flooded her eyes.

Madge took one look at her and pulled her inside. "Louie, what's wrong?"

Louisa could only shake her head as tears spilled

down her cheeks. Madge opened her arms, and Louisa went gladly into her sister's embrace. She soaked the shoulder of Madge's dress before she cried herself out.

Madge led her to a chair and eased her down. "Now tell me what this is about."

She sniffed. "Emmet asked me to marry him."

Madge smiled. "That sounds like good news to me."

"It's not. I had to say no."

Madge puffed out her cheeks. "Does he love you?"

"He said he did. And he kissed me." She pressed her fingertips to her lips. "It was sweet." She might never have a husband or children, but she had the memory of that kiss and would cherish it to her dying day.

"Then you didn't have to say no."

Louisa scowled at Madge. "Why must you insist on ignoring the facts?"

Madge grinned, as if Louisa's protests were laughable. "You would be surprised at how strong love is. Tell him the truth. Give him a chance to say if he loves you enough to want you despite your barrenness. If he loves you half as much as I think, I doubt it will be a barrier."

Dare she allow herself this hope? "I don't know if I could stand it if he withdraws his offer of marriage." Better to hold on to that dream.

"Would you prefer to live the rest of your life wondering if you missed the chance to be his wife, and a mother to Ellie?"

Louisa tried to convince herself the memory of a kiss, an offer of marriage would be enough. She knew, however, that compared with the reality of true love, they were but paper flowers left too long in the sun and would soon fade and grow brittle. They were dead.

"I'll have to think and pray about it."

"I'll pray for you. We both know God is able to do abundantly more than we ask or think."

"Thank you for that reminder." Louisa clung to the words, hung on to hope as she returned home. Rather than go directly to the house, she stopped in the garden to pull weeds and chase away grasshoppers—a losing battle, but one none of them was willing to abandon.

Lord, God, my savior, friend and guide. I need You to show me what to do.

She plucked a grasshopper from a tiny lettuce plant, tossed the insect into a bucket and examined the plant. Damaged but still lots of growth potential. Her mouth watered at the promise of fresh salad in a few weeks. She went down the row, rescuing plant after plant, then started on the row of potatoes. Meager as it was, this garden was so important to their survival. The gardens they'd grown when Father was still alive, before the drought hit and the Depression made life so difficult, had been lush and bountiful. Yet she and the others were grateful for every bit of food they could eke from this land.

She sank to the ground and stared at the tiny plants as something scratched the back of her thoughts.

Would she destroy this garden because it didn't measure up to the ones before the drought?

No—never. She tended it all the more carefully.

And yet it was only a garden—a bit of soil, a few plants. Here today. Gone tomorrow.

Like the lilies of the field.

If God so clothe the grass, which is today in the field, and tomorrow is cast into the oven; how much more will He clothe you, O ye of little faith.

Lord, I know You love me and will take care of me. That isn't the question.

Was it possible to believe that God had sent Emmet here to love her? Or was she wishing for something that was simply not so? What if she told him her problem and he backed away in horror and disappointment? How would she survive such a reaction?

Yet, how could it be worse than her rejection of his love?

Give him a chance.

Lord, would it be wrong to give him a chance? If so, stop me. Otherwise, I am going to tell him.

Nothing happened except more grasshoppers invaded the garden. She picked them off and pulled more weeds.

She returned to the house. Her peace must have been evident because Mother's tension released when she saw her. "Your talk with Madge seems to have done you good."

"It did. So did having a soul-searching talk with God."

Mother hugged her. "He gives us peace that passeth understanding, but too often we don't take it."

"Mother, I want to thank you and Father for raising us to trust God."

Mother's eyes sheened with unshed tears. "I couldn't ask for anything better than my daughters walking with God."

Sally demanded details. "This has something to do with Emmet, doesn't it?"

Louisa told her what happened. "I'm going to tell him the truth tonight."

Sally clapped her hands. "About time."

Mother dabbed at her eyes. "I'm so happy for you.

Since the doctor said you would never have children, I've prayed you would find a man who would love you for who you are. I worried you might shut your heart to love. This is an answer to prayer."

After supper, Louisa brushed her hair into submission and held it in place with matching silver combs. She wore her second-best dress and added a lace collar for good measure, but decided to forgo the gloves.

She stood before the door, ready to leave, then spun around to face Mother and Sally. "I'm scared."

They rushed forward, patting her arms and hugging her. "No need to be afraid. We'll be praying for you."

She tucked courage under her heart and pushed confidence into her limbs. She whispered a little prayer and drove toward Golden Prairie.

Her emotions bumped along in time to the rough road. Elation and hope, followed by fear and doubt. At times it seemed her heart stuck to her ribs, unable to function, then it took off at a gallop, leaving her breathless.

She laughed—a sound of self-mockery—as she drove down the street. Nothing like being one hundred percent sure of her actions. But she was going on faith here. Following what she believed was a God-given opportunity.

Pulling the truck to a halt before the Hamilton house, she sat and stared. The formerly faded wooden door was now a sickly shade of green. Not particularly an improvement, to her way of thinking. What did she do next? She really ought to have planned this out better.

The door eased open.

She held her breath and tried to guess if Ellie, Auntie May or Emmet would step into the opening. Or perhaps it was only a neighbor leaving after a visit.

Emmet stepped into the light and stood watching her,

the interior dark behind him, the setting sun highlighting his face. From this distance she couldn't see the color of his eyes, couldn't use that to judge his reaction to seeing her. But she took courage in the fact he didn't slam the door on her.

Instead he closed it with particular care and walked toward her. A crow flew overhead, cawing. Hopefully not a mocking warning of what was to come.

She pushed her fears and doubts aside as he reached the gate.

"Can I help you?" Guarded—but of course he would be.

"I'd like to talk, if you don't mind."

"You were pretty clear about what you felt."

"That's just it. I didn't tell you everything, and I think you deserve to hear it."

He studied her a moment, revealing nothing.

"Please let me explain."

"Very well. Do you want to come in?"

She glanced past him. "It's rather private."

"Ellie and Auntie May went to visit one of her old friends. Why don't we sit in the backyard?"

"Fine."

He held the door for her, and she stepped to the ground and followed him around to the back. He'd done a lot of work since she'd been here. "You fixed the fence and cleaned up some of the junk."

"I put a bench against the shade in the hopes that Auntie May would use it once in a while."

They both laughed somewhat nervously.

She sat on the bench at his invitation and waited, hoping he would sit too. But he stood, one boot resting on a bucket Auntie May had filled with dirt and planted with beans. And he waited. She felt his impatience even though he didn't indicate it, either by speech or restless movement.

"I'm not sure where to begin." She had rehearsed what she would say, but it had been much easier when she was alone. "I didn't want to hurt you by saying I couldn't marry you, but I felt I had no choice."

A muscle in his arm jerked.

"Not about hurting you. I don't mean that. But I felt I had to say no, even if it was the hardest thing I've ever done." She lifted her face to him, let her love and hope and desperation show, not wanting to hide any part of the truth. "Emmet, your love is the greatest gift I could ever hope for. I love you too—"

He dropped to her side. "Then why did you say no?"

"Because there are things about me you don't know." Her voice broke, and she couldn't go on.

He draped an arm over her shoulders and pulled her close. She didn't resist. The weight of his arm anchored her. Made her realize their love was worth telling the truth.

"Remember, I told you I'd been sick."

"Pneumonia? Right?"

"When I was younger. Last year it was influenza. Only for me, it was more. I had a raging infection throughout my body."

His arm tightened about her.

"The doctor said I was fortunate to survive it."

He rested his cheek against her head and made a rough sound in the back of his throat—a sound that indicated sympathy and pain at her suffering. "I'm glad you did."

She nodded, reveling in the way her cheek brushed against his shoulder. "I'm glad too. But I lost something in the illness."

"So long as you're alive."

The words gave her needed courage. "The infection left me barren." Blunt, but she had no idea how to couch it in gentler terms.

"What?"

Her pain erupted. She'd never told Mother or her sisters how much she'd lost when she lost the ability to have children. "All my life I dreamed of having a houseful of children." Tears gushed like a bottled-up waterfall. Her chest heaved in shudders. "Now." She could only manage one word at a time. "I." Sob. "Will." Sniff. "Have." Swallow hard. "None."

She felt him stiffen. Knew the news had shocked him. She waited for him to pull her close, dry her tears, assure her over and over it didn't matter. Love was enough.

He bolted to his feet and put a distance of two strides between them. "You can't have children?"

Her tears dried at the roughness in his voice. "Never."

He spun away, but not before she saw the look in his face. "To never have children—" He shook his head as if the idea was impossible to fathom.

"I'll see myself out." Never mind that she was already outside. She marched around the house. Cringed at the sound of something crashing.

It was what she had always feared. Expected, even. She shouldn't be surprised.

No, she wasn't surprised. She was devastated. He didn't want a barren woman.

Who was foolish enough to think love could be enough?

* * *

Emmet let her go. He didn't know what else to do. He'd seen the agony, heard the sobs, watched the tears flow. And he could do nothing to stop it. He couldn't marry her now and every day face the undeniable fact he couldn't protect her from this pain. He kicked the wooden bench, neatly removing one arm.

He knew how hard it was to live with failure. It had been his job to protect Jane. He'd failed.

Just as he failed his parents.

Everything stopped. His parents had died in an accident. An auto accident on a hilly road. He shook his head. He wouldn't think about it.

Just as he wouldn't think about Louisa and what she had lost. And how powerless he was to protect her.

He picked up the pieces of the shattered bench and repaired it.

By the time Ellie and Auntie May returned, there was nothing to indicate anything unusual had happened. Nothing but the acid burn in the pit of his stomach and a deep ache in the back of his brain.

Louisa made it home by instinct alone. She had no memory of the trip. The only thing she recalled was stepping into the house and knowing she would never be the same.

Sally and Mother waited for her return and rushed to ask how it went. One look at her, and they didn't need to voice the question. Mother reached for her.

"Louisa, come sit."

Sally closed the door, then helped Mother guide Louisa to the living room.

Louisa sat because they said she should.

She wasn't the least bit thirsty, but when Sally placed a cup of water in her hand she drank because she lacked the energy to argue.

"What did he say?" Sally asked.

"I can't remember." She didn't need to recall the words. His actions, his expression had said it all. "Having children is very important to him. I knew that. Why did I think it wouldn't matter?" She choked on her emotion and swallowed hard.

Mother sat at her side, rubbing her hands. "I can't believe this. I thought better of Emmet." She said it over and over, until Sally reached across and squeezed both pairs of hands.

"Sometimes things just don't work out the way we want."

Mother nodded. "But it isn't Louisa's fault."

Her mother's support was welcome, but it didn't change the facts. "He can't help what he wants either."

"I suppose." Mother rubbed Louisa's back. "I hope you aren't going to let this set you back."

"What do you mean?" She glanced at Sally, but her sister shook her head. She didn't know either.

"You've been so sick in the past. I can't bear the thought this might affect your health."

The words shook Louisa from her state of shock. "I'm not going to go into a decline, if that's what you mean. When Doc told me I was barren, I decided I would never marry, so this is but a little bump in what I had planned." Only she hadn't planned anything. She'd simply ridden along on necessity and opportunity. She'd taken the job tutoring Ellie only for the money, not out of a great passion or plan.

All that was about to change. It must. She had to

have something to aim at, some direction or, indeed, her mother's fears might come true.

"I'll be fine. Yes, it's a disappointment, but don't we all have to face them? I will pray about my future, and once I'm sure of what I want to do—what God wants me to do—I will begin making plans."

"There's no need. You always have a home. You know that."

"Yes, I do. And it is a great source of comfort, but I believe I'd like to do something with my life."

Sally chuckled. "You're not interested in becoming a cat lady?"

Louisa pushed at her sister. "I might have cats, but I think I'll aim a little higher." She knew what she'd like to do, but she wasn't sure how to make it happen.

Over the next few days she worked hard to get her feelings under control. She smiled to prove she wasn't upset and to keep her mother from worrying. Yes, she'd be okay. Did she have a choice?

She would move on.

For three days she planned and prayed; then she went to talk to Madge. "I want to become a teacher."

"Great. Glad to hear it."

"You don't think I need to stay home and take care of Mother?"

Madge sighed, as if Louisa's question signified faulty reasoning. "Mother will be okay. We'll see to it. Sally can get a job if necessary. Haven't we always managed?"

"Yes. And of course, once I start work I'll be able to help even more." Though there were teachers who didn't get their promised wages. The funds simply weren't available. However, that was a problem she'd deal with when she confronted it. "I don't have the money." She'd received her earnings for tutoring Ellie and given the funds to Mother. It had paid off the doctor's bill and eased Louisa's mind on that matter. "I could borrow the amount, but I only know of one person who could afford to lend it to me."

"Emmet?"

Louisa recoiled in horror. "I wouldn't ask him even if he had it." She hoped she could avoid him until she made her escape. "I mean Uncle Peter."

"But Mother—"

"I know. Will you help me ask her if I can write him?"

"You could write without her permission." Madge's tone indicated she didn't think it was a good idea.

"No. I don't want to upset her. Besides, I really want her blessing."

So Madge came over for afternoon tea. Sally had also promised to support Louisa's cause.

Louisa waited until the ordinary things had been discussed—the weather, the gardens, who had moved away, the houses the bank had foreclosed on, who was having a baby. She wondered if Mother would ever run out of topics.

Finally, Mother glanced around the table. "So what brings the three of you together in the middle of the week?"

The girls tried to look offended.

"Do we need an excuse to get together?" Madge demanded. "I'm here so often, I'm surprised you don't ask how Judd manages on his own?"

It wasn't quite true, but Madge did pop over often.

Mother fluttered her hands. "All of you have a let's-ask-Mother look. What is it you want to ask me?"

Sally and Madge turned toward Louisa, effectively informing Mother who wanted to ask something.

She swallowed hard, silently said a quick prayer and smiled, hoping to disguise the anxiety that suddenly threaded through her insides. Not until now did she realize how badly she wanted this. "Mother, I discovered how much I enjoy teaching, and Adele says I have natural talent for the task. I want your approval to go to Normal school. My earnings will help out once I get a job."

Mother studied her fingers a moment before replying. "I have no doubt you would make a fine teacher. My concern lies in the unsavory conditions some teachers must endure. I've heard stories of rural teachers practically starving to death, having to share tight quarters—" She fluttered her hands again. "I don't think you are up to that kind of hardship."

Louisa figured she could put up with almost anything she made up her mind to. She was learning that she could live and thrive despite a broken heart. How could physical challenges be any more difficult? "I would make sure I take a position that offers decent accommodations."

Mother nodded. "I suppose I must content myself with that. Very well, you have my blessing."

"Thank you."

A heavy, waiting silence descended over the table.

"There's something more?" Mother asked.

Louisa nodded. "I want to ask Uncle Peter if I may borrow the money from him to attend Normal school." She saw the beginning of a refusal on Mother's face and rushed on. "I know of no one else I could ask for money. And I intend to pay it back. Mother, please say it's okay. You must understand that I can't stay here and watch everyone else marry and have children while I sit around doing nothing but growing old. I need to do something."

Mother considered Louisa for a moment, gave the other girls a studied look. "It seems you are both in support of her idea."

Sally and Madge nodded.

"I confess my only objection to Peter is he kept himself distanced from the family. I know your father was hurt by it, although he insisted Peter had his reasons. I suppose I have been somewhat unforgiving toward him. I just never realized it. You go ahead and write him. Perhaps I'll include a little note of apology as well."

Relief fell from Louisa's shoulders. "Thank you, Mother."

She wrote the letter that very afternoon. Took it to town and mailed it, carefully avoiding the street where the Hamiltons lived. Not that it stopped her from thinking of the occupants. How was Ellie managing schoolwork? When would she see the doctor again? Would they leave as soon as Ellie didn't need crutches?

She stumbled. Blamed the rough road. Knew it was the weakness of her limbs at knowing Emmet would soon leave and she would never see him again.

All the more reason to move on with her life.

She delivered the letter to the postal wicket and released it with a degree of relish.

The first step in her future.

A future without Emmet and Ellie.

Chapter Fourteen

Emmet took the note Ellie brought home from Miss Ross. "Are you in trouble?"

Ellie shrugged, her gaze direct and challenging. She'd been moody for days. Since Louisa had said she wouldn't marry Emmet, but he refused to acknowledge it had begun then. Even as his own unsettled misery had begun at the same time.

He could live without her. Without marriage. Even if he had to remind himself how okay he was a thousand times a day.

He'd gone for walks. Heard the birds in the trees singing as if everything in the world was right. *Sing anyway.* Louisa's words mocked him. What did birds know about loss and pain and failure? They just laid eggs and were oblivious to the rest of the world. He wished he could find the same freedom.

The next afternoon, in response to Adele's request to meet her, he went to the classroom. Last time he'd been here he'd been with Louisa. He remembered noticing her generous smile, her chocolate-rich eyes, her—

That was then. This was now. No point in looking backward. It would only make him stumble.

Adele waited for him in the classroom and indicated he should sit in the front desk. He already knew he needed a shoehorn to pry himself in and out. Louisa, on the other hand, had slipped in with the ease of a child. She was slender as a willow branch. Moved as gracefully as one waving in the wind.

Enough. He had to stop seeing her in every corner of his house, remembering her in every corner of his life.

"You wanted to talk about Ellie?" He realized he sounded cross. He'd have to watch that. It wasn't Adele's fault he kept thinking of Louisa and resenting he couldn't erase her from his mind.

"Ellie has regressed. I'm wondering if there is something wrong to cause this."

"Regressed? How?"

"A number of ways. For instance, she says she can't read."

"She can read. I know it." Louisa's drawings and cards had made it easy for Ellie to learn. Too bad she hadn't made it easy for Emmet to forget.

"She says she can't remember. I'm afraid there's more. She is uncooperative and says things like her father generally lets her do as she pleases. Reminds us all that she doesn't have a mother, so she should be excused. I'm very sorry she is motherless, but I'm afraid I can't excuse bad behavior because of that."

"Of course not." But he had no idea what to do. He wasn't going to marry just to give Ellie a mother. Besides, he seriously doubted it would solve the problem.

"I think you need to talk to her. See if you can find out what's going on. Perhaps review her skills at home."

"I'll do that. For sure." He left a few minutes later, feeling as if he failed even at being a father. What did God expect from him? How could he find a degree of success? He didn't know.

The only thing that made sense was to return to the ranch as soon as Ellie was ready to go.

That night he pulled out the reading cards. "Let's play a game."

"It's Louisa's game."

"She gave it to you. It's yours."

"I don't want to read."

"Miss Ross says you need to practice at home." He shuffled the cards and passed them out. Ellie half-heartedly played. In the end he had the vast majority of matched cards.

"Miss Ross is right. You're being uncooperative. What's wrong?"

She shrugged. "I miss Louisa. Not that you care."

He scooped her up, sat with her on his lap and rocked back and forth, finding a modicum of comfort both in the warmth of her little body in his arms and the rhythmic motion. "Button, I care very much that you're hurting. But what can I do?"

"Ask her again."

"It's not that easy." He couldn't ask her. It made him feel as if he'd swallowed battery acid to think of her pain. And he'd never be able to make things better for her. He'd never be able to take care of her as he should.

The words struck a chord so deep in his thoughts that it startled him. It was as if he'd heard the words before. Of course he knew where they came from. When Jane died, he'd beat himself up mentally that he hadn't been able to protect her. But even then, they had a familiar ring. As if he'd heard them or said them before. But when? It didn't make sense, and he pushed the silly idea away.

Somehow they struggled through the next few days, Ellie barely making an effort to read or cooperate at school. He could hardly wait for the day he took Ellie to visit the doctor again. After that, Lord willing and the creek don't rise, they would head home. He'd originally planned to stay until Ellie finished the school year, but now it seemed a futile reason.

Finally the day to visit the doctor arrived. They drove to the office. Neither of them spoke. Emmet had no idea if Ellie worried about whether or not she would lose the crutches. Lately it had been hard to figure out anything when it came to Ellie.

Lord, help her be okay.

He marveled often that he turned to prayer even in his disappointment. Of course Ellie wasn't part of his disappointment. He could and would continue to pray for her well-being.

They walked into the office, and Doc waved them into the examining room. The nurse led Ellie to the X-ray room, and Emmet sat and drummed his fingertips together and tried not to remember the last visit to this room. Louisa had sat right beside him, waiting while the X-rays were taken. She'd smiled and laughed. He couldn't remember what he said. But he'd never forget the way he felt. As if music filled him. How could she be so cheerful, so gentle, so serene while all the time holding such a painful secret?

How could she say sing anyway? He wasn't sure he'd ever sing again. Certainly, he'd never feel music in his soul again.

Why was he feeling sorry for himself? He had a precious little girl and a ranch. Once he got back on familiar ground, both he and Ellie would feel better. Except—he could no longer deny the nagging question—how could he watch Ellie, keep her safe and at the same time run the ranch?

The doctor led Ellie from the other room and held up the X-ray.

"Good news all 'round. This leg has healed nicely." He nodded satisfaction. "Nicely indeed. Young lady, you can throw away your crutches."

Ellie handed them off to the nurse hovering at her side and marched around the room, as if to prove to everyone she needed them no more.

"She's okay?" Emmet wasn't ready to believe it.

"Should be as good as new, though it will likely take a few weeks for her to get her strength back." He turned to Ellie. "No more climbing trees. Okay?"

Ellie nodded. "Only little ones."

Doc laughed. "You got yourself a little tomboy."

"She needs to be. Ranch life requires she know how to ride and sometimes fend for herself."

The doctor gave him a few more instructions before they left.

"Thanks, Doc." On the way out, Emmet dropped the money for the visit on the desk. They returned to the truck. "Do you want to get a candy or ice cream?"

"I guess."

Hardly the enthusiasm one might expect, and no comparison to their last visit.

Ellie would get over her disappointment as soon as they returned to the ranch, but Emmet knew the rest of his life would be but a pale shadow of the few weeks he'd enjoyed Louisa's company.

They stopped at the store. Joanie saw her without crutches and cheered. "All better. I expect you're pretty happy about that."

"I guess."

Joanie blinked. "Wow, kid. Try to contain your enthusiasm."

Ellie shrugged. "What's so special about getting better?"

"Sure beats lying about in a body cast."

Ellie sighed. "It wasn't so bad."

Emmet knew what she meant. Being in her cast meant Louisa came every day. They both missed her visits. Not that he would wish Ellie back in a cast for such selfish reasons. "Pick out a candy stick."

Ellie didn't take any time making her selection. She took a licorice-flavored stick, stuck it in her mouth and headed back to the truck.

"She's just—" Emmet shrugged. He couldn't begin to explain Ellie's behavior. He dropped two pennies on the counter and left the store. They drove home without speaking. The only sound was Ellie slurping the candy.

Auntie May looked up as they entered the house. "Well, well. No more crutches?"

"Nope." Ellie crossed to her room and flopped on the bed.

"Shouldn't she be happier about this?" Auntie May asked. "Something wrong?"

"She's homesick. I'll take care of it." Emmet strode into the bedroom and closed the door. He sat on the edge of the bed. "Ellie, I know what will make you feel better."

"Humph."

"We're going home."

She didn't move. Didn't respond. Had she heard?

"We're going back to the ranch. You can ride your pony again—"

"I don't want to go home."

"Of course you do. Things will be better once we get back there."

"No they won't." Her voice rose to a screech. "Things will never be better, and it's all your fault. It's your fault Louisa doesn't come to see us anymore. Everything is your fault." She flipped to her stomach and buried her face in the pillow.

"Ellie?" He touched her back.

She shrugged from his hand. "Go away. Leave me alone. It's your fault and I'll never forgive you."

He stared at her a moment as the words raged through his mind. *It's your fault. It's your fault.*

Ah. The words hurt, they tore at his thoughts, they blasted at doors, they pounded at a memory.

Why couldn't he keep his loved ones safe? Why did he always fail?

Just like Mama.

He dropped his hands to his sides and stared into nothing. Where did that thought come from? How could this be like his mother's death? And how could it be his fault? He was only nine years old at the time of the accident. He remembered so little about it. Shock had dulled his memories.

Auntie May had always assured him it wasn't his fault.

Why would she say that unless there was reason he might believe he was to blame?

He fled the room, passed Auntie May without looking at her. He barely realized she watched him, her expression wreathed in sympathy. He flung out the door and strode away, down the back lane, out of town, across the prairie, as if he could run from his failure, his haunting accusations.

At the top of a rise, four miles from town, he ran out of steam and sank to the ground, panting. Had he done something that caused his parents' deaths? His mother's death?

Why hadn't he dropped Ellie and rushed to rescue Jane?

Was he doomed to be responsible for the death of loved ones all his life?

He sat staring across the undulating prairie, time and place forgotten. If only his thoughts would stop twisting and knotting. If only they made sense. Instead, words of blame and failure and fear tangled into a painful ball. *It's your fault. I can never keep anyone safe. I've failed. I'll fail again in the future.* He shuddered as the words reverberated through his brain. Why did he hear an echo of a voice not his own? Why did he feel sick inside?

Nearby a bird sang. Endlessly. As if mocking Emmet. Or trying to drive a message home. But what message?

Find the truth.

Right. He'd love to. But who could provide it?

Auntie May must know what happened and could perhaps explain why Emmet had such a sense of dread as he thought of his parents. He must talk to her.

Until he did he was stuck in this black vacuum, always feeling as if he couldn't keep his loved ones safe. It was what made him turn from Louisa—knowing he couldn't protect her from her pain.

He returned home. Ellie was up but wouldn't talk to him, though she had plenty of dark glowers to share.

This was not a conversation he wanted Ellie to hear, fearing what he learned might confirm her feelings that he was to blame, so he waited until he was certain she was asleep. "Auntie May, can I ask you some questions?"

"Of course, my boy. Whatever you want."

"Let's go outside."

She followed him out the door and sat on the bench. Right where Louisa had sat to tell him her terrible plight. He steeled himself to forget that moment.

"Emmet, you look worried. How can I help you?"

He pulled over an empty bucket and tipped it over to sit at her knees. "What happened to my parents?"

She pressed a palm to her throat. "Oh, my. What a question."

He waited as she stared out across the yard, sorrow and regret chasing across her face. Finally she sighed.

"I've always wondered how much you remembered. Was grateful you seemed to have forgotten. Yet I wondered if someday it would come back."

"What would come back?"

She brought her gaze to his and looked deeply into his eyes. "What do you remember?"

He shook his head. "Very little. Something about a car accident. That's all."

Her eyes clouded, and she nodded her head. "They died following a car accident. You were with them."

He jerked back. "I was?" A twisting road. Hills. His papa talking and laughing. "Papa liked his new car. He wanted to show Mama how well it handled on the road."

She nodded and waited, letting him find his words.

All he found was a blank. "I don't remember."

"You realize I wasn't there. I can only tell you what

the neighbors who found you said." At his encouraging nod, she went on. "Your father had indeed bought a new vehicle. Shiny and new. I suppose he wanted to take you both out for a drive. Or perhaps he had business in the next town. We'll never know."

Emmet remembered being excited. "We were going out for dinner at a restaurant."

"I see." She waited again, but still he remembered nothing. "The people said they didn't know if he was going too fast, or swerved to avoid something. All they could say for sure was the car went off the edge of the road and rolled. Your mother was thrown out and hurt. Your father was hurt badly as well. You had some cuts and bruises."

He glanced at the scars on his arm. Was that when he'd received them?

She touched the scars with her fingers. "It was a wonder that's all you got." Drew in a long breath. "Your father went for help and left you to watch your mother." She paused. "When they returned with your father—" She choked and paused another beat. "You sat with your mother's head in your lap. But she was gone."

He nodded, the memory edging closer. "I didn't know she was dead. I thought...I thought..." His throat tightened, and tears stung his nose. "I thought..." His voice fell to a whisper. "I was supposed to keep her safe. I thought I had."

She nodded, tears trickling unchecked down her cheeks.

"Papa told me to keep her safe." His father had pulled Mama from the rocks where she'd been tossed. He'd pressed back her hair and moaned. "Come here, boy." Emmet staggered to his side, the pain in his limbs drowned by a clogging fear. Mama didn't look like Mama. She looked like a beat-up doll.

"Sit here." Papa shoved him down by Mama's side. Lifted Mama's head to Emmet's lap. "I'm going for help. You take care of Mama. Don't let her die." He took a step away, then turned to speak to Emmet again. "Don't you let her die. Hear? It's your job to take care of her."

"I tried." He spoke aloud now.

Auntie May cupped her hand to his head. "There was nothing you could do."

"Papa came back."

All the time Papa was gone, he talked to Mama. "I'll look after you. I'll keep you safe." Over and over he said the words. He didn't know what else to do except pat her cheeks. "I'll look after you."

Papa limped back into sight, two men with him. Papa dropped down beside Mama. He called her. Shook her a little. Touched her cheek. Pressed his fingers to her neck. Then turned to Emmet. "She's gone. She's dead. I told you to look after her. What's wrong with you? You failed me, boy. You failed me."

One of the strangers pulled Papa away. "It's not the boy's fault."

Papa wailed like an angry bull Emmet had once seen. It was a very frightening sound.

The other man pulled Emmet away from Mama. "No. I'll take care of her. I will." He fought the man to escape, but he couldn't get away from this stranger.

Papa bellowed again. His eyes looked funny. He broke free of the constraining arms and knelt next to Mama. Tears flowed down his face. That frightened Emmet as much as holding Mama's head. He'd never seen Papa cry. Didn't know he could.

Papa lifted his tear-stained, gray-skinned face to Emmet's. "You let me down, boy."

Suddenly Papa fell to the ground. Emmet thought he wanted to lie down beside Mama. He wanted to die too. But the stranger took him away. Only later did he realize Papa had died as well, as seriously injured in the accident as Mama.

He hung his head and spoke quietly to Auntie May. "You knew Papa blamed me. That's why you kept telling me it wasn't my fault."

She stroked his arm. "It wasn't your fault. Your father was wrong to blame you. I was glad that you seemed to have blocked it from your mind." She made shushing, comforting noises for a few minutes. "You didn't remember it, but I think it has affected you anyway."

He jerked his head up. "What do you mean?"

"My boy, sometimes I think you try too hard to make sure everyone is going to be okay. Seems to me you tend to blame yourself if things go wrong." She leaned close and cupped his face between her palms. "There is so little in life that we truly have any control over. Ultimately, we must trust God. He holds us in the palm of His hand. Holds our loved ones too. Emmet, life is not your responsibility. Only loving and caring is up to you."

He didn't answer. Couldn't. How could he take a lifetime of self-blame and erase it in one thought?

Auntie May pushed to her feet. "You need to think about this. And while you're thinking, pray for God to help you sort out what you have charge of and what He has charge of. Might surprise you what you learn." She patted his head, then went inside.

Emmet continued to sit, his mind staggering with memories, regrets and yes, like Auntie May said, self-blame. He couldn't begin to sort out his thoughts.

Chapter Fifteen

Louisa received a reply from Uncle Peter within the week. "Come immediately," it read. Instructions on how to find his home were included.

She showed Mother and her sisters the letter. "I want to go right away. On tomorrow's train."

Mother shook her head. "It's not enough time to plan."

"What's to plan? I'll take enough clothes for a few days. I'll talk to Uncle Peter, and if he agrees to lend me the funds, I'll return to prepare for school." She couldn't wait to put distance between herself and Emmet. It was impossible to avoid him, as she'd discovered when she went to check the mail.

She'd seen his truck coming down the street and barely had time to duck out of sight around the corner of the hardware store. She peeked around the building to observe. Ellie had climbed from the truck without crutches. Joy flooded Louisa's heart. The child was all better. She'd be able to run and play now.

Emmet followed. He didn't look particularly happy. Perhaps he had decided it wouldn't be fair to pull Ellie from school a second time in order to move her back to the ranch. No doubt he was regretting the delay.

But the near encounter convinced her she must leave as soon as possible.

Sally and Madge sided with Louisa. "It will do Louisa good to go to the city."

Mother acquiesced. "No doubt you are right I'm just being selfish, not wanting to let go. But you proceed with your plans. I'll pray for a satisfactory outcome."

So Louisa sent a wire to Uncle Peter saying she would arrive on the train the next day, and she packed a small case for her visit. That night she fought a battle with fear and regret.

Oh, God, I am running from the man I love. But what choice do I have? He doesn't want me. Help me find a future full of promise and possibility.

The next day Louisa stepped from the train in Edmonton. They'd lived there seven years ago, and she tried to tell herself it was like coming home.

"Louisa." She turned at the sound of her name and stared at Uncle Peter. He was so much like Father that Louisa stumbled as her eyes filled with tears.

Uncle Peter caught her and steadied her. "It's so good of you to visit."

She nodded. He might change his mind once she'd told him the purpose of her visit.

He waited until they were in his charming home and had been served tea by his housekeeper to say, "I'm most happy to have you visit, but it is a surprise. I suspect there is a reason behind this rare pleasure. What is it?"

Louisa set her teacup aside, clasped her hands in her lap and prayed for uncommon courage and courtesy. She began by telling Uncle Peter of her experience in tutoring Ellie. "I enjoyed it and seem to have a little aptitude for the job. I'd like to attend Normal school."

"That sounds like a wonderful thing."

She twisted her fingers. It was hard asking for money.

"Can I help in any way?"

He sounded so much like Father, she had to swallow twice before she could answer. "I wondered if you could lend me the money to go to school." It sounded so brash said out loud. She couldn't meet his eyes.

"Is that all? Why, of course, I'll gladly finance your education. It's the least I can do."

"I'll pay you back."

"Nonsense. You'll do no such thing. I've never had children. Something I wish could have been different. You and your sisters are the closest I will ever have. It's my privilege to help any way I can."

She met his eyes, smiled. The two of them shared something—no children. It made her feel they had a special connection.

"Now you must stay and visit a few days...unless you have a young man waiting for you back home."

"No. No, I don't."

"I hear regret in those words. Is it regret that you have no young man or regret that he has designs on another?"

She smiled. "The former." So far as she knew, Emmet didn't have another woman in mind.

"Good. Because if it was the latter, I'd wonder if the man was blind."

Louisa's cheeks warmed, and she knew she blushed under her uncle's praise.

She spent two pleasant days in her uncle's company,

finding him extremely easy to talk to. It amazed her he'd never married, and finally she said so.

"I love a woman."

"But why—?" She broke off. It was none of her business.

"Why aren't I married? Why doesn't anyone know?"

She tried to pretend she wasn't curious, but he chuckled.

"Your father knew, but he kept his promise to never tell. Come, I'll introduce you to the one who has my heart."

She climbed into his car with him, expecting they would visit a cemetery. Instead they left the city and drove to a picturesque estate. A stately brick building set in a beautiful parklike setting.

He stopped in a gravel lot and led her inside. He greeted several women in nurses' uniforms as he led her to a room that looked like a well-fitted guest room in a fine house, except for the bed that was raised, as Ellie's had been.

In the bed lay a little gray-haired woman.

Uncle Peter crossed to the side of the bed and bent over. "Hello, Carrie Ann."

The woman's eyes lit up like dawn.

Uncle Peter held her hands. "She can't talk, can't feed herself. Can't sit up. My sweet, Carrie Ann had a stroke when she was but eighteen. A blood vessel ruptured in her brain, the doctors decided. I loved her before this unfortunate accident, and I will love her every day of my life." He stroked her hair back. "Sweetheart, this is my niece, Louisa. The oldest of the girls that I've told you about. She's come to visit us."

Tears pooled in Carrie Ann's eyes, and he wiped them away tenderly.

If only Emmet had that kind of love. A love undiminished by unfortunate circumstances.

If only.

Louisa wept.

Uncle Peter pulled her into his arms, while still holding Carrie Ann's hands. "Don't be upset. I've regretted not one moment. Carrie Ann's sweetness has been a blessing."

Carrie Ann tried to say something, but all that came out was unintelligible mumbles.

"She says not to cry for her."

"I'm not crying for her. I'm crying for me. I love a man, but he can't see past my health problems." The whole story tumbled forth, every pertinent detail. She even confessed her barrenness.

Uncle Peter made soothing noises and held her. Just as her father would have. Such sweet comfort.

"If he is worthy of your love, he will change his mind. If he doesn't, he is not worthy."

Louisa calmed, stood. "I'm sorry. I've made quite a spectacle of myself. It's just, you remind me so much of Father."

Uncle Peter caught her hand. "That is the best compliment I've ever received."

Over the passing days, she grew extremely fond of Uncle Peter. "The one good thing out of Emmet's rejection is that I have grown to know you. How did we miss all those years?"

"It is my fault. I wanted to protect Carrie Ann. And myself from people's pity, so I distanced myself from the family. It wasn't until your father died that I realized what I had lost. And by then it was too late."

"It's not too late. I admire you so much for how you have stayed at Carrie Ann's side. I hope I can find the contentment in my situation that you've found."

"Child, I would spare you the sorrow, but it isn't in my hands."

"Nor mine." She tried to prepare herself to return home, but dreaded confronting daily reminders of Emmet.

When Uncle Peter suggested, "Why don't you stay longer? Get to know Carrie Ann," Louisa readily agreed.

Emmet had not made any further plans about returning to the ranch. He couldn't. It was as if his life had hit a bump in the road, and he couldn't seem to get over it or around it or through it. He'd prayed, asking God to show him the answers. Auntie May was right. He wasn't to blame. He had been only nine years old.

But a persistent voice mocked, *What about Jane? You weren't a child then. And what about Ellie's accident? Where were you when that happened? Not protecting your child. That's for sure.*

And Louisa. How he missed her. Like a giant toothache that wasn't calmed by warm oil or a clove. He couldn't possibly protect her from something that had already occurred.

He wandered up and down back roads, praying and begging for an answer.

It was almost supper time when he turned his steps toward home. As he neared the yard, he heard Ellie and Leila playing. At least Ellie had found solace in her young friend.

One more loss she must endure when they left. Seems everything he did had a hurt associated with it.

The girls had the dollhouse and dolls out playing with them. Ellie guarded that gift carefully. More proof of her fondness for Louisa. Oh, if only he could prevent his daughter from experiencing further pain.

The girls arranged the family of dolls in the various rooms, having them talk in individual voices.

"Take the mommy out," Ellie said. "These children cannot have a mommy."

Leila removed the paper doll. Ellie stared at the remaining family. Took out all except the father and a girl doll.

Emmet stood in the back of the shed, unobserved, to watch and listen, sensing Ellie expressed her own life.

"Why did God take my mommy?" Ellie seemed to be speaking to the dolls. "Does He hate me?"

God hated them. Is that what Emmet thought? God was punishing him for not obeying his father, not keeping his mother safe?

Leila touched Ellie's hand. "God doesn't hate anyone. My mama always said He loves us all. No matter what."

Ellie considered the information. "But He took your mommy and daddy and sister. Why?"

Leila tilted her head. "It's awfully sad. But Matron says none of us are smart enough to know God's mind and understand Him. Bad things happen and we don't know why. But I'm glad God loves me."

Oh, for the innocence and trust of children.

But the words spoken by a child painted his thoughts. He couldn't keep people safe. Accidents happened. Illnesses happened. There was the uncertainty of weather and financial markets. But whatever happened, he could trust God. Even when he couldn't understand or make sense of it.

"I wish I could have a family like this," Leila said, putting the entire family into the playhouse. Her voice dripped with such sadness, it brought a sting to Emmet's eyes.

Ellie reached over and took two dolls—little girls, from what Emmet could see. "These two are sisters forever. Just like I wish you and me could be."

The girls bent to touch their foreheads together.

Emmet closed his eyes against a flood of pain, then called to the girls and entered the yard.

Both girls rushed toward him. Ellie flung herself in his arms and sobbed against his neck. He welcomed her gladly, even though he suspected she sought only temporary comfort. She would no doubt revert back to blaming him for driving Louisa away. When Leila hung back, he opened his free arm to her. With a strangled sob, she went to him and both girls snuggled close.

Oh, if only he wasn't a man alone, he would adopt this little child. The pair could be forever sisters. It tore at his insides to know he must leave Leila behind. How would the child survive without a family to love her?

She'd shown herself remarkably strong in face of her trials. He could only hope and pray she would continue to be so.

"You two can write each other. And maybe Leila can come and visit when she's a little older."

Two pairs of arms tightened about his neck.

After a bit, Leila lifted her head. "I wish you could be my daddy."

He knew his smile was very shaky as he studied her. "I would like that. But you need a mommy too."

At that, Ellie insisted on being put down. She pulled Leila to her side, and they returned to playing dolls. He suspected they both purposely kept their backs to him.

Leila stayed for supper and then he took her home, letting Ellie ride along. The pair whispered and giggled together on the trip.

Later, after he'd returned, put Ellie to bed and retired to his own bed, he lay staring in the darkness.

God, I have a long way to go yet, but I think I'm ready to start a journey of trust with You. I want to take the journey hand in hand with Louisa.

Would she forgive him for turning away from her pain? All he could hope was she would give him a chance to explain.

He waited until Ellie went to school the next morning, then headed for the Morgan place.

Their vehicle was missing. But perhaps she was home alone. That would be good. But no one came to the door to answer his knock.

His nervousness tripled. He had to speak to her as soon as possible. Perhaps Judd and Madge knew of her whereabouts. He jumped into his truck and raised a cloud of dust in his hurried departure.

At the Kirk place, he veered toward the barn where Judd stood in the doorway, a hunk of iron in his hand.

"What brings you out here in such a rush?" Judd asked.

"I need to see Louisa."

Judd leaned against the door frame and studied him. "You hurt her. I don't much appreciate that."

"I'm sorry."

"Yeah? That girl is well worth loving even if she can't have children."

"I don't care about that. I was only upset because—" It sounded stupid now, but he explained it as best he could. "I know now I have to trust God for things like life and death and everything in between. I want to tell Louisa. Hopefully she will give me another chance."

"I certainly hope you mean what you say, but I'm not sure—"

"I love her, Judd. I want to marry her."

Judd laughed. "I was about to say I'm not sure where she is."

"What?"

"She left a few days ago to visit an uncle. She plans to go to Normal school and become a teacher. Hear she was good at the work."

"Yes. But—you don't know where she is?"

"No. But Madge does. Let's see if you can convince her she should tell you."

Emmet followed Judd to the house.

Madge glanced up, and when she saw Emmet she frowned. "I'm not sure I want you here."

Only his determination to find Louisa and explain his reasons for turning away from her gave him the courage to face her displeasure. "I need to talk to Louisa."

"Seems to me you've said and done enough already." She stepped closer.

He gave a wary glance toward the big wooden spoon she shook at him. "I'd like a chance to change all that."

Madge hesitated. "How is that possible? You made it clear you want nothing to do with a woman who can't give you children."

"That wasn't my intention."

She crossed her arms, the spoon clearly evident in her grasp. "So what was?"

"She cried when she told me." His words were hoarse as his throat tightened. "I couldn't bear her pain."

Madge's expression softened. "So what's changed?"

"Me. I realized I can't protect everyone I love from life and its challenges." He wouldn't tell her more. That confession belonged to Louisa. "I think she would want to hear what I have to say." He didn't care that he sounded desperate. "I'm prepared to plead."

Madge turned to Judd and they communicated silently, then she moved to Judd's side and wrapped her arms around his waist, the wooden spoon hanging from her free arm. "I'm prepared to give you one chance, but if you hurt her again..." She brandished her weapon.

"You'll have the whole family to answer to," Judd added.

For a moment, Emmet hesitated. "I can't be responsible for her response."

Madge snorted. "I think you'll find my sister most reasonable."

The next day, address tucked in his pocket, he headed for Edmonton. He didn't explain to Ellie where he was going or why. Just in case Louisa rejected him.

God, I'm trusting You.

Of course, as Leila said, he couldn't begin to understand God's ways. That's why trusting was hard. And required faith. If he knew everything and understood all the reasons, there would be no need to trust anything but his own wisdom.

Louisa sat in a wicker rocker on the veranda of Uncle Peter's home. She had enjoyed every minute of her visit and planned to extend it until she must return home to pack for Normal school. Uncle Peter said but of course she would live here while she attended classes. She welcomed the idea. God willing, she would even find a job in the city when she graduated.

She turned her attention back to the sketchbook before her. Her intention had been to draw the flowers surrounding the veranda. Clematis crept up the side, almost blocking the view of the street. Yellow rosebushes stood grandly on each side of the entrance.

In the trees around the yard, birds sang. She'd identified the song of the vireo and even caught a glimpse of the shy bird. She'd seen an oriole, a tanager, robins, several species of sparrows and two kinds of hawks. She'd begun a journal of bird sightings, sketching them as often as possible. Maybe when she was a teacher, she would use this information.

Most of all, she enjoyed listening to the birds sing. She was getting her own song back, though it had a mourning quality to it. She would never stop missing Emmet. But she was learning to find peace in the midst of her pain.

One thing she had decided she would do was to pray for both his and Ellie's happiness. *Bless Emmet with happiness and peace. Bless Ellie.* She wasn't yet able to pray that Ellie would be blessed with a mother. But perhaps someday she would be able to.

A vehicle stopped nearby. She paid it little attention. Uncle Peter had gone to his office, and she knew no one who would call on her in the city. Perhaps one day she would feel ready to contact old friends, should there be any left living nearby. For now she was content to heal and prepare for the future.

A step sounded on the sidewalk, and she jerked about to see who approached the house. Through the canopy of leaves she almost thought it was Emmet. How many times would she look up at a man his size and build and feel her heart explode with hope?

She watched the man draw closer. Reach the step and mount to the porch. "Emmet?" Was she dreaming?

"Louisa. I've found you."

"I didn't realize I was lost." It was a silly thing to say, but she couldn't let herself believe he'd come for any special reason. "What business brings you to the city?"

"I'm not here on business. I'm here to see you."

She sat with her feet curled up beneath her and now dropped them to the floor. "Is something wrong? Mother? Sally? Madge? Did Madge get hurt helping Judd?"

"No one is hurt." He snagged a chair from the opposite side of the veranda and pulled it close. He sat facing her. "I've come to see you."

She stared. She would not hope. She would not try and guess what he wanted.

"Louisa, I want to explain."

"No need." She did not want to hear how he simply couldn't give up his dream of a big family. Something she could not give him. *No excuses, please. Please do not say it's not personal. Because it is.*

"You once asked me about how my parents died. You even suggested there was a big lump of something that stopped my heart. You were right. I just didn't realize it." He told the story of his parents' death. Of feeling he was to blame. His father's unfair accusation.

Long before he finished, she leaned forward, pressing her hands to his.

"I realize that I have always held myself responsible even for things I have no control over." He looked into her eyes, searching beyond the surface, exploring her heart.

She too sought the deeper meaning in his words at seeing his eyes fully unshuttered for the first time ever. Hope sprang fully bloomed, even though she warned herself she still could not give him what he wanted.

"Louisa, when you said you couldn't have children and I saw the pain in your face, heard it in your voice, I knew what a disappointment it was for you. I knew I couldn't fix it. All I could think was how could I see this pain in you every day and be able to do absolutely nothing about it? I failed before I started." He shrugged. "Talking about it, I realize how little sense it makes, but it made so much sense to me at the time. I couldn't think of how I would live with a pain I couldn't fix."

"I'm sorry, but I will never be able to give you the large family you've always wanted." She sat back slowly, pulled her hands to her lap.

"I don't care about that. Don't you see? It isn't not having a large family that matters. It's knowing I can't keep this pain from you." He grabbed her hands, knelt at her feet. "I love you, Louisa Morgan. So much that your pain seemed unbearable. But I realize I have to leave life and death and a whole lot of other things in God's hands." He told her how he'd overheard Leila and Ellie playing, and the words Leila spoke that made him realize he could do nothing but trust when life seemed unexplainable.

She chuckled at the picture he created of the girls playing with the dollhouse. "I'm so glad they are getting pleasure out of it."

Emmet still knelt before her, and she wished he would sit down again. He was making her nervous.

"Louisa, I love you. You are worth more to me than a dozen children. I want to share my life with you. I want you to be my wife and Ellie's mother. Please say you'll marry me."

She studied him, watched his eyes flash from blue to green. "Are you sure? There will never be children. The doctor was quite certain of that."

"Louisa, I would rather share my life with you than with anyone else. We have Ellie. We can love her."

She had to be sure. She had to know he was certain. "Ellie will be an only child."

"We'll see she has lots of companions."

"No sons. No babies. And me, an unhealthy specimen."

He lifted his head and roared with laughter. "You are anything but a weak, shrinking violet. You are strong as steel." He touched her chin. "Gentle as velvet. I know what I want, and it is you. Marry me?"

She smiled from a heart overflowing with assurance of his love. Free to open her own store of love, she spoke words that she had for so long ached to say. "Emmet, you are all I need. You are my sunshine and my rain, my heart's joy and contentment. You have filled my life to overflowing with love. If you are one hundred percent certain this is what you want, then yes, I will marry you, Emmet Hamilton. I love you and will do my best to make your days happy and—"

"My heart glad." He finished, pressing her palm to his chest. "Together we will face life walking at God's side. Whatever comes our way, we will stand together."

"Strong in God's strength."

His murmur of agreement burred against her lips as

he pulled her into his arms. He kissed her soundly, as if to make sure she understood all he felt.

By the time he finished and pulled away, she had no more doubts. They sat side by side, holding hands and kissing often as they discussed their future.

"I want to go back to the ranch." He sounded doubtful.

"I can hardly wait. Do you mind if I make the house ours?"

"It's been a long time since anyone has done much in the house. I'm afraid you will find it sadly in need of a woman's touch. I hope you will make it yours in every way."

"Ours."

"Ours," he echoed, kissing her again for good measure.

Uncle Peter returned a while later and stared at the pair of them.

Louisa jumped to her feet and introduced them.

Uncle Peter gave Emmet a hard look. "I'm not sure you're welcome here. You're the young man who broke my niece's heart."

Emmet faced the older man with dignity. "I don't blame you if you think I should be shot for that, but I plan to do my best to make up for it in the future. Louisa has agreed to marry me."

Uncle Peter's brows knit together. "Louisa, is that true?"

"Yes, Uncle Peter." She knew her happiness sounded in her voice. "It's an answer to a prayer."

"I have grown rather fond of my niece." He indicated they should all sit, and for an hour grilled Emmet on his plans, as if he hoped to detect some note of falseness in his affection.

Louisa's insides glowed with happiness at the way Emmet continued to speak of his love for her and how they would find their joy in loving each other and Ellie.

Finally, Uncle Peter relented and turned to Louisa. "I only regret that this means you won't be spending the winter with me."

"Uncle Peter, you must promise to come and visit us often."

"And you must come here as much as you can."

She looked up into the face of the man she had come to love like a father. "Will you come to my wedding and give me away?"

His eyes glistened. "I would consider it an honor." He kissed her cheeks. "Now go entertain your young man."

Emmet and Louisa had agreed to get married and return to the ranch as soon as school ended in June.

Emmet spent the night in one of Uncle Peter's guest rooms, and he and Louisa returned to Golden Prairie the next day.

"We need to speak to Ellie before we tell anyone else." Louisa wanted the child's approval.

"She'll be ecstatic. In fact, she figured I didn't know how to ask you. Blamed me that you said no." He grabbed her hand and pulled her to his shoulder, keeping one hand firmly on the steering wheel. "I never told her that I turned you down too. I'm sorry. I never meant to hurt you."

She kissed his chin. "I forgive you. I believe God used our time of separation to help each of us grow in faith."

They arrived back in town just as school got out and waited for Ellie outside the school. She saw Louisa and squealed. "You've come back." She shot a glance at her father and grinned. "Ohh."

Louisa chuckled. Ellie was much too smart for a seven-year-old. She and Emmet would have their hands full as this little one matured.

They had agreed to wait until they were alone to talk to her. They returned to the house and slipped to the backyard. Auntie May, smart woman that she was, stayed out of the way.

"Sit down, Ellie, we want to talk to you."

Ellie gave each of them a hard look and refused to sit. "Are you getting married?"

Louisa laughed at her demanding tone.

Emmet answered her. "Yes, we are."

Ellie squealed and threw her arms about Louisa. "I knew you'd be my mommy the minute you said you loved me." She squinted at her father. "I didn't know if you'd ever get it right."

Louisa grinned at Emmet, who shook his head sadly. "What did I tell you?"

Ellie backed away. "Can I have a sister?"

Louisa staggered back. She hadn't known Ellie would have the same dreams as her father.

Emmet caught Louisa's hand and pulled her to his side. "Ellie, Button, we can't promise a sister. Our future is in God's hands, but there might never be a baby."

Ellie made a noise of disgust. "I don't want a baby. I want Leila for a sister."

Louisa glanced at Emmet. At the look on his face, she knew he'd already thought of this.

"I'll see what we can do."

Ellie raced away to play.

Emmet took Louisa's hands. "What do you think of adopting Leila?"

She grinned. "I think it's a most excellent idea." Two little girls was more than she'd dreamed possible.

He caught her chin then and turned her face toward him. "You are one special lady. Have I told you that?"

She giggled. "Not recently. Besides, I don't think I'll ever grow tired of hearing it."

"You are special and I love you."

"I love you too," she managed before he kissed her.

Epilogue

Emmet checked the back of the truck, making sure all the gifts and extra furniture that Mother Morgan had donated, plus clothes for his growing family, were all secure. He tightened the ropes holding the canvas tarp in place. "It looks like it will hold until we get home."

He faced the crowd. Auntie May. Louisa's mother and sisters. Judd, of course, who had given him all sorts of advice for a married man. As if Emmet hadn't been married before. But this time was different. He was different. He had begun a walk of trust. And Uncle Peter, standing close to Mother. Louisa had commented how protective he was of her, and hoped they would now become friends.

"Are we ready to go?" Ellie demanded.

"We're ready."

Louisa circled her family, giving each a hug and receiving a whispered goodbye and, he suspected, a parting word of advice. Who'd have guessed everyone had so much to say about marriage and ranching? He couldn't remember such generous tidbits when he married Jane. Of course, he'd married away from home.

He followed at Louisa's side, getting hugs and good-byes. He paused before Auntie May. "I can never thank you enough for raising me."

She chuckled and patted his face. "I wish I could take credit for the man you've become, but we all know I can't. Now you behave. You write often. Send pictures and don't forget to visit."

"We plan to come back for Christmas, and all of you are welcome to visit us anytime."

They had been married only a week. He hated to take Louisa from her family, but it was time to start their life together—with his two daughters. Leila's adoption had been easy and rapid. The judge signed the final papers two days ago.

"Let's go home." He helped Louisa into the truck and lifted two chattering little girls in beside her.

Judd joined him at the window. "The way you're loaded down, it reminds me of the people moving out of the country, sick and tired of drought and poor prices."

Louisa leaned over to speak to Judd. "The difference is we're not running from the drought. We're headed to the future, with two precious little girls and a man who loves me. It's more than I asked or dreamed for."

Emmet leaned over and kissed her.

Leila clamped a hand to her mouth to hide her giggles, and Ellie sighed. "Guess what we'll have to put up with the whole trip?"

Emmet chucked her under the chin as the others laughed. "You'll have to put up with it a lot longer than that."

Ellie groaned, but her grin said how much she didn't mind. She reached for Leila's hands. "This is the happiest day of my life."

Three voices repeated her words in unison.

The happiest day of their lives. A great way to start the future.

They called a final goodbye and headed west.

* * * * *

Award-winning author **Dorothy Clark** lives in rural New York. Dorothy enjoys traveling with her husband throughout the United States, doing research and gaining inspiration for future books. Dorothy believes in God, love, family and happy endings, which explains why she feels so at home writing stories for Love Inspired. Dorothy enjoys hearing from her readers and may be contacted at dorothyjclark@hotmail.com.

Books by Dorothy Clark

Love Inspired Historical

Stand-In Brides

His Substitute Wife
Wedded for the Baby
Mail-Order Bride Switch

Pinewood Weddings

Wooing the Schoolmarm
Courting Miss Callie
Falling for the Teacher
A Season of the Heart

An Unlikely Love
His Precious Inheritance

Visit the Author Profile page
at Harlequin.com for more titles.

FRONTIER FATHER

Dorothy Clark

There is no fear in love; but perfect love
casteth out fear: because fear hath torment.
—*John* 4:18

This book is dedicated with my sincere thanks and gratitude to my readers. Thank you for your many, many letters about the previous five books about the Randolph family members. I am humbled by your compliments and encouraged by your comments and questions. I look forward to hearing from you.

To Nancy...
And Sam...
There are no words. Thank you.

Chapter One

Oregon country, 1841

It was not impressive. Not that it mattered. Nothing did anymore. Anne turned her back to the scattered log buildings that formed the Banning Mission, brushed the dust from her black wool cloak and walked to the back of her wagon. "Thank you for bringing me, Mr. Thatcher. I am grateful."

The tall man unhitched his horse from the tailgate and looked down at her. "Are you sure you don't want me to stay until you have met Mr. Banning, Widow Simms? I gave your sister my word I would see you safely settled."

"And so you have, Mr. Thatcher. Emma worries overmuch. What possible harm can befall me at a mission?" She gave him a polite, dismissive smile.

He frowned, glanced at the buildings behind her. "Even so. I will wait until you are safe inside."

Anne looked up at the man's set face and the protest on her lips died. Zachary Thatcher had guided their wagon train all the way from Independence, Missouri, to the site of the new town of Promise the emigrants were founding here in Oregon country. Now he had brought her on to the mission. He would not yield his position as protector on her whim. "As you wish, Mr. Thatcher. But I assure you, it is quite unnecessary."

She turned back toward the buildings. The one on the right had a large addition that formed a T on the far end. Smoke poured from chimneys at the gable ends, and from another centered at the juncture of the wood-shingled roofs. There was a beaten track through the grass that divided at the end to reach two doors. She lifted the front of her long skirts clear of the exposed soil and followed the path to the plank door in the main building. Its red paint was streaked and faded. And dirty. She gave the back of her skirts a shake to free them of any soil adhering to their hems, adjusted her bonnet and knocked.

The late October sun glinted off three small windows spaced along the length of the building. Dust encrusted windows. Her fastidious nature reared. She jerked her gaze back to the door and knocked harder.

A reluctant hinge squealed in protest as the door was yanked open. "What for you knock? Door open, you come in!"

Anne jerked back at the imperious words, then squared her shoulders and stepped into the dim interior. Behind her, hoofs thudded against the ground as Zachary Thatcher rode off. The stiffness in her spine relaxed. At last. Her final link with her family was broken. There was no one here she cared about. Her heart was safe.

"You sit. Mister come soon maybe."

The Indian woman issuing the order closed the door, crossed the room and disappeared through a doorway at the other side of the fireplace.

Anne stared after her, stunned to silence and immobility by the unaccustomed rudeness. She swept her gaze over the room, took in the crude furnishings made of wood and hide. Even in the dim light offered by the smoldering fire and one of the small, dirty windows she could see the dust that covered them. *And* the dirt and bits of dried grass on the plank floor. Her training to be mistress of a home surged to the surface. Why would Mitchel Banning's wife allow such neglect?

The hinge on the door behind her again squealed its protest. She turned, flinched as the flung-open door banged against the wall.

"By heaven, William, it is past time you got here!" A man charged into the room, stopped dead in his tracks and stared at her. The glad smile curving his lips and warming his hazel eyes died. Confusion took its place. He glanced around the room, frowned, looked back at her and made a visible effort to gather himself. He brushed at his shirtsleeves and ran his hands through his short, wavy, brown hair, scattering dust and tiny particles of some sort of grass or grain into the air. She could see them glittering against the sun coming in the open door behind him as they drifted toward the floor. He turned, grabbed a jacket off a peg beside the door and shrugged into it.

"Forgive my appearance, I was at the gristmill when I heard the wagon pull in, Miss…er…Mrs.…."

"Widow Simms."

He turned, swept his gaze over her black clothing and made her a slight bow. "Mitchel Banning, at your service. I beg your pardon for my…er…explosive entrance, Widow Simms. But when I heard your wagon arrive, I thought…" He gave a little shrug.

"That my brother, William Allen, had arrived?"

"William is your *brother*?" Mitchel Banning's broad smile returned. "Where is the scalawag? In the wagon?" He turned and peered out the door.

"No, Mr. Banning. William is in Philadelphia. His wife is with child and she took ill and was unable to make the journey."

Mitchel turned back, confusion on his face, a question in his eyes.

Anne straightened to her full height, which brought the top of her head somewhere close to the level of his chin. "William was loath to disappoint you, so I have come to teach school in his stead."

The man's reaction was instant and acute, his disappointment palpable. It washed over her like a wave. A frown drew his brows together. He lifted a hand and kneaded the muscles at the back of his neck. Her stomach clenched in a sharp spasm. If he should disapprove... "I am well qualified to fill the position, Mr. Banning." Her quiet words drew his gaze back to her. There was a harried look in his eyes.

He nodded and lowered his hand to his side. "Forgive my poor manners, Widow Simms. You must be weary after your long journey. We can continue this discussion later. If you would care to refresh yourself before dinner, William's— There is a spare room up those stairs." He gestured across the room. "I will have Sighing Wind bring you water. And if there is anything more you have need of..." His voice trailed off, left the words hanging there in indecision.

Anne took a deep breath. It would be of no advantage to delay. She must make her expectations clear. "I should like my trunks and personal belongings brought from the wagon to my room as quickly as possible, Mr. Banning."

Another frown darkened his face, was quickly erased. He made no answer, merely sketched her a polite bow.

Her stomach clenched tighter. Surely, he was not considering refusing her the position. She firmed her voice. "My teaching supplies can be carried directly to the schoolroom. I will begin organizing them tomorrow. For now, as you say, I am weary. But I should like to pay my respects to Mrs. Banning and express my gratitude for her hospitality before I go upstairs."

Something about him changed, went...still. He turned, closed the door, shutting out the fading sunlight.

"I see William did not tell you my wife has departed this earth for her heavenly home. It was her death that prompted me to write and ask William to come and help me in my work." He turned back to face her. "I wasn't sure William ever received my letter. It is over two years since her passing."

His words touched the rawness of her grief. *Over two years.* An eternity. How would she ever survive it without her beloved Phillip and their precious baby, Grace? The memories she struggled to keep buried surged upward. Familiar bands of pain clamped around her chest and throat. Her fingers twitched. "I am sorry for your loss, Mr. Banning." The words came out a broken whisper. It was the best she could manage with so little breath.

He stepped away from the door, came closer to where she stood in the center of the room. "And I, for yours, Widow Simms. May Almighty God grant you His peace and comfort during this time of your bereavement."

God. Every muscle in her body went rigid. Her face

drew taut. It was *God* who had taken her husband and child from her and left her to walk this earth in unbearable anguish. She wanted no comfort. Certainly not from God. Not from anyone. She wanted only to be numb. She swallowed, tried, but could not force polite words through the constricting barrier of her anger. She gave Mitchel Banning a small nod, thankful for the long brim of the scoop bonnet that hid her face from him, raised the front hems of her skirts off the dusty planks and walked toward the stairs, aware of his gaze on her every step of the way.

He was trapped. His choice a privilege that bowed to circumstance. Mitchel listened to the sounds of her things being carried to her room and stole another glance at William's sister. Her hair had been smoothly drawn back into a bun at her crown when she joined him for dinner. But all through the meal her curls had been popping free of any restraint and now formed a riotous halo around her head. Not a golden one, but one the deep-russet color of oak leaves in autumn. Color of such bold contrast to the rest of her solemn appearance it seemed almost to make it a lie. As did her eyes. They were the violet-blue of a bottle gentian, startling in a face with skin that put him in mind of the prized alabaster vase that had sat on his parents' mantel all his growing-up years. It gave him a shock every time she lifted those long, brown lashes and looked up at him. But those were not the only contrasts he had discovered in William's sister.

Mitchel scowled, stabbed his fork into the last bite of beef on his plate and carried it to his mouth. The woman's nature was strongly opposite to her fragile appearance. No matter what argument he set forth to prove her best interest lay in returning to the emigrant town being formed by those with whom she had journeyed to Oregon country, she would not be dissuaded from her determination to remain and teach school. And he did not need another person to look after! He had enough on his plate. He had been living on the hope of William's arrival expecting relief, not more responsibility. But what was he to do? Cast William's sister out into the wilderness? He did not have time to leave the mission to escort her to the emigrant town or Fort Walla Walla. There was too much work to be done in preparation for winter. And he dare not leave Hope in the care of the Indians. Their cures for sickness would kill her.

His heart seized at the thought of his toddler daughter lying ill in her bed. He had tried all he knew to help her, but— *Wait!* His heart lurched, pounded out an accelerated beat. In that last letter he had received before leaving to come west, William had written that one of his sisters was studying with their adopted father to become a doctor. Which one? Anne? No. Emma. He cast a speculative glance at the woman across from him. Which one was she? Had God answered his prayers for Hope's healing? No, that was senseless. Emma was working with their physician father in Philadelphia. Why would she come to the Oregon wilderness? Unless…unless she had married and lost her husband. *Please, Almighty God, for Hope's sake, let it be Emma.*

Mitchel put his fork down, looked across the table. The woman seemed so *delicate* to be a doctor. Still… *Please, God…* "Have you skill at tending the sick, Widow Simms?"

She placed her fork on her plate and looked over at him. "There is illness here at the mission, Mitchel—I mean Mr. Banning?" Pink tinged her face, crested on her high cheekbones. "Please forgive my lapse of manners. William always refers to you by your given name and I am accustomed to thinking of you that way."

"Ah, William. I miss him and our deep philosophical discussions greatly." Fondness for his friend welled. He pushed away his disappointment that William had been unable to make the journey and smiled. "As your brother is our connection, why don't we consider ourselves properly introduced and dispense with formality? Please call me Mitchel."

She gave a small nod. "You are very kind, Mitchel. Thank you for your graciousness in the face of my lapse." The merest wisp of a polite smile touched her lips, disappeared. "Please call me Anne."

Not Emma. His heart sank. He stared down at his plate, sought to find something encouraging on which to hang hope for his daughter's recovery.

"You were speaking of illness here at the mission?"

"Yes. My daughter, Hope." He cleared his throat of the lump lodged there. "I have done all I know to do, but she...does not improve." He looked into Anne's astonishingly blue eyes and silently willed her to be God's answer to his prayers. It was unfair, but he could not stop himself. "She is a baby, only two years old."

Anne Simms went as white as the snow on Mount Hood. Her long, dark brown lashes swept down to rest against her colorless cheeks, and her pale lips parted as if she could not breathe in enough air. Mitchel leaned forward. "Are you unwell, Anne?"

She gave a slight shake of her head. "No. I—" She opened her eyes, glanced at him, then looked down and placed her hands in her lap. "I am sorry to disappoint you, Mitchel, but I will be of no help to you. I know nothing of caring for the ill or…children. Now, if you will excuse me I am weary and should like to retire." Before he could stand, she rose and hurried from the room.

He stared after her, bitterness rising on a swell of anger at his dashed hope. For a moment he had thought— He gave a snort and shoved back his chair. It was impossible that Anne was the answer to his prayers. He'd prayed for *help,* not a frail beauty who looked about to swoon at the mere mention of Hope's illness. It was obvious Anne Simms was not strong enough to handle life on the wilderness mission, let alone teach Indian children. Well, he would not accept another burden! William's sister or not—when Adam Halstrum returned from his trip to Oregon City—Anne's belongings were going back in her wagon. Adam could take her back to the emigrant village.

"P-papa… P-papa!"

His heart squeezed at his daughter's sobbing call. He spun on his heels and hurried toward her room to comfort her.

Chapter Two

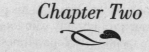

Anne rushed up the stairs, stopped and glanced around the room that had been barren but for a bedstead and washstand made from rough wood before all the furnishings from her wagon had been brought in. Trunks crowded along one wall. The dresser sat beside the small, dirty gable window. She darted her gaze to the bed. The dusty straw-filled mattress that had crackled when she touched it earlier, had been replaced by her two mattresses, the bottom one of horsehair, the top one of feathers.

So Mitchel had decided she could stay and teach in William's stead. Tension drained from her, carrying the false strength of her trepidation away. She ignored the sudden weakness, crossed to the bed, nestled under the roof that sloped upward from the front wall to the stone chimney radiating warmth from a fireplace below, and removed the striped blankets someone had spread overtop her bare mattresses. Thank goodness all that was needed for comfort William had provided in the wagon—even if the linens and other household items *were* originally meant for his mother-in-law. She was thankful for that. She wanted nothing from her own home. Nothing that would evoke memories. She wanted only to forget. And now teaching would fill her days so she would have less time to think, to remember, to *feel*.

She opened a trunk, pulled out sheets, spread them over the top mattress, tucked their hemmed edges beneath it, then replaced the blankets and added a woven coverlet. A few quick tugs and embroidered cases covered her feather pillows. She placed them on the bed, took out a towel and closed the trunk.

How fortuitously everything had worked out. William's expecting wife had developed the severe nausea that prevented them from making the journey, and their misfortune had provided her the perfect opportunity to escape her loving family's nurturing that, however well-intended, served only to keep her grief ever before her. Except for Emma. She had not escaped her adopted sister. Until now.

Anne frowned, hung the towel on a hook, moved the lit lamp from the washstand to the dresser, then lifted comb, brush and mirror from another trunk and placed them beside it. She burrowed through the trunk, extracted her toothbrush, tooth powder and soap and placed them on the washstand beside the china pitcher and bowl. She hesitated over the small crock of lilac-scented face and hand balm Papa Doc had made for her. She lifted it out, ran her fingers over the crock's smooth surface, flawed with a small bump here and there. Emma was so like their adopted father. She had refused to let her make the long journey through the wilderness alone in her injured condition. Even though that was what she wanted. After the carriage accident had wounded her and killed her husband and daughter, she had not cared if she survived. Indeed, had *hoped* she would not. But Emma would not let her be.

Anne shoved the balm back in the trunk, clenched her hands and cast another look around the attic room with its rough-sawn wood floor and beamed wood ceiling. Because of her adopted sister Emma's constant bullying and doctoring, she had lived. Now all she could do was hope teaching might give her life some purpose. She unclenched her hands, brushed one over the fabric covering her ribs, her twitching fingers searching out the raised scar caused by the carriage lamp when she had been thrown from the wildly careening vehicle. If only the finial of the lamp had penetrated deeper. Oh, if only it had. She would this moment be with Phillip and—

"Papaaa… Papaaaa…"

The baby! The toddler's calls sent pain ripping through her. Anne gasped, pressed her fingers to her ears to close out the child's crying. She succeeded only in muting it. Her breath shortened. She whirled around, looked for someplace to go, somewhere to hide from the heart-shredding cries. Nothing presented itself. She lifted the hems of her skirts and ran for the stairs, raced down them into the entrance room, then jerked to a halt. Mitchel Banning was entering the room holding his daughter, rubbing her back. The child's face was buried in the curve of his neck, her golden-blond hair curling over the blanket that swaddled her. "Did you need something, Anne?"

She closed her eyes to block out the sight of the toddler, but it was too late. A hot, prickly feeling swept over her. She gripped the back of the settee beside her, swayed, held tighter.

"Are you all right, Anne?"

Concern laced Mitchel Banning's voice. Anne forced air into her laboring lungs, opened her eyes and focused on his face, held her gaze riveted there. "Yes, I…suddenly felt the need for some fresh air. If you will excuse me…" She looked down at the floor, hurried to the door and yanked it open.

"Anne, wait—"

She closed the door on his words, leaned back against the house wall and gasped for air. What had she done? She had wanted to escape family and memories, had come to where there was nothing to remind her of her loss. And now— Oh, why had William not *told* her about Mitchel's child—

The squeaking hinge warned her. She pushed erect, stepped away from the house before the door opened.

"Anne, come inside." Mitchel Banning's voice was pitched low, his tone firm and unyielding. "There are Indian braves camped on the grounds and it would be best if you do not encounter any of them while you are alone."

Indian braves? She would far rather face them than the child in his arms. But her situation was too tenuous to anger him. She drew in a long breath and turned. The lamplight made his tall, broad-shouldered body into a silhouette framed by the doorway, the toddler in his arms no more than a deeper shadow. The child seemed to have fallen asleep. Perhaps it would be all right. She expelled the breath and nodded. "Very well. I have no wish to cause you concern, Mitchel. But it is a most pleasant evening." She took another steadying breath, moved toward the door.

"But chilly." He stepped aside to let her pass.

"A little, yes." A shiver slithered through her and she realized she had rushed outside without her cloak.

Was he commenting on her rash behavior? She must be more careful.

The door latch clicked into place. She watched as he lifted a bar in one hand and quietly dropped it into place across the door. Lamplight played over his face and she saw the worry in his eyes as he looked down at his child. Her heart contracted. Mitchel Banning was afraid for his daughter. She whirled and headed for the stairs, forcing herself to keep a sedate pace when everything within her was screaming *Run! Run and do not stop running!*

But where could she go?

Mitchel paced the floor, rubbing Hope's back, careful not to touch her elbows or wrists. She cried when he touched them. And tonight, she was feverish—her forehead hot and dry beneath his hand. Did that mean she was getting worse? The fear he couldn't conquer washed over him. He lowered his cheek to rest against Hope's hair and closed his eyes.

Soft footfalls sounded overhead, paced the length of the room, returned. He frowned, listened as the path was repeated. An image of Anne's face, pale and strained, as she had clutched the settee and stared at him, flashed into his head. What was wrong with her? Was she ill? His frown deepened. His determination to send Anne Simms back to the emigrant village strengthened. He didn't need another ill person to care for. He did not have time enough to care for Hope as he should. Far too often he had to leave her with Sighing Wind and Laughing Rain. And every time he returned after hours away from her he was afraid—

Mitchel sucked in a long breath, cast down the imagination and took the thought captive as the Bible instructed. He moved across the room and made himself place Hope in her bed. He had to hold on to his faith. He knew only too well, if God chose to call Hope home his arms could not hold her. No more than they had been able to hold her mother. The fear pounced again, tightened its hold.

"The weapons of our warfare are not carnal, but mighty through God to the pulling down of strong holds." Mitchel spoke the Scripture as a declaration, but even as the words left his mouth he knew the fear remained in his heart. He sank to his knees, placed his elbows on the small bed and rested his forehead on his clasped hands. "Please, Almighty God, I ask You to relieve Hope's pain and grant her restful sleep throughout the night. And, if it would be good in Your sight, Almighty God, in Your mercy, restore her to health I pray. Amen."

It was as close as he could come to giving his daughter into God's hands. He pulled the coverlet over her small, blanket-swaddled body, kissed her hot forehead, then turned to put more wood on the fire. The heat seemed to help Hope's pain.

The crying had stopped. Anne halted her pacing and listened to the silence. The child must have fallen asleep again. What was wrong with her? No, she would not wonder about the baby's illness, would not question the reason for her pain. For the toddler *was* in pain. Her mother's instinct told her that. Oh, why had William not told her about Mitchel Banning's toddler daughter!

She jerked her thoughts from the path that led to memories too painful to be borne, fisted her hands against the shaking she could not control and looked around the room that was supposed to have been her escape and, instead, had turned into a trap. *A two-year-old little girl. Grace would be almost two now.* The sickening grief washed over her. She pressed her fingers to her mouth and closed her eyes. When the baby cried, how could she not remember—

A muted thump echoed from the chimney. Another followed.

Oh, do not wake her!

Anne opened her eyes and tiptoed to the tower of stones, listened to Mitchel adding fuel to the fire, willed him to be quiet. She winced at the dull clank of a poker being lifted from its holder and prodding wood into place. And then there was only silence. She turned and leaned against the stones, letting the warmth radiating off them seep into her body.

At least she would no longer be cold.

She shivered at thought of the frigid discomfort of her wagon as the train traveled across the higher, snowy elevations of the mountains. The wind had howled and whistled as it rippled the canvas and insinuated its frosty breath between cover and wagon bed. It had been impossible to get warm, even beneath a pile of blankets. She frowned, ran her fingers over the scar again. The cold added to the jolting punishment of the wagon had made her newly healed ribs ache more than when they were broken in the carriage accident. But that was only physical pain. It was nothing compared to the rending agony of grief.

She stepped to the dresser, eased open the top drawer and removed her blue cotton nightgown and matching quilted robe. Her face tightened. She brushed her palm across the black fabric she had used to cover the embroidered rosebuds that decorated the gown's gathered bodice. Every stitch had felt as if the needle went straight into her heart. She tossed the gown and robe on the bed and tugged the combs from her hair. Her long, russet-colored curls tumbled free to hang halfway down her back. They had once reached to her waist. Phillip had loved her hair. But she hated it now. She had cut it as short as she dared when—

She caught her breath, thrust the combs on the dresser and began to undo the jet-black buttons on the bodice of her black wool gown. She wanted nothing to remind her of him. *Nothing!* But her hair had grown long again during the journey here from St. Louis. And now she had to keep it to look presentable. Mitchel Banning was already less than enthusiastic about her being here to teach in William's stead. She must do nothing to give him cause for dismissal. Though he could hardly put her out. There was nothing but wilderness around the mission. And that suited her purpose well. She wanted to be alone. She did not want her family or anyone she cared about close to her. Not ever again. She wanted to be safe. To never again suffer the pain of loss.

She hung her petticoat and gown on a peg protruding from one of the logs that formed the gable end of the building and slipped her nightgown on over her head. Her fingers twitched as she gathered the hated mass of curls, wove them into a loose braid and climbed into bed. She pulled the covers up to her neck and stared at the rough board roof that started at the floor and sloped up to the peak. She would relive the long journey from St. Louis to Banning Mission, every uncomfortable, painful moment of it. Perhaps that would be enough to help her sleep, to keep away the dreams…

Unless the baby cried.

Chapter Three

Anne broke a piece off the slice of coarse-grained bread on her plate, spread a dab of butter on it and held back a sigh. How much longer would Mitchel be at his breakfast? She wanted to be out of the mission before his daughter awakened. She stole a look across the table. Only a few bites of food remained on his plate. She bit back the admonition to hurry that sprang to her lips, placed the bite of bread and her knife on her plate and folded her hands in her lap. "If you have time, Mitchel, I should like to discuss the mission school. How many students attend? And what is the present schedule?"

He looked across the table, two small frown lines etched between his dark brown brows. "At present there *is* no school. I have had no teacher." He looked down, stabbed the last piece of bacon on his plate, then glanced back up. "Any schedule would have to take into consideration the Indians' way of life. They are accustomed to roaming free and are not amenable to schedules."

"I see." Indeed she did. If Mitchel's frown were any indication, he still felt he had no teacher. And was still intent on discouraging her from assuming that position.

She brushed a wayward curl off her temple and lifted her chin. "That being the situation, there is no need for further discussion. Would you be so kind as to show me to the schoolhouse, please?"

He stared at her for a moment, then wiped the frown from his face and nodded. "You will need your cloak. The morning air is quite brisk this time of year." He crossed his knife and fork on his plate and rose, started around the table.

She jumped to her feet, stepped away from her chair. He paused, gave her a questioning look. "I will get my cloak." She turned toward the door. Let him wonder about her lack of graceful manners in not waiting for him to assist her in rising from her chair. She did not want him, or any other man, touching her, erasing the memory of Phillip.

"Pa-p-p-paa!"

She stiffened, looked at the Indian woman coming into the dining room, Mitchel's sobbing daughter in her arms. The toddler's glassy-looking, blue eyes were flowing tears onto cheeks that were red with fever. Blond curls clung to the baby's small, moist forehead.

Anne sucked in air against a sudden light-headedness, dropped her gaze to the floor and pressed back against the table to give the woman ample room to pass.

"Papa is here, Hope." Mitchel's boots invaded her view as he stepped forward. The child whimpered, cloth rustled as he took the toddler into his arms. "I must see to my daughter's needs before I show you around the mission grounds, Anne."

"Yes, of course. I will get my cloak and await your summons." She walked from the room, hurried to the stairs and started to climb, tears blinding her vision.

Was it not enough that God had taken her husband and child? Must He bring her here where she would be confronted every day with a toddler baby Grace's age? Her toe caught in the hems of her long skirts and she plunged forward, caught herself and continued up the stairs.

"I am ready, Anne."

Mitchel Banning's deep voice drifted up to her, increased the tension in her shoulders. *Surely he would not take a sick child out into the chilly morning air. Surely he would not.* Anne rose from her perch on the edge of the bed, swirled her cloak around her shoulders and walked to the top of the stairs. Mitchel was standing at the bottom, his arms empty. She breathed out her relief and started down. He looked up at her and she read puzzlement, disappointment and perhaps a touch of censure in his eyes. Her spine stiffened.

"We go out this door." He depressed the thumb latch and opened the door on his right.

So there was to be no demand for an explanation of her behavior. Her defenses relaxed. She stepped down onto the bottom tread and her gaze grew level with his. The fear for his daughter shadowed the depths of his hazel eyes. Her own grief and sorrow rose in response. She reached up and pulled her hood in place, breaking the eye contact, the inner connection of mutual grief, then slipped by him and walked out the door.

"The mission does not have a schoolhouse as yet. There has been no need. My wife was to have been the teacher. However, in anticipation of William's arrival, I added a room on the back of the mission." He swept his arm left, toward a log addition with a sloping shed roof.

She turned toward the schoolroom door, waited for him to step out of her way.

"I think it would be well for me to show you around the mission grounds. You will need to know your way around when I'm not here."

Panic struck. What of the baby? She took a firm grip on the fear and looked up. "Are you gone often?"

He stared down at her, and the look in his eyes told her clearly he knew her thoughts and found her wanting as a woman.

"No more than is needed. I do not like to leave Hope. Still, I must see to the work around the mission. And there are sometimes emergencies..." He faced forward. "If you will come with me, we shall walk straight down this path."

His voice had cooled considerably, and the last thing she wanted to do was linger in his presence. All she wanted was to be alone. But she nodded and fell into step beside him.

"This large addition to the mission house on the right is the kitchen and pantry. And here, where the path curves behind it, are the kitchen gardens." He gave a rueful shake of his head. "I'm afraid they look sadly unkempt at the moment, but the Indians who help me decided they would rather go fishing. I shall have to finish gathering the vegetables and pulling the plants when I find time."

She glanced over the solid fence constructed of sturdy branches that had been cut to length and driven side-by-side into the ground and their tops lashed together. The earth had been overturned in spots and a few tiny potatoes still clung to the dead, exposed roots. Squashes and cabbages lay among limp stems and dying foliage. "It seems you have success in raising vegetables for your table."

"Since I dug the irrigation ditch, yes. The climate is dry in summer. I have put in a small orchard with apple, cherry and pear trees at the other edge of the garden, also. But they are only saplings and are not yet bearing fruit." He turned. "Now, here, beyond this fence—" she looked straight down the path they were on "—is the Halstrums' cabin. Adam runs the gristmill, and helps with the blacksmith work. His oldest son helps out, as well. His young son will attend the school."

"And Mrs. Halstrum?"

"She passed away before Adam came." He glanced her way, then looked back over the fence. "In that small barn, we keep the milk cows and the goats and chickens. The circular corral you see beyond the barn holds hogs. And that larger building, farther out to the left, by the river, is the gristmill." She looked in the direction of the sweep of his arm.

A rather grim look of satisfaction flickered across his face. "My efforts at converting the Indians from their heathen ways may not have met with much success as yet, but we do not go hungry. And there is enough food to share with those who come in need in the winter."

She saw no purpose in sharing with others a God who took a husband and baby from her, but the underlying frustration in his voice tugged at her. "Perhaps sharing your largesse will help you reach the Indians with your...message."

He glanced at her, a look of speculation in his eyes. He apparently had not missed her hesitation. Her shoulders inched back, her fingers curled into her palms and her mouth firmed. Her old childhood "I will not give in" posture, resurrected.

"That is my hope."

His quiet words deflated her defiance.

He turned and started down a path that led off to the left, motioned toward a small, narrow building. "That is the 'necessary.' There is a bar on the inside to lock the door. Indians are curious." He kept walking, matching his steps to her shorter stride, but she had not missed the warning note in his voice. What sort of place had she come to?

They emerged from behind the mission house and he started down a rutted path that angled toward the front of the building. Straight across the path were two more buildings. He nodded toward the first. "This small building on your right is the blacksmith shop where we do our repairs." He gave her a sidelong glance, waved his hand toward the other. "That large building is the stables. It has the granary attached. And this—" he indicated the path leading off to the right, the one she had followed to the front door last night "—as you know, goes to the mission house and the attached Indian gathering room."

"And the Indian camp?" She drew her gaze back from the Indians squatting and moving around a few campfires in the yard in front of the mission house to look up at him. "They were not here when I came. Do they gather here often?"

"Whenever they choose." He fixed his gaze on her. "As I told you last night, it would be best if you do not wander the grounds by yourself. Most of the Indians who come here are…agreeable, but not all. Until you learn their ways, it could be dangerous for you to encounter any of them. Even the friendly ones are suspicious and easily offended. I warn you because I do not wish you to come to harm. Nor do I want any troubling incidents that will undermine my work here."

"I understand. I shall stay a good distance from them." She tucked a curl that had fallen onto her cheek behind her ear and pulled her hood farther forward. "Have you more to show me, or shall we return to the schoolroom?"

He shook his head, looked beyond the river that flowed beside the mission. "Some braves are riding this way and I do not want it to appear as if we are spurning them. And I do not want you to go off by yourself."

The quietness of his voice sent a shiver down her spine. She looked the direction of his gaze and spotted three Indians astride horses with spots dappling their haunches. The same sort of horse Mr. Thatcher rode. "Are they coming to join the others in the camp?"

He shook his head. "The Indians camping here are Nez Perce. The ones coming are Cayuse." He shot her another look as the Indians splashed their horses through the river and thundered down the rutted path toward them. "Act natural, and go along with whatever I say."

She nodded, slipped off her hood and brushed the stray curls off her forehead.

"And keep that red hair of yours covered." His voice brooked no argument. "Indians are quite taken by blond or red hair. I don't want to have to fend off some brave intent on making you his squaw."

Anne shot him a look, yanked her hood back in place, then tugged it forward as far as possible to hide the errant curls. Being killed was one thing. To live life as the wife of an Indian, or any other man, was not to be borne. She stiffened her spine and prepared to stand her ground.

Chapter Four

The Indians raced toward them, the horses' hoofs thudding louder and louder.

"Stand still and stay quiet, Anne. No flinching or screaming…or swooning."

Anne drew her cloak closed and glanced up. Obviously, her actions around his daughter had caused Mitchel Banning to hold her in low esteem. "I'm not given to hysterics, Mitchel."

"Good. Because these Indians are testing our courage—bravery wins their respect, fear earns their contempt." He looked down at her. "I'll do the talking." She nodded, squared her shoulders as he turned his attention to the Indians who jerked their horses to a halt mere inches in front of them. "I bid my Cayuse brothers welcome."

The Indian in the middle grunted out a response. Mitchel nodded, replied in kind. Sunlight glinted off the hafts of the knives thrust into leather cases at the Indians' waists and glowed against the heads of the tomahawks suspended from long loops that dangled the handles against their legs as they slid from their horses.

Anne looked away, focused her attention on their mounts. The poor, gaunt beasts were ungroomed, their manes and tails dirty and matted. They looked—

The Indian closest to her stepped forward, his moccasins whispering against the packed dirt of the path, the long fringe on his buckskin pants swaying. He stopped, stood like a statue before her, his leather-bound braids resting against his bare chest, his piercing black eyes staring at her.

Indians are quite taken by blond or red hair. Her heart lurched. Were there any curls dangling on her forehead? Her fingers itched to reach up and check.

Mitchel looked at the brave, spoke.

The Indian grunted a reply, stepped closer.

His interest sent alarm tingling along her nerves. *Don't show fear!* She stood perfectly still, not allowing herself to inch toward the suddenly comforting presence of Mitchel Banning. The Indian walked around her, came back and stood staring at her. She lifted her chin and stared straight ahead.

A string of guttural words issued from the brave. From the corner of her eye she saw Mitchel nod, watched his eyes darken as the brave spewed forth another string of words and jabbed a dirty finger her direction then held his hand toward Mitchel, palm out, fingers spread. She stiffened, held her breath, wishing she could understand what was being said. Mitchel shook his head, grunted out an answer, then turned to her. "Go into the house, Anne. Tell Sighing Wind these braves want food."

She looked into his hazel eyes, read a silent "do as I say" message and turned and walked down the path toward the door she had entered on her arrival. She kept her pace normal, ignoring the impulse to look back over her shoulder. The squeak of the door hinge was comforting. She stepped inside, closed the door and expelled a long breath. She hadn't cared for the look in that Indian's eyes. And Mitchel had not cared for what the Indian had said. It was about her. Of that she was certain. There was no mistaking the intent of that dirty, pointing finger. Had it to do with her hair? *I don't want to have to fend off some brave intent on making you his squaw.*

Oh, surely it was not that. She would ask Mitchel about the conversation later. She shook off her unease and hurried through the dining room into the kitchen, stopped and stared. Flies buzzed around an uncovered pail of milk sitting just inside the open outside door and more hovered and crawled over a haunch of raw meat and a pile of dirt-coated vegetables on the work table. Her fastidious nature and housekeeping training sprang to the fore. She'd never seen such filth! Where was Sighing Wind?

She jerked the hems of her skirts above the grease-stained, dirt and crumb-littered floor and strode across the room toward the door. The Indian woman's bulky frame suddenly blocked out the light. She stopped, watched Sighing Wind grab the pail of milk in her free hand and pad over to set it and the small basket of eggs she carried on the table. More flies swarmed around the basket, joined those crawling on the meat.

The Indian woman looked at her and frowned. "Why for you here? What you want?"

"There are three Cayuse braves outside. Mr. Banning said they want food."

Sighing Wind grunted, grabbed hold of a knife stuck in the table top and slashed thick slices from the haunch. "Warriors want Mister's beef."

Anne clamped her jaw to keep from commenting as the meat slices, sluggish flies and all, were tossed into two large, food-encrusted iron skillets on the hearth and placed over the glowing red coals of the fire. It was little wonder Mitchel Banning's daughter was ill. It was a miracle Mitchel himself was in good health. Her stomach churned in objection to the thought of the two meals she had eaten since her arrival. One thing was certain. She would not eat another bite of food prepared among such filth! Nor would Mitchel or his baby. Her conscience would not allow it.

She jerked her thoughts from the toddler and stepped back out of the way as Sighing Wind grabbed a burlap bag hanging from a peg driven into one of the thick, square table legs, shoved the rest of the raw haunch into it and put the partially-fried slabs of meat on top.

"Give warriors."

Anne stared at the blood and grease stains spreading over the burlap bag Sighing Wind held out to her and gave a firm shake of her head. "No. I'll stay here. You give it to the warriors."

The Indian woman shrugged and started for the door, her moccasins scuffing across the puncheon floor.

Anne turned to the fireplace, grabbed the hem of her skirt, gripped the handles of the skillets and flipped them facedown over the fire as she had seen the women traveling with the wagon train do. The grease sputtered. She left the pans there to burn clean, and turned to survey the room.

The kitchen was well equipped. A large dry sink with a tub for washing dishes and buckets for carrying water on the lower shelf stood against the right wall. On the far wall, on either side of the dining room door, shelves held dishes, crockery and various sized baskets. The grimy work table claimed the space on her left. And behind it, in the corner beyond a door at the far end of the fireplace, was a straw broom.

She hurried around the work table, grasped the broom, then opened the door beside it. Air rushed out, moist and cool against her face and hands. A *buttery*. With a *well!* She rested the broom against the wall, glanced at the bench shelves and barrels sitting along the stone walls, at the beef, hams and slabs of bacon hanging from iron hooks driven into the slanting roof beams and stepped to the center of the small room.

Her throat tightened. The well was like the one at Uncle Justin's stables where she and Emma and William had learned to draw water for their horses. She touched the stone rim and memories rushed upon her. Longing for her family squeezed her heart. She yanked her hands away, brushed the feel of the cold stone off against her skirt and stiffened her spine. To love someone meant pain at their loss. It was better to be alone than suffer that agony again.

She took her thoughts captive, refusing all recollections of family and home, slipped off the rope loop to free the handle of the windlass and tossed the attached bucket over the rim. When she heard the splash, she allowed a bit more rope to play out, waited for the bucket to fill, then turned the handle to bring up the full bucket. Cold drops spattered her hands as she poured the water into the bucket sitting on the floor.

She sat the well bucket back on the rim and slipped the rope loop back over the handle as she'd been taught. The full bucket swung when she lifted it, sloshed water over the lip onto her skirt. She gripped the handle with both hands and carried it to the fireplace, grateful for the hard work ahead that would keep her too busy to remember, to feel.

The crane squeaked as she pulled it toward her. She hung the largest iron pot on the longest hook, poured the water into it then pushed the crane back until the pot hung low over the pulsating coals. By the time she had finished sweeping, the water should be hot enough to scrub down the table. She snatched up the empty bucket, shooed the flies away from the milk pail, carried both into the buttery and emerged, broom in hand.

The accumulated dust and dirt behind the baskets she pulled from beneath the shelves on the dining room wall were no match for her determination. The straw swished against the wide puncheons, pushing the dirt before it, the sound intensifying when she turned the broom edgewise and cleaned out the cracks. With every sweep, she could hear her adopted mother, *You shan't be as helpless as I was when I married Thad. All I knew then was how to manage servants. You shall learn how to do the work.*

Pain welled within her, stole her breath. She set her jaw and pushed the broom with greater vigor.

"What you do?"

"Oh!" Anne jerked her head up and spun around. Sighing Wind stood in the dining room doorway, curiosity gleaming in her dark eyes. Had the woman never seen a broom used? "I'm cleaning the floor." The dark eyes staring at her, flickered, clouded with confusion. She pointed to the pile of debris by the broom, then at the dust, dirt and crumb-littered floor in front of her. "The floor is dirty." She made a few sweeps, pushing the pile ahead with the broom, then indicated the floor she'd swept. "Now it is clean."

Sighing Wind came forward, squatted and ran her hand over the floor. "Clean." She scooped up a handful of the debris and threw it back down. "Dirty."

"Yes." Anne curled her nose and pointed to the unswept portion of the floor. "Dirty is bad."

The Indian woman nodded and straightened, gripped the broom handle. "Make clean."

Anne stared at her a moment, then nodded. "Very well. But you must do it all. Like this." She pointed under the dry sink and the table, took the broom, demonstrated how to clean in the corners and cracks, then handed the broom back to Sighing Wind. She pointed down at the pile of dirt and then to the open door. "Sweep it outside."

Sighing Wind nodded, took a few swipes with the broom, then nodded again and set to work.

Anne watched her a moment, then took a bucket from beneath the dry sink, tossed in a folded rag and a piece of soap and carried it to the fireplace to see if the water was hot enough to scrub the worktable.

Mitchel brushed his hair into place and turned from the mirror. It had been a long, hard day. That Cayuse brave who wanted to buy Anne Simms for his wife had been difficult to deal with. And the others had been demanding, as well. They'd wanted only those things he could give for their comfort, not his words of salvation. And now, because of Anne, he had to clean up and take time for supper. Supper. Corncakes and meat. It's what Sighing Wind always fixed. Not that it mattered. The vegetables he grew blessed others.

He frowned, dumped his wash water into the ceramic pail beneath the washstand, buttoned on his clean shirt and tugged his thoughts back to the story he was telling

Hope. "And all the piglets chased the rooster around and around the sty until he gave up trying to eat their corn and flew over the fence."

Hope giggled. "Me see piggies?"

The sound of her baby laughter, so rare since she'd become ill, pierced deep in his heart. He looked down at his daughter resting against her propped-up pillows. There was no fever flush on her face. She was having a good day. He dropped to his knees, brushed the back of his finger against the soft, baby skin of her cheek. "Not now, Hope, it's late. Perhaps tomorrow." Empty words. She was not well enough to go outside. He dare not chance her taking a chill. "Will you be a good girl and go to sleep for Papa so you can get strong?"

"Me good girl." Her small mouth opened in a wide yawn, but she did not stretch her arms or legs. Two years old, and his daughter had learned to be still because moving her limbs caused pain. He fought back a surge of anger, bent his head down and kissed her forehead. He could not afford anger, dared not let it turn his heart bitter. He had to hold on to his faith. *Heal her, Almighty God. In Your great mercy and love, heal Hope, I pray.* His face tightened at the repetition. How many times had he prayed that prayer?

He pushed himself erect, wishing with all his heart he could give some of his robust strength and health to his baby girl. He pulled the blanket up close under Hope's tiny chin and turned away. Fear for her dogged his steps as he shrugged into his jacket and strode to the dining room. If it weren't for Anne he could work on the mission's records while he ate. He was behind. As usual. He was always behind. He stopped short in the doorway, stared at the table. Blue and white patterned china rested on a white linen cloth. "What—"

"I found the china while I was searching through my trunks for table linen. I hope you don't mind if we use it."

He lifted his gaze. Anne stood beside the door to the kitchen looking up at him. For the first time since her arrival her violet-blue eyes were clear. The grief that shadowed them had given way to a look of purpose. Still, he needed *help,* not more problems. That brave had offered five horses for her. He would be back to offer more. It was certain his life would be a good deal easier had William come. He tamped down his frustration, shook his head. "Not at all. I only hope I remember my manners. It's been over five years since I've sat at a proper dinner table."

The sorrow flooded back into her eyes, the color left her cheeks. "It's been awhile for me, also…seven months." Her hand lifted, rubbed the black wool fabric covering her ribs.

He glanced down. Her hand stopped moving, dropped back to her side. He looked up, saw her draw back her shoulders, read a "don't question me" warning in her eyes.

"There are no dinner tables, proper or otherwise, in a crowded wagon. Only tin plates balanced on one's knees."

Her attempted smile was a mere curving of her lips. There was no amusement, no *life* in it. He nodded, remembering the effort smiling, for Hope's sake, had cost him when Isobel died. It still came hard. There wasn't much to smile about.

"I'll tell Sighing Wind you're here. That it's time to serve."

She would tell Sighing Wind? He stifled his shock, watched her hurry away. What had happened to make her take such authority on herself? And what had happened to her ribs? Was it connected to her husband's death? He tugged at his suit coat, wishing he could ease Anne's pain, knowing nothing but God and time could do so. Another situation where he was helpless. His life was rife with them. So often he found himself with no alternative but to pray and trust the Lord, when what he wanted was to *do* something to take care of the situation.

He scowled, vowed again to work on his impatience and stepped into the room, his attention snagged by the flickering flames of the fire reflected in the glass panes of the window. *Clean* window panes. Soft, yellow light shone through the smoke-free glass chimney on the oil lamp that sat on the table beneath the window. A table free of dust. He looked around. The entire room was clean. Something deep inside him lightened. He had been so busy, so overwhelmed with his fears and troubles, he had become inured to the accumulating dirt. He hadn't realized...

The hem of Anne's gown whispered against the floor. Sighing Wind's moccasins scuffed behind. He moved to the fireplace, picked up the poker and shoved the logs closer together. The smell of fresh-baked biscuits teased his nose. He put the poker down, watched them place pork chops, potatoes, carrots, green beans and a linen-lined basket of biscuits on the table. Sighing Wind shuffled back to the kitchen and Anne slipped onto a chair.

He stepped to the table and took his own seat, his throat swelled to a painful fullness. The lonely, empty existence his life had become pressed upon him, weighted his heart. He cleared the tightness from his throat, bowed his head and asked God's blessing on the abundant food He'd provided. But he couldn't help wishing God would provide something to fill his hungry heart.

He frowned at his lack of thankfulness, sent a silent prayer for forgiveness winging upward. Hope was enough. *Please God, heal Hope. Please let her stay with me.* He filled his plate with meat and vegetables, split a warm biscuit and reached for the butter.

"Mitchel, what did that Indian warrior say about me?"

He glanced across the table at Anne, sitting so erect in her chair, looking vulnerable but defensive. And lovely. William's adopted sister was a beautiful young woman, though a bit prickly for his taste. Isobel had been so… amenable. He looked back down and spread the butter, prepared himself for a scene. Prickly and defensive or not, Anne might be frightened by the truth, and he'd seen her close to swooning twice. "He gave you a name." He glanced up. "Little Crow."

"Little Crow!"

He nodded. "Because of your widow's garb—and your size." He reassessed the possibility of her swooning. She had gone stiff as a board and her violet-blue eyes were fairly flashing with sparks of anger.

"I am *not* that short!"

A sore point, obviously. He would not debate the issue with her, though a woman that barely reached his chin did not seem overly tall to him. "Perhaps not. But you are very slender and…small." The starchiness drained from her. The shadows returned to dull her eyes.

"I've been…ill." She looked down, ran her hand over the black wool fabric covering her ribs. "I suppose the name is…understandable." She lifted her head. "What did the Indian say when he pointed at me, and held up his five fingers."

His instinct to protect rose strong within him. His fingers tightened on the knife he'd picked up to cut a piece of meat. "He said you were frightened, but very brave. That you were worthy to be a warrior's wife. He offered me five horses for you."

She stared at him, a gauntlet of emotions sweeping across her face—shock, astonishment, anger, horror, fear and outrage. She drew her shoulders back, lifted her chin and looked straight into his eyes. "And what was your answer, Mitchel?"

"I told him you were my woman, and you were not for sale."

She gave a sharp intake of breath. "Your—you had no right to say such a thing! Phillip is my husband."

He met her furious gaze, shook his head. "Your husband is dead, Anne. He is not here to protect you from that brave, or from those who might offer for you in the future. I am. And the best way I know to protect you is to tell them you belong to me. You'd best not deny it."

Chapter Five

Anne rushed outside, pulled the door closed on the toddler's cries and sagged against the wall. Her arms trembled, her heart ached with the need to hold her baby girl. She thrust away the broom she'd been using and pressed her hands to her mouth to hold back the sobs crowding into her throat. She'd come here to escape! To forget! How was she to survive when every day the child's cries were a constant reminder of—

She opened her eyes, forced away the memory. Her face tightened, her jaw set. Where was Mitchel? Why was he not— No. That was unfair. Mitchel worked harder than any man she knew. And he spent his every spare minute with his child. She frowned and pushed away from the wall. All the same, she could not face going back into that house until the child was asleep.

She snatched up the broom and looked at the lean-to schoolroom attached to the back wall of the mission. Mitchel had said nothing more about her teaching, but she could at least look at the room.

Cold, stale air rushed out when she opened the door. She stepped inside and looked around. The roof, festooned with cobwebs, sloped from the log wall of the mission to the lower, outside wall opposite it. A stone fireplace stood in the center of the low wall, a fire laid and ready to be lit.

Why did the toddler cry so often? What caused her pain?

She sucked in her breath, concentrated on the room to dispel the unwanted thoughts. In front of her, three long, rough wood bench desks with low, backless seats marched the length of the room toward a table. Beneath a small window in the far wall sat the two trunks of school supplies William had purchased in anticipation of teaching here at the mission. On her right, a large wood box, filled with firewood, crouched in the corner beside the door. The room and furnishings were rough and crude.

Did Laughing Rain know how to care for the baby? Or—

Why could she not stop thinking of the child? She clenched her hands on the handle, advanced into the schoolroom and laid about her with the broom, swished and whacked, until every filmy cobweb was gone and its creator dead. Mitchel's daughter's care was none of her concern.

She turned her attention to the dusty floor, jabbed the broom into the corners, angled it into the grooves between the wide, rough boards. Tending the sick was what Papa Doc and Emma cared about. She did not care. She *would* not care!

Whatever was wrong with the baby was serious. Mitchel was afraid—

She stiffened her spine, worked harder, coughing from the dust raised by her furious sweeping. The unbidden, unwelcome thoughts remained—plucked at her conscience. She whirled about, drew back her broom and sent the pile of dust and dirt flying out the door—straight onto a pair of black leather boots. She lifted her head, stared at Mitchel Banning.

"I saw the door was open and came to investigate. The Indians do not consider it wrong to take whatever they want." His startled expression changed to one of concern. "What's wrong, Anne?"

"Why...nothing." She cleared the tightness from her throat. "I'm cleaning."

"You're crying."

Was she? She jerked her hand up, felt a streak of moisture on her cheek. "The dust..." She blinked her eyes and wiggled the broom.

He didn't answer, simply looked at her. She whirled about and began sweeping the low, bench seats. He was a minister. Had her evasion angered him? Would he refuse to let her teach? Perhaps make her go back to Emma? No. He didn't know Emma was in Oregon country. But he knew about the town the emigrants were founding, and—

His boots thudded against the floorboards. He was coming inside! She swept faster.

"I'm afraid this table will have to serve as your desk. I've nothing better. I'll bring you a chair."

He was going to let her stay and teach! She stopped sweeping, looked down the length of the room. "The table will be fine. And a chair would be helpful. Thank you."

He nodded, looked at her, his eyes shadowed with doubt, questions. "You will have to be firm with the Indian children. Especially the boys...if any come." His brow furrowed. "In their culture the women and girls do all the work. The men and boys hunt and fish and go to battle against their enemies. As I said before, they are undisciplined and unaccustomed to schedules or responsibilities." The furrows in his brow deepened. He looked out the door, looked back at her. "There is more I have to say, but I have work to do in the fields while there is light. We will discuss the other things tonight."

"Very well." She turned back to her work, listened as his footsteps drew near, caught her breath when they paused beside her. She kept her head bent and the broom moving, watched through her eyelashes as he continued on out the door, then dropped the broom and sagged onto the bench.

He knew there was something wrong. She would have to be stronger, do better at hiding her emotions. She couldn't tell him the truth. He would never let her stay if he knew she couldn't bear being around his daughter. He would take her back to the emigrant town for certain. And that would mean being with Emma. And the memories.

Pressure settled in her chest. She gripped the edge of the bench and looked around. If only she could begin teaching and spend her entire day in this room. She would be safe here. But she needed students. Until then, she would spend her time in the kitchen teaching Sighing Wind about housekeeping and cooking. The child's cries were not as loud there.

She carried the broom outside, closed the door and walked toward the gate in the garden fence. She would go in through the kitchen door. She didn't want to chance running into the Indian nanny, Laughing Rain, and Mitchel's daughter.

* * *

Mitchel watched the calf struggle, nodded with satisfaction as it gained its feet. It had been a difficult birth, but both the cow and her calf would live. He would keep them in the barn, safe from the weather and predators, for a few days. He tossed some fresh hay in the stall, stretched his back and arms and went outside. The temperature had dropped considerably.

He started toward the mission house looming black in the darkness, its windows spilling yellow lamplight into the night. The ever-present fear quickened. Had Spotted Owl brought in wood so Laughing Rain could keep Hope's fire going? Or had he gone hunting instead? He so often turned surly when asked to do work. *Please let Hope be all right, Lord. Please let her be all right.* He heard her crying as he neared her window. She was having a bad day. He broke into a run.

Mitchel washed off the barn smell, dried his face and hands and continued the story of the calf's birth. "So the mama cow lowered her head and nudged her baby. And when the little calf stood up, its legs wobbled like this." He made his ankles go slack and swayed back and forth, his knees jutting and bending at extreme angles.

Hope looked up at him, her eyes glassy-bright in her fever-flushed face. Her little lips trembled, but she stopped crying. He bent over and lifted her, blankets and all, into his arms, cuddled her as close as he dared. His heart ached with the need to comfort her with a hug. He suppressed the urge for fear of hurting her. Resentment kindled, the angry flames lashing at his spirit the way the tongues of fire were licking at the new wood he'd brought in to replace what had been consumed.

Don't let that happen to me, Lord. Don't let me be consumed by the anger and fear. Please strengthen my faith lest I fail You. Lest I fail Hope. I believe in Your Word and in Your son, Almighty God. I believe. Help Thou my unbelief.

He swallowed back the lump in his throat, laid his cheek against Hope's golden curls and walked around the small room praying for her pain to ease so she could sleep before he joined Anne for dinner.

Anne took a bite of squash, laid down her fork and looked across the table at Mitchel. He looked tired with a weariness beyond that caused by hard, physical labor. Worry and fear for a child did that. It was— She shifted her gaze to her plate. It was *not* her concern. Mitchel's burdens had nothing to do with her.

She picked up her fork, jabbed it into her potatoes, laid it down again and clenched her hands in her lap. She couldn't swallow. Must *everything* in this house remind her of her loss! She snatched the napkin off her lap, placed it on the table and raised her head. "Mitchel…"

"Yes?" He looked up.

She knew so well the pain that shadowed his eyes. She closed her mind to it. "You seem tired after your day's labors. Perhaps, you would care to postpone our discussion?"

He shook his head. "That's thoughtful of you, Anne. But one day is as busy as another. And there are things you need to know. However, you're right. I am tired. If you will join me in the other room, we shall have our discussion there."

"Very well." She glanced up as he rose from his chair.

The worry was so evident. "Would you like to have an after-dinner coffee there?"

"That is an excellent suggestion."

She poured out the dark brew, handed him the cup, then led the way into the other room and seated herself near the hearth, on the chair closest to the stairs.

Mitchel stood by the fire, took a sip of the hot coffee. He raised his brows, stared down at the cup. "This tastes different."

"Better, I hope."

"Yes. Much better." He gave her a quizzical look. "What did you do to it?"

"I cleaned the pot."

"And a lot more." He looked around the room, brought his gaze back to rest on her. "I have been remiss, Anne, in not thanking you for taking upon yourself the task of cleaning the mission. As you have discovered, Sighing Wind has little knowledge of housekeeping or cooking. Your efforts have made a great difference. The meals are excellent. And the mission looks…" He stopped, rolled the cup between his hands. "I'd forgotten…"

What it was like before his wife died? Did one ever forget? "It is not necessary to thank me, Mitchel." She looked down, smoothed a fold from her skirt. "With no students to teach as yet, overseeing the cleaning of the mission and the preparation of meals has…given me a purpose." She glanced up, caught her breath at the flash of understanding in his eyes and jerked her gaze away lest he say something that would penetrate her defenses and cause her buried grief to rise.

"You should have students soon."

"Truly?" Her relief spilled out in her tone.

He nodded, took another swallow of his coffee. "I

have sent word among the Indians that the mission is to have a school where their children can learn to speak and write the white man's tongue and learn the white man's numbers so they can trade with wisdom." He gave her a wry smile. "That last should gain you at least one or two male students." His smile faded. "But you must be prepared for dealing with the Indians, Annc. They are very different in their outlook."

He drained his cup, placed it on the mantel and shoved the logs together with his booted foot. "The mission is situated close to both the Nez Perce and Cayuse nations." He turned back toward her, a frown creased his brow. "The Cayuse have proven to be less than welcoming. A few are friendly, but most are insolent and demanding. They tolerate our presence for the goods the mission provides them. They consider us as traders, nothing more. The Nez Perce are more open to our ways. You will find their children to be—"

"Papaaa... Papaaaa..."

Mitchel jerked his head toward the doorway on the other side of the room.

She jumped to her feet, turned toward the stairs.

"Papaaa..."

He glanced back her way. "We'll talk tomorrow, Anne. I have to go to Hope."

"What causes your daughter's pain, Mitchel?" The words were out before she could stop them. Words that had been roiling about in her head all day. Emma's words. Papa Doc's words. She took a breath, clenched her hands.

He stopped, shook his head. "The doctor at Fort Walla Walla died before Hope took sick, and I—I fear she would not survive the longer journey needed to see another." He cleared his throat. "I don't know what sickness has struck her. I only know I would give my *life* to spare her. Now, I must go to her. I can sometimes soothe her by holding her, though I must be careful of her joints."

Her joints. Emma's discussions with Papa Doc swarmed into her head, their words came out of her mouth. "Are they red and swollen? Warm and fevered to the touch?"

"Yes." His gaze locked on hers. "Anne—"

She shook her head, backed up a step. "I was injured…" She sucked in her breath, fought the trembling starting in her hands. "I have an ointment that may ease her pain." She whirled around, grasped her skirt and lifted the hem out of the way and ran toward the stairs, saw Mitchel hurrying across the room as she climbed.

She didn't want to do this! Didn't know enough… The pressure squeezed her chest. The lack of breath threatened darkness. She willed it away, went to her knees in front of the trunk and fought the twitching of her fingers that made it difficult to open the latch. If the ointment would ease the child's pain she would stop crying. And if the toddler stopped crying the memories would stop haunting her. It would all be better in the end, if she could hold on…

She lifted out the sealed crock of ointment, set it aside and pulled out the narrow rolls of red flannel Emma had used to bind her injured ribs. They were much too long for a toddler's small limbs. She blinked the tears from her eyes, took her scissors from her sewing box and cut one of the rolls into short lengths. She pressed her hand against her lap to control the shaking and slit one end of each length in half to make strips that could be used to tie the bandage in place.

When she finished, she gathered the short red flannel strips into a pile, draped them over her arm, picked up the crock of ointment and hurried down the stairs. Her steps lagged as she crossed the room. The pressure in her chest increased at the sound of the toddler's quiet sobs.

She stepped up to the open door, saw Mitchel pacing the room, his little daughter in his arms, and the hot, prickly feeling washed over her. She stepped back and leaned against the wall, her breath coming in quick, short gasps.

She forced her lungs to yield, drew in long, slow breaths. The threat of fainting subsided. She stepped away from the wall, raised her hand and rapped on the door frame.

Chapter Six

Mitchel turned at the quiet knock. Anne stood in the doorway, her posture rigid, her face pale in the flickering firelight. Her lashes were lowered, her eyes hidden beneath their lush darkness.

"Here is the ointment. And some cloths…"

He glanced down at the crock in her hands, the red cloths hanging over her arm. The cloths fluttered. She was *shaking*. Perhaps the illness she'd spoken of was a recurring one. He squelched a frown, pushed the thought aside to be considered later. "Come in, Anne."

She hesitated a moment, then stepped to the washstand by Hope's bed. She set down the crock and turned to the rocker by the hearth, leaned down, the gold of the firelight outlining the mass of red curls on her crown. "I'll hang these here for you. Papa Doc and Emma say it's soothing to have the cloths warm when you wrap the sore joints."

"Warmth does seem to help. I keep the fire going all the time." He rubbed Hope's back, watched as Anne draped the cloths over the arm of the rocker. She straightened, buried her hands among the folds in her long skirt.

Did she hope he wouldn't notice their trembling, the twitching of her fingers?

"I cut ties into one end of the cloths." She started toward the door, her eyes still hidden by her lowered lashes. "I hope the ointment helps."

"Please don't leave, Anne. I need your help. I've never done this."

She halted. Froze would be more accurate. He stared at her stiff back, frowned. "Please. I don't want to hurt her."

She rubbed her palms against her skirt, turned. "Very well."

Why would she not look at him? "I'll put Hope in her bed."

She nodded, moved to the washstand and removed the cover from the crock.

The fire crackled and popped, spit red sparks up the chimney. He laid Hope on her bed, caught a whiff of herbs and camphor and gave a loud sniff, hoping to distract her from the pain of movement. "Do you smell that, Hope?"

She nodded, her blue eyes swimming with tears.

"That's an ointment. Anne will put some on you. It will help the hurting."

"Me b-be better, P-papa?"

There was a sharp intake of breath. From the corner of his eyes he saw Anne's skirts swirl out as she spun about and hurried toward the hearth. "I pray so, Hope." He uncovered her, placed the blankets at the foot of the bed.

Anne returned, the red flannel strips quivering in her hands. She placed the cloths on the bed, turned, picked up the crock of ointment and knelt beside the bed.

"P-papa…"

"I'm here, Hope." He went to his knees, brushed a blond curl off her moist forehead. *Please, Lord...*

Anne moved. He glanced sideways, watched as she reached across Hope, undid the ribbon ties at his daughter's tiny wrist and gently slipped the sleeve of her nightgown up above her elbow.

He stroked Hope's hair, murmured words of comfort to take her mind off any pain Anne caused, kissed her fevered forehead to soothe any fear and looked back at Anne. His stomach knotted. He'd never seen anyone so pale, so...tense. She looked *brittle,* as if she would shatter into pieces if he spoke to her or touched her. If she swooned... But that didn't seem likely. She was working efficiently. It was the inner stillness and silence about her that was worrying. *Almighty God, I don't know what is wrong with Anne. But You do. Please heal her. I offer myself as a vessel for You to use should it be Your will. Amen.*

The fire snapped. He glanced over his shoulder to make sure no live ember had flown out into the room, turned back. Anne had bared Hope's other arm and placed red flannel strips beneath Hope's elbows and wrists. He held his breath, offered a silent prayer as she dipped her fingers into the ointment and began to rub it onto Hope's joints.

He leaned toward his daughter, ready to offer what comfort he was able to give. She was staring at Anne, her teary blue eyes wide, her quiet sobs abating. Would the ointment work that quickly?

He kept his hand on Hope's soft, blond curls and watched Anne wrap his daughter's treated joints, tie the flannel bindings in place, then slip the sleeves of Hope's nightgown down over them and tie the ribbons

at her tiny wrists. She turned slightly, lifted the hem of
Hope's nightgown and treated and wrapped her ankles
and knees. When she finished, she pulled the nightgown
down into place and rose.

He covered Hope with the blankets, tucked them
under her chin.

"Me be...better...Papa..."

He looked at his daughter's closing eyes, rubbed his
finger against the warm, silky skin of her cheek, his
heart flooded with gratefulness that she could sleep.
He cleared the lump from his throat, looked up as Anne
placed the crock back on the washstand. "Thank you,
Anne."

She nodded and turned toward the door, the black
wool of her gown rustling softly as she walked away.

The wood on the hearth crackled. Firelight flickered
through the dark, silent room, lit the empty doorway.
He listened to her footsteps fade, stepped to the hearth
and added another log to the fire, his heart burdened
with a new care.

Anne soaped her shaking hands again, scrubbed
them together and swished them through the water in
the washbowl. The soft, silky feel of baby skin stayed on
her fingers, the sweet baby smell lingered in her head.

She yanked the towel off the nail on the wall, rubbed
her hands, then buried her face in the damp cloth. She
had to stop remembering, had to do something to force
the thoughts away. She jammed the towel back on the
nail, caught a glimpse of the moon hanging in the night
sky, its silver face limned by the darkness.

"'O thou pale orb, that silent shines, While care-un-
troubled mortals sleep!'" She turned to the window,

pressed her hands down on the log sill to still her twitching fingers. "'Thou seest a wretch that inly pines, And wanders here to wail and weep!'"

Her face tightened. Quoting Robert Burns only made her think of Emma and her atrocious attempts at a Scottish accent.

She spun from the window, wrapped her arms about herself and strode down the length of the room. The Constitution. She had memorized it at school in the orphanage. That would be safe. "We the people of the United States, in order to form a more perfect union, establish justice, insure domestic tranquility—" *Domestic tranquility...*

The shaking grew more violent. She whirled toward the bed, snatched off the coverlet and draped it around her shoulders, grasped the edges and continued pacing. Was there nothing she could think of that did not bring back some painful memory? That did not increase the chill inside her? She was so tired of being cold.

She glanced at the bed, rejected all thought of climbing beneath the blankets. If she fell asleep she would dream. She walked to the chimney, leaned against the stones to absorb what warmth they offered, though they could not warm her inside.

Tea.

The thought came, strong and tantalizing. The image of the hot, steaming cup in her hands, the warmth of the tea sliding down her throat to relax the tightness in her chest. Tea would chase away the cold, at least for a few minutes.

But she could not go downstairs. The risk was too great. Although, it *was* quiet.

She pushed away from the chimney and hurried to

the top of the stairs, listening. There was no sound from below. The child must be sleeping. Was Mitchel sitting with her? Had he retired? She draped the coverlet over the railing and inched partway down the stairs, scanned the living room. Empty. Should she chance another encounter?

She gripped the railing and continued down, the whisper of her skirts blending with the quiet crackle of the fire. She released her held breath and hurried to the dining room, rushed through it into the kitchen. Sighing Wind had banked the fire before going home to her tepee behind the mission.

She uncovered the live embers, added bits of bark and a few twigs and blew softly. The embers glowed red hot, the bits of bark burst into flame catching the twigs afire. She stacked a few small pieces of firewood around them, checked the iron teakettle for water, set it on a trivet over the fire and reached for the tin of tea and the pewter teapot on the mantel. She lifted them down to the table. The lid on the tin defeated her shaking hands. Her trembling fingers lost their grip, slipped off. She heard a sound and froze. Boot heels struck against the wood floor. *She should have stayed in her room.*

"Allow me."

Mitchel stepped close beside her, grasped hold of the tin. She jerked her hands away, stepped back and clasped her arms around her waist to hide the shaking.

"I heard you come downstairs." He pulled the lid off the tin, dumped a portion of the dark, dry leaves into the teapot and replaced the lid. "Why don't you tell me what's wrong, Anne?" He turned toward her, the firelight playing over his strong, handsome features. "And please don't say 'nothing.' It's obvious you are in distress. I'd like to help…if I'm able."

The concern in his voice brought her perilously close to tears. She cleared her throat, moved with brisk purpose back to the fireplace to check on the water. "There is nothing you can do."

"I'd like to try. And I'm certain William would want—"

She spun on him, her hands clenched, her chest heaving with her effort to breathe. "Very well, Mitchel. Are you able to bring the dead to life? Can you call my husband and my baby daughter from the grave and restore them to me, the way Jesus called forth Lazarus?" She saw shock pass over his face and tried to stop, but the words kept pouring out. "Go ahead. Call them! My husband's name is Phillip. And my baby's name is Grace. I named her that because I so longed for a child and I was certain God had answered my prayers and graced my life with her. Of course, I didn't know, then, that He was going to take her from me!" Pain ripped through her. Her chest squeezed and her laboring lungs emptied. The darkness came, the blessed darkness where there was no memory.

She tried to ignore the voice calling her, to stay in the darkness where there was no pain, but the cold on her forehead was too intense, making her shiver. Something wet trickled down her temple into her hair. She frowned, raised her hand to wipe it away, touched the warm, firm flesh of a hand and opened her eyes. She was lying on the hide-covered settee in the living room, Mitchel kneeling on the floor beside it looking down at her. Memory flooded back. The scene she'd created in the kitchen replayed in her mind. She'd let her fury with God break free, given voice to her anger. Well, there was no help for it now. Mitchel was certain to send her away.

"Are you all right?"

His words were soft, concerned. But foolish. Oh, so foolish. The anger surged back. She swept the dripping cloth from her head and handed it to him. "I am *conscious*. I doubt I shall ever be *all right* again."

He nodded, dropped the cloth into a bowl beside him, set the bowl on the chest and rose to his feet.

Guilt smote her. Her pain was not Mitchel's doing. She pushed to a sitting position. "I'm sorry, Mitchel. Please forgive me. I didn't—"

"There's no need to apologize, Anne. I understand your anger." He fastened his gaze on hers, and she knew he was speaking the truth. "When Isobel died, the pain of her loss was terrible—and I was helpless to stop it. It made me furious. That, and the…betrayal." He leaned down and picked up the bowl, turned toward the kitchen. "Wait here. I'll be right back with the tea."

Betrayal. She pushed a wet curl off her forehead and stared after Mitchel, aware of something deep inside her breaking open. She was not at all certain she wanted to examine what was being exposed.

She rose and stepped close to the fire, letting the warmth chase away the outward chill.

"This should help warm you."

She turned, watched Mitchel moving gingerly toward her, his gaze glued to the cups in his hands. She stepped forward, glanced at the cups, hesitated. Her fingers were twitching too much to chance holding the full cup.

"Did I put in too much cream?"

"No. I—" She rubbed her hands against her long skirt, stopped when he looked down.

"Seems like that fire could use some encouraging. I'll set these here." He placed the cups on the chest beside the settee and stepped around her to the woodbox. "I'm sorry about your baby daughter, Anne. I didn't know." He selected two pieces of split log and added them to the fire.

"Nor could you." She sank down on the settee, folded both hands around a cup, tightened them to control the twitching, and took a swallow of the rich brew. The delicious warmth slid down her throat. She stared at the tea he had prepared for her, looked up and met the warmth and compassion in his gaze. "I didn't mean to sound ungracious, Mitchel. I thank you for your…sympathy." Her throat closed.

She looked down, took another swallow of tea to ease the tightness, pulled in a breath. "It's only… I haven't spoken of…" Her hands jerked. The tea sloshed close to the brim. She placed the cup on the chest and clasped her hands in her lap. "I try not to think of…that day."

"Would you like me to pray with you?"

She snapped her head up, met his gaze. "To a God who took my husband and baby from me and left me alive to suffer this agony of bereavement? Certainly not!" She surged to her feet, her hand sliding across the hated black wool and seeking the raised scar tissue on her ribs. "I should have died that day, too. Why didn't He take me, too?"

"Sometimes illness—"

"There was no illness. It was an accident." She stared at him, not bothering to hide her bitterness. "We had gone into town to buy gifts to celebrate Grace's first birthday and, on our way back to cousin Mary's, Phillip…lost control of the carriage. It overturned." She stared off into the distance, rubbing at her ribs. "I was thrown from the seat, struck the carriage lamp and Grace…flew from my arms." She shuddered, drew back her shoulders and clenched her hands into fists. "When I came back to consciousness, I was in bed, with William watching over me. Emma was— She tried all she knew, but my baby…died in her arms. Phillip had died immediately."

She sought his face, looked straight into his eyes. "That was in April, when William was preparing his wagons to join the wagon train to come here and teach in your school. When Caroline became too ill, carrying their baby, to make the journey, I came in his stead. In spite of my injuries, I survived the journey. Though I hoped I would not."

She rubbed the scar on her ribs again, lifted her chin. "And now you know why I am here. And why I will not pray. Not ever again." She took a breath. "I know that is unacceptable to you, Mitchel. That you want a person of faith to teach in your mission school. My faith died with my husband and child. I should have been honest with you about that when I arrived. Again, I ask your forgiveness. I will pack my things."

"Anne—"

She lifted her trembling hand, shook her head, turned and headed for the stairs.

"I need a teacher, Anne. I want you to stay."

Her steps faltered. She turned, looked at him, at the quiet strength, the resolve on his face. "You're certain?"

"I'm certain. I am no stranger to the struggle to maintain faith in the face of grief." He turned and walked to Hope's room, disappeared inside.

The tears started then. She whirled around and ran to the stairs, stumbled up them and threw herself on her bed to muffle her sobs with her pillow.

Chapter Seven

Not another one! Anne frowned at the whisper of moccasins against the floor. All afternoon the Indians who helped around the mission had been coming to lift the towel and poke their dirty fingers into the large bowl of rising dough on the hearth, their eyes going wide, their mouths forming round circles from which emitted sounds of amazement. It seemed risen bread was unknown to them, and word had spread by way of Sighing Wind.

Her frown deepened. In spite of her past lectures on cleanliness, the Indian woman had come in after gathering eggs that morning and thrust her fingers deep in the soft mass. Tiny bits of nesting material had stuck to the dough, but the dirt did not bother Sighing Wind. She had shuffled outside, oohing and aahing and babbling with excitement.

Anne glanced toward the floor. She'd quickly made a second batch of dough and hidden it so there would be bread for Mitchel's table that evening. And it was well she had. The Indians came and stabbed the dough on the hearth, and when they tired of that, roamed around the room peering into things and handling whatever took their fancy. And she had learned, by their angry scowls and stiffened postures, not to refuse them.

She glanced at the brave squatting on his heels poking at the dough and resisted the urge to lift her hems and peek into the covered basket hidden beneath them. The dough should be ready. When the brave left she would punch it down and put it into the pans she'd found on a shelf behind some crocks. Hopefully, that would be soon. She dare not move and expose the basket, and she wanted to cook Mitchel a good meal, to show him he would not regret his kindness in allowing her to stay on at the mission after her "lack of faith" confession last night.

She sighed, and pulling the cabbage she was cutting into wedges closer, cut through the last half. Learning to cook without a stove was difficult. Now she had these Indians wandering in and out of the kitchen to make it even harder.

A spate of deep, guttural words, different in tone from the exclamations over the dough, froze her hands in mid-slice. She looked up. Her heart jolted. A fierce-looking brave with a puckered scar running across his cheek and a knife and tomahawk dangling at his waist stood in the doorway. Her mouth went dry. This was no mission Indian, this was a warrior. And his interest was not in the bread dough—his dark eyes were focused on her.

Her hair! Had any curls slipped free of her black turban bonnet? Her pulse stuttered, raced. She dropped her gaze back to the cabbage, listened to Sighing Wind speak with the warrior. She severed the last cabbage wedge and reached for the washed carrots. *Where was Mitchel? Was he close enough to hear her if—*

The soft brush of leather against wood knotted her stomach. She swallowed hard, tightened her grip on the knife and lifted her head, darted a glance toward the doorway, stared at Sighing Wind's round bulk. The warrior was gone. And so was the Indian who had been squatting on the hearth. She dropped the knife and sagged against the table.

"Barking Fox find Mister. Talk much school."

She straightened, looked over at Sighing Wind. *"School?"*

The Indian woman nodded, scuffed over to the hearth and stirred the corn kernels that were roasting over the fire. "Him son, Running Wolf. Him come maybe yes."

She was to have a student? Perhaps? She seized the knife and continued cutting the carrots into large pieces. Sighing Wind's conversation was hard to understand. She would wait and ask Mitchel at dinner tonight. Meanwhile, she would go to the schoolroom and see what supplies William had bought. She wanted to be prepared.

Running Wolf. The name sent a jolt of apprehension through her. She had not thought of possible students as *Indians*...merely as children. What if those who came didn't speak any English? She hadn't considered that. She would have to teach them to speak English before she could teach them to read or write. Something akin to panic gripped her. She had to get to the schoolroom, devise a plan.

She lifted the overturned crock in front of her, snatched up the large chunk of beef she'd hidden beneath it and stepped over the basket to the fireplace, dropped the meat into a large iron kettle, snagged the end of the crane with the hook and pulled it toward her. She chose her hook, settled the heavy kettle onto it, tossed in the cabbage and carrots and an onion, covered them all with water from the teakettle and pushed the crane back until the pot hung over the fire.

Sighing Wind pulled the pan of corn kernels off the coals, lowered her bulk into the rocker and closed her eyes.

Anne spun toward the table. She grabbed the bowl of dough out of the basket, punched it down, molded it into loaves, put them into pans for the second rising and shoved them in the basket.

"Sighing Wind..."

The Indian woman opened her eyes.

She pointed to the pot over the fire. "That is Mister's supper. Do not let anyone touch it." She reached her hand toward the pot, slapped it with her other hand, scowled and shook her head. "Not for braves. For Mister. Do you understand?"

Sighing Wind frowned, nodded. "Braves no eat."

"Yes." She gave an exaggerated nod. "I am going to the schoolroom. You clean the table." She waved her hand over the vegetable scraps. "For the pigs."

Sighing Wind huffed out a breath, nodded and closed her eyes.

At least she had given an answer. Anne gripped the basket handle and headed for her room to get her cloak.

Mitchel gave a firm shake of his head, pivoted and strode into the building. *Please, Lord, let him accept this.*

Sharp, guttural words and the quick tread of moccasins put an end to the prayer.

If this went badly, Hope and Anne— Almighty God, be with me! He stepped to the forge, took a tight grip on the poker, jabbed at the fire, turned and faced the Indian. "No trade."

Words spewed out of the warrior.

Mitchel's face tightened. He closed both hands on the poker, edged toward the hammer he'd been using to pound the hot metal into shape. "I'm sure your sister is a fine woman, Eagle Claw, but hear my words—I will not trade Little Crow. Not for horses, not for your sister, not for anything. Our God says that is a bad thing to do. White men do not sell their women." He lifted his right hand from the poker, chopped it through the air to show an end to the talk of trade, then lowered it to his side, inches from the hammer.

The Indian's face darkened. He spit out words, grabbed the knife at his waist and brandished it in the air between them.

Mitchel shifted his stance to hide his hand, closed his fingers over the smooth, wood hammer handle. "I do not wish to fight you, Eagle Claw. My heart is good toward you and your people, and my ways are ways of peace." He looked straight into the Indian's black eyes, kept his voice even and firm. "But my God is a powerful, *strong* God, and He is with me. You will not have Little Crow." He raised the hammer level with his chest, held the poker ready at his side and balanced on his toes, ready to spring aside if the warrior lunged.

Hoofs pounded against the ground, stopped outside. There was a muted thud, soft footsteps. *Moccasins!* He saw the knowledge of them bring confidence leaping into the brave's eyes and braced himself.

"You in there, Banning?" A wiry, lean form appeared in the doorway. Keen blue eyes swept the interior of the smithy, glittered with alertness when they skimmed over the knife in the warrior's hand. The man stepped to his left, grounded his rifle and casually folded his hands on the barrel. "Go on with your parlayin'. Don't let me interrupt nothin'."

Eagle Claw straightened, lowered his knife, then spun about and strode outside.

Mitchel stepped to the door, watched the Indian leap on his horse and thunder off, the braided rawhide leads of the horses he'd brought with him clutched in his hand. "You saved my bacon, Will. Thank you."

Will Cooper's lips curved a path through his dark beard. "Didn't do nothin' but show up. An' seems as how you had things pretty well in hand." He glanced down. "Break a man's arm easy with that poker. An' that there hammer would make short work of a knife... or a head." He frowned, shook his head. "I see you're still not carryin' a weapon."

"I can't very well teach peaceful ways if I go about with a knife on my belt." Mitchel put the hammer and poker down. "Will you stay and share supper?"

The mountain man shook his head. "Appreciate the invite, but I got to move on. Heard tell there's some folks lost their guide and tried to come on through to Oregon by theirselves. They're lost up in the mountains somewhere. I'm goin' to try an' find them. Bring them down 'fore they all freeze or starve to death. Stopped by to give you this here letter." He reached inside his fringed jacket, pulled out a crumpled missive. "Fella at the fort give it to me."

He handed him the folded paper and strode out the door. "You shouldn't go unarmed, Banning." He mounted, looked down at him. "You'd best consider what would happen to that little girl of yours if some

brave caught you out in the field with no way to defend
yourself." He lifted a hand, wheeled his horse and heeled
him into a lope.

"Stay alert, Will! Eagle Claw could be waiting in
ambush."

The mountain man raised his rifle into the air, guided
his horse onto the path that led through the trees to the
rolling hills at the base of the mountains.

Mitchel stood staring after him, a sick, hollow feeling in his gut. *You'd best consider what would happen
to that little girl of yours if some brave caught you out
in the field with no way to defend yourself.*

Their vulnerability, surrounded by warring Indians,
slammed into him with new force. Fear tightened his
chest. He clenched his hands, heedless of the crunch of
the letter. Life on the mission field was not as the board
members had depicted it. And rules or no rules, from
now on he would carry a knife. He had to live for Hope's
sake. And now Anne's, as well. If he were killed…

He shoved the letter inside his shirt, spun on his heel
and strode into the smithy, his jaw clenched, his stomach churning. He pumped the bellows until the small,
charred pieces of wood glowed red and heat pulsated in
waves off them, then grabbed the tongs and shoved the
piece of iron he'd been working with into the coals. It
would take on a new shape now, that of a bar lock for
the inside of the schoolroom door. If Eagle Claw caught
Anne alone—

His mouth went dry. He jerked his thoughts from the
direction they were traveling, grabbed the bellows and
pumped harder. He didn't need this! He didn't need another helpless person to look after and protect. He'd written and asked *William* to come teach at the mission, not

his *sister.* He wanted a *man* that could help him, fight with him if necessary, not another burden to carry.

He jerked the piece of iron out of the bed of coals with the tongs, held it on the anvil and beat it with the hammer, every sharp clang of steel against iron a proclamation of his frustration and fear.

The door opened, banged against the end of the woodbox. Anne jerked her head up, took one look at Mitchel's face and rose to her feet. "Is something wrong?"

"I thought you were in the house." Something hit the floor with a clang. He grabbed the door, shut it none too gently. "I told you not to go wandering around by yourself."

She stiffened, lifted her gaze from the black iron objects at his feet. "I hardly think walking from the kitchen to the schoolroom is *wandering.* And I made certain there were no Indians around when I left the house."

His face tightened. He stared at her a moment, then gave a brief nod she took to be a concession of the point. She turned back to the trunks, lifted out another slate board and placed it on the table. That made seven. "Did you want something?"

"Yes. I want you to obey what I say. You shouldn't be in here by yourself. I've told you these Indians are...curious. One could come in here to see what you are doing."

Why was he so angry? She turned back to face him, holding her own rising anger in check. "I've done nothing wrong, Mitchel. The door was *closed.* How would an Indian know I was here?"

"The same way I did...smoke." He shot a look toward the fireplace.

"Oh." Her flare of temper fizzled. "I didn't think..."

"Exactly." He turned toward the door, stooped, selected one of the pieces of iron and straightened. There was a hammer in his hand.

"What is that?" She left the table, moved to stand by the woodbox where she could watch him.

"A bar lock." He fitted the piece on the door frame, nailed it in place, grabbed the other piece and nailed it to the door. A narrow piece of iron bar dangled from it, held in place by a nail with a flattened head.

She watched him flip the bar up and drop it behind the bent-up pieces of iron on the lock, grab the door handle and yank. It didn't budge.

He nodded, turned and looked at her. "Keep this locked whenever you're here by yourself."

She stared at the lock, looked up and studied his face. A chill trickled down her spine. "What is wrong, Mitchel?" She saw the small muscle along his jaw twitch, looked into his eyes and knew he wasn't going to tell her. She stepped close, placed her fingers on the cold iron bar. "If there is danger, I have a right to know. Why do I need this lock?"

He didn't want to tell her. That was plain. His mouth tightened, as if to hold back words. She looked into his eyes, waited.

"That Cayuse brave who wanted to buy you for his wife came back today. He made another offer. I told him I would not trade you for any price. That our God says it is wrong, and white men do not sell their women." Something flashed in his eyes, too quickly masked for her to discern. "He's not disposed to take no for an answer, and if he comes back, I don't want him to find you alone."

His hard, calloused fingers brushed hers as he reached out and raised the bar, the sudden warmth of his touch a comforting contrast to the cold of the iron. His eyes darkened, his gaze locked on hers. The warmth crept from their fingers to her cheeks. She jerked her hand away, stepped back. He cleared his throat, opened the door. Cold air rushed in, sent a chill shivering through her.

"Flip the bar in place when I'm gone. And keep it there." He stepped outside, turned back. "If any Indians ask to come in, tell them I said no."

She nodded, shut and locked the door, stood staring at the iron bar and rubbing the place where his fingers had touched hers. For that one tiny instant she had felt her heart stirring...

She frowned, shook her head and went back to finish sorting through the trunks. She pulled out two crocks of chalk, found more slates beneath them and added them to the stack on the table. That made ten slates. Or was it twelve?

She counted the pile on the table again, looked down at the trunks, glanced at the lock on the door. Mitchel's worries and fears for her wormed their way past her defenses, pierced her determination to not care. She closed the trunk lids and walked to the fireplace. The dough was ready to be baked.

She put on her cloak, carried the basket to the door and reached to lift the bar. The feel of the cold metal brought the thoughts she'd been fighting swarming to the fore. She jerked her hand away, scrubbed her fingers against her wool cloak, but she couldn't erase the memory of the warmth of those hard, calloused fingers on hers. Mitchel's touch had penetrated the numbness she had struggled so hard to attain.

She set her jaw, flipped the bar and stepped outside

into the cold. She would have to be more careful to maintain a merely polite relationship with Mitchel. She wanted no part of friendship. Allowing others into her heart only led to pain.

Chapter Eight

"Me like 'tatoes wiff bwown stuff, Papa." Hope's head emerged from the nightgown he'd slipped over it. Her blue eyes sparkled up at him. "And *bwead*."

Mitchel smiled and eased her arms into the long sleeves. She had not cried during her bath, only whimpered a time or two when he treated and bandaged her joints. Anne's ointment was truly a blessing. As was the supper she'd prepared. He tied the ribbons at the neck of the gown, then tapped his daughter's tiny nose. "That 'brown stuff' is called gravy, Hope. And I like it, too. And the bread. Did you have honey on it?"

She nodded, grinned. "Me like honey, too."

He studied her face, his heart sinking at the telltale flush on her cheeks, the feverish brightness in her eyes. Still, she wasn't hurting as much. And she was sleeping better. And now, thanks to Anne, she was eating better, too. As was he. It had been years since he'd had any bread other than the coarse flatbread the Indian women made from ground corn. And the potatoes and gravy—

"Tell me 'bout the aminals, Papa."

He smiled at her familiar request. Noah building the

ark was her favorite Bible story. "All right. But first I'll tuck you in. It's bedtime." He felt her hair. It was dry, thanks to the roaring fire he'd built to keep her from getting chilled while in the tub. He tugged free a long, silky curl that was caught in the neck of her nightgown, lifted her into his arms and laid her in bed, tucked the warm blankets around her. She didn't cry out. Such an odd thing to be thankful for.

He handed her the stick doll Laughing Rain had made her and went back to take care of the tub. "When Noah finished the ark, all the animals came in as God had commanded." He picked up the damp towel and hung it over the edge, stared at the small tin tub sitting beside the hearth. Hope would be outgrowing it soon. Her nightgowns were already getting small for her. He would have to send word to Lieutenant Fields's wife at Fort Walla Walla, have her make some new ones for Hope.

"'Piders, too, Papa?"

He glanced over at Hope, grinned at her wrinkled nose, the tiny crease between her small, arched blond brows. His daughter did not like spiders. "Spiders, too, Hope. But they were very *nice* spiders. They knew Noah's wife was frightened of them, so they climbed *alllll* the way to the very top of the ark to build their web. And they stayed there the whole forty days."

He set the tub outside the door to empty later and went back to sit on the edge of her bed. "There was a terrible racket when all those animals started talking to one another! The bears growled—" He hunched his shoulders forward and hung his hands loose in front of his chest "—Grrrr! And the lions roared—" he lifted his head, opened his mouth wide and swung his head side to side "—Raarrr! And the dogs barked…Arf, arf!"

"Do piggies, Papa!"

"And the piggies oinked and snorted—" He sucked in air, made grunting noises deep in his throat. She giggled. A beautiful sound. "You try it."

She shook her head. "Me do cow...moooo..."

"That's a good cow."

She nodded, yawned. "Me like aminals, Papa."

"Yes, I know you do, Hope. You go to sleep now." He watched her eyes close, leaned down and kissed her forehead. *Thank You that she can sleep, Almighty God. But I pray You will heal her. Please heal her, Lord. Let her run and play again, I pray. Amen.* He rose and went to empty the tub.

The room was chilly tonight, with a dampness that presaged rain. Anne shivered, pressed closer to the chimney. The sounds from downstairs had stopped. The child must have gone to sleep.

She wrapped her arms about herself and paced the room for warmth. There'd been no crying, only a few whimpers. Perhaps the sickness was a temporary one and Mitchel's daughter was better. And perhaps she was simply trying to avoid what she knew she must do.

Oh, why, why, *why* had she ended up in this situation? All she wanted was to stay numb and feel nothing. Now...

She clenched her hands, walked to the stairs. It *was* quiet. Perhaps Mitchel had retired, though it was still early evening. The faint glow of lamplight on the steps ended that hope. She gripped the railing and started down, paused. He was sitting at the desk writing, his brow furrowed in concentration. Firelight flickered over his back and shoulders, gilded the crests of the slight waves in his brown hair. He turned his head, looked up at her, and she caught a glimpse of sadness in his eyes. She was intruding on a private moment.

"I didn't mean to disturb you, Mitchel. Good evening." She turned to go back upstairs.

"Please stay, Anne. I would be glad of your company. I will finish my letter later." He wiped the nib of his pen, stoppered the ink well and rose. "I have not had anyone to converse with during the evening hours since Paul died."

"Paul?" She shivered, continued down the stairs and across the room, lured by the warmth of the fire.

He joined her by the hearth. "Paul Dodge, the man who came west with Isobel and me to start the mission. Did William not tell you of him?"

She shook her head, ignored the pang of homesickness for her adopted brother and turned the conversation from him. "What happened to Mr. Dodge? Did he take sick?"

"No. Two of our horses came up missing and Paul went after them. He didn't come home." An expression she couldn't read flashed in his eyes. He sucked in air, looked away, stared down into the fire. "Anyway, I waited two days, then followed his tracks up into the mountains. I found his body at the base of a deep chasm. He'd…fallen off a cliff."

There was a sudden tenseness about him. She shouldn't have inquired into his friend's death. She wanted no questions about the deaths of her loved ones. "How terrible to find your friend like that. I'm sorry, Mitchel. I should not have asked."

"I think, perhaps, it's good that you did."

"In what way?"

He looked down at her, squared his shoulders, shook his head. "An idle thought. Anyway, Paul's death was over two years ago. He…died, a few weeks after Isobel passed away."

Shadows darkened his eyes, and she knew he was remembering. Her heart ached in sympathy. "That must have been a difficult time for you."

"Yes." He stooped and added a log to the fire. "The worst part was the fear. Hope was a tiny baby, and I, a new father with no knowledge of caring for her. I kept wondering if I would lose her, too. I still wonder…"

She caught her breath, raised her hand and placed it on her chest, rubbed at the gathering tightness.

He straightened, looked down at her. "Now I must apologize, Anne. I should not have—"

She raised her hand, shook her head to stop the words she didn't want to hear. Again turned the conversation back onto safe ground. "Please go on. How did you care for your daughter?"

"Isobel never recovered her strength after Hope's birth, and we hired a Cayuse woman as a wet nurse. She stayed on when Isobel passed. Then, a few days after Paul died, Mr. Overbeck and Mr. Newhouse and their wives stopped on their way to found a mission among the Yakimas. The weather being unfavorable for travel they stayed on awhile. The men helped me finish the buildings Paul and I had started, and the ladies took over Hope's care. They bathed her, and fed her. The wet nurse became offended and went back to her village.

"When the missionaries left, I imitated what I had seen the ladies do. And I hired Laughing Rain to care for Hope when I was unable to be here. I had the mission to run. And the Indians started coming in ever larger numbers."

She felt the tension growing in him again, knew, intuitively, he needed to keep talking, to relieve the pressure with words. "Isn't that what you wanted?"

"Yes. I was very pleased."

Was?

"The Cayuse and Nez Perce were welcoming, and seemed to accept my message of Christ. Some were baptized." He looked over at her. "That's when I wrote William about the school."

Seemed? She studied his face, something in his eyes sent a chill skittering over her flesh. "But that has changed?"

He looked at her for a long moment, then nodded. "The Indians do not like to be told that warring and stealing and taking slaves and trading women are wrong. They resent it. They say their life was better before I told them it was bad to do those things."

"Then you shall have to convince them otherwise."

"Yes. I suppose I shall. If any come back to hear my messages. Most of them have stopped coming to my Sunday services." He rubbed his hand across the muscles at the nape of his neck, rested his forearm on the mantel and looked at her. "Eagle Claw is right. You have a strong spirit and a brave heart. It's surprising, when you look so...so—"

"Like a *crow?*" She looked down, brushed at her skirt, lest her aggravation show on her face. The unflattering name rankled.

"I was going to say...fragile." He cleared his throat. "I haven't asked—had you a purpose in coming downstairs? Was there something you wanted?"

Her hands stilled. She glanced toward the open door across the room, forced out the words. "I wondered… There's been no crying…" She inched back her shoulders, looked at him. "Has the sickness gone, Mitchel? Is your daughter well?"

The shake of his head killed her hope.

"She is much improved, thanks to your kindness. Her pain is greatly lessened by the ointment and wrappings you provided, and she is able to sleep because of them. But the pain is still there. And she still has a fever."

There was such sadness on his face. She had to tell him. "Mitchel, you said the other night that you had not taken your daughter to a doctor because of fear the journey would injure her further." She looked down at the dancing flames, fought for control, spun away from the hearth and moved to stand behind the hide-covered settee. "My sister Emma is a doctor."

"Yes, I know. William wrote—"

"She is here. In Oregon country. At the new emigrant town."

He straightened, stared at her, hope blazing in his eyes.

She lifted her hand, rubbed at the scar on her ribs. "Emma came on the wagon train because she would not allow me to travel alone with my injuries. I don't know if she can help your daughter, but she's a very good doctor. I thought you should know she was here." The words came out in bursts, flat, without emotion. She had become adept at hiding the pain. She turned toward the stairs.

"Wait, Anne!"

She froze.

Mitchel rushed around the chair, gripped her upper arms. "Where is the town?"

She went rigid, glanced down at his hands then relaxed. He didn't even realize he was holding her. She took a breath, shook her head. "I'm sorry, Mitchel. I didn't think—I don't know."

He stared at her, released his grip and stepped back. "No. Of course you wouldn't..." He bowed his head, rubbed at the back of his neck. "How far away is it?"

"It was three days' travel in the wagon."

"The *wagon*." He jerked his head up, looked at her. "Hope would be protected from the weather in your wagon."

"Yes. You are welcome to it."

"But the jolting..." He looked toward his daughter's doorway, his shoulders slumped. "The jolting would be too painful for her. It might harm her."

She couldn't stand watching the hope fade from his eyes. She lived with hopelessness. She wrapped her arms about herself and rubbed where his hands had gripped her, erasing the warmth, the memory of his touch before it could steal into her heart. "There was a toddler on the train who was injured falling from her wagon during a storm. Emma found her and treated her injuries and then refused to move her wagon until the child had regained consciousness." She looked up, met Mitchel's intent gaze. "Mr. Thatcher made a sling bed and hung it by leather thongs from the ribs that supported the cover. It protected the toddler from the jarring and bouncing of the wagon. Emma described it to me. I could tell you."

He stood there nodding, staring into the distance. "Clever. That would work..." He lifted his hands, rubbed his right fist against his left palm and strode around the room. "I'll find out where the town is located. The Indians will know." He shot a look in her direction. "And I'll prepare the wagon so we're ready to go when Halstrum gets back. Make sure the wheels are tight and the hubs are greased..."

We're? Surely he didn't think— She clenched her hands and walked to the stairs.

"We'll need lanterns and bedding and food. And Hope's clothes. And the ointment and... Horses." He stopped pacing, looked at her. "Is there anything special you need?"

To protect my heart. She gripped the banister, shook her head. "No, Mitchel. I will do all I can to help you prepare for the journey, but I'll not come with you. Laughing Rain can care for your daughter." She turned away, lifted the hems of her long skirt with her free hand and climbed the stairs.

Mitchel stared down at his sleeping daughter, his throat so tight he could not swallow. Was God answering his prayers? Had Anne been the answer all along and he had not understood because of his own desire for William to come and help him?

He sank to his knees, crossed his arms on Hope's bed and lowered his head to rest on them. "Almighty God, I thank You Anne came to teach in William's stead. And I thank You that Emma came along on the wagon train to care for Anne. If it be Your will, use them to heal Hope I pray."

The words were muffled, strained. He drew in air to ease the pressure in his chest, rose and went to add wood to the fire. He wanted to believe Anne was God's answer, but if that were true, why would she refuse to care for Hope? The doubt he'd battled since Isobel and Paul's death, that had grown since Hope's illness, rose, strangled his faith like weeds in a wheat field.

His chest squeezed, ached. He gripped the mantel with both hands, hung his head between his arms and stared down at the fire. How could he know? How could he believe God heard and answered prayer when so much had gone wrong in spite of his own fervent prayers to the contrary?

And now the Cayuse were becoming more and more belligerent. Or were they? Had they only feigned friendship and pretended to accept the white man's God in order to receive food and the services the mission rendered them? Services and food they had demanded with increasing boldness since he was alone at the mission.

The thought came again. The one he'd been suppressing ever since it occurred to him during his conversation with Anne. Had Paul fallen over that cliff—or been pushed?

His stomach knotted. He didn't want to believe the Indians would do such a thing. But Paul had been on that trail dozens of times without incident. And he'd been too wary to allow an unknown Indian to come close. And his horse hadn't come home. It should have, *would* have unless something or *someone* prevented it. He knew that now, though he'd been too green to realize it at the time. And it was since Paul's death the attitude and behavior of the Cayuse braves had changed. And now…now he had been openly threatened.

Mitchel looked at Hope, clenched his hands and strode over to the chest at the foot of his bed. He lifted out the leather belt he'd worn on his way across the wilderness. The knife was snug in its sheath, the hatchet dangled from its loop. He closed the chest, tested the edge of the hatchet's blade, brushed the pad of his thumb against the double-edged knife. He would hone them in the morning.

He laid them on the chest, kicked an ember that popped out onto the floor back into the fire and strode to his desk in the other room and turned up the wick in the oil lamp. Yellow light spilled across the paper he'd left there. He sat, lifted the stopper from the inkwell and dipped his pen.

I have written you of the Indians' antipathy toward Sunday services. And, also, of the opening of our school. I am hopeful that educating them in our ways will lead to them a greater acceptance of the Christian message.

To conclude, gentlemen: It is with deep regret, I inform you that things on the mission field here in Oregon country are not as you suppose them to be. The Indians are far different than I was led to believe. They do not listen or accept truth as you imagine. A very few of them are tolerant and slowly accept some of our ways, but many of the Cayuse are troublesome. They are increasingly threatening in their behavior.

Mission work viewed from our native land is peaceful and godlike. Here, on the field, it is a harsh, dangerous reality. I am concerned for my young daughter should I lose my life. It is for this reason I am breaking the "no-arms" rule set forth by the mission board and will go armed beginning tomorrow. I will do whatever is necessary to preserve my life, that my daughter might live.

I realize you will wish to recall my posting due to this insubordination. To facilitate the matter for you, I will remain at my position until my replacement arrives.

In His service,
Mitchel Banning

He folded the letter, directed it to the American Board of Commissioners for Foreign Missions, applied his wax seal and rose to place it on the mantel to wait for the next mountain man who stopped by the mission on his way east.

God grant that it might be soon.

Chapter Nine

"You come."

Anne looked up, saw Sighing Wind's bulk disappear from the dining room doorway and frowned. She'd given the Indian woman the task of sweeping and dusting the living room because she did not want to go in there. It was too close to Mitchel's daughter's room. No matter how hard she tried to ignore them, she heard every little outcry, every sob. But they were less frequent since she had given Mitchel the ointment.

She had to go see what Sighing Wind needed. She jabbed the threaded needle through the cotton fabric to hold its place, rose and laid the apron she was making from one of Mitchel's mother-in-law's tablecloths on the chair. She listened intently, heard no sound from the child. If she hurried… She shook out her long skirt, rushed through the kitchen and dining room to the living room.

"What is it, Sigh—" She stopped short, stared at the two small Indian girls standing just inside the front door, a bearded man wearing buckskins and holding the barrel of his grounded rifle beside them.

The man whipped off his fur hat, dipped his head. "Good day to you, ma'am. Name's Joe Means."

She lifted her gaze to him.

"I heard tell the mission is startin' up a school, and I've brung my children."

His children? She shifted her gaze back to the little girls in their fringed skirts, moccasins and bead-decorated tunics. Their dark hair, parted in the middle, swept down over their ears, accentuating their small round faces, then hung in braided loops against their chests. Their eyes, blue like their father's, proclaimed their mixed blood.

"This here is Iva." The man laid a broad, scarred hand on the tallest girl's head. "She's seven years. And this here one is Kitturah. She's five come December."

He lifted his gaze back to her. "I want they should have an education, learn my people's ways. My squaw's settin' up camp 'mongst the trees next to the river so they won't be a trouble to you. She won't bother you none." He gave a brisk nod, slapped his hat on his head. "I'll be back to fetch 'em come spring."

Spring! Before she could gather her wits to respond, he yanked open the door and slipped outside. "Wait!" She rushed to the door, opened it and hurried outside, looked around. "Mr. Means?" There was no sign of him.

What was she to do now? She hadn't expected to begin school today. She wasn't *prepared*. She blew out a frustrated breath, went back inside and closed the door. The girls were standing silent and still as shadows, those startling blue eyes fastened on her. She smoothed the front of her long skirt, raised a hand to check that no curls had escaped her black turban bonnet. "Well, I suppose the first—" She stopped, looked at the oldest girl. "You *do* speak English, Iva?"

"Yes, ma'am."

"Me do, too."

"*I!* Not *me*."

Kitturah's offering earned her a scowling correction from her older sister. She pressed her little lips together and looked down at the floor.

Anne's heart squeezed. The little girl looked crushed. How well she remembered feeling that way when Emma or William corrected her. She frowned, buried the sudden rush of empathy beneath a brisk, businesslike attitude. "I'm very pleased that you both speak English. It will make my job much easier."

What now? Her plans for the day fell away. Prepared or not, she was a teacher now. A tiny jolt of anticipation tingled through her. Perhaps her life *would* have a purpose. She walked to the fireplace, lit a candle stub and looked at the girls. "Come with me, please." She cupped her hand around the candle flame and led them out the back door, turned toward the lean-to on their left.

"This is the schoolroom." She glanced down at the two sober faces, felt another tiny jolt of purpose at the betraying gleam of excitement in their blue eyes. "Open the door please, Iva." The girl hastened to obey, then stepped back beside her little sister. Obviously, discipline would not be a problem. But overcoming their taciturn ways might prove difficult.

A gust of cold wind swept down the path, swirled back upon itself in the cul-de-sac formed by the mission house and the attached kitchen and schoolroom. The candle flame flickered. Anne shivered, shielded the candle with her body and stepped inside, her two silent shadows at her heels. "Close the door please, Kitturah."

She hurried to the fireplace and touched the burning candle to the laid fire. The tinder caught with a whoosh, flames licked at the short lengths of encircling small branches, found the dry bark to their liking and began to burn in earnest. Smoke rose, pooled at the top of the firebox, hovered and roiled, then found escape up the chimney.

"There now—it will soon be warm in here." She blew out the candle, set it on the mantel and turned. The girls were standing just inside the door. "Please, come sit close by the fire where you'll be warm." She indicated the bench closest to the table at the front of the room. The whisper of their moccasins against the rough planks of the floor blended with the crackle and pop of the burning wood as they obeyed her bidding.

"These will be your seats. You will sit here whenever you come to school. Do you understand?" Their dark heads nodded in unison. "Good. Now then, I know your names but you do not know mine. You will address me as…" *I told him you were my woman, and you were not for sale. You'd best not deny it.* "As…Miss Anne."

Wind gusted down the chimney, smoke puffed out into the room, swirled around her head, crawled up the sloped roof. She coughed, moved away from the hearth and wiped tears from her smarting eyes. "Can you read, Iva?"

The girl's blue eyes clouded. "I don't know 'read.'"

"I see." A shiver raised goose bumps on her flesh. She rubbed her upper arms and wished she had taken the time to go upstairs for her cloak. "Do you know the alphabet?"

A frown drew Iva's dark, straight brows together. "I do not know what is 'al-phabet.'"

"Then that is where we shall begin." She hurried to the table at the front of the room, picked up slates, grabbed chalk sticks from the crock, hurried back and placed them on the table. "Now then I shall write—" She stopped, looked at the girls who were staring at the slates and chalk, their eyes wide, their hands drawn back behind their small bodies.

"It's all right. These are slates…" She lifted hers, tapped the cold, dark stone enclosed in the wood frame. "Repeat the word after me…*slate*." They chorused the word. "Very good." She lifted the white stick. "And this is chalk. Say *chalk*." Again they chorused the word. "Yes, very good. Now, I will *write* on the *slate* with the *chalk*. Like this…" She drew a circle.

The girls gasped, covered their mouths with their hands and stared at the slate, making small sounds of amazement, like the ones the Indians who had poked her bread dough had uttered.

A smile tugged at her lips. She ignored it. "Now you do it." She placed their sticks of chalk in their hands, tapped their slates, then pointed to her own. "This is a *circle*. You make a *circle* on your *slate* with your *chalk*."

They stared up her, their eyes as round as the circle she had drawn. She nodded and pointed to their slates.

Kitturah looked at her sister.

Iva set her mouth in a determined line, put her chalk to her slate and made her hand go around. "Whaah!" She dropped the chalk, stared at her slate.

Kitturah stared at Iva, gripped her chalk tight and bent over her slate. When she lifted her head, her eyes were sparkling with delight. *"Circle."*

Anne couldn't stop her smile. It came from deep within, a smile of true pleasure, a sensation she had not felt in a long time. She added a stem and two leaves at the top of her circle, held her slate forward. "Can you tell me what this is?"

"A apple!" The answer was spoken in unison.

"Yes, it's *an* apple." She placed her chalk on the bench desk and looked at her young students. "Before I go further, I must tell you one of the rules of the schoolroom. Only one person is to speak at a time. When I ask a question to which you know the answer, please raise your hand...like this." She lifted her hand into the air palm forward. "That tells me you wish to answer the question, and I will then choose which one of you may do so. Do you understand?"

Their blue eyes stared at her raised hand, their braids bobbed up and down against their beaded tunics as they nodded. She lowered her hand, waited until they looked at her. "Let's try it. What is your father's name?"

Kitturah caught her lower lip with her small top teeth and shot her hand into the air, palm out. Iva's response was more restrained, but her eyes betrayed her desire to be called upon to answer. She looked back at the youngest child. "Kitturah, what is the answer?"

"Papa's name is Joe Means!"

The little girl blurted the answer and stared up at her. "Thank you. You may lower your hands once I choose someone to answer." They immediately lowered their hands to the desktop. She nodded, shifted her gaze to oldest girl. "Is Kitturah's answer correct, Iva?"

The girl stared at her, frowned. "I do not know... cor-rect."

"*Correct* means is her answer true."

Iva's frown disappeared. She nodded.

"Answer aloud, please."

"Kitturah speaks the truth. Her answer is *correct*."

"Very good. Now, don't forget to raise your hands when you wish to answer a question. Or when you wish to ask me about something you do not understand." She placed her slate on the desk table so they could copy it and gestured toward their slates. "Please make your circles into apples."

She watched them pick up their chalk and bend over their slates, less tentative this time. She waited a moment to be certain they didn't need her, then stepped to the woodbox, picked up a piece of firewood and carried it to the hearth. She placed it on the fire and turned back to check their work. "Those are very good apples. Now listen carefully. Words are made of *letters*. And each *letter* has a name—as you each have names. Letters also have a sound."

She glanced at the girls, felt a thrill at their rapt expressions. No wonder William loved teaching! "Now watch carefully. I am going to show you how to make the first letter in the alphabet." She looked back at her slate. "The name of this letter is *a*. Capital *A*—" She drew one at the top of her slate. "And little *a*." She pointed to the lowercase *a*. "This letter says '*aaaa*'—" she drew out the sound "—as in *aaapple*." She glanced at the girls. "Iva—"

The door opened. *Mitchel*. He must have seen the smoke of her fire and come to check on her safety. A sense of well-being flowed over her. She looked toward the door, saw moccasins and fringed leggings. Her heart stopped, lurched into a racing beat. She raised her gaze from the sheathed knife and dangling tomahawk, slid it over the bare chest visible beneath a buckskin vest and up into the cold, black eyes of the warrior with the puckered scar on his cheek. His straight, stern lips parted. He spoke. Harsh, guttural, *frightening* sounds. She strained to hear him over the roar of her pulse in her ears, to make some sense of his words.

Movement caught her eye. She glanced down at Iva and Kitturah, drew a breath. Would they be in danger? She couldn't let anything happen to them, they were her responsibility. She darted a glance toward the poker leaning against the stone of the fireplace, then looked back at the warrior. "I do not understand your words. Do you speak English?" She took a step toward the hearth, stopped when the warrior grunted out more words.

"He said he does not speak your tongue."

She jerked her gaze to Iva. Relief whooshed through her, foolish when the girl was only seven—but at least she could now understand the warrior. "Thank you, Iva. Please ask him what he wants."

The young girl nodded, rose and faced the Indian. She listened to the two converse, watched the warrior's face for a clue as to his purpose in coming, looked down when Iva turned back to her.

"He says he is Barking Fox, a war chief of the Cayuse. He has brought his son Running Wolf to the white man's mission school to learn the marks white men put on paper. He would have him know the white man's ways of trade."

War chief! Her knees went wobbly. A desire for one of her Uncle Justin's pistols in her hand made her fingers curl inward to touch her palm. "Thank you, Iva." *Fear earns their contempt...bravery their respect.* She stiffened her spine, raised her head and looked at the warrior. "Please tell Barking Fox I welcome Running Wolf to the mission school. I will teach him to know the white man's marks."

Iva spoke. The war chief nodded, stepped outside, grunted out some words and walked away. A young Indian boy, of perhaps eight or nine, took his place in the doorway, swept the room with an imperious, intelligent gaze. He looked at her, spoke. She looked at Iva.

"He asks where is the man who will teach him the white man's marks?"

You will have to be firm with the Indian children. Especially the boys... Mitchel's words again rang in her head, though she'd not given them much heed at the time. She looked at the young boy's arrogant bearing, the challenge in his piercing black eyes, and knew that Mitchel was right. She drew back her shoulders and put a firm note in her voice. "Tell Running Wolf I am the one who will teach him. And tell him to close the door and come forward and sit down. It is time to begin."

Mitchel looked down at Anne, watched her take a sip of coffee. She was so delicate and refined. So out of place here among the rough crudeness of the log building and branch and hide furniture. Yet she made the mission feel like a home. And today, she had made the mission school he had dreamed of a reality. He scowled, shifted his gaze to the dark brew in his cup. He should feel grateful, not...irritated.

"Do you think I handled the situation correctly, Mitchel? I remembered what you said about being firm with the Indian children...especially the boys."

"I think you handled it very well." He twisted his wrist, watched the dark liquid swirl around in the cup, then took a swallow of the strong coffee. It was getting cold. He set the cup on the mantel, looked down and met her gaze. His gut tightened. He hadn't known God made eyes that deep violet-blue color until he'd looked into hers. "What happened after you had Iva tell Running Wolf to come in and sit down?"

The shadows that haunted her eyes gave way to a glow of satisfaction. "She looked up at me and said, 'Do you want me, also, to tell Running Wolf to raise his hand before he speaks? Indians do not know about rules.'"

He stared into her eyes, sharing that moment of success with her, then turned and booted a log on the fire into place with his toe. "Precocious child, isn't she?"

"Yes. I'm so thankful for Iva. I don't know what I would have done when Barking Fox came into the room if she hadn't been there."

Barking Fox, a Cayuse war chief. Mitchel grabbed his cup, swallowed the rest of the cold coffee to relieve the tightness in his chest. "The door would have been locked if you'd been alone."

She stared at him a moment, then looked away. "Yes."

There was a tautness, a withdrawal in her soft voice. His own fault. He had sounded churlish. But the thought of that warrior—

"I noticed you were wearing a knife and a hatchet when you came in from the fields today, Mitchel. And I realized it was because of me." She rose, came to stand beside him, looked straight into his eyes. "I told you what happened with Iva and Kitturah and Running Wolf today because I wanted you to know what I have taught them… so you can continue." Her voice broke. She looked down, reached for his cup. "I have brought you trouble, Mitchel.

And, in spite of the school opening, I now believe it would be best if I left the mission."

It was what he had wanted ever since she arrived. So why did it feel as if a buffalo bull had run over him? He sucked in air, shook his head. "You're wrong, Anne. The trouble has always been present. It's only that my eyes have been opened more fully in the past few days." He looked down at her, realized his heart had changed, that he wanted her to stay…for purely personal reasons. *Selfish!* "But for your sake, your safety, it would be best if you leave."

He took another breath, handed her his cup. "When Halstrum returns, I will put your things back in your wagon and you will go with me when I take Hope to the emigrant town to see your sister."

Chapter Ten

The rain the sky had been promising for two days drummed on the roof, splatted against the small window.

Anne shivered, pulled her black, wool gown over her head, shoved her arms into the long sleeves and settled the fabric over her shoulders. She rubbed her cold hands together, fumbled over the small buttons that paraded down the front of the bodice.

The drumming increased. Lightning flickered white light through the murky darkness outside. Thunder rumbled. She sat on the small wood stool she'd placed against the chimney and buttoned her shoes. Would Iva and Kitturah come to school during a storm? Would Running Wolf come even if it were a nice day? It was obvious the Indian boy did not like being taught by a woman. Still, he would probably come in obedience to his father's wishes.

Another shiver shook her. She wrapped her arms about herself, pressed back against the warm stones and watched the rivulets of water chase each other down the small windowpanes.

She didn't want to leave.

Despair gripped her throat. She leaned her head back, closed her eyes. She had found purpose in planning and preparing meals, in overseeing the housekeeping chores of the mission. And it had nothing to do with Mitchel or his daughter. She had been careful to maintain her distance, to stay aloof from them—other than giving her ointment to help the child's pain and fixing special meals to encourage the child to eat.

The grip on her throat tightened. She rubbed at its base, drew a breath. Doing those things didn't mean she cared. *Anyone* would do what they could to help a sick child. And she could not live with the dirt, or eat meals prepared in a filthy kitchen. If Mitchel benefitted, she was pleased. He worked hard all day. And the faint glow of the oil lamp bathing the stairs, the sounds of him moving about below while he worked on the mission records, continued long after she had retired. And always, he tended his daughter.

She lowered her hand to her lap, swallowed. He'd told her the ointment and the meals were a blessing. That his daughter said she liked the potatoes with "brown stuff"—her name for gravy. And especially the bread...

She blinked her eyes, stared up at the rough beams and boards overhead. The ointment *had* helped. The child's cries were less frequent, quieter, her sobs softer. She no longer heard her at night, if she covered her ears with the blankets. And now she would be in the schoolroom all day. It was what she wanted.

She rose, shook her long skirt into place and stepped to the dresser. There was no time to brood about leaving. She had to speak to Sighing Wind about her tasks for the day, then prepare breakfast and make bread dough for supper. She would take it with her to the schoolroom.

She refused to allow Sighing Wind to touch the dough or prepare their meals. The Indian woman did not grasp the meaning of cleanliness.

She shuddered, pushed away thoughts of the meals Mitchel and his daughter would eat after she was gone. It was not her concern. She peered into the hand mirror she'd propped against the wall and settled her black turban bonnet over the bun formed by her mass of russet curls. She tugged the front edge of the bonnet farther forward, tucked in every errant wisp of hair, then adjusted the bonnet's sewn-in crown.

It had seemed, on her arrival, that she had blundered into the worst possible situation. But it was all working out. And now she had to leave. How long would she have until Mitchel's helper returned? How many days until she would have to go back to Emma and face all the memories?

Her fingers twitched. She turned and looked around the roughly constructed, sparsely furnished room so different from the luxurious home she was raised in. Or the home she had shared with Phil—

She whirled back to the dresser, poured her wash water from the washbowl to the pail and rinsed the bowl. How could she go back to the emigrant village? She would have to live with Emma. Mitchel would have her wagon to protect his daughter from the weather.

Her face tightened. Why had this happened? She wanted to stay and be a teacher. She wanted to forget. And in the schoolroom, she did. But she could not stay at the mission at the cost of Mitchel's safety. Or of the child's.

She pressed her lips together, turned down the wick and snuffed the lamp. She had no choice in the matter. For the sake of Mitchel and his daughter, she had to go back.

Lightning glinted at the window, cast wavering light into the room, receded. Thunder growled, rumbled away into the distance. The storm was coming closer.

She stared out the rain-rinsed window, lifted her gaze toward the brooding, overcast sky. Once again, God was using a man and a child to rip her life apart. But this time her heart was safe.

She inched her shoulders back, lifted her chin and grabbed her cloak off the peg on the wall. While she was here, she would hang it downstairs on the pegs by the back door where it would be handy for her trips to the schoolroom.

A bolt of lightning streaked through the darkness, thunder crashed. The child screamed. She whirled and ran for the stairs—and remembered. It was not her child. She would never hold or comfort her baby again. The wave of grief drove her to her knees. She hunched forward to ease the pain rending her heart and buried her body-shaking sobs in the cloak clutched in her hands.

The heifer lifted her head, bawled, then trotted toward the small herd of cows on the hill, her calf gamboling at her heels.

Mitchel reined his horse around to face the way they had come, and touched his heels to her sides. The bay mare broke into a lope. He glanced over his shoulder for a last look at the calf, faced front again, the muscles in his face taut. You'd never know, from the way the calf was kicking up his heels at his new-found freedom, that he'd almost died at birth. *Please, God, grant that Hope will one day run and play again.*

The wind chilled his face, plucked at his hat. Lightning flashed, brightened the dark sky above the mission buildings. Thunder muttered in the distance. The storm was returning, any field work was out of the question. He tugged his hat down tighter, corrected course, and urged his mount to a faster pace as they headed for the barn. He'd work on the wagon now instead of waiting until tonight as he'd planned.

He dismounted, led the mare inside, stripped his gear off her and forked fresh hay into the rack on the wall at the head of her stall. Light flickered through the dim interior. He frowned, tossed his jacket over the rail of an empty stall and ran for the river.

The water whispered along the grassy bank, rushed off into the distance. Mitchel rolled up his shirtsleeves, knelt down, reached into the cold water and dragging the wagon wheel out onto the ground, gave a grunt of satisfaction. The overnight soaking had worked. The dried out wood had swollen until the iron rim was tight again.

Lightning winked. He shot a look at the black clouds tumbling his way, clamped his hands around the wet wood and cold iron, tugged the wheel to waist height, then gritted his teeth, transferred his grip to the underside and shoved the wheel upright.

Raindrops hit his upturned face, others spattered against his hands, tapped his shoulders. Lightning flashed again, closer this time. Thunder growled a warning. He took a firm hold on the wheel, braced his feet and pushed. The wheel rolled forward. He grabbed another spoke, dug in his heel and pushed with his other foot. With one firm grasp after another he rolled the large, heavy wheel across the uneven ground toward the crippled wagon sitting under the long, slanted roof overhang of the smithy.

The rain came in earnest. He propped the wheel against the building, crooked his elbow and blotted the moisture from his face with his rolled-up sleeve. Wind gusted through the sheltered area beneath the roof, chilled his wet forearms and damp shirt, sent a shiver through him.

He stepped inside the smithy, grabbed a rag and dried his arms. The heat from the smoldering coals of the fire he always kept going chased away the chill. He added a few small chunks of hardwood to the dying fire, then carried the rag and the pail of grease he'd set inside to soften overnight out to Anne's wagon.

He set the pail on the ground, shook out the rag. She had been so obstinate the night she'd said she would not go with him when he took Hope to the emigrant village. He thought about the loss of her child, understood. He didn't want her to suffer because of him or Hope, but all the same, he was grateful she'd changed her mind. He could not go off and leave her here alone, not even when Halstrum came back. Not with Eagle Claw around.

He glanced in the direction of the schoolroom. Smoke streamed into the sky from its chimney, the plume looking almost white against the thunderclouds overhead. She was there, teaching her students.

He squelched an urge to go to the lean-to and make certain none of the Cayuse braves, who were butchering the pig he had given them as payment for their help around the mission, had wandered into the schoolroom. Anne was so beautiful. And with that mass of red curls...

Not that he ever saw them.

He scowled, swiped the rag around the inside edge of the wheel's hub to remove the mud from the riverbank, jammed his fingers into the pail, then smeared the warm grease all over the inside of the hub. He *hated* that black thing she wore on her head. It made her look so wan and lifeless. Except for her eyes. She had incredible eyes— even when they were shadowed by sorrow and grief. Or darkened by anger. And when she looked up at him...

He frowned at the stirring in his gut, stepped to the wagon and smeared grease around the bare, back axle. He had no business thinking about Anne or his growing attraction to her. He'd best keep his emotions under control and his mind focused on the facts. He was a widower with a small, seriously ill daughter. Anne was a widow, still grieving for her husband and baby girl. She wanted no part of him or his child. She'd made that plain.

He wiped his hand on the rag, grasped the wheel and rolled it over to the wagon. One strong heave had it up and wobbling on the end of the axle.

Rain poured down, blew in under the back side of the roof, dampened the pants stretched over his calves. He drove the linchpin into place with three hard, quick blows of the mallet.

Lightning snapped, sizzled to the earth. Thunder crashed with a force that made his chest vibrate. He jerked his head up, looked toward the window in his daughter's bedroom. That would have frightened her. She was afraid of loud thunder. He tossed the mallet into the wagon, ducked his head and raced through the rain toward the mission house.

Anne flinched at the crack of thunder, slid the oil lamp closer to her slate and chalked, a rather sad, but she hoped distinguishable, buffalo. "Who can tell me what this is?"

Iva and Kitturah raised their hands, looked at her with expectancy brightening their blue eyes. Running Wolf snuck a peek at her drawing, then sat like a statue, his gaze fastened on his own blank slate. "Running Wolf—" she held the slate in front of him, tapped it with her finger "—what is this?"

The boy looked at the drawing. *"Qoq'á lx."*

She tapped her slate again. *"Buffalo.* In the white man's language it is a buffalo." She pointed to her mouth, *"buff-a-lo"* then pointed to him. Waited.

"Buff-a-lo."

"Yes. Very good, Running Wolf." She nodded, smiled. He looked away, but not before she had caught the gleam of pleasure in his eye at the approval.

She lifted her chalk, drew *B b* on her slate. "This is the *letter B.* Repeat the letter's name as I point to you please." She pointed to Iva, then Kitturah, received their answers, and pointed to Running Wolf. He gave the girls a sidelong look, glanced at the slate and then looked up at her and answered. She nodded and smiled.

"Very good, everyone. Now listen carefully." She pointed to the letters. "*B* says *bu*—" she pointed to her drawing "—as in *bu*ffalo. Repeat that please." The girls chorused the answer. She looked at Running Wolf. He answered. She nodded, smiled at them all and had them repeat it in unison a few more times. "Now all of you draw a buffalo on your slate."

She put her slate down on the bench desk where they could all see it, pointed to her drawing, then tapped Running Wolf's slate. He caught her meaning and began to draw.

Rain pounded on the roof. Lightning flashed outside the small window, thunder crashed and rumbled. Anne moved to the hearth, checked her bread dough then turned and studied the children's bowed heads. School was going well, better than she had expected. Running Wolf was a very intelligent young boy and was becoming less surly in his attitude as the days progressed. Iva was quick and helpful. And Kitturah... She glanced at the youngest child, at her small hand holding the chalk, and turned away. It was better to think of the children as students, not as individuals. Her heart would be safer that way.

The patter of the rain outside blended with the murmur and crackle of the fire and the scratch of Mitchel's pen as he worked on the mission's record book.

Anne tilted the fabric toward the light from the oil lamp on the chest and took another stitch along the fold that formed the hemmed edge of one of the apron's ties. Only a few stitches to go and she would be finished with this one.

Her temple twitched. She laid the needle on the fabric, slipped a fingertip beneath the edge of her turban bonnet and scratched at the spot, frowned and removed the hat. Wearing it all day made her skin itch. She rubbed at the curls flattened against her temples and the nape of her neck, then picked up the needle and took another stitch.

A burned log on the hearth collapsed with a hiss. The log atop it fell onto the hot coals, flamed up, then died down to a steady burn. She rested her hands on her lap, stared at the pulsating coals and dancing flames. Did Iva and Kitturah's mother have a fire? Or was it damp and chilly in their tent?

"A fire is a comforting thing on a night like this."

She jumped, lifted her head. Mitchel was standing at the end of the settee.

"Sorry, Anne. I didn't mean to startle you."

"Not at all. I was simply lost in thought." She bent her head, took up her sewing. "I was wondering if a tepee was warm on a cold, damp night like this."

"They keep a fire going in the center and put their pallets around it. But I imagine it gets cold around the outside."

She nodded, looked up as he added wood to the fire. He straightened, turned his right hand toward the firelight and dug at the pad at the base of his finger with the thumbnail of his left hand, winced. "Have you injured yourself?"

He glanced her way, shook his head. "I picked up a sliver when I was working on the wagon wheel, and it's in a most inconvenient spot. Every time I curl my fingers it jags me." He went back to digging at his hand.

"Mother used to take slivers out of William's hands with a needle." She knotted her thread, snipped it off and held her needle out to him.

"A splendid idea. Thank you." He moved the chair closer to the light, sat and took the needle, poked at his right hand.

She watched his clumsy attempts at removal as long as she could stand it. "I could try to remove it, if you would like."

He looked up. "Thank you. That would be very helpful. It's awkward using my left hand." He handed her the needle, held his right hand out, palm up.

She scooted forward on the settee until their knees almost touched, braced her elbow on her lap and wrapped her fingers around his, knowing immediately she had erred. Her hand trembled.

He looked up, a question in his eyes.

She forced a polite smile. "I hope I don't hurt you."

"Not with that needle."

She nodded, pulled his hand into position and bent her head over it, pushed away a strong impression that was not what he wanted to say. She focused on removing the sliver, tried to ignore the firm calloused fingers folded ever so slightly over the tips of hers, the warmth uncoiling deep inside her. She broke through the calloused skin, exposed the tip of the splinter. Two more gentle probes and the tiny sliver of wood was out.

He flexed his fingers, looked into her eyes, his face so close she could see gold specks in his. "You got it."

"Yes." The word rode the last bit of air out of her lungs. She slipped the tips of her fingers from beneath his, rose and gathered her sewing, snatched up her turban bonnet and fled the room.

Chapter Eleven

Perhaps she was wrong. Anne gathered the children's slates, carried them to her table and wiped them clean. Perhaps it was best that she return to the emigrant town. All day she'd fought the memory of Mitchel's fingers curled atop hers, the increased pressure when she'd looked up and their gazes met. She couldn't block it out—not even when she was teaching. But it was the tentative stirring in her heart at his touch, like a bud about to open, that disturbed her.

She frowned, stacked the slates, swirled her cloak around her shoulders and slipped her wrist through the drawstrings of the small bag she had made from the left-over pieces of fabric from the apron. It was only that she allowed no one to touch her since that day. Yes. That was it. She would feel the same no matter who touched her.

She slipped the small loop of roping over the wool-covered button at the neck of the cloak and reaching for the next, glanced at the hearth. The fire was only a pile of coals. It was safe to leave it. She paused with her fingers on the next button, and stared at the winking coals. When she came in tomorrow morning a fresh fire would be laid. Mitchel had one waiting for her every morning. All she need do was touch a burning candle to the tinder. He was very thoughtful of her comfort.

She stiffened, finished buttoning her cloak. That was pure foolishness. Mitchel was simply taking care of the children. The same way he cared for his daughter. And that was how she wanted it. She desired no obligation or friendship between them. She refused to allow that. She was *not* going to be hurt again.

She pulled the hood up over her turban bonnet and strode to the door, threw back the bar-lock and stepped out into the damp, chilly air. The wind whistled around the corner of the lean-to, plucked at her cloak and the hems of her skirts. At least it wasn't raining...for the moment. She shivered, held on to the hood and tipped her head back to look up at the sky. The gloomy, gray expanse full of dark clouds wasn't hopeful. Perhaps Sunday would dawn with a clear sky.

A hammer clanged against iron. Mitchel was working at the blacksmith shop. A stroke of good fortune. She ducked her head against the wind and hurried down the path and looked around the corner. No Indians. The hammer clanged again. She straightened, adjusted her hood, crowded close to the protection of the mission building, then braved the wind and angled across the path toward the smithy.

"Mitchel."

He turned, looked down at her. Something flashed in his eyes. Something reminiscent of the tiny, flickering flames consuming the coals she'd left burning on the hearth. She lost her breath and voice.

He turned away, tossed the mallet he was holding into the back of the wagon, snatched a dirty rag off the tailboard and wiped at the black, greasy smudges on his hands. "Did you need something, Anne?"

She looked away from the ripple of muscles beneath the shirt stretched taut across his shoulders. "I'm going to begin teaching numbers on Monday, and I plan to use some small stones. I did not want to roam about looking for them without your knowledge."

He turned back, his expression polite, concerned. "There's no need to roam. You'll find all the stones you want along the riverbank."

She nodded, looked at the wagon. A thick length of log propped beneath a front corner held it upright. The missing wheel leaned against the side. Her heart gave a hopeful little skip. Perhaps they wouldn't be able to leave. "Is there something wrong with the wheel?"

"The iron rim was loose because the wood was dried out. I've been soaking them in the river overnight." He reached out and touched the rim. "This is the last one. When I put it back on, the wagon is ready to go. Except for the packing. That has to wait until the day we leave, lest the Indians discover our preparations and we have nothing left."

An image of the wagon as it had been packed on the journey across the country from Missouri flashed into her head. This time there would be a sling bed cradling an ill toddler. How would she bear it? She took a breath, lifted the drawstring bag. "I'd best go collect the stones. I have a meal to prepare."

"Anne."

She looked up, wished she hadn't.

"I don't believe there are any unfriendly Indians around, but stay close. I don't want you out of my sight."

She nodded, stepped out from under the sheltering roof and hurried toward the river, knowing he was watching her, and helpless to stop the safe, protected feeling stealing through her.

"Thou shalt not steal. Thou shalt not kill." Mitchel scanned the faces of the braves sitting cross-legged on the floor, staring up at him. Most worked at the mission and were here because he required their attendance at his Sunday meetings. Chief White Cloud, Strong Heart and Red Squirrel had accepted the Christian faith and came every Sunday to learn more of their new God. There were a few he had never seen before, but from their expressions, it was likely they had come because they had heard about the meal he provided after he'd shared his message. "These are the words of God."

"White man's god, squaw god. He afraid to fight."

There was a chorus of affirmative grunts. Even the Indians who worked at the mission had joined in. Mitchel shook his head, looked down at the Cayuse brave who had spoken, chose his words of translation carefully, so as not to give offense. "Your heart is good. But your words, for lack of knowledge, are false. I do not speak of a 'White man's god.' I speak of a God who is Father to all men—white or red. A *powerful* God, strong and *mighty* in battle. But His ways are ways of peace. As are the ways of His children when He lives in their hearts."

The brave jabbed a hand toward him, his pointing finger accusing, his black eyes glittering. "If your words true, why you have knife and tomahawk? Knife and tomahawk no for peace. Knife kill. Tomahawk kill. My ears hear you no have knife and tomahawk. You put him far away."

So he would be defenseless? The thought drew him up

taut. He glanced toward White Cloud. The old chief sat huddled in his blanket, his gaze fixed straight ahead on the brave who had spoken. Something about the elderly Indian sent a prickle crawling over his flesh, raised the hair at the nape of his neck. *Lord, give me wisdom...*

He shifted his gaze back to the belligerent brave and shook his head. "It is not the knife or tomahawk that kills. It is what is in the *heart* of the man who wields the knife or tomahawk that kills." He slowly moved his hand to his belt, drew his knife and laid the blade flat against his other palm, held it out in front of him for all gathered to see. "My knife can slice rope or leather. It can butcher an animal and cut a fish—or I can use it to defend myself and my family. These are things of peace."

"You fight, you kill. No peace. Your god angry. You bury knife and tomahawk."

Another request for him to remove his weapons. His sense of danger strengthened. He shook his head. "No. My weapons stay at my side." He sheathed his knife, swept his gaze over all the braves. "The Almighty God of whom I speak has eyes that see into a man's heart." The Indians stared up at him, uttered sounds of amazement. His heart thudded. They were *listening.* He pressed his point. "If I am attacked, it is not in *my* heart to kill. To *kill* is in the heart of the one who attacks me. The Almighty God, my Father, sees this and He makes me strong to protect myself and my family. His ways are of peace, but if His children's hearts are good, and they are attacked by men with bad hearts, He makes them powerful warriors."

"I would hear of such a warrior."

Grunts of agreement came from every direction.

He glanced at Chief White Cloud, noted the warning in his eyes and nodded. "Many years ago, in a land far across the big water, there was a brave called David, who was small, not yet grown into a man." He held his hand level with his shoulder, received nods of understanding. "A tribe of giants—braves of great size—" he stretched his arm above his head and went on tiptoe to reach as high as possible "— came to make war on David's people."

There were scowls, mutters. These braves understood war.

"One warrior of the giant tribe called Goliath, bigger than all the rest, challenged any of the warriors of David's tribe to meet him in a battle. If the giant lost, his tribe would leave David's tribe in peace."

Feathers bobbed as the assembled braves nodded. They swelled their chests, clenched their hands on their knees to show they would accept such a challenge.

"The warriors of David's tribe were afraid. They turned their backs to the challenge."

Whoops of derision and scorn burst from the braves.

He held up his hand, spoke into the resulting quiet. "But David knew the Almighty God, His Father, lived in his heart and would make him strong and brave! He had no spear, no shield. He picked up a stone, put it in a sling—" He mimed the action so they would understand a sling.

The braves tensed, waited, their black eyes glistening with excitement.

He looked at the warrior who had challenged him to put down his weapons. "The giant cursed David from his bad heart, raised his shield and spear to kill him. But David called on Almighty God and threw his stone." He hit his forehead with his fisted hand. "Almighty God made David so strong the stone sunk in Goliath's head. The giant fell dead. David's tribe was safe."

"Whaah!" The sound of amazement echoed around the semicircle. Excited chatter broke out among the braves. The one who had challenged him scowled, rose and stalked from the Indian room, two others with him. The smell of beef roasting over an open fire flowed in the opened door. The rest of the braves rose and filed outside, eager to get their free meal.

The tension drained from him. He had averted the danger this time, but when would the threat of attack rear again? He had to get Anne to the emigrant village, for all their sakes.

"David strong warrior...brave heart."

Mitchel turned. Chief White Cloud had crowded close to the hearth, warming his old bones by the fire as was his wont when the weather grew cold. "Yes. But it is God Almighty who gave him courage and made him strong."

The old chief nodded, pulled the blanket he clutched closer around his bony shoulders. "That good. Maybe so Almighty God do samelike with you." His keen gaze sharpened. He stared toward the open door, squatted, picked up two small pieces of wood and drummed on the firebox. "You know two trapper come all time to mission?"

Mitchel frowned, tried to follow the old Indian's thoughts. "Bonner and Turner? Yes. I remember."

"Last time come, you sell horse. They go away."

"Yes. Bonner's horse broke a leg in the hills and they had to shoot it."

White Cloud shook his head. "They lie from their bad hearts. They no trap animals. They kill my people, steal furs." He looked up, fastened a stern gaze on him. "Halstrum hide furs in house that growls like angry bear."

Mitchel stared at the old Indian, speechless with shock. He'd never known White Cloud to lie—color the truth and exaggerate, yes—but not lie. So this wasn't only about Anne. He sucked in air against the sudden, sick feeling in his gut and squatted on his heels facing the chief. "I'm sorry your people were killed, White Cloud. But I've never seen any furs. Are you certain Halstrum had a hand in this? Are you sure he hid furs Bonner and Turner had stolen from your people in the gristmill?"

The chief nodded, drummed out a staccato beat. "Horse no break leg. Fast Like Wind shoot with arrow. Trapper kill Fast Like Wind, run to mission. Halstrum hide fur. Trapper buy horse, go fast to fort, take boat to town by big water so my people no kill."

The sick feeling in his gut worsened. He rose, motioned to White Cloud. "Come with me to the mill. If Halstrum hid the furs we'll find them and you can take them back to your people."

The chief pinned another keen glance on him. "You sit. Furs not in house that growls."

He stared at the Indian, his thoughts tumbling, landing where he did not want them to go. He had to ask, but he was afraid he already knew the answer. "Where are they?"

"Halstrum take in wagon to fort. Wagon go on boat to town by big water. My people see. Little Elk follow. My people wait." The old chief's eyes glittered up at him. "Trapper come back, hide in hills. Him wait for my people to catch much furs. My people watch trapper. Watch Halstrum come back. Watch you."

The drumming took on a beat that raised the hair on the back of his neck. "I didn't know about Halstrum and the furs, White Cloud."

The chief looked up and met his gaze, nodded. "All same, Eagle Claw and Limping Bear—he who speak sharp words about your God—have much anger. Him heart is bad toward you. Fast Like Wind him brother. I talk truth, tell Eagle Claw and Limping Bear you have good heart toward my people. They no hear. They tell my people you have bad heart. You make wagon fix. You take furs and run to town by big water likesame Halstrum."

His stomach roiled. It made horrible sense in a twisted way. He fixed a stern look on the chief. "Those are false words from a bad heart, White Cloud. I would not steal from your people. My God says it is bad to steal. He would be angry with me."

The chief grunted, continued drumming.

He pressed his case. "My heart is good toward your people. I feed all who come. None leave my mission with hunger in their bellies. I give your people meat when the days are short and the mountain snows deep and the hunting bad. I teach them to know the white man's ways. I teach them to know Almighty God. My words are straight. Hear my words now."

The chief glanced up.

Please, Lord, let him believe me. "Eagle Claw and Limping Bear spoke truth about the wagon. I have fixed it. But the rest of their words are false words from their bad hearts. White Cloud knows my daughter lies in bed with sickness upon her."

The chief's gaze sharpened, the drumming stopped.

"There is a doctor...a healer...at the new town. Rain

and cold are bad for my daughter's sickness. I need the wagon to keep the rain and cold from my sick daughter when I take her to the doctor. That is why I fixed the wagon. That is why I asked Spotted Owl to tell me where the village sits. My words are true."

White Cloud stared down at the hearth. The fire whispered and crackled in the silence. Mitchel sat back on his heels and waited.

The chief tossed the pieces of wood into the fire and lifted his head. "You open ears, hear my words. You no go in wagon. My people say you have bad heart, attack wagon. You wait Halstrum come, make wagon safe." He pulled his blanket about his shoulders and rose.

Mitchel surged to his feet, extended his hand. "Thank you for the warning, White Cloud. My ears have heard your words. It is good to know your heart is still good toward me, my friend. My heart is good toward you and your people always."

The old chief dipped his head, pulled his arm back under the blanket and walked to the door, looked back. "Eagle Claw and Limping Bear seek blood. You watch good. Keep knife and tomahawk sharp. You no David. Stone no good."

Boot heels thudded against the floor. Anne placed the cover over the bowl of bread dough she had placed in the basket to set for tomorrow and lifted her head. Her heart lurched. Mitchel was striding toward her, a pistol and a lantern in his hands. She looked at his set face and stepped around the work table to meet him. "What is it, Mitchel? What's wrong?"

"I've decided it would be best if you were able to protect yourself in case I'm…not around." The muscle along his jaw twitched. "Get your cloak and join me out back, Anne. I'm going to teach you to shoot." He pivoted toward the back door.

"Wait!" She grabbed hold of his arm.

He looked down at her hand, turned and looked into her eyes.

She caught her breath, brought her hand back to press at the base of her throat. "I—" It was only a whisper. She tried again. "I know how to shoot, Mitchel." She got control of herself, lowered her hand to touch the Colt Paterson revolver he was holding. "William had pistols like this one. He taught both Emma and me to shoot with them. It turns out we were both quite good at it."

"Aiming and hitting a target is one thing..." That muscle along his jaw twitched again. "Could you shoot an Indian?"

Tension radiated off him. She lifted her gaze to his face, found it ensnared by the look in his eyes. Her stomach knotted. "Are we talking about Eagle Claw?"

His eyes darkened. He gave a curt nod. "And his brother. Perhaps a few others."

"Oh, Mitchel..." She swallowed against a sudden surge of bile pressing at her throat, clenched her hands, lifted her chin. "Yes. I could shoot Eagle Claw to protect myself or...or someone I— Someone in danger." *His daughter!* She swallowed hard again. "I'm so sorry I have brought this trouble on you, Mitchel. But it will stop if I leave. I'll go at dawn tomorrow."

She pressed her hands to her temples, her thoughts racing. "If you will loan me a horse, I will pay Spotted Owl to take me to the emigrant village." She shot a look at him. He seemed about to explode. "I'm an excellent rider, and Spotted Owl will bring the horse back to you." She looked away. "You are welcome to the things I brought in the wagon in exchange for the loan of the horse. Emma has all I will need…"

"That's enough!"

She glanced at him, took a step back. She'd never seen anyone look so angry.

He stepped close, locked his gaze on hers. "I have never heard anything so *foolhardy*. Your skill as a rider will be of no avail when you know nothing of the country or of Indian ways. You will remain here until Halstrum returns and I take you to the village."

"No, Mitchel. Think of your daughter. Of what would happen to—"

Pain flashed in his eyes. "I *am* thinking of Hope. I'm thinking of us all." He set the lantern and pistol on the work table, walked over and barred the kitchen door. "Should we be attacked here, or on the trail, I will welcome your shooting skill. It might make all the difference."

He came back, held out the pistol. "Keep this with you at all times, even in the schoolroom—*especially* in the schoolroom. And here in the kitchen where the door is never barred."

She thought of him out in the fields, or in one of the outbuildings and the bile pushed at her throat again. "You will need the pistol."

"I have one." He thrust the Colt Paterson toward her. "This one belonged to Paul. Do you know how to load it?"

She nodded, willed her hand not to tremble as she took the pistol.

"Anne."

His voice had gentled. She looked up, sucked in her breath at the pain, the sadness in his eyes.

"The danger is not because of you. I found out this evening it has to do with Halstrum. I did not know, but it is I that have placed you in danger by allowing you to stay here at the mission. All I can do now is try my best to keep you safe until Halstrum comes back and things are...resolved... We would be in great danger if we left before then. So no more talk of leaving...please."

Her heart ached to help him, to take the fear and sadness for his daughter from his eyes. She curled her fingers around the cold, hard steel of the weapon and nodded. "I'll stay."

Chapter Twelve

Mitchel filled the second bucket with the dying plants and vegetables, straightened and rotated his shoulders while he gave a casual glance around.

Movement caught his eye. He tensed, looked toward the trees on the wooded trail that led to the hills. Joe Means's squaw and children walked from the shadowed area into the open, their arms loaded with branches, more than was needed for the night. They moved to their tepee, dumped their loads onto a pile of branches large enough to supply firewood for several days and headed back to the woods.

He frowned, glanced up at the sky. Dusk was falling, but the sky was clear. There was no sign of a storm in the offing. Still, Indians had an uncanny way of knowing when the weather was going to take a turn for the worse. He eyed the dwindling stack of firewood beside the kitchen door. Spotted Owl must have gone off fishing again. He'd bring more wood from the large pile behind the smithy tomorrow. It would give him an excuse to stay close to the mission house and schoolroom.

He did another quick scan of the area, picked up both

buckets and hurried toward the pig sty. The braves who normally helped him had gone off somewhere, and he needed to be done with the chores and in the house before night fell. He would be at a serious disadvantage in the dark should Eagle Claw or Limping Bear strike. He was no woodsman, and Indians could move as silently as shadows.

The porkers snorted and came running, milled about, bumped against the fence. He dumped the buckets, slapped the ham of a large sow trying to crowd the other sows from the feed, grabbed the hind legs of a piglet and pulled the squirming, squealing creature out of the water trough. It burrowed between the legs of a full grown sow and, small hooves digging at the mud, shoved its way into the center of the pile of plants and vegetables.

He picked up the buckets, walked to the river and dipped them in the water, set them on the bank and swiped his wet hands on his pants. He took another casual look around, skimmed his gaze over Halstrum's cabin and the idle gristmill.

Adam Halstrum…a *thief.*

The thought sickened him. He didn't want to face it. Didn't want to believe he had brought a wolf among the sheep he'd come to tend. But Chief White Cloud's words made sense of things he'd noticed and pushed aside as not worth troubling about. Things like the way Bonner and Turner suddenly showed up at the mission when he'd never seen them on the trail, and always at night. He'd simply assumed it was natural for men who trapped animals in the wilds to travel at night. Now he knew it was because the sins of men like darkness. But they never had furs with them. So how—

He turned, stared at the idle mill wheel, suddenly, acutely aware of the gurgle and slap of water against the wheel paddle that was half buried in the river that powered the mill. A river that drained the surrounding mountains. He lifted his gaze, followed the meandering course of the tree-lined banks to the hills beyond. The winding river provided a perfect, hidden back door approach to the gristmill—to Halstrum, who would have hidden the furs while the trappers came on to the mission house. No wonder he'd never seen Bonner and Turner coming. But the Cayuse had. And they believed he had a part in it all.

A chill chased through him. He stooped, grabbed hold of the bails on the buckets and carried the water back to the sty. Halstrum knew the Cayuse and their ways. He knew that if the Indians discovered their furs were being hidden at the mission, they would seek revenge. And he, unarmed, and innocent of any knowledge of the lost Indian lives and the stolen furs, would be unprepared to defend himself or Hope.

Anger flared, burned like a hot coal in the pit of his stomach. The man had driven off with his sons and his ill-gotten gain in the wagon without a thought for the fate of a helpless, sick two-year-old. And Halstrum knew the Cayuse's vengeful, warring ways. He *knew*.

The muscles along his jaw twitched. He dumped the water into the trough, hung the buckets on a fence post and headed back to the mission house, the grunts, snorts and squeals of the feeding pigs fading with every long, muscular stride. Adam Halstrum had a lot to answer for. And he would…if he lived to reach the mission.

If.

The full weight of the precarious position he was

in hit him, froze his feet to the ground. Fear uncoiled, turned the burning coals in his stomach to ice. Did Halstrum plan to return? Or was leaving him here to suffer the Indians' revenge part of the scheme?

No. That didn't figure. He took a breath, hurried on toward the house. White Cloud said the trappers had already returned. That they were hiding in the hills waiting for the Indians to begin their winter trapping. They didn't know the Cayuse were watching them. And neither did Halstrum. He would be back. His *greed* would bring him back. And then the Cayuse would kill him. And Bonner and Turner. But would that be enough to quell their anger, to slake their bloody thirst for revenge? Could Chief White Cloud hold the Cayuse warriors in check once they had been loosed on the war trail? Or would they come after him, also?

He opened the door, stepped inside. The warmth of the fire, the faint odor of dinner cooking greeted him. His heart ached, his breath caught. It was all so peaceful…so like a home. And it was all a lie. They were surrounded by danger. *Almighty God, be with us I pray. Give me wisdom to know what to do to save Hope and Anne, and the strength to do what is needed. Save us, Almighty God! I ask it in the name of Your Son. Amen.*

He took a deep breath, pasted a cheerful smile on his face and went to check on his daughter.

"So Chief White Cloud told you that Eagle Claw and Limping Bear want to…to *kill* you because they do not believe you are innocent of the fur theft that resulted in their brother's murder?"

"Yes." Mitchel looked down at Anne, so lovely and elegant, even with shock that approached horror filling her eyes, and a thought struck him so hard it took his breath. The consuming anger he'd been fighting to control flared. "I never should have told Eagle Claw you were my woman."

She gave a small, trembling wave of her hand. "You thought you were protecting me, Mitchel. And I'm sure if Eagle Claw and his brother lead the Cayuse warriors in a revenge attack on the mission, nothing will keep me safe." She rose from the settee and stepped to the hearth. "Certainly, hiding my red hair will not help. I no longer need this." She removed her turban bonnet, tossed it into the fire and turned back to face him. "I learned one very important thing from watching our wagon master as we came west to Oregon country, Mitchel. Mr. Thatcher anticipated…problems, and was always prepared. Have you a plan?"

He lifted his gaze from the burning bonnet and studied her. Anne Simms was a courageous woman. The shock was still in her eyes, her voice quavered, but there was determination in her squared shoulders, the tilt of her chin. Burning her bonnet had been *defiance*. Perhaps a denial of her fear. "Yes. But I shall need your help."

She gave a small nod.

His stomach knotted. *Lord, help me. Lead me in the way that I should go. Don't let me err, Lord.* "Chief White Cloud warned me not to use the wagon until Halstrum returns because the Cayuse would misunderstand my purpose and attack."

Her gaze locked on his, demanded truth. "And do you believe Mr. Halstrum will return?"

He nodded. "Adam does not know the Cayuse are aware of his complicity in the fur thefts. As long as he thinks it is safe, I believe his greed will bring him back."

He took a breath. For her safety, she had to know all of it. "What I don't know is if the Cayuse will spare any of us when they come after Halstrum."

She stared at him, the fear in her eyes growing. "Your child—" Her voice broke. She raised her hand to the base of her neck, rubbed at her chest, drew a breath.

He noted her pallor, the tremor in her hands, and hated himself for adding to her distress. But he had to... for Hope. "Yes. I need you to help me with Hope."

Her eyes closed. He thought she was going to collapse. He took a step toward her, stopped when she opened her eyes and looked at him. "What must I do?"

"I don't know what will happen, Anne. But I want us to be prepared to leave at any moment if I sense there is a greater danger in staying. If the Cayuse attack, they will likely strike Halstrum's cabin and the gristmill first. That will give us a few minutes to escape. We'll not be able to use the wagon or horses. They leave too plain a trail. So, as we will be walking, we must pack very light, take only the barest necessities."

"The ointment..."

"Yes." His throat closed. Rage shook him. He forced it down, concentrated on laying out his plan. "I have chosen a path through the hills to the emigrant village. It is a long way around, but I am hoping that will throw any warriors who may come searching for us off our trail. I'm hoping they will think we will head for Fort Walla Walla as it is closest to the mission."

He rubbed his right fist into his left palm, paced. "I asked Spotted Owl where the village was located, but that was a few days ago and I said nothing that would make it seem important. And Chief White Cloud knows I want to take Hope there to see your sister."

"Will he tell the warriors where to find us?"

Her voice sounded stronger. He glanced her way. Her color had improved. "I don't believe he will. But I am taking the circuitous path in case. Though it will mean we will be on the trail for five or six days." He sought her gaze, held it with his. "We must go on as usual here at the mission. It is important no one guess what we are planning. That's why I need you to hide what we pack for Hope in your room, along with what you are taking. Sighing Wind and Laughing Rain never go to your room. Will you come with me now, while Hope is sleeping, and get her things? She must not know, lest she mention it to Laughing Rain."

She took a breath, rubbed her palms on her skirt and nodded.

"We must be quick. Hope has a fever and is restless tonight." He led the way to his daughter's bedroom, his heart clutching at the sight of her sleeping face. "Her things are there, in the dresser. Top drawer. Choose what you deem best." He opened the chest beneath the window, pulled out a blanket.

"Mitchel…?"

He closed the chest at Anne's soft whisper, walked over to stand beside her.

She gestured toward the open drawer. "The child will need to be dressed for warmth. Where are her coat, bonnet and shoes? I find nothing here but nightgowns." The firelight played over her refined features, revealed the concern in her eyes.

He frowned. "That is all Hope has. And those too small. The husband of the woman at the fort who makes Hope's clothes has not brought her by in some time, and I've not been able to get away with Hope being so ill."

He lifted the blanket in his hands. "A nightgown will have to do. I'll wrap her in this blanket."

She stared up at him a moment, then nodded and turned back to the drawer. She selected a nightgown, turned to the nightstand and lifted the crock. "I have a smaller crock in my room. I'll put most of the ointment in it and bring this one back." She headed toward the door, turned back to look at him. "If you go to the kitchen and build a small fire, I'll bake some biscuits to take along." She whirled toward the door.

"A moment, Anne." He hurried into his room, opened his chest and pulled out two leather pokes, carried them back and held them out to her. "Cap and ball for the pistols. I have more."

She stared at them a long moment, then clasped the necks of the bags with her free hand and hurried from the room.

He turned back to tend the fire.

"Papa."

He jerked his gaze to Hope. Tears were pooling in her overbright blue eyes. Had she seen or heard—

"Me hurt, Papa."

"I know, Hope. I know." He rushed to her bed, scooped her up, blankets and all, and carried her to the rocker. He brushed the damp curls off her forehead and cuddled her as close as he dared, his heart seared with a pain that took his breath.

"Please, Almighty God. Please." All his pain and fear for his daughter rose in his prayer. He lowered his head against Hope's soft curls and rocked.

Anne scooped the face and hand balm into the slop bucket and carried the small crock back to her dresser.

The lilac scent clinging to her fingers brought memories soaring back. Anger shook her.

She jammed her trembling fingers into the ointment, scraped them off into the small crock and stabbed them into the ointment again. The astringent odor stung her nose, overpowered the mild, floral scent. Her eyes teared. She would *not* have another man and child ripped from her life. She would *not!* They were not hers. She had been very careful to keep her heart safe from them. But still… The child was little more than a baby. And she needed her father.

The anger welled to fury. She added enough ointment from her fingers to fill the small crock, scraped the rest off against the lip of the large one and replaced the covers.

Tears blurred her vision. She blinked, swiped her sleeve across her eyes and soaped up her hands. The ointment came off, even in cold water. She dried her hands, grabbed up the large crock and hurried downstairs and across the sitting room to the child's bedroom. "Mitchel…"

Silence greeted her whisper. She peered into the room. Firelight danced across the child's sleeping face, highlighted the fevered flush, touched the blond curls on the pillow with gold.

Pain streaked through her. She moved forward, compelled by a hunger stronger than the pain. She placed the crock on the nightstand, knelt by the bed and touched her trembling finger to Hope's soft cheek. The scab covering her heart split open, pain from its wound poured out through hot tears that flowed down her cheeks. Her body quivered. *Not again, God. Not again.*

She drew a long breath, wiped the tears from her face

and lifted the edge of the covers, looked at the small hand and exposed wrist, smoothed the covers back in place, rose and walked from the room.

Chapter Thirteen

"I put the ointment on the nightstand in your daughter's room."

Mitchel glanced over his shoulder. Anne was coming down the length of the kitchen toward him, her face set, resolve in her every step. Dim light from the lowered wick of the oil lamp he'd set on the heavy, wood table shone on her face, caught the flowing movement of the long skirt of her black gown setting it apart from the surrounding darkness. "Is she still resting quietly?"

"Yes."

Quiet, abrupt. "I don't want to talk about your daughter" clearly spoken without saying a word. He nodded, placed another small chunk of wood on the greedily feeding fire, brushed off his hands and rose. He understood her distress in being around Hope, but there was no other choice. He was trying to keep them all alive.

She ducked her head as she crossed in front of him, but not before he saw the flickering light of the fire glittering on the sheen of tears in her eyes. Resentment flashed at being forced to cause her pain.

"Do you think the Indians are watching?"

"From a distance, yes."

"Well, making biscuits should seem innocent enough to them, I suppose." She snatched the apron she'd made off a nail in the wall and tied it around her waist. He looked down, stretched and flexed his fingers. He could probably span her waist with his hands. The intense longing to do so jarred him.

"Thank you for starting the fire."

He looked up, watched her move about the room gathering various containers and carrying them to the long table. He listened to the soft fall of her steps, the whisper of the hem of her dress against the puncheon floorboards and anger constricted his chest. *Why did You allow her to come here, Lord? She belongs with her family back east, where she'd be safe.*

"It doesn't take long for biscuits to bake." She spooned ingredients into a large bowl, picked up a fork, looked at him. "When they are done, I shall snuff the lamp and then take them to my room while you bank the fire. Anyone watching will not be able to see, and Sighing Wind will be none the wiser when she comes in the morning."

She stopped stirring, dropped the fork she'd been using onto the table, pushed a curl off her forehead with the back of her hand. "I need milk."

"I'll get it." He walked into the buttery, waited for his eyes to adjust to the darkness, searched out the pail of milk. He turned toward the door, stopped. Faint as it was, the light coming in the door created shadows among the rough stone of the walls and gave form to the well in the center of the small room. He stared at the door. Only one man could come through it at a time. And two people, armed with Colt Paterson revolvers and crouched behind the well for protection, would have no trouble stopping them. For a time.

He glanced up at the iron hooks driven into the center beam, the coiled ropes that held hams and slabs of bacon and sides of beef, then back at the door. It could be tied shut. Not that it would keep determined attackers out forever, but it would make it more difficult for them to reach them. Give them time to get in position, to prepare...

His face drew taut. He didn't like the idea of being trapped inside, but if they couldn't sneak away, this would be the best place to make a stand. Stone didn't burn.

The knots that had taken up residence in his stomach twisted tighter. How had his life come to this?

"Mitchel? Did you find the milk?"

Anne's soft whisper made his heart squeeze. "Yes, coming." He took a stronger grip on the pail and carried it to the worktable. "Here you are."

"Thank you." She dipped a cup into the milk, poured it into the bowl and stirred with the fork. "Do you think she will be all right, Mitchel? I mean, if the Cayuse attack and we escape and make the journey to the emigrant village in this cold, rainy weather?"

Her words brought the constant, gnawing fear for his daughter surging to the fore. Her innocent life was threatened by so many things. He gripped the handle of the pail, lifted it down from the table. "I don't know, Anne. I pray—"

She jerked her head up, looked at him, her eyes dark in the reflected light on her face. "That doesn't work, Mitchel." She tossed flour onto the smooth, clean work surface and dumped the contents of the bowl onto it. "If God answered prayer, my baby would be alive."

There was so much pain in her voice. He forced aside his own fear, his own doubts about prayer and grabbed hold of his remaining faith. Without God, they did not stand a chance. He made his voice firm, confident. "God does answer prayer, Anne. Though not always as we want or expect Him to. The things men do have consequences and—"

"Consequences." She breathed the word, stopped kneading the biscuit dough and looked up at him, her eyes shadowed, her face tense. "Like an overturned carriage." She caught her breath, swallowed. "I don't understand why Phillip didn't stop, Mitchel. I begged him to slow down, to stop racing. But he only laughed and urged the horses on. And then our wheel hit a rut and the carriage rocked…"

She blinked, folded the dough toward her, placed the heels of her hands against the pile, pushed, folded, pushed. "There was a large stone at the side of the road. The carriage wheel climbed it and we overturned. I flew against the carriage lamp and Grace was torn from my arms. The rest you know."

He nodded, wished he could comfort her, take her pain. He watched her narrow hands patting out the dough into a large circle and ached to hold them, to let her know by his touch that he understood and he cared. "I'm sorry, Anne." Such inadequate words.

She gave a small nod. "Do you remember when you told me one of the most painful things you suffered at your wife's death was a sense of betrayal?"

"Yes."

She picked up the tin cup, pressed its rim into the

dough and twisted, paused. "I didn't know, until that moment, why I was so furious with Phillip. And I was ashamed of feeling anger for my beloved husband when he died. But I know now it was the betrayal. If he had only slowed the horses…" She lifted the cup, pressed it into the dough and twisted out another biscuit. "Phillip's love of racing took him from me. And it took my baby, also. He betrayed his vow to—"

The mass of russet curls at her crown quivered at the abrupt shake of her head. "But that is not important now. You have the danger at hand to think of. I only wanted to thank you, Mitchel, for helping me to understand. I may not have a chance…later." She looked up at him, curved her lips in a sad little smile and went back to cutting out biscuits.

He bent and picked up the pail to fill his hands so he wouldn't reach for her, wouldn't take her in his arms and hold her safe where nothing would hurt her again. He couldn't do that. No matter how he ached to protect her. There were too many obstacles, too many impossibilities—they faced grave danger, she still loved her husband, and she couldn't bring herself to speak his daughter's name. He carried the pail of milk to the buttery, set it inside and closed the door.

Anne hung the small nightgown and the blanket Mitchel had given her over the edge of the chest, filled a pillowcase with the rest of their supplies and carried it to the chair sitting close to the top of the stairs. The crock of ointment, the leather pokes of cap and ball for the pistol hit the chair seat with a dull thunk. She draped a petticoat over the pillowcase and strode to her bed.

Not again, God. Not again. The words echoed in her

head, replacing fear with determination. She yanked back her covers and sheet, grabbed the scissors from the sewing box she'd taken from the chest and cut along the edge of the India-rubber sack that had protected her mattress from any water that might flood into the wagon while fording rivers on the way across the country.

She cast a glance at the window, furious at the idea that there were Indian braves out there watching the mission. They could not see in the small upstairs window, but they could see her light, and Mitchel said they must go on as usual. She frowned, folded the large, flat piece of India-rubber sheeting she'd cut free, laid it on the stool beside the chimney and remade her bed. She could not cover the window, but she refused to snuff the lamp. How could she sew without light?

She bent to adjust the edge of the coverlet, stared at the dark area beneath the bed, straightened. If she cleaned off the washstand and pulled it a bit closer, sat the chair at the other end of the bed, at the same distance away, then stretched the coverlet between them and the bed…

Mitchel frowned, listened to the faint scuffing sound from overhead. What was Anne doing? He rose from the chair, put his cleaned and loaded rifle back on the hooks over the mantel. Paul's rifle hung above it, cleaned and ready to shoot. He stared up at them, clenched his hands and turned away, a stony weight in the pit of his stomach. He was preparing to fight the people he had come to minister to. But, for all the messages of Christ's love and Christian ways he'd shared with them, the Cayuse still followed their heathen path. And now some had turned on him. Treachery was a common practice among the tribes. It was disheartening, but not surprising they would believe it of him.

The scuffing sound came again, stopped. He tried to place it, failed. It was too soft for him to hear well. He stood listening for a moment, then picked up his gun-cleaning equipment, put it back in the chest and closed the lid. White Cloud had said the warriors were watching Bonner and Turner, waiting for Halstrum's return before they struck and captured the two thieves.

He sucked in air, fought back a surge of bile at the thought of what the trappers and Halstrum and his sons would suffer at the hands of the angry, vengeful Eagle Claw and his followers. He would wish that on no man. Not even one who had endangered all he held most dear. And Halstrum's sons… *The things men do have consequences.*

The bile surged again. He gripped the mantel, hung his head between his arms and breathed deep. There was nothing he could do. No way he could warn Halstrum about the trap. *He* and Hope and Anne were already ensnared. The Cayuse were out there, watching the mission, watching them. One false move and—

He jerked erect, thudded the heels of his hands against the log mantel. He looked at Hope, at her closed eyes with the light brown lashes that rested on her rosy, fevered cheeks, at her tiny, tip-tilted nose and her little mouth that looked always ready to smile, even in her pain, at her soft, blond curls lying against the pillow. Fear seized his throat. He clenched his hands, forced words through the constriction.

"Father God, I need *help.* You know my weapons and plans are pitiful against the horde of warriors that will descend on us. Hope is but a baby, and Anne innocent of any wrongdoing in these thefts. My guilt lies only in hiring Halstrum to work here at the mission. Spare us, Almighty God, I pray. But if my life must be forfeit, then I ask that You please save Hope and Anne."

Tears burned at the backs of his eyes, pain at thought of what would happen to his little, ill daughter without him to protect her or care for her seared his heart. "If it is Your will that I die, I beg You please…put it in Anne's heart to love and care for my daughter. I ask it in the name of Your beloved Son, Jesus. Amen."

It worked. The room was dark but for the splash of light on the floor beneath the coverlet. Anne crawled into her cramped work space, pushed the oil lamp over against the wall, then spread the blanket Mitchel had given her out on the floor and cut it in half crossways. She folded one half of the blanket and put it under the edge of the bed out of her way, measured the length of the small nightgown, added several inches and cut a circle to her measurement out of the other blanket half.

Tears stung her eyes. The last time she had made a cloak, it had been a little green velvet one with gold ribbon ties for Grace. She'd been wearing it the day she died.

Anne pressed her lips together, blinked to clear her vision, folded the blanket circle in two, then doubled it again and cut a tiny quarter circle out of the pointed end for a neck hole. She hadn't been able to save her baby, but she could see that Mitchel's child stayed warm and dry on their way to Emma. She laid the circle of wool blanket out on the floor, measured the neck hole and cut an adjoining slit so the child's head would fit through.

Ribbon ties attached to the hemmed edges would hold the slit together.

She jumped, looked toward the base of the chimney visible between the legs of the washstand. What was that thud? It didn't sound like Mitchel adding wood to the fire. It was too soft a sound for that. Perhaps it was something to do with his preparations for their departure or a possible Indian attack.

She lowered her hands to her lap, stared at the joining of the rough floorboards and the smooth chimney stones. Would she soon be dead at the hand of hostile Indians? How odd if it should happen now, when she was beginning to feel alive again, when she was beginning to believe her life might have a purpose after all.

A vision of Mitchel standing by the hearth, the firelight playing over his strong, handsome face, flashed before her. Her pulse quickened. Memory of the look in his eyes when he'd fastened his gaze on her brought heat rising to her cheeks. She'd wanted to go to him, to put her head on his shoulder and feel his strong arms holding her. A longing, no doubt brought forth because of her awareness of danger, of the knowledge of the possibility of imminent death. Mitchel was a strong, courageous man, resolute and unwavering in his determination to protect his daughter. Of course, his strength would draw her. He made their situation seem…manageable.

She frowned, went back to her sewing. She could do nothing about the Indians or their intent, her purpose was to care for Mitchel's child with whatever tools lay in her hands. And the first thing was to keep her warm and dry should they have to run for their lives.

She eyed one of the scrap pieces, picked it up and tugged at the cut edge. The tight weave held its shape, did not ravel. There would be no hemming needed. That would make the work go apace. She heaved a sigh of relief, cut out a piece to make a hood and pieces for loose-fitting trousers which she would sew closed at the bottom to protect the child's feet from the cold. But what of her little hands? Tears surged again. The child was so little and helpless. She wiped tears from her cheeks and cut a second cloak from the rubber sheeting. The blanket and sheeting pieces together would provide the child with a warm, rainproof cloak. She pulled the oil lamp close, threaded her needle and took long, running stitches around the outside edges, then sewed the top seam of the hood together.

The child cried, called for her papa.

Anne ignored the flash of pain, blocked the child's sweet face, the soft, smooth feel of her too-warm cheek from her mind and joined the hood to the neck hole in the cloak, easing in the fullness, and making the seam strong with small, neat stitches. Hope would not suffer from the weather—not if she could help it!

Chapter Fourteen

Wind gusted down the chimney, puffed smoke into the room.

Anne turned her head, coughed her lungs clear of the acrid smoke irritation and closed her eyes against the sting. Tears welled, momentarily easing the dry, burning discomfort that was the cost of her sewing projects. But the fruits of her labor were worth the loss of a night's sleep and tired eyes.

Everything was finished and stowed away in the pillowcase she'd lined with a leftover piece of the India-rubber sheeting. Everything but the small nightgown she had cut from her warmest cotton petticoat, and the pistol. That was in the large pocket she had sewn into the side seam of the skirt of her gown. The weight of it dragging at her waist band was quite uncomfortable— but comforting.

She shook her head at the incongruity of the thought, pulled the crane toward her and forked the large chunk of ham off the plate she held into the iron pot. She added the wedges of onion, blinked her eyes clear of a second spate of tears and ladled in enough water to cover the meat. A small push of the crane and the pot hung over the fire.

Everything must be as usual. Yet, nothing was.

She stepped back to the heavy, wood table, ladled water over the dried green beans she had waiting in a bowl and began cleaning the carrots. The door opened, cold air rushed in. She tensed, lowered her hand to her side and raised her head. A shiver passed through her. She released her hold on the pistol. "Good morning, Sighing Wind."

The plump Indian woman grunted, put her backside against the door and pushed it wide, stepped inside, a milk pail in one hand and a basket of eggs in the other. A quick bump with her round hip slammed the door closed. "Rain she go. Snow she come, maybe so." The fringe at the bottom of Sighing Wind's long, buckskin tunic swayed as she scuffed her way to the table, plunked down the pail and the basket of eggs, then shoved the rocker closer to the fire and sat.

Anne glanced at the eggs, at the bits of nesting material clinging to them. At least it was too cold for flies. She moved them away from her soaking beans, picked up a knife and cut the cleaned carrots into large chunks and piled them on the plate. She carried them to the hearth, added them to the ham and onions to simmer while she was teaching. Would they eat this meal? Or would they be running toward Emma and the emigrant town? Or would they be—

No. *Not again, God. Not again.*

She put the lid on the iron pot, carried the pail of milk and the basket of eggs into the buttery. There would be cream enough to make butter now. Would they even need butter? No matter. Everything must go on as usual.

She closed the buttery door, removed her apron and hung it on the nail on the wall. The weight of the revolver pressed against her thigh, reminded her of their danger. Mitchel was at work outside. Was he safe?

She thrust the thought away, pushed the hair combs deeper into the pile of curls on her head and looked toward the hearth. *Sighing Wind*. The name put her in mind of slender tall grasses and supple tree tops swaying gracefully in a breeze. An odd fit for the solid, stoic Indian woman in the rocker. Did she know about the furs Mitchel's helper had stolen?

She took a deep breath. "Sighing Wind, I have to go to the schoolroom. I would like you to please wash the table. And when the cream has risen to the top of today's milk, add it to the cream already saved in the crock, and churn butter."

A grunt was her answer. She smoothed her hands over the front of her skirt and walked to the dining room, the pistol bumping against her leg with every other step. She continued on across the small room to the parlor, headed for the back door at the foot of the stairs, stopped and looked over her shoulder. The bedroom door at the other end of the parlor was open. She clenched her hands, looked back at the door and willed her feet to move, but they stayed stubbornly in place.

She gave in to the need to see the child safe in her bed, turned and walked the length of the room, pressed close to the wall and peered around the door frame into the bedroom.

Laughing Rain was adding wood to the fire. The child was propped against her pillows, holding a doll made of sticks in her hand, the red flannel wrappings on her wrists visible beneath the too-short sleeves of a cotton nightgown. The child was so small, so ill.

Tears surged, clogged her throat. She blinked her eyes, covered her mouth with her hand and ran on tiptoe back to the door, snatched her cloak off the peg on the wall and rushed outside. She would help the child in every way possible, but she would not risk her heart.

The rain had stopped. But the damp, chill air of the past few days had taken on a new bite. Mitchel frowned, looked toward the low hills. He should ride out and check on his cows, but it was too far. He couldn't bring himself to leave the area around the mission house.

He turned back to the pile of firewood, set a length of log on end, took a firm hold on his axe and swung from the shoulder. The sharp steel bit into the log, split it dead center. He set up the halves, split them and threw the chunks into the wagon.

It wasn't as if he didn't have enough work to do around the place. Spotted Owl and all the other Cayuse braves who helped him around the mission had disappeared. They'd simply wandered off, one by one. Not an unusual thing in itself. The Indian lifestyle was not given to disciplined schedules. The braves worked when they wanted, and when they tired of whatever job they were doing they simply threw down the tools and went hunting, fishing or raiding. But they had never before gone all at once. His uneasiness grew. He didn't like it.

He split a few more lengths of wood, tossed the pieces on the wagon to top off the load and walked to the head of the horse standing quietly between the traces. "Come on, girl." He took hold of the reins and walked her out onto the path that led to the rear of the mission house.

Hoofbeats thundered against the ground. He looked to the trail that led by the mission, tensed. Four—no five—Cayuse warriors were approaching, the two in the rear each leading a string of horses. A raiding party then. Hopefully their success would have them in good humor.

He stopped the horse with the wagon barring the path, checked to make sure his knife would easily slip free of its sheath and stood waiting. The mare tossed her head, snorted as the Indians came close. He reached up and stroked her neck. "Whoa, girl. It's all right. Everything is all right." *Grant that it may be so, Lord. Be with me.*

"Why you do squaw work, Mission Man?"

Mitchel ignored the sneer of the leader, the laughter of the other warriors. "A white man's squaw does not gather wood. A white man cuts wood with his sharp axe to keep his family warm when the air bites and snow hides the ground."

"Whah! Squaw hunt meat? Raid village get horse you ride?"

The warriors glanced at each other, laughed at their leader's mockery of the Mission Man.

Mitchel shook his head. "No. I raise my meat, and buy my horses. I do not steal. It is bad in the eyes of my God."

The warrior's gaze sharpened. "You no talk about your God. You no tell bad to steal. Our bellies hungry. You give meat." He raised his hand, pointed an imperious finger at the sows in the round corral attached to the sty.

He met the warrior's angry gaze fully, nodded. "I am happy to share with my Cayuse brothers the meat my God puts in my hand. No warrior leaves my mission with his belly empty."

The warriors slid from their horses, ran for the corral and leaped the fence. The sows ran around the enclosure, snorting and grunting, spun, with teeth bared, and charged the whooping braves chasing them. Piglets squealed and squirmed out of their captor's hands, raced in and out between the warriors' moccasin-clad feet, tripping them and sending them headlong into the churned up mud to the hooting delight of their friends.

It was bedlam. And a blessing. Mitchel grabbed a bucket, ran and scooped it full of dried bark and wood chips, rushed into the smithy and grabbed a small, iron pot of hot coals and hurried toward the corral. The bark caught fire immediately, the chips smoldered, then burst into flames. He ran to the wagon, grabbed an armload of firewood and ran back.

One of the warriors gave a cry that made the hair on the back of his neck stand up. He looked into the corral, saw the brave astride a huge sow, watched him lean forward and slice his knife across its throat, and whooping with victory, ride it until its knees buckled and it collapsed. Another followed suit. He turned away from the carnage, threw more wood on the fire. When the warriors had finished their butchering, and their custom of eating parts of their kill raw, they would haul it to the fire. He wanted it ready.

He turned and walked back to the wagon, approached slowly so as not to spook the Indian mounts, grasped the reins and led the mare toward the corral. *Lord, please, let those Indian ponies follow.* He wanted them as far from the mission house and the schoolroom as he could manage.

"What is *that?*" Earsplitting whoops, squeals of pigs drowned out her voice. Anne dropped the stones she

held, pressed her hand to the base of her throat. An ululating cry quivered on the air, raised goose bumps on
her flesh.

"That victory cry!"

Mitchel! She slid her hand into her pocket, ran to the
door, yanked it open and rushed outside. He was leading a horse pulling a wagon toward the pigsty.

"Get inside and lock that door!" He hissed the words
at her without pausing, without so much as looking her
direction.

She turned, her legs wobbly with relief, and almost
fell over the children standing beside her and laughing at the mayhem in the pig corral. "Inside, children."

She spread her arms and herded them back into the
schoolroom, leaned against the door and took a deep
breath. The children stood like little statues watching
her. She motioned them to their seats. "Please put your
slate and chalk on my table, then you are free to go.
School is over for today." There would be no danger to
them from the warriors. But if they stayed...

"You afraid Indian."

She stiffened at the trace of satisfaction and scorn in
the quiet words, buried her trembling hands in the folds
of her long skirt and looked at Running Wolf. "I was
startled by the yelling. Men do not behave in such a man-
ner where I come from." She held her hands at her sides
though she was itching to throw the bar-lock in place. "I
am dismissing school because of the goings-on outside.
It is impossible to teach if I have to shout to be heard."
She fixed a steady gaze on the young Indian boy. "And
when did you learn to speak English, Running Wolf?"

He placed his slate on her table atop those of Iva and

Kitturah, drew himself up straight and looked up at her. "Me go fort. Me listen white man much good."

"I see." She looked at his proud stance, decided not to make an issue of his devious behavior in holding back the truth from her. "It is good to know. From now on, you will speak English in school. And Iva will no longer translate my instructions to you."

She smiled at her three young students, stepped back and opened the door. "Good afternoon, I shall see you tomorrow."

They filed out, ran around the corner of the kitchen and disappeared. She closed and locked the door, sagged against it. She must never show fear in front of the children again. Especially Running Wolf. It would cost her all the respect she had thus far earned.

She took a long, slow breath, walked to the bench desk and picked up the small stones she had dropped, searched for one that had gone missing. She needed all of them to teach the children their numbers, and the rudiments of ciphering. She found the stone under the second bench, placed it in the small, drawstring bag and put it on her table. A few quick prods with the poker separated the burning logs of the fire so they would simply smolder and go out.

She swirled her cloak around her shoulders, turned down the wick on the lamp, cupped her hand over the chimney and blew out the flame.

"Piggies crying, Papa."

"Yes they were, Hope." Mitchel looked down at the frown on his daughter's face, sought the right words to explain away her concern. "Sometimes pigs get hurt and they cry." He tapped the end of her tiny, tip-tilted nose and smiled. "The same as little girls cry when they hurt."

"Papas don't cry."

Oh, but their hearts do, Hope. Their hearts do. "That's because we're big and *tough!*" He stopped the rocker, sat up ramrod straight, put a fierce look on his face. She giggled. A beautiful sound that filled his heart with tears. It was so seldom she laughed. He relaxed back in the chair, pushed against the floor with his toe and set it rocking again.

Her frown returned. "Piggies hurt all better?"

"Yes. The pigs do not hurt anymore."

"Me glad. Me don't like to hurt, Papa."

Another wound to his heart. It would soon drown in its tears. "I know, Hope." He kissed her soft, warm cheek, too choked to say more.

"Lady make me better."

Her voice faded. He looked down at her heavy-lidded eyes, rose and carried her to her bed. "Time to go to sleep, Hope." He tucked the covers up under her chin, leaned down and kissed her forehead. "Happy dreams, Hope."

"Me dream…horscy…"

Such a simple dream for a child. But not for Hope. Pain and anger surged. He stood looking down at his daughter, struggling to control his emotions, to fight his way through the knowledge of all that threatened her and find the faith that had once come so easily to him. "I believe, Almighty God, I believe. *'Help Thou my unbelief.'* Keep Hope safe, I pray. And someday, Lord, make her well so she can ride her horsey. Amen."

Mitchel wrote another sentence, paused, forced himself to keep his gaze focused on the paper. Not an easy task. All he need do was take a few steps across the room to satisfy the growing demand in him to be close to Anne, to share these quiet night hours with her. God alone knew—

He shoved back from the desk and went to stand by the hearth. What purpose did record keeping serve given the peril of their present situation? What did it matter if the Cayuse warriors slaughtered three pigs for sport?

He poked at the fire, leaned the poker against the stones and allowed himself to drink in the loveliness that was Anne. The way the firelight kissed the long, brown lashes shielding her eyes, drew a golden whisper across her high cheekbones and the tip of her patrician nose took his breath.

He told himself he should look away. But what did it matter if he let his heart dream? What harm would imagining do under the circumstances? It was only the shared danger that heightened the attraction, that made him want to be close to her, to share his thoughts, his hopes and his fears with her. Anne could not bear to be around his daughter. And he could never truly care for a woman who did not love Hope.

"Have you finished your day's accounting?"

Anne lifted her head and he caught a glimpse of the smudges of weariness beneath her eyes before she returned to her sewing. Reality replaced his wandering thoughts. What should he tell her? That there was no purpose? He shook his head. "It's difficult to muster enthusiasm for the task tonight."

Her hands stilled. She looked up, nodded. "Yes, I imagine it would be hard under the circumstances."

He read the understanding in her eyes, wanted to take the knowledge of it from her, to spare her the worry and protect her from the fear. He was helpless to do any of it. "And you?" He nodded toward the small pile of fabric on her lap. "Are you almost finished with your sewing?"

"Yes." She took a stitch, pulled the thread taut, then reached for her scissors and snipped the needle free. "I've finished the hem. Now I've only to attach the ties." She lifted the garment by its narrow shoulders, shook it out.

He stared, reality and imagination merged, hope flared. "You've made a nightgown for Hope?"

She nodded, picked up her needle and a short length of ribbon, bent her head over her work. "You said the child suffered with the cold, and that her nightgowns are too small." She placed the ribbon at the edge of the neck opening, jabbed the needle through to the underside of the fabric, turned it and pushed it through to the top again. "Emma and Papa Doc would never forgive me if I did not see that your daughter had warm clothes for our journey to the emigrant town."

The child...your daughter... The flare of hope fluttered and died, left disappointment, an unexpected bleakness in its place. So much for the foolishness of dreams. He turned and strode into the kitchen to make sure the door was barred.

Chapter Fifteen

Mitchel yanked down the brim of his hat, lifted his head and scowled at the white flakes swirling on the wind. They were coming faster, would soon cover the ground. He should ride out and check on the heifers and their calves. He should. But he wouldn't. It was too far.

He pulled the collar of his buckskin jacket up around his neck, grabbed another piece of split wood off the wagon and slapped it onto the stack in the sheltered corner between the Indian room and the front door. With no help around the place, he had his hands full caring for the stock and keeping the woodpiles for the fireplaces full. He'd stacked the wood for the kitchen yesterday. This afternoon he'd refill the stack by the schoolroom. At least the work kept him close to the mission house and—

He jerked his head up, listened. Hoofbeats, coming fast. His stomach knotted. He loosed his jacket, checked his knife and stepped out in front of the building where he could see who was coming. *Please, God, be with us.*

The horseman emerged from the trees that lined the trail that led to the hills, thundered toward him, the tails of his covering blanket flew in the wind.

Red Squirrel. The son of White Cloud's dead brother. A friend. The knots in his stomach eased, tightened again as the brave jerked his horse to a stop and leaped to the ground in front of him.

"You come! White Cloud him much hurt. Him want talk in your ear. Hear words of Almighty God before him die!"

His heart lurched. "Chief White Cloud is hurt?"

Red Squirrel nodded, lifted his arm and pointed back the direction he had come. "Him on trail. Bad hurt. You come!"

"I'll saddle my horse."

Mitchel turned and ran for the stables, swerved to the schoolroom, opened the door. "Anne, White Cloud is badly injured on the trail. He sent Red Squirrel to bring me back." He stared at her startled face, saw fear shadow her eyes. "It's all right. He wants me to pray for him. If it's possible I will bring him back here to the mission to care for him. There are no Indians around, or—"

"I understand, Mitchel. White Cloud needs your help. *Go.*" Her hand lifted, made a little pushing motion in the air.

"I'll be back as soon as possible." He yanked the door closed and ran to saddle his horse.

Anne took a deep breath, squelched the apprehension flooding through her. Mitchel would not leave if there were any danger. He'd told her Chief White Cloud was one of the few Indians who had accepted the message of salvation. Surely the chief would not endanger Mitchel's life.

A spate of Indian language broke through her thoughts. She pulled her attention back to her teaching.

"That is enough, Running Wolf. You are to speak English." She glanced at Iva, looked into her bright blue eyes. "And you, Iva, are not to translate for him. Why did you do so?"

Iva straightened, lifted her head. "You spoke with excitement, and too fast for Running Wolf to understand. He wished to know what was said." The little girl looked abashed. "I thought the rule not to translate was for schoolwork."

"I see. Well, as long as it does not happen again."

She shifted her gaze. "From now on, if you have a question, Running Wolf, you are to ask me, not Iva. Do you understand?"

The boy stared up at her, nodded. But there was a pensive look in his eyes.

"Is something troubling you?"

The boy frowned. "Iva say Mission Man go help Chief White Cloud. She say Mission Man bring Chief mission to—" He looked at Iva, grunted out words.

The little girl pressed her lips together, shook her head.

"To take care of him!" Kitturah's eyes widened, she clapped her small hands over her mouth and pressed her forehead against the bench-desk.

Anne repressed a smile, laid her hand on Kitturah's head, snatched it back at the feeling of fondness the touch engendered. "It's all right, Kitturah. But do not do it again."

She turned her attention back to Running Wolf. He was still frowning. "What troubles you?"

"Does Iva speak truth? Does Mission Man bring Chief White Cloud to mission to make better?"

"Yes. Of course. Chief White Cloud is Mr. Banning's

friend. Mr. Banning will do all he can to help your chief heal from his injuries. It is what friends do. They help each other." She studied the young boy's face, tried to discern his thoughts. "Why do you doubt this, Running Wolf? Mr. Banning helps all who come to him. Does he not give your people food in the winter when the game is scarce, and the braves cannot find meat?"

Running Wolf nodded, stared at her, his expression intent, his gaze unwavering. It was as if he were absorbing her thoughts.

"Have you another question?"

"You tell Mission Man go help Chief?"

"Well, of course. He's injured."

"Him Indian."

She stared at him, taken aback by his tone. "That is not important, Running Wolf. Chief White Cloud is a *man* who needs help. Mr. Banning will willingly give him that help. And so will I."

She turned her thoughts back to her teaching before the interruption. "Now, to continue our lesson." She lifted her slate. "Kitturah, please tell me the names of the letters as I point to them."

Mitchel shivered, ducked his head against the onslaught of wind and trotted his horse after Red Squirrel's appaloosa. The snow came faster as they climbed. Here in the hills it already spread a white blanket over the ground.

He stared at the snow, hoped the chief had a warm blanket to cover him. How serious were White Cloud's injuries? Would the chief be alive when they reached him? Would they be able to move him to the mission house?

His horse lunged up a steep rise, found its footing and trotted on. How much farther? They had come a good distance already. He looked up to ask, found Red Squirrel had stopped his horse across what looked like a footpath that branched off to the right. "No go here. There." The brave waved his hand ahead.

Mitchel drew rein, stared at the path behind the brave, wondered at its destination. "Where is Chief White Cloud?"

"Him at big rock." Once again Red Squirrel pointed ahead.

Mitchel stifled a twinge of unease, nodded and urged his horse up the steep path, looked around. The unease grew to wariness. He'd never been this way before, but the country looked familiar. He studied the way the trail ahead narrowed and wound around a sharp curve in the hill, tensed. It was a perfect spot for an ambush. Is that why Red Squirrel had dropped behind him? To close off any possible route of escape?

But Red Squirrel had always been friendly. Was he only imagining possible treachery because of the situation? Or was it real? Alarm streaked through him, settled in his gut. Was this a ploy to get him away from the mission while the Cayuse attacked? No. What would be the purpose? They wanted revenge and Halstrum had not returned. Or had he? Was he even now on the trail to the mission? The Cayuse had been watching the fort. They would know. And if it were true—

Almighty God, be with me! He shifted in the saddle to camouflage his movements, slid his left hand beneath his jacket and drew his knife. In a slow, easy motion, he reached forward, transferred the knife to his right hand and took a firm grip on the reins with his left. One war whoop could frighten his horse into a lunge that would carry them both over the edge onto the rocks below.

Is that what had happened to Paul?

Another shiver shook him, and this one not from the snow and wind. This was from a chill deep inside. That was why this country looked familiar. It was not the same path, but this was the area where he had found Paul. He adjusted his feet in the stirrups, shortened his grip on the reins and clenched his jaw. If he were ambushed, by God's grace, he would be ready.

Chapter Sixteen

"And now it is time to practice our numbers." Anne pulled a stone from the drawstring bag, placed it on the desk table in front of the children. "How many stones are on your desk? Please write the number on your slate."

She checked each answer, nodded and smiled. "Very good. One is the correct answer." She drew out another stone and placed it by the first. "And now how many stones are there? Count them and write the answer."

Kitturah frowned and gripped her chalk. It screeched against the slate as she drew the number two. She shot a surreptitious glance at Iva and grinned.

Iva frowned and shook her head, the black loops of her braids swinging against her beaded tunic.

Anne repressed her own grin. She had little to do in the way of discipline for her youngest student. Kitturah's older sister kept her well in line. She checked all the answers and nodded. "You are all correct. Now listen carefully, for I am going to teach you to add numbers as white men do."

Running Wolf straightened, fixed an intent gaze on her.

She picked up the stones. "To add numbers is quite simple. But you must understand the word *plus*. All of you, say *plus*."

They chorused the word.

She nodded. "*Plus* means to add. Thus—" she laid down a stone "—one stone, *plus*—I am *adding* another—" she laid down another stone "—one stone, equals two stones." She repeated the cipher, touching the stones as she spoke. Three frowns greeted her when she looked up. "All of you, hold out *one* hand to me."

Three small hands were extended.

"Now hold out your other hand."

"How many hands have you?"

"Two!"

She smiled at their excited answers. "Yes. One hand, plus one hand, equals two hands." She picked up her slate and drew the numbers as she spoke. "One, plus—" she made the plus sign "—one—" she drew the line beneath them "—equals two."

There was a clatter of hoofbeats, the rumble of wheels outside. She stiffened, listened. Mitchel must have come back to get a wagon to use to bring Chief White Cloud to the mission. "Copy the cipher on your slates three times, children."

She went to the small window at the end of the room, but could see nothing but falling snow. Would Mitchel return before night fell? Or would she be left alone with his child? She thrust that thought from her mind. It didn't bear thinking on.

Cold radiated off the small, glass windowpanes. She cast another look out at the snow, shivered at the thought of Mitchel being caught out in the storm. Had he thought to take blankets?

She crossed to the fireplace, added wood to the fire and frowned. If he didn't return before dark, she would have to make certain there was wood enough in the child's room and the parlor to last through the night before she barred the doors. Did Indians attack at night?

The thought sent a shudder through her. She refused to think on it. There had been no Indians around the mission for days, save for those warriors who had killed the pigs. It was perfectly safe, or Mitchel would have never gone off and left his daughter.

The ululating cry from above him split the silence, rose to a nerve-shattering crescendo.

Mitchel kicked his boots free of the stirrups and lurched from the saddle as an Indian, dressed only in leggings, loincloth and war paint, launched himself off the wall of stone and dropped onto his horse's haunches, a scalping knife in his hand.

The Indian rolled, slid to the ground as the horse screamed in fear and bolted wild-eyed up the trail. Red Squirrel thundered by in pursuit.

Mitchel crouched on the balls of his feet, his gaze fastened on Eagle Claw's eyes, his left arm bent to ward off deadly knife thrusts, his own double-bladed skinning knife held low. He felt the readiness in his body and knew he hadn't forgotten.

A wall of stone rose on his left, the earth fell away in a sheer drop on his right. He registered the facts, accepted that there was no place to maneuver, no way to feint. It would be a face-to-face battle of cunning, strength and skill on the narrow trail.

He ignored Eagle Claw's taunts. Stayed loose. Waited. He took a firmer grip on his knife and let his instincts take over. They had never failed him coming across the country.

The warrior rushed him, slashed with his knife. Mitchel jumped back, planted his right foot and propelled himself at his off-balance foe. His knife found the thin skin stretched taut over the warrior's ribs.

Eagle Claw recovered his balance, edged toward the wall of stone, black eyes glittering with hatred.

Mitchel dropped back into his defensive crouch, braced himself for another rush.

The warrior came low, drove the scalping knife toward his groin. He brought his left arm down in a slashing blow that deflected the eviscerating, killing thrust. Before he could withdraw, Eagle Claw's blade sliced through the sleeve of his leather jacket, drew a line of fiery pain across his upper arm. He closed, thrust his own blade straight and true. It hit Eagle Claw's ribs, slipped between them. Blood warmed his hand.

The warrior grunted, caught him in a bear hold and pushed him toward the edge of the trail. He wrapped his arms around the warrior's torso, staggered back, planted his left foot and stopped, grappled for the killing blow.

His foot slid back. He dug in his toe, pushed. The ground crumbled away, his foot and leg slid into nothingness. His grip on Eagle Claw broke. His hands slid down the brave's leather-clad legs. Eagle Claw's victory cry quivered on the air.

He twisted his hand, grabbed a fistful of the long fringe on the brave's moccasin, swung his other hand over, grabbed around his ankle and held on. He lifted his legs, pushed against the cliff, tried to gain a purchase and climb.

Eagle Claw teetered, tried to step back.

He felt the warrior's foot slip. Dirt peppered his face. Eagle Claw toppled off the trail and they both fell into nothingness.

Hope! Air whistled past as he plunged toward the rocks below. He slammed against the ground. The breath gusted from his lungs, burst out of his nose and mouth. His neck snapped backward. Pain exploded in his head. Dark descended.

"And now I have a surprise for you." Anne lifted three slates off her table and carried them back to the children. "We have not learned all of the letters of the alphabet, but I thought it would be good if you could write your names."

She put the slates down on the bench-desk. "The slate in front of you has your name written on it in the white man's language. This one says Kitturah." She pointed to the word, smiled at the wide-eyed wonder on the little girl's face as she stared at her name.

"And this one says Iva." She watched the seven-year-old struggle to hold her excitement in check, felt a rush of pleasure when the child couldn't stop herself from reaching out to touch the slate.

"And this one says Running Wolf." The boy held his face impassive, as befitted a warrior, but his eyes shone with pleasure.

"Copy your name three times on your slate. Make your letters carefully, so—"

The door opened, banged against the woodbox.

Her heart lurched. She jerked her head up, stared at the stocky, bearded man who stepped into the schoolroom, followed by a younger, taller version of himself.

"Been looking for you, Banning." The man stomped

his boots free of snow. "Wanted to let you know me and Seth are back. Tom took sick, he's at the fort—" The man looked up, gaped at her. "Who are you? Where's Banning?"

Halstrum! It had to be. It must have been his wagon she had heard earlier. Were the Indians watching? A quiver started in her hands and arms, spread through her. She had to get the children out of here! Get to Mitchel's daughter. But Halstrum didn't know. And she couldn't let him find out. He might do something to precipitate an attack.

She squared her shoulders, mustered a cool look. "I am Widow Simms. I am the teacher here at the mission." She kept her voice quiet, calm, refused to let her racing thoughts and inner quaking affect it. "May I help you, Mister..."

"Halstrum." The man gave a polite nod. "Pleased to make your acquaintance, Widow Simms." He jerked a thumb over his shoulder. "This here's my boy Seth. Where's Banning?"

She nodded at the young man, gave his father an edited version of the truth. "Chief White Cloud has been injured. Mr. Banning went to see if he could help him."

Cold air poured in the door. The fire flared from the draft, smoke swirled, drifted up the sloped ceiling.

She shivered, resisted the urge to rub her arms with her hands. The poor children! She should ask him to close the door, but she wanted him to leave. Perhaps if she ignored him.

She looked down at the children. They had stopped work, were sitting as still as statues looking up at her, their faces tense. Running Wolf's gaze was wary. Clearly, they sensed her apprehension. Perhaps it was all foolishness on her part. Perhaps there was no danger. But she wanted the children out of the schoolroom. She wanted them to go home where they would be safe... in case.

She forced a smile. "Children, put your slates and chalk on my table." There was a soft rustle as they moved to obey.

"When did Banning leave?"

She shifted her gaze back to Halstrum, shook her head. "I don't know the time. It was earlier—".

"Banning."

The call sent a prickle chasing through her.

The Halstrums spun around.

A tall, wiry man appeared in the doorway, flicked his gaze over the room, saw her and snatched his hat from his head. "Begging yer pardon, ma'am. But it's urgent I find Banning."

Halstrum shoved his son aside, stepped closer to the man. "What's wrong?"

The man looked down. "Trouble's afoot. The Indians caught themselves two trappers this morning, drug them off to their camp. I didn't hang around to see more. I been riding full out to get out of the hills. Had to stay off the trails. I stopped to warn Banning. Figured he'd want to prepare to fort up, 'case there's an uprising."

She caught her breath, heard Iva behind her, whispering to Running Wolf.

"Two trappers, you say?" Halstrum's voice was tight, gruff.

"Yeah, fellows name of Bonner and Turner. Don't know what they done, but them Cayuse was mad as hornets and twice as mean." The man slapped his hat back on his head. "If Banning makes it back, tell him

I traded horses. Mine's plumb wore out and I've got to get to the fort and warn them." He ran off.

If Banning makes it back. Her heart seized, her lungs froze. The quivering took possession of her body.

"What're we gonna do, Pa? If the Cayuse have Bonn—"

Halstrum spun on his son. "Shut yer yap. Let me think!"

His angry voice caught her attention, snapped her out of her momentary paralysis. She took a deep breath.

"The Cayuse must've found Bonner and Turner stealing their furs." Halstrum rubbed his hand over his chin, looked up at his son. "They'll soon tell the Cayuse our part in it. We've got to get out of here."

He turned back, looked toward her. No, *beyond* her, toward the children. She read his intent in his narrowed eyes. Anger steadied her. She slipped her hand into her pocket.

"Get them kids, Seth. The Cayuse won't attack us if we've got their kids with us."

The young man turned.

She pulled the pistol from her pocket, leveled it and thumbed back the hammer and placed her finger on the trigger. "You'll not touch these children."

Halstrum lunged.

She shot.

He dropped to his knees, cursing and clutching his shoulder.

His son stared at her, crouched, poised to attack.

She leveled the pistol at him. "Tell your son to stay where he is, Mr. Halstrum. The shot in your shoulder was not an accident. I never miss my mark. Now please leave. I have no wish to kill either of you. But I *will,* if you try to take these children."

Halstrum wiped the anger from his face, struggled to his feet. "Be reasonable, lady. We're dead if we try to run without those kids for protection."

Outrage made her hand tremble. She took a breath to steady it. "You should have thought of that before you stole the Indians' furs, Mr. Halstrum. Now leave."

The man's face tightened. He pivoted and headed for the door. "Come on, Seth. I gotta stop this bleeding. There's no place to run. We'll fort up in the gristmill."

She rushed to the door, watched them run toward their cabin, turned back. "Hurry children! It's not safe for you to stay here!" She motioned them to come outside. "Run home! Quickly now. Don't let them see you!"

She shoved the pistol in her pocket, gave Iva and Kitturah a little push to start them on their way, turned to Running Wolf. He was simply standing there. "Run home, Running Wolf! Quickly! Go!" She reached for his shoulder to urge him on.

He stepped back, shook his head. "You go! It not safe you stay."

Her heart swelled. She shook her head. "I've nowhere to go, Running Wolf. Now hurry!"

He grabbed her wrist. "You come. Me show you hide."

Tears stung her eyes at his concern. "I cannot go. I have to take care of Mitchel's child." She loosed his hand from her wrist, whirled and ran for the door to the parlor. He would go when she was inside.

What should she do about Sighing Wind and Laughing Rain? She rushed into the house.

"Paa-p-paa!"

The sobbing cry froze her in her tracks, then lent wings to her feet. She ran to the child's room, found her propped in her bed, the stick doll in her hands. She glanced around, saw no one. She took a breath to calm her racing pulse, leaned over the child and smiled. "Hush, little one, don't cry. It's all right, I'm here."

She heard a sound behind her, spun. Running Wolf stood in the doorway, the cloak she had left in the schoolroom in his hands.

"Not safe, here. You bring her. Come hide! Come fast!"

She stared at his set face torn with indecision. What about Mitchel? *If Banning gets back.* "All right. Thank you, Running Wolf. Wait here!"

She snatched her cloak from his hands, swirled it around her as she ran out into the parlor and up the stairs. She grabbed the pillowcase and rushed back down. "I'm ready." She handed him the pillowcase, leaned over Hope and wrapped the blankets around her, feeling the child's soft whimper in her very soul. She scooped her up into her arms. "We are going for a walk, Hope. Won't that be fun?"

The small blond head nodded against her shoulder. "Me go see horsey?"

"Not this time, Hope. Perhaps next time." She blinked the stinging tears from her eyes and followed Running Wolf outside.

Chapter Seventeen

Running Wolf hurried past the tepee. Anne slowed, glanced inside the opening. Kitturah and Iva and their mother were gone. A shudder ran through her. With every moment, every step, the danger became more real.

"Me want Papa."

The child's sob was soft, frightened.

"I know, Hope. We will see Papa tomorrow." Oh, how she hoped it might be so! She adjusted her grip on Hope to ease the burden on her arms and increased her pace to keep up with the young Cayuse boy. He veered off the path, entered the deep woods. She hesitated, looked back toward the mission buildings. Smoke drifted from the chimneys, mixed with the falling snow. It all looked so peaceful.

"You come!"

She started at the hissed words, nodded and plunged into the darkness beneath the trees. Running Wolf strode ahead of her, walking with the sure-footedness of a child striding down a walkway in Philadelphia.

Dusky light fell through the overhead branches. She quickened her steps, anxious not to lose sight of the white pillowcase he carried slung over his shoulder. Her toe bumped something. She stopped, looked down, fearful of tripping over a fallen branch or exposed root with Hope in her arms. It was a stone. She stepped around it, looked up. There was nothing but darkness ahead of her. "Running Wolf!"

He appeared from out of the darkness. "You no talk. Trees have ears."

"I couldn't see you."

"Whah! Forget you have white eyes." He took hold of her cloak, marched straight into the darkness. "You get down. Hurt head."

She ducked. Something brushed the pile of curls on the crown of her head. She took a firmer grip on Hope and bent lower, walked with hesitant steps in the direction of the tug on her cloak.

"You get up."

She straightened and looked around. Dim light filtered through narrow slits in a layered rock arch overhead. He tugged her cloak, pulled her toward the darkness ahead. A trickle of water came from the depths. A dark shadow along one earthen wall turned into a log as they neared.

"You stay here." He put the pillowcase down, swept his arm around the shadowed area. "No go there." He indicated the lighter area, pointed to the slits above. "You no talk. Warrior hear, come see."

He stepped farther into the darkness. She stared after him, made out his small form kneeling on the ground when her eyes adjusted to the lack of light. There were soft rustling, brushing sounds. He bent down, straightened, did something with his hands then rose. A fire, little more than a candle flame in size, gleamed bright, chased away the darkness around it. Her heart lifted.

"You come."

She moved to his side, a student, learning from her teacher. At his right, a heaped pile of short pieces of small branches took form. At his feet, the tiny fire licked happily at four short pieces of branch arranged like a tepee.

"You no make fire big. Smoke go up. Warrior smell smoke, come see." He bent down, picked up a small piece of branch in each hand. "You *plus* one and one, no more."

The instructions were given in a barely audible whisper.

She nodded. "I understand. I'll not add more than two pieces at a time."

He started away, came back, pointed to Hope. "Her cry, warrior hear long way. You make stop." He covered his mouth with his hand, nodded. A frown knit his dark brows together. "I hide track, warriors no find you. You no go outside make more track. Big fight done, warriors go, you go outside. Go fort. Go down river to town by big water. Be safe."

"Running Wolf."

He turned back at her whisper.

"Thank you for helping me, for hiding us." She swayed, patted Hope who was beginning to whimper. "And thank you for the fire. It's—" her voice broke "—comforting."

He drew himself up straight, stuck his small chest out. "You friend Running Wolf. Save from white man with bad heart. Running Wolf save friend from Indian with bad heart. All same good."

She blinked tears from her eyes, had a sudden longing to hug the proud, nine-year-old warrior but knew it would embarrass him. "And Mr. Banning is also your friend, Running Wolf. He is the one who brought me here to teach you the white man's ways so you can trade with them. And he is my friend. And the child's father." Her voice choked again. She cleared her throat. "If Mr. Banning comes home, please bring him to us."

"Him come, me see, me bring." He turned and disappeared.

Silence. Nothing but the trickle of water. A shiver slid down her spine, slipped down her arms and legs.

"Me c-cold. Me want P-papa!"

"I know, Hope. I know." She wanted him, too. Oh, how she wanted his quiet strength to lean on. She pushed the enervating thought away. Mitchel was not here, she was alone. And his daughter needed her.

She glanced up at the slits in the rock arch. Was the light growing dimmer? Her stomach knotted at the thought of total darkness. Thank goodness for the fire. Still, she would have to hurry.

She sank down onto the end of the log closest to the fire and smiled at the toddler in her arms. "I have a surprise for you. Do you like surprises?"

Hope stared up at her, her blue eyes swimming with tears.

"I made you some clothes to keep you warm. And a big girl cloak like mine." She drew the bag close, pulled out the small piece of India-rubber cloth she'd had left over and spread it on the ground close to the fire with her free hand. It was large enough to protect a pallet for Hope.

She reached in the bag again. "See these pants. They will keep your feet nice and warm."

"Papa wear pants."

"Yes, he does." A lump filled her throat again. She unfolded the blankets. Tears welled into her eyes at the sight of the red flannel wrappings on Hope's joints. She slipped the pants on over the toddler's little feet, pulled them up to her knees. "Can you stand up for me, while I pull them on, Hope?"

The toddler, nodded. "Me a big girl."

"Yes, you are. It will be cold when I take off your blankets, but the clothes will make you warm soon." Anne stood her on the piece of rubber sheeting, pulled the pants up and tied them at her waist. "Do you want to play a big girl game?"

Hope stared up at her, nodded.

She dropped the blankets onto the sheeting, stripped off the too-small nightgown and slipped the new warm cotton one on over Hope's blond curls. She put her face close to Hope, filled her whisper with suspense to hold the child's interest while she dressed her. "We are in a *secret* place. And while we are here we must speak *very quietly.* And not ever, *ever* speak or cry loudly." She eased the toddler's arms into the sleeves of the nightgown, draped the floor-length, wool-lined, India-rubber cloak about her little shoulders, pulled the hood up and tied the ribbons under her tiny chin. "Can you whisper like me?"

"Me whisser."

Anne smiled. She could hardly hear her. "That's very good, Hope." But would a toddler remember? She finished tying the cloak closed, then folded one of the blankets into a thick pad and laid it on the rubber sheeting. The other she folded for a cover.

"Would you like me to tell you a story while you eat a biscuit?"

"Me like aminal story."

"All right." She lifted Hope onto her lap, handed her a biscuit from the bag, then pulled her own cloak over the toddler for extra warmth. Hope snuggled into the curve of her arm, rested her head on her chest and took a bite of biscuit.

Tears welled at the feel of the small body in her arms. Hope was so little, so precious.

Almighty God, please protect Hope. Please help me to care for her. And please, please bring her father back to her. Oh, God, please save Mitchel. Please let him be alive.

The prayer rose unbidden from her heart. She leaned back against the earthen wall and swallowed back another rush of tears. She had not prayed since Phillip and her precious baby had died. But here in the cave, with the toddler in her arms, the dim light fading, and danger all around, it felt right to pray. In the middle of the trouble and the worry and the heart-stopping fear, God was real to her again.

She cleared her throat, looked down at Hope's adorable face and began to whisper an "aminal" story. "Once upon a time there was a little girl who had a pony named Pepper…"

The violent shivering woke him. The fire must be out. Mitchel frowned, raised his head to rise from bed. Pain clamped on his temples, sent shafts of light exploding behind his eyelids.

He opened his eyes, stared into a swirling darkness. Bile climbed his throat. He rolled his head to the side, let the sourness spew out of his mouth. The pain of his movement brought another surge of nausea, and another.

He struggled onto his hands and knees, let his head hang down between his trembling arms and retched his stomach empty. His body ached. His head pounded. And his upper, left arm had a line of searing heat across the muscle.

He wanted to shake his head to clear it, to make the swirling stop, but he didn't dare. The pain was too great. Fear clutched his empty gut. What was wrong with him?

Hope! Who would care for Hope if he were ill? He drew his body backward to try and get into a position so he could rise. Rough, gritty soil rubbed against his dragging palms. He froze, closed his eyes as it all came roaring back—Eagle Claw's attack, and the ensuing fall off the cliff.

The shivering made him want to cry out for mercy. It made every ache and pain worse. But he welcomed them. They meant he was alive. *Oh, God, let it be only me the Cayuse wanted. Let Hope and Anne be safe. Protect them I pray.*

He opened his eyes, blinked away the blurriness, stared at the spinning, moonlight-silvered pile of dirt and gravel beneath him. *Help me, Lord, help me!* He drew in a long, slow breath, exhaled and drew in another, prayed. The whirling stopped. *Thank You, Lord, for Your mercy.*

He took another breath, lifted his head. Moonlight shadowed rocks and boulders at his side. If he had struck those… He braced himself for the pain, placed his hand on the rock nearest him and pushed himself erect. His legs were wobbly, but they held his weight.

He rested against the tallest rock to let the throbbing

in his head subside, glanced at the glint of moonlight on an object sticking up from the crack between two rocks on his right. A knife.

He moved slowly along the pile of boulders, reached to grasp the weapon, drew back. Eagle Claw's broken body lay wedged among the rocks. He stared at the dead Indian, fought the fogginess to order the thoughts tumbling through his head.

Why hadn't the Cayuse come for Eagle Claw's body? Red Squirrel knew the ambush spot. Or hadn't he returned? Perhaps he didn't know Eagle Claw was dead. Or was he not talking to spare himself Chief White Cloud's anger? Or perhaps night had fallen before they could reach this place? Or had his earlier thought been correct, and Halstrum had returned, and the Cayuse had been busy raiding the mission? So many possibilities. But no matter which was true, he had to get out of here. The Cayuse *would* come for Eagle Claw. And he was in no shape to fight them.

His gut tightened at the notion. He picked up the knife, slipped it into the sheath on his belt and looked about to get his bearings. Red Squirrel had ridden in from that direction, but he would have to stay away from any trail.

He scanned the area for more weapons, then started over the pile of boulders. If he could reach the creek on the other side, he could follow it out of the valley.

Pain flared with his every move, streaked through him with every step. He gritted his teeth and climbed faster, the need to know that Hope and Anne were safe driving him on.

Anne shivered, added two small pieces of branch to the dwindling fire and glanced at Hope. She had again comforted the frightened toddler and coaxed her to sleep on the pallet, but the child was *hurting*.

Anger boiled. She rose, paced the area the light of the fire reached, shot a glance at the slits in the stone arch, discernible now only as a lighter darkness. It must be the middle of the night. Surely, there were no warriors around to smell smoke if she built a real fire. It would ease the child's discomfort and fear. *And* burn up all the wood before daybreak, leaving them in total darkness. No, better the suggestion of warmth and the comfort of the light.

She pulled her arms through the slits in her wool cloak and wrapped them around her waist. If only she could stop shivering. But the cold went bone deep. And Hope's joints already ached from her sickness. She could only imagine how the toddler must hurt.

She looked over at the sleeping child and her stomach knotted. She didn't know what the future held for them. But if something should happen to Mitchel or Hope or her, it would be because of Mitchel's helper Halstrum and his two trapper partners in the fur thefts from the Cayuse. This time she would not blame God.

Where was Mitchel? Tears surged. Sobs pushed at her throat. She ran to the log and sat, yanked her hands from inside her cloak, grabbed the hem of it and held it against her mouth to stifle the cries she could not stop.

What would happen to them? To Mitchel, to Hope— *What time I am afraid, I will trust in Thee.*

The words of Scripture flowed into her heart and spirit—the body-racking sobs eased. Yes. This time she would not blame God. This time she would trust Him.

She wiped the tears from her cheeks, closed her eyes and lifted her heart to God in prayer.

Chapter Eighteen

Anne tensed, placed the two pieces of wood on the fire and hurried to the edge of the lighter area, looked up at the slits in the layered stone. The dim light was strengthening. Dawn was breaking.

It came again, stronger. Not so much a sound, as the suggestion of a sound. A slight quivering... She ran to the log, placed her hands on the earth wall behind it. There was a slight tremble.

The tremble grew stronger against her palms. And then she heard the faint sound. Hoofbeats—muffled by the soft earth of the wooded path. Her heart thudded. If she could hear and feel the hoofbeats of the Indians' horses, this end of the cave must not be far from the path. The tremble stopped.

She drew her hands from the wall and spun about, ran to the edge of the lighter area and strained to hear any sound of movement. Nothing. Only silence.

And then it came. An ululating cry from a multitude of Indian throats that quavered on the air, rose to a heart-stopping pitch and died away. Hoofbeats thundered, dirt trickled down the wall.

"*Papa! Papa!*"

Anne snapped out of her paralysis, whirled and ran to Hope.

"P-pa-pa."

"Shh, baby, shh…" She scooped the toddler into her arms, cuddled her close, cupped the back of her head and tucked her little face in the curve of her shoulder, leaned her cheek against her soft blond curls. "You mustn't cry, Hope. Remember our game. We only whisper here in our secret place. Shh, shh…"

She swayed back and forth, walked farther into the darkness away from the slits where sound would escape. She placed her mouth against the hood covering the tiny ear and hummed the lullaby she had sung to her baby.

Hope's sobs stopped. She lifted her head, looked up, her blue eyes awash with tears, her lower lip quivering. "Me no like yell. Me scared."

She had whispered! "I know, baby. But the yell is only noise, it can't hurt you." Then why was she shaking? She tucked the extra length she had left on Hope's cloak around her little feet. "It is only the Indians playing a game."

"Like whisser game?"

"Yes. Like our whisper game."

Hope nodded, cuddled back against her shoulder, sighed the sweet sound of a child yielding to sleep.

Anne walked back toward the stone arch, strained to hear any sound. It was frightening not knowing. She heard the sharp crack of a rifle—muted but distinguishable. Another. And another. Were those war cries, or only her imagination? Her stomach churned at thought of what was happening at the mission house—at the gristmill.

Mitchel! He didn't know they were hidden and safe. If he returned now—

The strength left her legs. She sank to her knees on the dirt floor, held Hope close in her arms and rocked to and fro, trying to ease the consuming fear.

What time I am afraid...

Yes. Yes, she must trust God. She closed her eyes, whispered into the silence of the stony, earthen shelter.

"Almighty God, don't let Mitchel come back now. Please don't let him come back while the Cayuse are attacking the mission. Please keep him safe, Lord. Please keep him safe."

The light filtering in through the slits was brighter. Was it noontime? Had the morning passed? It seemed like an eternity.

Anne smiled down at the toddler lying on the pallet. "Your arms will feel better soon, Hope." She pulled the sides of the wool-lined, rubber cloak over the toddler's treated arms and fastened the ties. "I'm going to do your legs now, so they will feel better, too."

She lifted the hem of the cloak, unfastened the ties and slipped the footed, cotton-lined, wool pants off Hope's legs. Her heart swelled at the child's whimper. She forced a smile. "It's your turn. What other animals were on Noah's ark?"

"Chickies." It was a hesitant whisper.

Anne pushed a tone of teasing fun into her voice. "Oh, no. You already said 'chickies.' Pick another animal." She worked quickly to free the red flannel strips while Hope was distracted.

A tiny, vertical line formed between Hope's blond

brows. "Kitties!" Her round blue eyes brightened. "Me like kitties."

"Oh, yes. I like kitties, too." She dipped her fingers into the small crock of ointment she had set by the fire, spread the warm balm on Hope's knees and ankles, then replaced the red flannel strips and tied them in place.

"I had a kitty when I was a little girl." She slipped on the small footed pants, tied them and pulled the cloak back down to cover Hope's legs and feet. "The kitty was black and white, and I called her 'Fluffy,' but mother called her 'Trouble,' because she kept getting underfoot.

"There! All done." She put the crock back in the pillowcase and smiled at Hope. "Are you hungry? Would you like a biscuit?"

The toddler's eyes lit up. "Me want honey on it."

Anne picked her up, sat on the log, spread the blanket over her and fished a biscuit out of the bag. "There is no honey for your biscuit. But when it is all gone, I have a surprise for you."

"Me want 'prise now."

"Nope." She tapped the end of Hope's little tip-tilted nose. "Not until you eat your biscuit."

A scream split the silence, shrill and full of agony, even muted by the walls of the cave. It was followed by another. A chill slithered down her spine, set prickles rising on her flesh. She closed her eyes, swallowed to control the nausea that swirled in her stomach.

Another scream came, shriller, more piercing than the others. Her stomach roiled, pushed sourness up her throat.

Not Mitchel, Almighty God. Please don't let it be Mitchel.

"Indians play game."

She opened her eyes at Hope's whisper, nodded, swallowed again before she could answer. "Yes. The Indians are playing a game. And we must not forget to play our whisper game. It's very, very important."

She sat there with Hope on her lap eating her biscuit, and tried to act as if everything was fine, tried to shut out the agonized screams, and the whoops of the Indians, tried not be sick, tried to pray and trust in God. But, inside, with every scream, every whoop, her fear grew.

"Me all done. Me want 'prise now."

She managed a smile, pulled a small, drawstring bag from the pillowcase and handed Hope a slice of dried apple.

Mitchel opened his eyes, stared at dirt and dried leaves. He'd gone unconscious again, this time flat out and face down. He frowned, braced himself and dragged his hands back to push himself off the ground. Something pricked his hand. He lifted his head, stared at the snow-covered thicket of bushes around him. He didn't remember any bushes.

He pushed to his hands and knees, felt a weight on his back. He shoved erect, stared at the horse blanket that slid to the ground. *His* horse blanket. He dropped down below the level of the bushes, gripped the handle of his knife and scanned the area. There was no one in sight. No tracks in the snow as far as he could see. How long had he been unconscious?

He frowned, glanced up at the sky. The sun was sinking below the hills. An entire day then. The sun had been rising when he'd left the creek to cut across the hills. He'd lost an entire day!

Urgency gripped him. He fought it down. He could

not save Hope and Anne if he were killed. He wrestled the fogginess in his head, fingered the blanket. Red Squirrel must have come back to the ambush site and found Eagle Claw dead and him gone. A chill shot through him at the thought of how easily the warrior had tracked him, and how vulnerable he was when found. Obviously, he was not thinking as clearly as he supposed. He would have to be extra cautious, not move until after dark. There was no way to hide tracks across snow.

The shadows from the bushes lengthened. He glanced at the sky. The sun was sinking fast. He would soon be able to move. He looked at the surrounding area, took a bead on a tall tree in the distance, scooped up a handful of snow, swallowed it, held another handful to his aching head and closed his eyes. The throb subsided to a dull ache.

The light against his eyelids faded. It was time to move. He rolled the horse blanket, shoved it out of sight among the bushes, looked around, spotted no sign of danger. He broke cover, crowded against the side of the hill and started in the direction of the mission. His cold, aching muscles protested every movement.

He gritted his teeth and pushed himself to greater speed. Once he reached that tree he knew the area well, and he would be able to stay under cover and still make the mission in a few hours.

He reached the level ground and broke into a lope, blocked out all thought of what he might find. He needed the strength of hope and faith to get him there.

Anne glanced at the fading light filtering into the cave, prayed night would come. The tortured screams had finally stopped, but the whoops and yells of the Cayuse still rose and fell in spurts. She refused to think of what might occasion those whoops of celebration. She only wanted them to stop. Her nerves were raw. If darkness would bring an end to the horror of this day, she would welcome it.

"Papa come soon?"

Tears sprang to her eyes. Her throat constricted. The knots in her stomach twisted into a painful snarl. She couldn't bear to hear Hope ask for her father and was running out of distractions. She looked at the toddler sitting on the pallet she had used to pad the log and form a back rest for her and forced another smile. "Soon, Hope. Perhaps tomorrow."

And if he didn't come?

She thrust the thought from her, went to tend the tiny fire. There was wood enough for tonight, and perhaps part of tomorrow. She picked up a small piece of branch, reached to put it in the fire then drew it back. There was a round knob on the end. She set it aside, fixed the fire then picked up the knobby piece of wood and sat on the log.

"I have another surprise for you, Hope." She dug to the bottom of the pillowcase and pulled out the scissors and roll of red flannel she had brought to tend Hope's joints. "Watch me carefully, and tell me what the surprise is." She cut off a short length of flannel, folded it in half and cut a small hole in the center.

She watched Hope's eyes grow wide and bright with interest, and her heart swelled with thankfulness for the piece of wood that had given her the exact distraction she needed. She raised the hem of her gown, snipped a ribbon from the ruffle on the bottom of her petticoat, then pushed the stick through the hole in the flannel and tied it in place with the ribbon—once under the knob for the neck, and again a short way down on the stick for a waist. Once more she gripped the scissors and with the tip made two tiny circles on the knob for eyes and scratched in a curved mouth.

"It's a dolly!"

"Yes." She smiled at Hope's excited whisper, helped her slip her little arms through the slits in her cloak, and handed her the doll.

"Me gonna—"

"Shhh!" Anne scooped Hope into her arms, hurried into the dark area behind the fire, her heart pounding, her body shaking. She cuddled Hope close, placed her mouth against the hood over her tiny ear. "You mustn't talk, Hope! Not even a whisper. And don't cry. It's very important that you not cry!"

There was a spate of guttural exchanges overhead. Fine particles of dirt fell from the slits in the stone arch. Wavering light danced against the earthen wall. Her heart stopped. Her lungs froze.

A warrior rushed into the cave, a torch held high, his tomahawk raised to strike. He advanced, his moccasins making soft padding sounds against the earth floor.

Torchlight fell on her face, blinded her. She took a breath, slid her hand toward her pocket.

The warrior stopped, lowered the torch, dropped his tomahawk into the leather loop at his side.

She blinked, stared at the puckered scar running across the warrior's cheek. *Barking Fox! Running Wolf's father.*

He pointed at her, covered his mouth with his hand, shook his head, pivoted and ran to the entrance. He shouted what sounded like a command. An answer came from outside. He turned back, again covered his mouth with his hand, pointed at her.

She nodded, raised her hand and covered Hope's mouth, then her own.

He lowered the torch, ducked his head and disappeared out the entrance.

Hope squirmed, lifted her little face. She leaned down, placed her ear by the toddler's sweet rosebud mouth.

"Indian play whisser game?"

Mitchel passed the cows, snow-covered, butchered trophies of vengeance scattered over the hills where they'd been struck down and ran on. The moonless night was too dark for him to make out the mission buildings in the valley, but the glow of burning embers, visible through the rapidly falling snow, told him what he would find. Hope, his precious daughter, and Anne the woman he loved, lost to him forever.

His mind told him it was true, that it was no use, but he refused to accept it. He raced down the hill, heedless of the dark, of the slippery snow, numb to the pain in his body.

The mission house was gone, the roof collapsed, only the stone fireplaces, the buttery and part of the Indian room still stood.

He climbed beneath the broken beams and sections of roof not wholly burned, searched through the charred wood, burned his hands and feet on hot coals protected from the snow. They were not there.

He walked by the burned stables and smithy, the fire still going in the forge, and on past the trampled fence of the round corral and the burned sty. He passed the ashes and charred wood of Halstrum's cabin and moved with wooden steps to the burned gristmill—the blackened wheel tilted at a crazy angle against the riverbank, found what was left of Halstrum and his oldest son.

He turned, headed for the trail that led to the closest Cayuse village. Limping Bear would want Anne as part of his revenge. Hope—Hope he would kill.

Pain, rage, burned in him. He started up the wooded path, stopped, stared at the broken branches on the tree on his right. Indians didn't break branches. His heart lurched, his pulse thundered in his ears. Had Anne gotten away? Had they chased after her?

He plunged into the trees, knocking snow off the branches, taking the clearest path. "Anne!" He stopped against a wall of darkness, turned to search the trees, find another broken branch, something to give him direction. "Anne! Can you hear me?" He cupped his hands around his mouth, turned. "Anne!"

"Mitchel! Oh, Mitchel, you're alive!"

He spun around, saw her emerging from the wall of darkness, Hope in her arms, and rushed to meet them, crushed them in his arms, buried his face in her hair. "I thought I had lost you. Thank God, I've found you. Oh, thank God! I thought I had lost you forever."

Tears of thankfulness stung the backs of his eyes. He tightened his embrace.

"Papa! Me hurt!"

Hope's cry, muffled from being crunched in his embrace, brought him to his senses. He loosed his arms from around Anne, snatched his daughter up into his arms and hugged her close. "Hope… Oh, *Hope,* my precious child. I thought I'd lost you."

Chapter Nineteen

Anne stepped back, watched Mitchel cuddling his daughter close, listened to the agony in his voice as he spoke of losing her.

Tears stung her eyes, clogged her throat. For a moment, in his embrace, she had thought… But that was foolishness. Hope had been in her arms. Of course he had embraced them. *Them.* Not her. Yet, for that moment, secure in his strong arms, it was as if her heart had come home. But that, too, was foolishness, brought on by the surcease of the horrible, unrelenting fear that he would not return.

She blinked her vision clear, shrugged off the unjustified sense of abandonment and focused on Hope's happy laughter as Mitchel reined kisses on her adorable face. Her tears flowed, melted the snowflakes landing on her cheeks. *Thank You, God, for bringing Hope's papa back to her.*

A tree limb cracked. Her heart lurched. She spun to her right, toward the rustling, crashing sound of movement among the trees, slipped her hand toward the pistol in her pocket.

"It's all right. It's an animal. Sounds injured. Probably a wounded cow coming home."

Mitchel's warm breath flowed across her cheek, tickled her ear. She looked up at him and nodded. His gaze held hers, and the shadows in his eyes brought the horrible fear plummeting back to land like a stone in her stomach.

"We have to leave, Anne. We have to travel through the night. I want to get as distant from this place as possible before morning. The Cayuse want my blood. They will come back to search for me tomorrow. And you."

Icy cold slithered down her spine, crawled along her skin. She nodded, turned toward the cave. "I'll get our things." She led him to the entrance, glanced over her shoulder. "You'll have to duck your head."

He nodded, winced.

She stopped, turned to him. "What's wrong, Mitchel? Are you hurt?"

"I'm all right."

The tension in his face said otherwise. The heaviness in her stomach grew. She hurried into the cave, rushed to the log, rolled Hope's blankets and the rubber sheeting and stuffed them into the pillowcase.

He followed, stepped around her, looked down at the small fire. "How did you find this ca—ummph."

She whirled at the odd sound. Hope had her little hand on Mitchel's mouth.

"Papa in secwet place. Play whisser game."

He lifted Hope's hand, looked at her. "Whisser?"

"We played a whisper game to stay quiet." She stared at his left arm, at the dark stain soaked into the leather around the slit in the sleeve. "You're wounded." She shook off the shock, gathered her senses. "Come sit on the log and I'll tend—"

"Later, Anne. We have to leave."

She looked at his face, knew he would not relent, knew he was right and hated it. She squared her shoulders, stepped close to him, put down the pillowcase and held out her arms. "I will carry Hope."

He shook his head, and she saw a flash of pain in his eyes. What was wrong with him?

"I'll carry Hope. She's too heavy for you."

He was wounded, yet willing to take the burden of carrying Hope from her. Phillip wouldn't even stop racing the horses to protect her and their child. She thrust the disloyal thought away and lifted her chin. "I have managed thus far." She studied his face, knew she would not win that argument. "The weather is cold, Mitchel. My cloak will cover Hope and holding her next to me will help to keep her warm and lessen her discomfort."

She watched his eyes, knew he saw the wisdom in what she said, though the crease between his brows shouted he didn't like it. She pressed her case. "Also, if we are attacked, you must be ready to protect us. You cannot fight with Hope in your arms."

Anger darkened his eyes, the muscle along his jaw twitched, and her heart ached for him. Mitchel had no choice. Neither did she.

"You'd better have this." She reached in her pocket, drew out the gun and placed it in his left hand, unfastened her cloak and took Hope into her arms. She wrapped her cloak around the toddler, gripped the top edge in her hand so it could not blow open and smiled. "There, we're all snug and warm and ready to go for a walk. And this time your papa is coming with us."

* * *

Thank goodness for her hood! Anne blinked her eyes, stared at the large, fluffy snowflakes piled on Mitchel's head and shoulders and on the pillowcase he had slung on his back. The snowfall was so thick she had trouble seeing him.

"Me tired. Me go home, go bed?"

Anne glanced down at Hope, shook her head. "No, Hope. Papa's taking us for a walk, remember?"

The toddler's lower lip pouted out. "Me tired."

Her face tightened. Hope didn't deserve any of this! None of them did. "I know, Hope. Put your head on my shoulder and close your eyes." She tilted her head, pressed her cheek against Hope's head to shield her from the snow and hummed her way across the field.

The gristmill loomed, a heap of snow atop half walls, crazily tilted timbers and collapsed roof, the undersides scorched and blackened. *There's no place to run. We'll fort up in the gristmill.* An image of Halstrum and his son flashed before her. Tortured screams echoed in her head. Tears welled into her eyes, trailed a hot path down her cold cheeks. No one should die that way.

She jerked her gaze from the coals still burning hot where the snow didn't reach, looked down lest a worse horror appear, and followed the impressions of Mitchel's footprints in the snow. They dissolved into a blur of snow, dirt and dead leaves.

"Anne."

She stopped, lifted her head. The snowfall had lightened, the flakes hampered in their descent by the intermingled branches of surrounding trees. River water gurgled and rushed somewhere close by. Mitchel was a dark form holding a less dark object over his shoulder.

She blinked to clear her vision, but nothing changed. *White eyes.* A smile touched her lips at thought of the young Cayuse boy who had saved them. "Yes?"

"We are hidden now and it's highly unlikely any Cayuse are out in this storm. They don't like inclement weather, and I've not seen a storm this bad since I came west to found the mission. Still, they'll be out searching for us tomorrow and we've a long way to go until dawn. I'll carry Hope."

His deep voice, warm with concern flowed over her, brought foolish tears swimming into her eyes. It was the exhaustion. She'd had no sleep last night and little the two nights before. But she didn't have a wounded arm and whatever made him wince when he moved his head quickly. She shook her head. "She's sleeping, Mitchel. And she is warm and snug with my cloak covering her. I'll carry her until I tire."

Mitchel looked up at the lightening sky. Dawn was breaking. It was time to stop. He eyed the stand of pine at the top of the wash and altered course to approach it from the side. It would mean a little steeper climb, which he was reluctant to put Anne through in her exhausted state, but it was the safest way.

He chose the easiest path, reached the pines, led the way to a campsite beside the babbling rill that drained the hill into the river, then went back and looked down the wash. The snow had already obliterated all trace of their passage. He made his way through the trees until he could see up the fold of the hill, found nothing alarming and went back to camp.

His head was throbbing and his bruised body was screaming for rest, but his heart lifted at the sight of his daughter sitting on a blanket pad, draped with another blanket and eating a biscuit.

"I'm gonna have a 'prise, Papa."

"You are?" He glanced at Anne.

"I brought dried apples. I give her a slice when she finishes her biscuit."

She was kneeling on the snow-covered ground, a small mound of pine needles in front of her and the flint and steel he had given her to pack away in her hands. She looked exhausted and perturbed. "I can't seem to make this work."

Her voice quavered ever so slightly. He hadn't the heart to tell her you couldn't start a fire with damp pine needles.

"Perhaps I can help." He glanced around, spotted a rotting stump, brushed aside the snow at its base and grabbed a handful of the dried, crumbled wood from the underside, broke off a few slivers of the dried wood. "This should work."

He squatted beside her, made a "nest" of the tinder in the top of her pile of pine needles and took the flint and steel into his hands. Four quick strikes and the tinder started to smolder. He leaned down, blew gently. The tinder flamed. He fed the fledgling fire the slivers of wood, rose and gathered pieces of dead branch, added enough to make a small fire.

The burning pine crackled and snapped, made the small, hidden area among the tall trees seem more comforting, the snow sifting through the branches overhead more bearable.

"Me all done, want 'prise now."

He accepted the dried apple ring Anne pulled from a small bag and handed it to Hope, spotted the tin cup on the ground beside his daughter and helped her drink the water.

"If Indians come near, will they see the smoke from the fire?"

He glanced at Anne, handed her the cup when she held out her hand. "There is very little smoke when you burn dried wood. And what smoke there is will be lost among the branches of the trees."

She nodded, stepped to the rill, filled the cup, brought it back and placed it close to the fire. She picked up a stick, pulled some warm ashes from the fire and set a small crock on them. Her hands were shaking.

Fear or weariness? Likely both. He clenched his hands to keep from reaching for her. "Why don't you rest while you're able, Anne?"

"In a bit." She glanced at Hope, leaned toward him and lowered her voice. "She was crying with pain before I distracted her with the biscuit and the apple. I want to treat her joints while there is some heat from the fire to warm the ointment."

"Anne and Papa play whisser game?" Hope's eyes widened. She looked around. "This be secwet place?"

He glanced at Anne, clenched his hands and jaw. What had she suffered alone with his daughter in that cave while the Cayuse raided and burned the mission? He sucked in air to calm the anger, went on his knees in front of Hope and took her tiny hands in his. "We may have to play the whisper game often, Hope. And, sometimes, we may not be able to tell you it's time to play the game. So if Anne or I do this—" he placed his finger across his lips "—it means you are not to talk. Do you understand?"

She frowned, shook her head. "Ind'an do this!" She

pressed her hand over her mouth, then pointed a tiny finger at him.

His heart stopped, lurched into a staggered beat. He turned to Anne. "What Indian? What is she talking about? What happened?"

She met his gaze, looked away. "It was Barking Fox— when the Cayuse were…searching the woods." She took a breath, rubbed her hands over the cloak covering her knees. "I heard them talking and walking around overhead. I picked up Hope and ran into the dark at the back of the cave. But a few minutes later an Indian came in carrying a torch and his tomahawk."

His stomach twisted, his pulse raced. He took a breath, reminded himself they were all right, strained to hear her over the roaring in his head.

"He came toward us and the light of his torch blinded me." She looked over at him, her eyes wide and puzzled. "And then he lowered the torch and I saw the puckered scar on his cheek. I knew, then, it was Running Wolf's father. He did as Hope said, he placed his hand over his mouth and pointed at us. When I repeated the motion and nodded, he left and the searchers went away." Her voice broke. Her hands trembled. "Barking Fox saved us."

"Anne—"

She shook her head, reached into the pillowcase and handed him a bag. "I will put the ointment on Hope while you eat. And then I will tend to your wound."

He opened the bag, smelled the biscuits she'd baked the night he'd told her they should be prepared to leave. His throat closed. He'd come so close to losing them both. *God in Heaven, help us. Give me strength to protect them and wisdom to get us safely to the emigrant town, I pray.*

Strength. He needed strength to protect and care for Hope and Anne on the long journey ahead. He took a biscuit from the bag and took a bite.

Mitchel chewed on a piece of dried apple and watched the deft movement of Anne's fine-boned hands as she made her preparations. Two ribbons were snipped from the ruffle of her petticoat, quickly joined by a cut-off length of the cotton cloth. He frowned, vowed to replace her ruined garment, then realized that would be inappropriate. But a bolt of material would be acceptable.

"You made the pants and cloak for Hope from the blanket I gave you to bring along?"

She nodded, cut a square off one end of the length of material and set the rest aside. "I thought it would be as warm and much easier to carry her."

He nodded, watched her drop the square of cloth into the cup of water warming by the fire.

"I'm ready. Take your arm out of your jacket please."

He slipped his jacket off his left shoulder, grabbed hold of the end of the sleeve and pulled it off his arm. She gasped, paled. He looked at his shirtsleeve, from the slit down it was stiff with dried blood, and some fresh. He frowned. "The wound is not that bad. It bleeds when I use it."

She nodded, picked up her scissors. "I shall have to cut off your shirtsleeve." She held the sleeve away from his arm, slid the scissors into the knife slit and began cutting.

"Where did you get the India rubber for the cloak?"

"William had the mattresses in the wagon encased in India-rubber sacks to protect them at river fordings and such. I cut the top from one sack." She dropped the bloodied sleeve on the ground, squeezed the excess water from the rag in the cup and began washing his arm.

"Clever of you to think of using it for Hope's cloak." He looked at his sleeping daughter, thought of how the clothes Anne had made her kept her snug and warm and protected from the weather from the top of her head to the bottom of her little feet. It kept him from thinking about the softness of Anne's hand on his arm.

"Not really. It was raining that day. That's what made me think she would need protection as well as warmth." She dipped the cloth again, gently cleaned the wound. "How did this happen, Mitchel?"

"Red Squirrel lied about Chief White Cloud. It was a trap. I was ambushed on the trail."

Her hands stilled, then continued to cleanse the wound. "Was it Eagle Claw?"

"Yes."

She dropped the bloody rag on top of the shirtsleeve and picked up the length of cotton. "I have no unguent to put on the wound. I hope cleaning it well will be enough to help it heal." She placed the cotton cloth over the wound, held one end and wrapped the rest of the length twice around his arm. "Hold that please."

He felt the light touch of her fingers on the swelling on the back of his head. "How did this happen?" She tied one of the ribbons around the bandage on his arm and picked up the other.

"We fell off a cliff."

She stared at him a moment, then tied on the other ribbon. Her hands were shaking against his arm. "Is that when you lost your weapons?"

"Yes."

"How fortunate that you gave me your partner's pistol to carry."

He looked down at the Colt Paterson stuck in the belt that carried his knife and tomahawk and nodded. "It is indeed."

"I'm finished, you may put your jacket on."

"Thank you, Anne. My arm feels much better."

She nodded, picked up the cup. "This must be cleaned." She turned toward the rill.

He stepped to her side, took the cup from her hand. "No more, Anne. I'll clean the cup. And it's time to put out the fire. You lie down on the pallet and share Hope's blanket. You need to rest while there's time."

That stubborn little chin of hers jutted into the air.

"And what of you, Mitchel? When will you rest?"

"I'll keep watch while you sleep this morning. I'll sleep this afternoon."

She stared up at him a moment, then nodded. "Very well." She stepped over to the pallet, slid beneath the blanket and curled up beside Hope.

He picked up a branch, spread the burning wood apart and started for the rill to clean the cup.

"Mitchel."

Her voice was heavy with approaching sleep.

He turned and looked down at her. Her eyes were closed, her long lashes dark smudges against her pale skin. "Yes, Anne."

"I forgot...to tell you. Pistol has...empty chamber." Her eyelashes fluttered, lifted, closed again. "I shot... Halstrum." She gave a long sigh and fell asleep.

Mitchel stared at her, lying beside his daughter beneath the snow-covered blanket, the hood of her cloak pulled forward to cover all but the profile of her face against the pallet. She was so lovely, so delicate. And so incredibly frustrating. How could she say such a thing and then fall asleep and leave him standing here with every muscle tensed and twitching, every nerve jangling?

I shot Halstrum.

Had she been dreaming?

He pulled the pistol from his belt, squatted beside the dying fire and checked the chambers. One was, indeed, empty. Shock caromed through him, jolting from nerve to nerve. Anger ricocheted in its wake. He clenched his jaw, looked up through the falling snow and the tree branches to the awakening sky.

No more, God, no more. She has suffered enough. Keep Anne from all danger I pray. If there is more trouble to come, let it come to me.

He reached into the pillowcase, grabbed the bags of cap and ball, reloaded the pistol then rose, placed the pistol back in his belt and leaned against a tree keeping watch over his child and the woman he was trying his best not to love.

Chapter Twenty

"We're ready."

Mitchel looked at Anne, at his daughter held close in her arms, Anne's cloak wrapped snugly around her. A perfect picture of mother and child. If only it could be so.

He closed his heart to the wish. Every day his attraction to Anne grew stronger. She was wonderful in her care of Hope *and* him, but there was a reserve about her, a holding back of her heart he couldn't overlook. He could not wed a woman who did not give her heart wholly to him and his daughter, no matter how much he loved her.

He clenched his jaw, picked up the pillowcase and gave one last look around the campsite. His effort to hide any evidence of their stay here would not bear close scrutiny by a Cayuse warrior, but a passing glance would not betray them. He fixed his thoughts on the need to move on and led the way through the trees. The clear sky and the dry feel of the air signaled trouble. Temperatures could plummet quickly in the mountains. He would prefer to stay in camp and keep Hope and Anne close to a fire, but two days spent in the same spot was dangerous if the Cayuse had picked up their trail.

"There is a valley at the top of this hill, Anne. When we reach it, we will go straight across, then follow the fold of the hill that angles down to the right. At that point, we will be halfway to the emigrant town."

"Halfway to 'Promise.' That's what they named it."

He nodded, skirted around an outcropping of stone. "A good name choice for the first town those making the long, hard, wagon journey to Oregon country will encounter."

"Yes. That was their feeling when they chose the name. It was how they felt when they arrived."

He glanced over his shoulder. "But not you?"

"I was not looking for a promise. And I had my destination."

Her quiet words brought a rush of guilt. She had suffered so much since coming to the mission.

He stopped, grasped her elbow beneath her cloak and steadied her while she carried Hope over a tree fallen across their path. "Keeping to these tree-lined washes helps hide our trail, but it makes the walking more difficult."

She looked up at him and nodded. "I understand your purpose, Mitchel."

He looked into her eyes, dark in the moonlight, their beautiful dark blue color hidden but to his memory. "Do you ever complain, Anne?"

"Bitterly, when it's deserved. But not to someone who is trying to save our lives." She curved her lips in a soft smile.

His heart kicked like a mule. The bone-chilling cold fell away. The ache in his arm, the dull throb in his head ceased to exist. He held Anne's gaze, tightened his grip on her elbow, leaned down.

Don't do it! Turn away, get moving again. The thought came, lost itself in the beauty that was Anne Simms.

Her breath came in a soft gasp, clouded the air between them. She looked down, shivered beneath his hand.

He snapped back to his senses, lifted his hand and tugged Hope's hood a little farther forward, dropped a light, highly unsatisfying, kiss on his daughter's cold cheek, turned and continued up the wash.

"Me c-cold."

"I know, sweetie." Anne hitched Hope higher in her arms, took more of the toddler's weight on her shoulder. "Put your face against my neck. It will help keep you warm."

Her hood fell away as Hope lowered her head and burrowed her little face into the curve of her neck. Chills chased down her spine as the cold air bit at her ears and neck. A shiver joined the tremble that began with Mitchel's touch.

She raised her head, looked at him walking so strong and sure before her. She had to stop misreading his intentions. When he had leaned toward her she had thought—

Foolishness! It was Hope who Mitchel cared about. As well he should. She slammed the door on the image floating at the edge of her will and focused on the trail, the crunch of snow beneath Mitchel's boots. He had no hat. She poured over a mental list of the items in the pillowcase, puzzled over a way to fashion him a hat of sorts. It was a fruitless effort, but it kept her from thinking about the sudden yearning in her heart.

* * *

The cold air made his lungs burn, snow squeaked with his every step. His worry had become reality. Mitchel stopped at the edge of the trees, shivered with the lack of motion.

"Mitchel, I'm w-worried about Hope. The cold—"

"I know." Anne's teeth were chattering. He frowned. The cold would be even worse when they left the protection of the trees to cross the open valley. He set the pillowcase down, reached inside and drew out a blanket. "I'll put this around you—"

She shook her head. "Take off my c-cloak. Put it inside. Where I can h-hold it on."

He jammed the rolled blanket between his thighs, fumbled with the loop and button at the neck of her cloak, his fingers thick and awkward with the feminine fastenings.

She lifted her chin to give him freer access. "Is that b-better?"

He looked down, met her gaze and sucked in a deep breath. Frigid air invaded his lungs. He broke into a coughing fit, then returned to his task, kept his gaze firmly locked on his hands. The button came free. He lifted the cloak from her shoulders.

Hope whimpered, burrowed closer to Anne's neck. "D-don't put it in the s-snow."

He glanced around, frowned and pulled the hood over his head, let the cloak hang down his back. He shook out the blanket, folded it in half, stepped close and draped it over Anne's shoulders, pulled it forward, crossed the ends over Hope, pulled up enough to cover her small, hooded head.

"G-give me the edge s-so I can hold it."

He nodded, pulled the blanket over the top of Anne's hand and tucked the edge into her palm where her fingers could grip it. He snatched her hood off his head, swirled her cloak over the blanket around her shoulders and fastened it at the neck, eased the edges around Hope's neck and finished fastening the loops and buttons down the front.

"Thank you, Mitchel. That's b-bet—" Anne pulled her head back, stared up at him. "What are you d-doing?"

"Letting your hair down to protect your ears and neck." He slipped the combs from her hair.

"No! I—"

Russet curls fell over his hands, tumbled down her back and shoulders. His gut tightened. He sucked in another breath, coughed, dropped the combs in the pillowcase and slid his hands along her neck, captured the silky mass of curls and held them prisoner against the nape of her neck. His heart thudded. He freed one hand, reached over her shoulder and grasped her hood, pulled it far forward to protect her face, stepped back and cleared his throat. "That should help keep you warm."

"And what of you, Mitchel? What will protect your neck and ears? What will keep you warm? It will do us no good if you sicken." Her voice sounded tight and small.

"This will do." He pulled the other blanket from the pillowcase, tossed it around his back and shoulders, pushed the edge high around his ears, then rolled the edges together at the base of his throat, snatched up the pillowcase in his other hand and led the way out into the valley.

* * *

"Walking downhill is as hard as walking up. I thought it would be easier." Anne gave Mitchel a rueful smile, wiped a small dry stick clean on her petticoat and stirred the dried apple and water heating in the cup. A poor excuse for dessert. "If you hadn't held my arm and supported me, I would have slipped many times."

"It's the least I can do, Anne. You're carrying my daughter."

She heard the frustration in his voice, read it in the way he snapped a branch over his knee and added it to the fire. The warmth caressed her skin, the comforting crackle and snap coaxed her to rest.

She shook her head to fend off her weariness, looked at the large, heavy branches that slanted from the trunk of the evergreen to brush their green-needled tips against the ground.

The abundant boughs encircled and sheltered them, masked their presence and held in the heat from the fire. A thick layer of fallen needles provided a soft, dry carpet, with only here and there a clump of snow that had toppled off one of the branches.

She watched the smoke rise, weave in and out through the spaces between the limbs and drift away.

"Eat your biscuit, Hope. It's time for you to go to sleep."

"Me want honey, Papa."

"There is no honey, Hope." Pain, frustration and anger flashed in Mitchel's eyes. How hard it was on him to see his child suffer.

"Oh, but we have something much better than honey!"

Mitchel shot a look her way, raised a disbelieving brow.

She took Hope's biscuit, broke it open, used the stick to cover it with some of the gooey, cooked apples and handed it back. The toddler took a bite.

"Me like it."

Anne smiled at her, split open another biscuit, smeared it with some apple and handed it to Mitchel, summoned up the energy to give him a saucy look, then prepared one for herself. She took a bite, chewed slowly, her body warmed by the fire, her heart warmed by the surprised grin on Mitchel's face.

Anne's eyelids fluttered and slid downward. Mitchel shoved the last of his biscuit in his mouth and lunged for her as she slumped sideways. He caught her in his arms, rolled to a sitting position and pulled her onto his lap.

"You tell Anne aminal story, Papa?"

His heart lifted. The warmth of the fire had cheered Hope. He smiled and shook his head. "Anne is sleeping." He pulled the cover from Hope, lifted Anne in his arms and laid her on the pallet. "Time for you to go to sleep, too, Hope." He kissed his daughter's warm cheek, snuggled her close beside Anne and pulled the cover over them.

"Thank You, Almighty God, for the blessings of this day. Thank You, for—"

"You play…whisser game wiff God, Papa…"

He smiled and nodded. "Every night and every morning, Hope." *And lots of times in between.*

His face tightened. This journey of escape wasn't over yet. He thought one more day of travel, perhaps two. He moved the cup holding the apples away from the fire, pulled the pistol from his belt and leaned against the tree trunk, the Colt Paterson ready in his lap.

Chapter Twenty-One

Mitchel moved into the thick growth of pines at the base of the mountain. "We'll camp here today."

Anne nodded, glanced up toward the sky. Dawn was approaching, announced by the gray light that filtered down through the branches. But it had stopped snowing.

He held back a branch for her, stopped, tilted his head. Her heart stumbled, raced. "What is it?"

"Water."

The tension fled, her pulse slowed. She firmed her trembling legs, listened. A river rushed and chuckled over rocks somewhere close by.

"That's the river I've been aiming for, Anne. We must be getting close to the emigrant town. We've only to follow the river now."

There was relief in his voice. *Their journey was almost over.* Tears stung her eyes. She forced her weary body to move, trailed through the pines after him watching for stones or raised roots in the murky light. The river's song grew stronger. "How far is the town?"

He glanced over his shoulder, smiled at her. "Perhaps another day's journey. We'll make camp today and—"

He stopped, touched his fingers to his lips.

Her mouth went dry. She put her mouth on the hood over Hope's ear. "Do not talk. Be very, very quiet." She held the toddler close, put her chin over top of her little head and looked at Mitchel.

He stood, eyes narrowed, face taut, the pistol ready in his hand. The pillowcase sat at his feet.

A hoof struck a stone. Her heart jolted. She jerked her gaze back toward the edge of the pines. The hoofbeats were coming from the direction they had traveled. A Cayuse following them? Her stomach roiled.

No! We're almost there! She released her hold on her cloak, lifted her hand to cup Hope's head, to hold her safe.

The hoofbeats stopped. A horse snorted. Something brushed against a pine branch. Bile pushed into her throat. She pressed Hope close, looked at Mitchel. *Protect him, God. Protect us—*

The horse nickered, snorted.

"Horsey!"

She clapped her hand over Hope's mouth, looked at Mitchel. He was standing, pistol pointed, a puzzled look on his face. He motioned her to stay, started toward the spot where they had entered the woods.

She turned, heart pounding, and looked through the trees. A horse stood in the small clearing, nose thrust their direction, ears pricked forward. A large roan stallion with spots on his rump.

Comanche!

Her heart soared. "Mitchel, wait!"

He spun at her urgent cry, dropped into a crouch, pistol held steady.

She shook her head. "There's no danger, Mitchel.

That is Mr. Thatcher's horse. He will run off if you go near him."

He rose, stared at her, shock written all over his face.

"The horse won't let anyone but Mr. Thatcher and—" her voice broke, tears welled "—and *Emma* touch him."

A sudden longing to see her sister overwhelmed her. She blinked the tears from her eyes, cleared the lump from her throat. "Hello, Comanche."

The horse tossed his head, whickered.

"Horsey!"

"Yes, sweetie." She patted Hope, kept her attention on the horse. "Where is Mr. Thatcher, boy?"

The roan snorted, pawed the ground.

She glanced over at Mitchel, fought to keep her voice calm. "Mr. Thatcher must be somewhere close by. He was going to build a trading post somewhere in the mountains." Tears stung her eyes again. She swallowed hard, took a deep breath. "Mr. Thatcher was our wagon master. He will be able to lead us to Promise."

He looked doubtful. "Thatcher may be injured, Anne. Or worse. Otherwise the horse would be with him."

She shook her head. "Comanche always runs free. If we follow him—" She took another breath, fought down her expectation lest she be disappointed. "Go home, Comanche. Take us to Mr. Thatcher."

The horse snorted, moved down the hill.

Hope wiggled in her arms. "See horsey, Papa!"

Mitchel looked up at the lightening sky, frowned. "All right, we'll follow the horse. But only until dawn fully breaks. Then we make camp and wait until night to travel on. He'll leave tracks." He picked up the pillowcase, kept his pistol in his hand.

She nodded, took a firmer grip on Hope and started

after Comanche, the hope of finding Zachary Thatcher's trading post giving her strength to continue on after their long night's trek. The big roan wove in and out of pines in a winding path down the hill.

Mitchel looked down, frowned. "Maybe the horse *will* lead us to your friend, Mr. Thatcher. He seems to use this path often. There are a lot of tracks going both ways, and they all appear to be the same. I don't see any tracks of unshod horses."

There was relief in his voice. She looked up at him. "Do you suppose that means Mr. Thatcher's trading post is near?"

"I don't know, Anne. It could—"

He gripped her arm, rushed her off the path, pushed her behind a tree and stood shielding them with his body. She listened to the thunder of Comanche's hoofs against the ground. Her heart thudded. Comanche was running off. Had something startled him? Indians?

Time froze. She stood motionless, her back against the tree, Hope in her arms, Mitchel in front of her facing the path. She could feel his warm breath on her cold cheeks, see his pulse beating in his temples. Comanche's hoofbeats faded. Silence descended broken only by the twittering of birds welcoming the day.

Mitchel stepped back, motioned her to stay put and moved off through the trees, following the direction the horse had taken.

She closed her eyes.

"If you are praying, your prayer has been answered."

She snapped her eyes opened, looked at Mitchel's grinning face. "You found Mr. Thatcher's trading post?"

"Better." He took hold of her elbow, led her onto the

path and walked her around a curve. "We're safe, Anne. There is Promise."

She stared out over the snow-covered rolling hills stretching from the mountain to a plain that reached as far as she could see. Her breath caught at the sight of log cabins clustered along the river that crawled out of the mountain and snaked its way through the hills and the plain. One log cabin stood alone on this side of the river, its only company two barns, and the horse and man standing in front of one of them. Zachary Thatcher.

Mitchel tightened his grip, led her out into the open, lifted his other hand and waved it through the air.

Zachary Thatcher waved his hand, leaped onto Comanche's bare back and raced toward them.

They were safe.

The trembling started in her shoulders and arms, traveled through her body into her legs. Darkness hovered, swirled. She handed Hope to Mitchel, sighed and collapsed in a heap at his feet.

Mitchel grasped the reins and saddle horn in his left hand, tightened his right arm around Hope and swung down from the saddle.

"Go on in and warm yourself and the little one by the fire, Mr. Banning. Emma will be with you as soon as she takes care of her sister."

Mitchel glanced at the man taking hold of the horse's reins. "Thank you for your help, Mr. Thatcher. And please, the name's Mitchel." He held out his hand. It was taken in a strong grasp.

"No thanks needed, Mitchel. People have to help each other out here in Oregon country if we want to survive. And the name's Zach."

Mitchel nodded, took the pillowcase Zach handed him and hurried up the steps and across the porch. He reached for the door latch, caught a glimpse of Zach leading the horse toward the barn, Comanche plodding after him. He would forever be grateful to that horse. But he would never forget the feeling of having his heart wrested from his chest as he watched Zachary Thatcher take Anne in his arms and ride away on him.

The knot of worry in his gut tightened. He opened the door, stomped the snow from his boots and stepped inside. Warmth from a fire rushed to greet him. His cold flesh tingled from its touch. He stepped to the hearth of the stone fireplace, looked at his sleeping daughter. *Let them be all right, God. Please let them both be all right.*

The memory of the prayers he'd said for his wife's healing, for Paul's safe return haunted him. *The actions of men have consequences.* Yes. Isobel and Paul had joined him in his missionary work and both had died. Isobel for lack of a doctor's care after Hope's birth, and Paul at the hands of the Indians he had come to minister to. Would he lose Hope and Anne, as well?

He tightened his hold on Hope, smaller, frailer now for the lack of nourishment. Anne was in the same condition. He'd watched her beautiful face grow thinner, the fine bones become more pronounced over the days they'd walked the hills and mountains.

Please, Almighty God, please! Let me have gotten them here to the doctor in time. Please let them live. Please heal them, and let them live.

The silence of the empty room answered him. He closed his eyes, grabbed on to his remaining faith and released it in prayer.

A latch clicked. A door sighed open, closed with another soft click.

He braced himself, opened his eyes. A brown-eyed, blond-haired woman walked toward him. Anne's sister, Emma. The knot in his gut twisted. He wished with all his heart it was his blue-eyed, red-haired Anne coming to him. *His.* No. Only in his heart. Forever in his heart. He took a breath, forced out the question gnawing at his very soul. "How is Anne, Doctor Allen?"

"She will be fine, Mr….Banning?"

"Yes." *Thank You, God. Thank You that Anne is all right.*

Her lips curved in a warm smile. "May I call you Mitchel? William speaks of you so often, I think of you by your given name."

"Of course, Doctor—"

She gave a quick shake of her head. "Emma." Her smile widened. "But back to Annie. She slipped from being unconscious into natural sleep without waking—" her brown eyes took on an assessing glint "—from exhaustion I'd guess, judging by her appearance…and yours." Her gaze dropped to the blanket-wrapped bundle in his arms. "And who is this?"

Emma's a good doctor. She saved a toddler on the wagon train. He cleared his throat. "My daughter, Hope. She's two years old, and she's…not well."

"I see." The look in her brown eyes sharpened, her entire countenance changed. She held up her arms. "Why don't I take a look at her, while you tell me what's wrong, Mitchel?"

Please, God. He placed his daughter in her arms. "She is often fevered. And her joints pain her. Cold bothers them, makes them hurt more."

"Then we shall keep her right here in front of the warm fire." She laid Hope on a blue settee, knelt on the floor and unwrapped the blanket from around her. She stared at the hooded cloak, the footed pants. "Very clever. The rubber sheeting must have kept her dry and warm in all this snowy and windy weather."

"Anne made them."

She shot him a look of astonishment, dropped her gaze and untied the fastenings on the cloak and pants.

Hope opened her eyes, blinked, stared up at the strange woman. Her lower lip quivered. "P-pa-pa!"

"I'm here, Hope." He leaned over the back of the settee, smiled down at her. "This nice lady is Anne's sister. She's a doctor and is going to try and make you better."

Hope's lower lip, pouted out, tears flowed into her eyes. "Me w-want Anne."

"Anne is sleeping, Hope. She's very tired." He brushed the back of his finger against her soft, warm cheek, comforted her as Emma slipped the cloak and pants off her.

He heard a delicate sniff, glanced at Emma and saw the flash of surprise in her eyes when she lifted the hem of Hope's nightgown and spotted the red flannel bandages. A smile curled her lips upward, widened into a grin.

"I see Annie has been doctoring Hope." She slipped the sleeve of Hope's nightgown up beyond her little elbow, nodded. "Do all of Hope's joints pain her, or is it her wrists and elbows, knees and ankles that hurt?"

He fastened his gaze on Emma's face, not wanting to miss a nuance of her expressions. "Those you named." Again, that little nod, as if that were the answer she expected. His heart thudded. Did she know what was wrong with Hope? *Oh, God, use this woman to heal Hope I pray.*

He watched her unwrap the bandages, study Hope's joints.

"How long has she had these joint pains, Mitchel?"

"Since late September."

She nodded, pulled Hope's nightgown back in place, covered her with the blanket and rose. She bent over and brushed a curl, flattened by the hood, back off Hope's cheek. "I shall be right back, sweetie. I have some ointment that will make your arms and legs feel better."

She walked into another room, came back with a crock, a roll of red flannel and some scissors. She uncovered Hope and treated her joints, her movements deft and sure. "Do you remember, Mitchel, if Hope had a bad cold or if her throat hurt her before the fever and the joint pains started?"

What was wrong with Hope? He fought down a rising fear, thought back. "Yes, she complained of her throat hurting a few weeks before. She wouldn't eat because it hurt her to swallow the food."

Again the nod came. He was beginning to dread those nods.

She pulled Hope's nightgown in place, leaned down and placed her ear on Hope's chest, an intent expression on her face. She lifted her head, covered Hope with the blanket and smiled. "Are you hungry, sweetie?"

Hope looked at him. "Me want 'tatoes wiff bwown stuff, Papa."

Emma shot him a quizzical, amused look.

"Potatoes with gravy."

She laughed, lifted Hope into her arms. "The very thing I was about to suggest. With a goodly portion of meat thrown in for your papa. Tell him to come along. We'll get you both fed, and then I shall take you in to sleep with Anne, while I take care of your papa's arm." She gave him a look over her shoulder and led the way into her kitchen.

Chapter Twenty-Two

"Can you heal Hope?" Mitchel set his cup of coffee on the table and looked up at Emma.

"I'm sorry, I don't know of any cure, Mitchel. However, Hope's heartbeat is steady and strong. The illness makes her uncomfortable, but it does not endanger her life." She tossed the rag she'd used to clean his wound into a bowl of clean water and pulled a small, covered crock toward her.

He swirled the brown liquid in the cup, his head echoing with the yet she did not say aloud.

Zach drained his cup, rose and picked up the bowl of dirty, bloody water. "If there's a way to help your little one, Mitchel, Emma will find it. I married one stubborn woman."

"Tenacious."

Zach grinned at his wife. "Different word, same result."

Mitchel shifted his gaze to the hearth. The look the two exchanged made his heart hunger for what he would never have with Anne.

Zach opened the kitchen door and tossed the dirty

water out on the ground. The fire flared in the draft, settled back to a steady burn when he closed the door.

Emma dipped her fingers in the crock, spread salve on his wound. "Hope also has a good appetite, which is a favorable sign. Hold your arm out, Mitchel." She wound a clean, white bandage around his arm and tied it in place. "That wound should heal quickly now."

She took the chair opposite him, fastened her gaze on his. "I will not lie to you, Mitchel. Hope's illness can be a dangerous one."

Her words stabbed deep, made his heart bleed. He clenched his hand around the cup and nodded.

"But I helped Papa Doc with several of his patients and I know it is the weak, the undernourished, the *uncared* for who do not survive. Your little Hope is none of those things. And, given what little I have seen of her, I believe she has a fighting spirit. Our job will be to keep her quiet—rest is very important—and to see to it she has a reason to keep fighting."

She smiled, rose and picked up her medical supplies. "Now if you gentlemen will excuse me, I will go check on my two patients."

The brush of the hem of her long skirt across the wide planks of the kitchen floor blended with the crackle and snap of the fire, faded away as she swished out the door. Mitchel lifted his cup, drank the cold coffee.

"Sorry about that bacon."

He lifted his head. Zach had that lopsided grin on his face.

"Emma's still learning about the cooking part of being a wife. She tends to leave the meat on the fire a bit too long. But she makes good soup and *great* apple dumplings." Zach turned, reached into the cupboard behind him, opened a wooden box with holes in the top and took out two apple dumplings. He put them on plates, added a fork, set one down at his place and slid the other down the table to him. "Best part of breakfast!"

He picked up the fork and stabbed it into the dumpling.

"I meant what I said earlier about Emma, Mitchel."

He raised his head, studied Zach's now sober expression.

"Emma's a top-notch doctor. There's a lot of folks here in Promise that wouldn't have made it across country if she hadn't been on the wagon train. If there's a way to help your little one, Emma will find it. She's a fighter."

The pressure in his chest eased a little. He nodded, speared a piece of apple with his fork. "It must run in the family."

"What's that mean?"

"Adam Halstrum worked for me at the mission, ran the gristmill. He and his son stole some furs from the Cayuse, and when he learned they were coming after them, he decided to use the Cayuse children Anne was teaching as hostages so they could escape. Anne warned him off, and when he tried to take them anyway, she shot him…in the shoulder."

"Good for Annie!" Emma swept into the kitchen, a frown on her face. "What sort of person would put children in harm's way to save his own life? I shall have to write home about *that*." The frown turned into a smile. "Mother always said you couldn't push Annie, you had to coax her. She insisted it's the red curls."

Zach laid his fork down, grabbed the pot and poured more coffee. "I didn't ask before, figured it was none of my business, but this Halstrum—is he the one who sliced you?"

He shook his head. "No. It was a Cayuse warrior named Eagle Claw. He ambushed me on the trail. But Halstrum had a part in it. It was all the same day and all for the same reason, because Halstrum and two trapper friends of his stole the Indians' furs. The Cayuse figured I had a part in it, and they wanted blood for revenge. They burned and looted the mission."

"That's why you were afoot in the mountains?"

His face tightened. He nodded, took a sip of coffee before he could speak. "Chief White Cloud warned me the Cayuse would attack if I left before Halstrum got back from his trip to sell the furs. It was the first I learned about his thefts."

The weariness washed over him in an overwhelming wave. "I told Anne, warned her we had to carry on as usual but be ready to leave in a moment, and that we would have to walk in order to hide." He looked at Emma, saw a glint of tears in her eyes. "Your sister is one of the bravest people I've ever known. She made those clothes so Hope would stay warm and dry in the snow. And she baked biscuits to take along. And when Halstrum tried to take those Cayuse children, she shot him. Then she took Hope and hid in a cave while the Indians tortured Halstrum and his son and raided and burned the mission."

He swallowed, cleared his throat. "Eagle Claw ambushed me the day the Cayuse were taking their revenge." He shook his head, rubbed his dry, burning eyes to stay awake. "Our fight ended when we fell off a cliff. I knocked my head, and lost the whole day. By the time I made it back, there was nothing but charred wood, and hot coals burning where the snow couldn't reach them. I—I thought I had lost them both. And then Anne came out of that cave carrying Hope in her arms—" He shook his head, put his elbows on the table, lowered his head into his hands and toppled sideways.

Zach shot out a hand to brace Mitchel, rose and stepped behind him, slid his arms under Mitchel's armpits and dragged him back from the table. "Hold the chair, so I can get a grip on him, Emma. I'll help him in to lay him on the rug in front of the fire. Then I'll ride into town and talk with Hargrove and Lundquist and some of the others. When I tell them that story, they'll want to help, too."

Emma nodded, wiped the tears from her eyes and came around the table and gripped the chair. Zach leaned down, draped Mitchel's uninjured arm over his shoulder, grasped Mitchel's wrist then straightened and grabbed him around the waist. "C'mon Mitchel, let's get you in the other room."

"I'll help." Emma reached for Mitchel's other arm.

"No, Emma. He's too heavy for you. I don't want anything to happen to that little filly of mine you're carrying." Zach gave a lunge.

Mitchel moved his feet, half walked, half stumbled along, collapsed with a yawn onto the rug by the hearth in the parlor.

Emma ran into the bedroom, brought back a blanket and spread it over him. She watched Zach shrug into his jacket, then went on tiptoe and gave him a kiss. "Whatever you men decide, Zachary Thatcher, you make certain it means Mitchel Banning will stay here in Promise. That baby needs care, our town needs brave, good men like Mitchel, and that man loves my sister!"

"Yeah, that was sort of plain." Zach returned her kiss and hurried out and closed the door.

Emma leaned back against it, looked down at Mitchel Banning, shook her head and smiled. "Thank You, God. You sure are working it out in a mysterious way, but I think Annie is going to have her dream."

She lifted her gaze to the wood and beam ceiling, lifted her heart in faith. "That leaves William, God. And I sure don't know how You're going to fulfill his dream of coming to Oregon country and teaching the Indians when the mission has been destroyed, but I have learned to trust You to work everything out for the good."

She patted her swelling stomach under her skirt and headed for the kitchen to clean up the breakfast dishes and start some soup for supper.

Anne stirred, yawned, felt the softness of a mattress beneath her and bolted upright. A shaft of bright sunlight poked her in the eye. She turned her head, looked around the strange room. Where was she? *Hope.* Where were Hope and Mitchel?

She shook her head to try and clear her thoughts, threw back the covers and slid out of bed, her heart pounding. She would worry about where she was and how she had got here later. She had to find Hope, take care of her. Was she hurting or hungry? Soft fabric slipped down her legs.

She jerked her gaze down, stared at the yellow cotton nightgown, the white ribbon ties on the bodice, the hem that pooled on the floor at her feet.

"There you see, sweetie, I told you Annie was awake."

Emma. Tears welled, spilled out of her eyes and ran down her cheeks. She looked up, saw her sister at the door. Hope, dressed in her white nightgown and blue blanket pants, was in her arms. She burst into tears.

"Oh, Annie, don't cry." Her sister's arm came around her shoulders and pulled her close. Emma's cheek, warm and soft and blessedly familiar, pressed against hers. "Hope is fine. Mitchel is fine. And so are you. You're all safe now."

She nodded, wrapped her arms around Emma and rested her head on her shoulder.

"Me hurt." Hope wiggled between them.

She drew back, took Hope into her arms, suffered another rush of tears at the feel of the toddler's small arms sliding around her neck, her little head burrowing against the side of her neck. She hugged Hope close, swayed side-to-side, looked at her sister. "I was s-so afraid for her, Emma. She's not w-well."

The tears flowed again. She sank down on the side of the bed, forced a trembling smile. "I'm sorry, I can't s-seem to control my tears."

"It's little wonder after what you've been through." Emma sat beside her. She felt the warmth of her sister's arm come around her again and leaned into its comfort. "Though Mitchel did say you are one of the bravest people he's ever known."

Emma drew back, fixed her brown-eyed gaze on her. "Annie, did you really shoot that man?"

"I did." She stiffened her back, jutted her chin. "And, after what he put us through, if I had it to do again, I wouldn't aim for his shoulder!"

Emma burst into laughter, hugged her tight. "Welcome back, Annie." Her voice choked. "Mother was right about those red curls of yours. Now—"

She looked up as Emma rose and held out her arms.

"Let me carry Hope, Anne. You hold up that night-gown so you don't trip over it, and we'll go to the kitchen and get you something to eat. You are looking downright *gaunt,* my little sister."

She surrendered Hope, rose, lifted the hem of the nightgown and followed Emma out the bedroom door.

"And then—" Emma glanced over her shoulder at her "—when you are finished eating, we will see about altering some of my dresses so you have something to wear. Your black gown was quite stained, and torn and tattered beyond decent repair. I threw it away."

Anne stood by the fire holding Hope, soaking up the heat and ignoring the questions about Mitchel that begged to be asked. His whereabouts and his affairs were none of her business.

She glanced down at the soup Emma was ladling into a bowl from the iron pot on the crane. It looked good. It was hard to believe Emma had made it. Domestic skills had never interested her sister. All Emma had ever wanted was to be a doctor. And all *she* had ever wanted was to be a wife and mother. Phillip had destroyed that dream with his love of racing horses.

Until now.

She frowned, changed the direction of her thoughts. "I can't seem to get warm. I can feel the heat of the fire, yet I'm shivering. It's very annoying."

Emma pushed the crane back to dangle the pot of soup over the fire and carried the filled bowl to the table. "You haven't been eating anything but biscuits, Annie. And few of those. And you've been trudging over snowy mountains in frigid weather for days. It's not surprising you feel cold. The shivering should go away when you get some hot, nourishing food in you. Come and eat."

"Me want some."

Anne studied the toddler's eager expression. "I guess eating nothing but biscuits and dried apples the past few days has improved Hope's appetite. Mitchel said she ate very little at home."

"Until you began fixing her special meals to coax her to eat." Emma smiled and ladled soup into a small bowl. "Her first request when she woke was for ''tatoes and brown stuff.'"

"Me *like* 'tatoes and bwown stuff."

Emma laughed and put the bowl on the table. "Well, you get soup tonight, little one. Now come sit with me and let Anne eat."

Hope frowned. "Me not little, me Papa's big girl."

"Wonderful. Big girls eat all their soup." Emma carried Hope to the table and settled the toddler on her lap.

Anne sat in the chair closest to the fire, her gaze fastened on Hope.

"What is it, Anne?"

She lifted her gaze to Emma, shook her head. "I don't know. At the mission, Hope was so listless. All she did was lie in bed. And she cried often. She was not like that on the journey. And now, she acts so…different."

Emma nodded, helped Hope manage the spoon that was too big for her little hands. "Mitchel said she had a Cayuse nanny. Perhaps, Hope didn't understand her words. She is a very smart, very social little girl. It sounds as if she was enjoying being in the company of you and her papa on the journey."

"Then it's not— You haven't—"

"No, Annie. There's nothing I know to do beyond

easing her discomfort and keeping her quiet and rested. The rest is in God's hands."

"Does Mitchel know?"

"Yes. But I also told him some of the children I visited with Papa Doc improved vastly and led quiet, but normal lives. I am trusting that Hope will be one of the blessed ones."

Trusting, yes.

What time I am afraid, I will trust in Thee.

She let the prayer rise from her heart and picked up her spoon.

Chapter Twenty-Three

Anne lifted the hem of the nightgown from the floor and followed Emma into the parlor. The soft, cotton gown brushed against her legs, a flash of brightness with every step. Yellow, a happy color. Simply looking at it lifted one's spirit. A smile tugged at her lips. She would make Hope a dress of yellow with warm, matching pants.

She shook her head, clenched the cotton in her hands. Hope was not hers. Mitchel would be moving on and Hope would go out of her life. She pressed her lips together, lifted her chin. Nonetheless, no more black widow's garb for her. She was free of wearing those somber, depressing clothes that forever reminded her of her loss and sorrow. Emma had no black dresses for her to alter.

She looked around the room searching for distraction from her gloomy thoughts. Pride surged through her. The emigrants must think very highly of Emma's doctoring skills to have built her such a fine, large cabin, with its added-on kitchen, and the good-size bedroom or two.

She stared at the second door a short distance from the open one to Emma's bedroom. No doubt it was her room for treating patients. Her sister's dream of being a doctor had come true.

She glanced at the stone fireplace throwing warmth into the cozy room and— *Cozy.* She paused, swept her gaze over the oil lamp sitting on the mantel beside a small stack of books, the two wooden pegs protruding from the stone above it. She gave a passing thought as to what purpose the pegs served, then glanced at the blue settee sitting at a right angle to the fireplace, the two padded chairs facing it, the rug that covered the plank floor between them. Where had Emma gotten such fine furniture?

She eyed the desk and chair sitting beside the small, multipaned window on the side wall and her pulse quickened. She hurried into the bedroom, smiled at Hope who was lying on the bed holding a piece of red ribbon, her eyes heavy with sleep. "The emigrants have built you a lovely, spacious cabin, Emma. But where did you get such fine furniture? Have you been to Oregon city? Has one of Uncle Justin's boats arrived?"

Emma shook her head, continued searching in the trunk, then stopped, sat back on her heels and looked up at her. "I forgot you don't know, Anne."

"Don't know what?"

Emma gave a soft laugh. "The emigrants didn't build me this cabin, Zach did. And Zach bought the furniture from a widow who was returning to New York. We're married. I'm Mrs. Zachary Thatcher."

"Married!" Her mouth gaped. "You're married to your nemesis Zachary Thatcher!"

Emma laughed. "I am. And I've never been happier. Oh, Annie, he's such a wonderful man! So thoughtful and caring and loving. And—" her laughter stopped, her hands crossed over her abdomen "—I'm going to have a baby, Annie."

Her sister's words were soft, hesitant. She was afraid to tell her. "Oh, Emma…" Anne went to her knees, hugged her older sister with all her strength. "I'm happy for you, Emma. Truly happy for you." Memories washed over her. She pushed them away. She had made her family suffer much too long because of her fear of being hurt again.

She rocked back on her heels, wiped tears from her eyes. "I suppose Mr. Thatcher wants a son." Phillip did. He'd been disappointed when Grace was born. Pain squeezed her heart.

"Actually, Zach insists he wants a little girl. A blond one, as stubborn as me." Emma laughed, patted her abdomen. "He calls the baby his 'little filly.' I am the one that wants a son. One who is strong and adventurous and handsome, like Zach."

She tried to stop it, but envy crept into her heart and spirit. It wasn't that she didn't want Emma to have a wonderful husband and lovely children. It was that she wanted them, too. She wanted them with all of her heart. But not simply *any* husband and child. Her gaze lifted to the toddler asleep on the bed, and her whole body went still with the knowing. She wanted Mitchel and Hope.

"Emma!"

Anne jerked her head toward the door, looked a question at her sister.

"It's Lydia Hargrove." Emma scrambled to her feet, headed for the open door. "Come along, Anne, we'll look for dresses to alter when she's gone."

She shook her head, grasped the front of the nightgown between her thumbs and index fingers and held it out from her body.

"Oh, poof!" Emma gave a dismissive wave. "Lydia's seen women in nightgowns before."

"Well…" Anne followed Emma, glanced at Hope sound asleep on the bed, closed the door and turned.

"Oh!" She stared at the women stomping snow from their shoes, others who were crowding through the open door and froze in her tracks. Heat climbed into her cheeks.

Lydia Hargrove took off her cloak, tossed it on the wood bench by the door and looked her way. She fisted her hands on her plump hips and nodded. "Glad to see you're some rested, Anne. But you look a mite peaked. Better than what I expected though after what you've been through." She shook her gray head, advanced into the room. "It was hard enough trekking through them mountains in a wagon, let alone walking and carrying a little one, and with no comforts to speak of."

There was a chorus of amens.

"Anyway, the men told us about what happened at the mission. How you lost everything you had and all. And we figured you had some needs. Thought maybe we could help 'til you can make plans and get started again. Here's a length of wool I was saving to make me a skirt. Should be enough for a dress for you."

There was a chorus of laughter. Lydia joined in, then sobered, placed the material on the settee and stepped aside. "The others can speak for themselves."

Anne looked down at the green wool fabric, swung her gaze to the others—they were all holding something. And she knew the cost was dear to most of them. Tears stung her eyes. She swallowed hard, forced words past the lump in her throat. "I—I don't know what to say, ladies. I treated you all so—so shabbily on our journey here. I refused your company when you offered—" she swallowed back a rush of tears "—to befriend me. I'm undeserving of your kindness and generosity."

"Oh, pshaw! We've all had our bad times. This here's a tablecloth, come from the old country. Figured you could make yourself a pretty shirtwaist from it." Olga Lundquist stepped forward, placed a beautiful lace-trimmed tablecloth on top of the green wool.

"I heard 'bout the little toddler you brought safe from them heathens' grasp, an' I brung one of my Jenny's dresses for her." Lorna Lewis stepped forward, placed a small blue dress on the pile, then gave her a fierce look. "An' don't you be sayin' nothin' 'bout not deservin' it. If it weren't for Dr. Emma I wouldn't have my Jenny!"

Anne nodded, became more and more choked up as one by one the women stepped forward and added their sacrifices to the growing pile. Every object given was a loved treasure or a protected necessity the women had brought with them on the long, arduous wagon journey from their homes back east to Oregon country.

Her heart filled, overflowed with gratitude and affection for the women's generosity in so readily forgiving her for holding them at a distance during the journey. How wrong she had been to turn her back on the love and understanding they had so freely offered then, were freely offering now. This time she would not withdraw to protect her heart. This time she would accept their friendship and give hers in return. *Bless them for their generous hearts, Lord, I pray. And show me how I may become a blessing to them.*

She blinked the moisture from her eyes and moved forward to thank them.

* * *

"I've only been to the mission once, Mitchel—when I brought Anne. I'm not familiar with the wide range of the country, but I'm sensing we're getting close to Indian territory. Do you know where the Cayuse are located?"

Mitchel looked over at the man sitting astride the roan stallion as if he'd grown there. There was little resemblance to the affable rancher of Promise. Zachary Thatcher's features had sharpened, his bright blue eyes glinted with a hardness that provoked pity for the man's enemies. "We're getting close to their territory. There's a large village a mile or so to the north of that next hill."

Zach nodded, held up his hand. The men following reined in, walked their mounts close, waited. "Mitchel says we're getting close to Cayuse territory. I don't expect there to be any braves standing lookout, and I know it's dusk, but Indians can see a tic on a dog's back at a hundred yards in the dark, so we'll take to the woods here and rest our mounts. Charley, you scout ahead, find us a way to pass them in the night."

A small, wiry, dark-haired young man dressed in buckskins nodded, walked his mount forward, then touched his heels to his horse's sides and disappeared against the backdrop of the trees.

The rest of the men dismounted and led their horses, single file, into the woods.

Mitchel slid from the saddle, gripped the reins and glanced up at the sky, willing night to fall. He wanted to get this trip to the mission over with and return to Hope…and Anne. He shook his head and moved forward into the murky light of the woods. Hearts were foolish things. At least his was. It didn't know enough not to go where it wasn't wanted.

* * *

"I heard Zach tellin' Axel it won't take 'em more than two days ridin' to get to the mission."

To get to the *mission?* Fear pounced. Anne shifted her gaze from Olga Lundquist to Emma, the buzz of conversation overcome by the roaring of her pulse in her ears. She wet her dry lips, forced out the question. "Mitchel and Zach have gone to the mission?"

"Not alone, Anne. Several of the men went with them. They don't know what they will encounter, or how much they will find at the mission that is salvageable." Emma wrinkled her brow in thought. "I saw Charley Karr and Luke Murray…and Seth Applegate in the yard."

"An' Axel and Garth an' Ernst joined 'em when they come by. Garth and Ernst figured they might could help herd back any stock still alive. An' Axel knows how to rig up a wagon fit to carry things out of next to nothing!" There was pride in Olga Lundquist's voice. She took a sip of cider, looked across the table at Lydia Hargrove. "What about Matthew?"

Lydia nodded. "My Matthew went along. But that's the men's affair. We ladies have got other important business to talk about."

There was a murmur of agreement. Every eye fastened on her. Anne straightened, looked at Emma, who shrugged and shook her head.

"Well get to it, Lydia." Hannah Fletcher frowned at the older woman. "We all got chores waitin'. An' don't none of us want to leave here without knowin'."

"That's right." A murmur of agreement swept around the table.

Lydia tapped her cup against the table. "If you'll all hush, I'll speak my piece."

Anne clenched her hands in her lap, fought the urge to squirm when all the women quieted and looked her way. What did they want of her?

Lydia Hargrove cleared her throat. "Well, it's this way, Anne. When our wagon train was forming, way back in Independence, we women had us a meeting and we made our husbands promise that, as soon as ever possible, after they settled in the place where they'd found our town of Promise, they'd build us a church and a school."

Affirmation sprang from the women's lips.

Anne glanced at Emma. There was a tiny smile playing at the corners of her sister's mouth. A tingle of excitement spread through her. Could it be?

Lydia tapped her cup for quiet. "A town isn't rightfully a town without a church and a school. And while we're right sorry for the trouble at the mission, when Zach told Mr. Hargrove what happened, he called a town meeting and we all agreed it could be turned into a blessing for everyone. Our cabins are all built and our husbands declared it was time they kept their promise to us."

She was certain now. And so was Emma. Her sister was beaming. Her heart began to pound.

"So Mr. Hargrove and the men met with Mr. Banning, told him they were gonna build us a church and offered to give him land and build him a cabin if he'd be our pastor."

The pounding in her heart stopped, her breath stuck to her lungs, refused to release.

"He said yes, so the men went with him to see what he could find to bring back for his new home."

Mitchel was staying. Her heart and lungs worked again.

"And we women had us another meeting." Lydia fixed her gaze on her. "We all know you left Promise and went on to the Banning Mission to teach school to the Indian children. So we came to ask would you teach our children? We can't pay you anything yet. But our menfolk will build a cabin for you. And we'll see you don't want for food or firewood. Of course if you want to go back east after all you been through, we'll understand."

She looked around the table at their anxious expressions. *Thank You, God, for showing me the way to be a blessing to them.*

"Say 'yes,' Annie."

She looked at Emma and grinned. *"Yes."*

Chapter Twenty-Four

Mitchel slapped the snow from his hat brim, crouched beneath the beam supporting a scorched section of fallen roof and heaved. The beam slid to the left, caught on a protruding stone on the shoulder of the fireplace. He ground his feet into the ashes and cinders on the puncheon floor, placed his hand against the edge of the beam and shoved. It slid off the stone, crashed to the ground where the kitchen door once stood.

He leaned down, scrubbed the black char from his hands in the snow, then straightened and looked at the fireplace he'd exposed. An iron stew pot hung from a hook on the crane. Spiders of different sizes sat on the hearth beside the iron teapot on its trivet. Large iron spoons, a two-tined fork and half-melted pewter porringers hung from iron nails in the mantel. The poker and fire tongs leaned against the stone. An oil lamp sat on the mantel.

It wasn't much, but at least he would be able to cook—once he learned how. An image of Anne, making biscuits in the darkened kitchen with fear in her beautiful eyes, her small chin raised in defiant purpose, flashed into his head.

He gritted his teeth, set the oil lamp at the edge of the floor. Anne was out of his life now. She was back with her sister. There was no mission, no school and no reason for her to be with him. Anne had made it clear she still loved her husband and wanted no part of any other man. Or child, though her care for Hope during the Cayuse raid and their long journey had given him hope. No, that was of necessity. It did not mean she was beginning to care for his daughter. She thought as highly of the Cayuse children. She had shot a man to protect them.

He pulled his thoughts back to the present, gathered the utensils and iron pots into a pile by the oil lamp, pushed aside part of a collapsed wall and what remained of the worktable and peered into the buttery. The walls were intact, the ceiling collapsed around the well. His stomach twisted at the thought of what would have happened to them had they taken refuge there.

He picked up a bucket, undamaged except for a little char around the edge, and turned to survey what remained of the rest of the kitchen. The dining room wall with all the shelves had burned and fallen in.

There was nothing more in the kitchen, or dining room. And little hope of anything at all from the parlor or bedrooms.

He hopped down off the floor, walked through the snow to where the schoolroom had been and shoved aside the burned bottom section of the stairs. The support posts of the landing creaked, settled a little farther toward the schoolroom, stopped. He went to his knees, peered into the dark area. What looked like a burned trunk sat there, debris atop it. He frowned, looked up at the gaping hole where the ceiling had been. The trunk must have fallen from Anne's room.

He tossed aside the pieces of blackened wood on the floor to clear a path, grasped the scorched end and pulled. The handle and attached wood came off in his hand. He scooted farther forward, gripped both sides of the trunk and hauled it out into the open.

The trunk was scorched beyond use. He lifted the lid, stared down at the neatly folded bed linens, blankets and towels. His chest tightened. At least being at the mission hadn't cost Anne everything. He could return these to her. And perhaps more.

He pushed the trunk aside, ducked his head and scanned the dark area again. His desk, the legs burned off, lay on its end, the drawer partially open, the spilled contents a pile of ashes. The oil lamp, the base intact, the globe shattered, sat on the floor beside it. And in the corner, its cover stained with ink from the broken ink-well that rested atop it, was his Bible.

He drew it out, brushed a film of ashes from it. Hoof-beats jerked him to attention. He dropped his Bible onto the linens in the trunk and gripped his pistol.

"Hello, Mitchel! Look what we found in the woods!"

He rose, peered through the snow as Garth and Ernst Lundquist rode out of the wooded path. Three cows, one of them limping, and a calf trotted in front of them. The calf that had almost died at birth. For some reason he didn't understand, the sight of that calf gladdened his heart. He hopped down from the floor onto the snow-covered ground and walked toward them.

Axel Lundquist and Matthew Hargrove came out of what was left of the stables and joined him. "Found some harness and a saddle that can be saved with a good oiling. But that's the whole of it."

His lips quirked. He would be able to ride—as soon as he could buy a horse.

Axel squinted up at his sons. "What's wrong with that cow?"

Garth frowned. "She's got a nasty gash on her hip. 'Pears like she might have caught a glancing blow from a tomahawk."

"Well, she'll likely live if she's made it this long."

Zach strode up to him. "Nothing in the gristmill or Halstrum's cabin, Mitchel. The Indians seemed to take particular care to ruin everything there."

Mitchel nodded, clenched his hands. "That's probably where he hid the furs the trappers stole from the Cayuse." He looked at the men coming from the direction of the smithy. "Seth, Luke, did you find anything?"

"Nothing but the anvil. They either took the tools or threw them in the river. We looked around the ground some. Couldn't find anything."

"You find anything, Mitchel?"

He looked at Zach, nodded, brushed the ashes off his hands. "Some iron cookware and some dishes. My Bible, blankets and bed linens. And an oil lamp. Odd how something that delicate could survive the fire."

Zach nodded, turned his back to the rising wind. "That's it then. No use wasting more time." He peered up at the snow falling thicker and faster out of a gray sky. "Looks like God's granting us favor. We can't sneak through the Cayuse territory herding cows and carrying clanking pots. But Indians don't like the cold. The Cayuse will stay close to their villages. And not even an Indian can see through a snowfall thick as this."

Zach motioned the man standing watch over their horses to bring them over. "Charley, you ride out and scout the trail, but don't get too far ahead. This storm shows signs of getting serious, and I don't want anyone getting lost. Garth and Ernst, you follow Charley with the cows."

Zach shifted his gaze to him. "Mitchel, divide up the stuff you found and we'll carry it among us. Cold as it is, those blankets might prove a real blessing. The rest of you, mount up, take what Mitchel gives you and head out. And all of you, stay close together."

Mitchel gave each man a blanket or sheet to drape over their shoulders and warm their backs, then parceled out the iron pots he had collected. He tore the wet tablecloth in half, used one piece to pad the dishes in the bucket then hooked the bail over his saddle horn. He wrapped the oil lamp in the other piece of tablecloth and put it in the iron stew pot, tucked his Bible inside his shirtfront. One quick swing of his leg and he was in the saddle. He balanced the stew pot in front of him, reined his horse around and followed after the others.

The wind gusted, blew snow down his neck, chilled his fingers holding the iron pot. When they reached the spot at the top of the hill where he always stopped and looked down on the mission buildings below, he glanced over his shoulder. There was nothing to see but stone fireplaces standing sentinel over blackened beams rising from the snow.

He turned and rode on toward his daughter, toward his new life as pastor of the church in Promise. A life without Anne.

Wind whistled around the chimney, rattled the glass panes in the small window. Anne shivered, tucked the covers more closely around Hope and added another piece of wood to the fire.

Mitchel was out there in the storm. Where was he? And Zach and the other men? Were they in the woods where they would have some protection from the howling wind, or out on the plain at the storm's mercy? Would they be warm enough? Did they have food to eat? What if they lost their way in the blinding snow?

The questions pummeled her. Fear for Mitchel's safety gnawed at her. *What time I am afraid...* She was afraid now. She had this insane desire to be out there with him so she would know he was all right.

She walked to the window, stared at the snow plastered against the glass. William said Mitchel had told him the winters in Oregon country were mild. Not this one. This one had weather that put her in mind of the occasional blizzard back east.

What if he didn't make it home?

She shook her head, felt her long, loose curls, still damp from her bath, brush against her back. Mitchel had no home. But the promise of one. And the one in her heart. That was Mitchel's home, though he didn't know it. And didn't care to have it so. Hope was his only love.

She shivered, walked back to the fireplace to absorb some heat. When had she changed? When had her fear of being hurt again, of suffering the devastating pain of a loved one's loss, been overcome by her need to love and be loved? When had her desire to stay numb succumbed to her desire to live again? When had she fallen in love with Mitchel Banning?

And with Hope?

She looked at the toddler asleep in the bed, her cheeks rosy with warmth, her soft blond curls framing her adorable face. She could not bear to lose her. But she would. Hope was not hers. Only in her heart. Her foolish, *foolish* heart. Why couldn't it have stayed unfeeling? Why must she again suffer the loss of a man and a child she loved?

Because she would rather have Mitchel's love and Hope for a short time than to live the empty existence that had been her goal before she met Mitchel.

She took a deep breath, inched her shoulders back, raised her chin and clenched her hands. Mitchel's love and his adorable daughter were worth fighting for. And God hadn't given her red hair for nothing.

Anne stepped into the small room with a roof that began high on the kitchen fireplace chimney and sloped steeply to the ground. She sniffed and the astringent odor of crushed herbs carried her straight back to her childhood. She wrinkled her nose at Emma and smiled. "It smells like Papa Doc in here."

Emma laughed, gave a tiny bow of her head. "Thank you. You couldn't say anything that would please me more."

She scanned the shelves on the wall filled with crocks and stoppered bottles and rolls of bandages, looked to her sister working with mortar and pestle beneath a hanging oil lamp that spread a golden circle of light on the small table. "So this is your apothecary. Very smart attaching it behind the kitchen fireplace, it's nice and warm in here."

"It was Zach's idea. He's very clever at coming up with solutions to a need or problems."

She laughed. "I remember when you didn't find Zach's solutions clever. You found them…combative."

Emma nodded, spooned the crushed herbs in the

mortar into a bottle. "I was so focused on the sneer-
ing rejections I had suffered at the hands of other men
I thought he was disdainful of my doctoring skills, as
well. I couldn't have been more wrong. Are you ready
to leave?"

"Yes, Hope is down for her nap. I should return be
fore she wakes."

Anne grabbed her hood, ducked her head against the
driving snow and eyed the small ferry on the other side
of the slow-flowing river. It looked like a long, floating box with doorways in both ends. Another of Zach's
clever solutions to a need, no doubt. But how did one
use it?

She stepped to the anchored post on the riverbank
and slid her gaze along the taut rope that fed through
the pulley on top. The rope was affixed to iron rings on
the corner posts of the ferry. From there it fed through a
pulley atop a matching anchor post on the opposite bank
and returned. An experimental tug on the bottom loop
of the rope brought the ferry away from the far bank.
She smiled and tugged the bottom loop, hand over hand,
until the near end of the ferry nudged up against the riverbank in front of her.

She lifted the dragging hems of Emma's too-long
dress and stepped through the gaping doorway onto the
ferry, felt a dip and hurried to the center of the floating
box. River water lapped at the bottom of the hip-high
wall, then slipped beneath the ferry and flowed away.
A few strong pulls on the top rope brought her across
the river. A smile curved her lips at sight of the large
bell atop a solid post with an iron arm. The carved sign
swinging in the wind on small chains from the iron arm

read "Dr. Emma." A warm feeling settled around her heart. God had granted her sister her dream.

Hope swelled. Perhaps God would grant her dream, as well. He had once. And then Phillip had taken it away. Grief for her lost husband and child rose, a sorrow that would always be a part of her. But she was ready to live again. To dream again. She glanced up through the falling snow to the overcast sky. "I will trust in Thee, God. Thy will be done." The wind tore the words from her lips.

She grasped the edge of the hood, pulled it forward and ducked her head as she made her way across a large open space, skirted a pile of logs. Small chunks of raw wood littered the ground. She lifted her head, stared at the notched logs that formed the beginning of a cabin. *Mitchel's* cabin? Her pulse quickened. Could it be? Right here? Directly across the river from Emma's and Zach's home?

Lydia would know. She ducked her head and continued across the space toward the clustered cabins. Emma had said the first cabin on the right belonged to the Hargroves. She hurried to the door and knocked.

"I shall be happy to advance you any amount you need, Widow Simms. Simply tell the merchants to present your accounts to me for payment."

Anne rose from the chair and smiled across the desk at the portly, gray-haired man. "Thank you, Mr. Hargrove. I will settle my debt with you as soon as I receive a letter from home."

The man's bushy eyebrows drew together. "You do understand that banks charge interest on money advanced to their clients, do you not, Widow Simms?"

She nodded, held back a frown at his pontifical tone. "I am well versed in the matters of finance thanks to my mother and my uncle Justin. Their businesses are many and varied. *Banking* is one of them." She allowed that information to soak in for a moment, then again smiled at the pompous banker. "Good afternoon, Mr. Hargrove. And please—call me Anne. I find the 'widow' appellation wearisome."

She glanced at Lydia's bemused expression, gave her a warm smile and stepped outside into the blustery cold.

The next cabin on the right. She repeated Emma's instructions, hurried on to the next cabin, saw the sign affixed to the logs beside the door—Thomas Swinton, Merchant. Enter.

She opened the door. A small bell rang. She stomped the snow from her boots, stepped inside and closed the door with another tinkling of the bell. Warmth from a fire greeted her. She moved to the shelves along the wall, studied the items displayed.

"May I help you, Anne?"

She turned, smiled as Pamelia Swinton limped toward her. "I am interested in sewing notions."

Pamelia nodded, smiled. "I thought you might be. Let me show you what we have to offer."

Chapter Twenty-Five

Anne cut the last skirt panel from the green wool, added it to the pile of other skirt pieces and eyed the leftover fabric spread out on the floor. If she planned it right, there should be enough left to cut out a bodice and make a dress.

"Me want Papa."

She looked up at Hope. The toddler's lower lip was quivering, the packet of buttons she had given her to play with lay on the bed beside her. "Your papa will be home soon, sweetie." *Please, God.*

Tears glistened in the toddler's eyes.

She put down her scissors, rose and snatched Hope's cloak off the chest against the wall, sat on the bed and pulled it around Hope's shoulders. "You and I are going outside for a walk." She tugged the hood in place and tied the ribbons.

"Me see aminals?" Hope's face brightened.

"As many as we can find." She laughed, scooped Hope into her arms and headed for the parlor, crossed to the front door, stepped out onto the porch and tapped lightly on Emma's office door. "I'm taking Hope to the barn, Emma. I'll be back shortly to help with dinner."

The sky was overcast, large, fluffy snowflakes drifted lazily through the cold air. "Watch me, Hope." She waited until a snowflake floated close, stuck out her tongue and caught it.

Hope giggled, clapped her small hands. "Me do it." She tilted back her head, stuck out her little tongue and leaned backward to catch a snowflake. It landed on her eye. She giggled, stuck out her tongue and tried again... and again...and again.

Anne laughed, kept a firm grip on the squirming toddler and headed for the river. The sharp thunk of an ax biting into wood accompanied the swish and gurgle of the water rushing along the bank. "Look across the river, Hope. Do you see those men working?"

The toddler looked, nodded.

"They are building a cabin for you and your papa. Soon you will have a lovely, snug home. Won't that be nice?"

"An' a horsey?"

Anne laughed, hugged Hope close. "I don't know about a horsey. You will have to ask your papa about that. But we can go see if there is a horsey in the barn." She turned and headed for the large log barn, careful not to trip over the long skirt of Emma's gown.

"Piggies!"

"Yes. I hear them."

"Me wanna see piggies. Piggies do—" Hope made an attempt at a snort.

Anne choked with laughter, leaned against the barn to keep from collapsing in a heap on the ground. "Oh my, Hope. You have to show your Aunt Emma—" *Aunt*

Emma. Only if— She sobered. *If it is Your will, God. I put my trust in You.*

She straightened, lifted Hope higher on her shoulder. "Let's go see the pigs. And then we'll see what animals we will find in the barn."

"Is she all right? I didn't harm her by taking her outside this afternoon, did I?" Anne lifted her gaze from Hope to Emma.

"She's fine, Anne." Emma released Hope's tiny wrist and tucked her small arm back under the covers. "What has you worried?"

"She's sleeping so *soundly.*" Anne glanced back down at Hope, tucked the covers more closely beneath her tiny chin. "She's not made a whimper since I put her to bed."

Emma nodded, yawned. "Well, you've no cause to worry. Her sleep is a natural, healthy one." She grinned at her. "From what Mitchel told me of Hope's life these past few months, the child has done little but lie in bed. My diagnosis is that you simply wore her out this afternoon, Anne."

She let out a long sigh. "Well, that's a relief. I thought perhaps she had turned for the worse, though I could detect no sign of fever." She looked up at her sister. "I'm sorry, I disturbed your rest, Emma."

Her sister gave a soft laugh. "I'm a doctor, Annie. I'm accustomed to being awakened at all hours. *And* to dropping right back to sleep when whatever crisis that prompted the awakening is over. I intend to do that right now." Emma yawned, headed for the door, looked back. "You should get some sleep, too."

She smiled and nodded. "I shall. But I want to get more sewing done first." She glanced down at the green wool fabric draped over the chair by the hearth. She had been working on it every moment she was not caring for Hope. It was already a dress. But there was trimming and hemming to do.

"I guess there are some things more important than sleep. Things like looking your best in a new gown when your beau comes home."

Emma's voice held a teasing note. She jerked her gaze up. "Mitchel is not my beau."

"Not yet. But wait until he sees you in that dress. That *is* the reason you are working on it so furiously, is it not?" Emma gave her a saucy grin, turned and waltzed out of the room. "Better hurry, Annie. If Zach was right, and the storm did not delay them, the men could be back tomorrow."

The words floated into the room on Emma's soft laughter.

Tomorrow. She grabbed up the green wool, picked up her needle and continued stitching the hem of the right sleeve. She would soon be finished with sewing the dress and then she could start adding the trim.

She glanced at the notions she had purchased at Swinton's store and smiled. The green wool was a sober color and Mitchel might think she had chosen it to replace her ruined widow garment. But he would not be able to mistake the message of the gold metal buttons and the braided gold ribbon trim. Such decorative accoutrements on the new gown would firmly announce that she was no longer in mourning. Her pulse quickened.

If it be Thy will, God. Oh, please let it be Thy will.

She took the last stitch in the sleeve hem, secured the thread and snipped her needle free. Now for the ribbon.

* * *

Anne gathered her mass of shiny, red curls into an unruly bun at the crown of her head and secured them with her hair combs. The length of gold ribbon was long enough to wrap twice around the bun, then tie into a bow and let the ends dangle among the wispy curls at the nape of her neck.

She stepped back from the mirror, smoothed her hands over her fitted bodice, felt the raised scar from the carriage accident beneath her fingers. It was getting smaller. She moved her hands down over her small waist and smoothed the front of the long skirt. A smile touched her lips. The gown fit perfectly. She was ready. She stepped into the doorway. "Well?"

"Oh, Annie…" Tears glistened in her sister's eyes. "It's so good to see you—" Emma choked off her words, smiled. "You look beautiful. Mitchel will not be able to keep his gaze from you."

She laughed, did a slow pirouette. "That is my goal. Now, let me—" She frowned, at Emma's sudden, broad grin. "What is it?"

"The buttons and ribbon trim. Very subtle."

She wrinkled her nose, grinned. "As long as their message is clear?"

"Oh, it's clear all right, especially to someone who wants so much for it to be so. And I don't mean me." Emma chuckled, rose from the settee and headed for the kitchen.

"Emma!" Anne scooped Hope into her arms and hurried after her sister. "What did you mean about Mitchel? Why do you think he is…interested in the state of my widowhood?"

"Because I am neither blind nor deaf." Emma pulled

on an apron, added wood to the back of the fire, stepped into the pantry and came back out carrying a small slab of bacon and three eggs. "The man could not stop talking about you. And the look in his eyes…" She shook her head. "He's in love with you, Annie."

She held the words close in her heart for a moment, then sat Hope on a chair and donned an apron in self-defense. "Why don't I cook the bacon and eggs, Emma? You needn't do all the cooking."

She sliced strips off the slab of bacon and placed them in a spider, pulled hot coals forward with the fire rake and placed the frying pan over them. The bacon sizzled, hot grease popping.

She straightened, stepped back and looked at the fireplace.

"Is something wrong, Annie?"

"Noooo… It's only— It would certainly be easier on a woman's back if the hearth could be raised." She laughed, shook her head and picked up the turning fork to tend the bacon.

"Me want bwead wiff honey." Hope scrambled to her knees and stretched her arm out to try and reach the bread in the middle of the table.

Anne dropped the fork and reached for her.

Emma caught hold of her arm, held her back. "When did Hope last complain about pain in her joints, Anne?"

"I don't remember." She stared at Hope, raised her gaze to meet the contemplative gleam in Emma's eyes. Her hopes soared. She tamped them down, forced herself to remember. "I treat her joints every morning and again every night before she goes to bed. And— Oh, Emma—" tears welled, she choked them back "—for the past two days, she hasn't even whimpered."

* * *

"Hold still, sweetie. I'm almost finished." Anne smiled at Hope wiggling with impatience on the settee beside her, and stitched the edge of the hood to the head of the stuffed doll she had made. She snipped the thread and handed the toy to the toddler. She would add refinements when Hope went to sleep.

"Look, Emma. Me gots a dolly!" Hope held the doll in the air, then hugged it to her chest.

"My, she's lovely! You shall have to give your dolly a name."

Anne rose from the settee, carried the sewing box into the bedroom. She tried not to go to the window, but her defiant feet carried her there.

Dusk had faded to dark. Maybe tomorrow. She swallowed her worry and disappointment and strolled back into the parlor, looked at Emma and saw her concern reflected in her sister's eyes.

Emma rose, brushed her hands down the sides of her skirt. "I'm going to the apothecary. It might make me feel better to crush and grind some herbs to a powder."

She nodded, curved her lips in a feeble smile. *Almighty God, please bring Zach back to Emma and their unborn child. Please, let my sister have her dream.*

Mitchel. What if Mitchel didn't return? Her heart squeezed, shrank to a small, empty shell. Her fingers twitched. What had she done, allowing herself to love him?

No. She inched back her shoulders, clenched her hands and lifted her chin. She would not run from her love for Mitchel. If he did not return she had the memories of the time she had spent with him. And she would have Hope. She would take her for her own and love her and care for her as long as God gave them life.

She moved to the settee and lifted Mitchel's child into her arms, kissed her warm, rosy cheek. "Do you want me to tell you a bedtime—"

The clatter of hoofbeats sent her heart leaping right into her throat.

"Emma!"

"I hear—"

There was a thud of footsteps on the porch. The door opened and Zach straight and tall and grinning from ear to ear strode into the room, swept it with an all encompassing gaze. "Where's Emma, Anne?"

"In the apoth—"

"I'm here, Zach!"

He pivoted, trotted into the kitchen.

The door closed.

She turned her head, met Mitchel's gaze full on hers. The look in his eyes made her heart stop, her lungs freeze.

"Papa!"

Hope twisted in her arms, leaned toward him. Mitchel crossed the room in three long strides, took his daughter into his arms and covered her laughing face with kisses.

How pitiful was a heart that envied a child? Anne took a breath, lowered her empty arms to her sides.

"You *hurt,* Papa."

Mitchel drew his head back, lifted his hand and rubbed the back of his finger over his daughter's cheek. "I'm sorry, Hope. I forgot about my whiskers."

"Me gots a dolly." Hope held the stuffed toy in front of his face.

"I see. And a very nice dolly it is." Mitchel raised his

hand and lowered the doll, looked at her over the top of Hope's head. "Hello, Anne."

So polite. Emma was wrong. The message of the gold buttons and gold ribbon trim worthless. She squared her shoulders, summoned a smile. "Hello, Mitchel. Was your trip to the mission successful?"

"Papa, we gots a—a ca—" Hope frowned, looked at her.

"A cabin?"

Hope's blond curls bounced. She looked back at her father. "We gots a cabin!"

He looked a question at her. She nodded, wished she could flee to the bedroom and release the tears pressing at her throat and eyes. "The men have started building your cabin. I took Hope to show her your new home."

"An' to see the piggies, an' the chickies. An' a horsey!" She wiggled with excitement. "An' we finded eggs! I ate 'em."

"Were they good?"

Hope nodded, twisted toward her and held out her little arms. "Me go see cabin."

She took her in her arms, shook her head. "It's bedtime, Hope. I will— Your Papa will take you to see the cabin tomorrow."

"We'll all go see the cabin, tomorrow." Mitchel leaned forward, kissed Hope's cheek. "You be a good girl and go to bed, Hope. I have to take care of the horse and some other business. I'll see you in the morning."

"Me be good girl, Papa." Hope turned and looked up at her. "Me want aminal story."

She glanced up, caught a fleeting look of surprise on Mitchel's face before he turned away.

* * *

She was a coward. She had dragged out Hope's bed-time preparations and story as long as possible. Though Hope had fallen fast asleep close to an hour ago, she couldn't make herself go out into the parlor.

She added another log to the fire, walked to the window and stared out into the night listening to the deep rumble of Mitchel and Zach's voices through the closed door. She couldn't face him tonight. She needed time to compose herself.

She jumped, whirled toward the door as it opened.

"Oh, good, Hope is asleep. Come join us, Annie."

She could think of no excuse. She stiffened her spine and followed Emma into the parlor. Mitchel stood at the hearth, wearing his soot-stained leather pants and a clean shirt. He was clean-shaven and so handsome it made her lose her breath to look at him.

She moved toward the chair opposite the settee where Emma sat with Zach's arm around her, found Mitchel in her way. She took a breath, looked up.

"I thought, perhaps, you would be kind enough to show me my cabin, Anne?"

Her temper flared. How much was she to endure in one night? She looked down at the long skirt of her new gown. "It's dark."

"The moon is out. With its light on the snow, it's almost like daylight."

She gritted her teeth, shook her head. "Hope is sleeping. I have to—"

"I will watch over Hope, Annie."

She shot a look at Emma, got a sweet smile in return. "Very well." She jutted her chin and sailed to the door, swirled her cape around her shoulders, yanked the hood in place and marched outside and across the porch and down the steps.

The door closed. Mitchel's boots crunched snow behind her.

"This way." She headed toward the river, acutely aware of him moving up to walk beside her. She hurried her steps.

"Is something wrong, Anne?"

"I thought you were going to take Hope to see your cabin tomorrow."

"No. I said we are *all* going to see my cabin tomorrow." He caught hold of her shoulder, stepped in front of her. "Tonight, I want to see it with you. I've been thinking about you while I've been gone." His voice was soft, husky. And that look she'd seen earlier, when he first came in the door, was back in his eyes.

Her heart faltered, forgot how to beat.

"But, of course, I had to respect your widowhood." He lifted his hands, slid off her hood, touched the high collar of her gown with his finger. "Gold braid, Anne? Gold buttons?"

Her lungs forgot how to breathe.

"When I walked into that room tonight and saw you standing there holding Hope as if she were your own child—" He shook his head, drew his finger along her jaw. "It was the image of what has been in my heart for a long while, Anne. But I could not marry a woman who did not love Hope as her own."

What was he saying?

"And then Hope told me all the things you did with her that you didn't need to do. Still, I wasn't sure—" He drew a breath, brushed a curl off her temple. "While you were putting Hope to bed, Emma told me of your care for Hope and I remembered the way your face went soft with love when you took my daughter into your arms. The barrier is gone, Anne. My heart is free."

He cupped her face, tilted her chin up and drifted a smoky gaze over her face. "Do you have any idea of how beautiful you are? My mind can't find words to tell you." He lowered his head.

She closed her eyes. His lips brushed her eyelids, trailed heat down her cheek, seared her mouth. Her heart lurched to life. Her lips parted, yielded as his claimed them. His hands, warm and strong, slid inside her cloak, pulled her to him. She melted against him and her world went spinning.

He lifted his head, drew a ragged breath. "I love you, Anne." He kissed her temple, pressed his cheek against her curls. "I know this isn't fair, that I should wait. A small cabin, an ill child and my heart are all I have to offer you right now. But I don't want to wait any longer, Anne. Will you marry me?"

His husky words brought a joy she'd never known. She reached up and laid her hand against his face. "I would marry you if you lived in a cave, Mitchel Banning. I love you. And Hope is not ill. She's gaining strength every day." Tears stung her eyes at the happiness that lit his face. "But I'm afraid I'll have to insist on a barn quite soon. Hope's going to need a horsey."

Chapter Twenty-Six

"Hold still, sweetie, you'll make me drop you." Anne smiled, took a firmer hold on Hope.

"Me get down. Me wanna walk."

"When we get to the cabin. We're almost there."

"Good morning, Anne. Are you out enjoying this lovely day after all that stormy weather?"

She stopped, switched Hope to her other side, smiled at the plump woman standing in her doorway. "I didn't see you, Lydia."

"Not much wonder. You've got your hands full of squirming youngster. Good morning to you, Hope."

"Mornin'. Me got mocc'sins!" Hope stuck out her small, leather-clad foot.

"Been to Carrie Fenton's, I see. She does fine work. She's shod half the children in this town." Lydia Hargrove pretended to examine Hope's moccasins, nodded her head. "Those are fine." She straightened, looked at her. "How's your wedding dress coming along, Anne?"

"It's almost finished. I'll have it done soon. Now, if you'll excuse me, Lydia, I have to get to the cabin."

"Of course, the sooner that cabin is finished, the

sooner I have a new neighbor. We'll chat tomorrow—er—later."

"Later?"

"Why, yes. When the cabin is done." The elderly woman waved to Hope and ducked inside.

Anne frowned, settled Hope on her hip and hurried down the trodden path that would one day be a wooden walkway. She'd never seen Lydia Hargrove act so... unstrung.

"*My* cabin." Hope pointed a tiny finger at the new log building.

Anne smiled at the possessive note in her voice. "Yes, it is. And it will be ready soon." Her stomach fluttered. She hurried in the doorway, glanced around. Mitchel had finished and hung their bedroom door.

A scraping sound drew her to the kitchen. Mitchel was at the fireplace fitting a stone into the cooking shelf he was making her. The muscles in his shoulders rippled, strained the shirt across his back.

"Me here, Papa."

His body tensed. She smiled. That reaction was not for Hope. The fluttering increased.

Mitchel settled the stone, wiped his hands on his thighs and turned. His gaze locked on hers. He took Hope in his left arm, slid his right arm around her and drew her close for a heart-pounding, world-spinning kiss.

"Papa! Me gots mocc'sins."

He lifted his head, gave her a look that said he would have liked that kiss to continue. She gave him a saucy smile in return.

"You wait, wench." He growled the words, released

her and lifted Hope's small foot and examined the moccasin, made appropriate exclamations.

She laid her head against his upper arm then stepped around him and looked at the fireplace that stretched along the end wall. The door beside it led to what would be their washing, bathing room. An idea birthed by Emma's cozy, warm apothecary.

Her hands itched with the urge to cook. The fireplace was divided into a normal hearth for heating the room and the hip-high cooking shelf. She moved forward, ran her hands over the stone surface. "Mitchel, this is *perfect*. Every woman in Promise will be begging her husband to make her one after they see it."

"Wonderful. The men will probably run me out of town." He lowered Hope to the floor, came and folded his arms around her, tugged her back against his strong, lean body and chuckled, a rumble she felt in his chest. "We'll have to find that cave you said you would live in with me."

She laughed, rested her crossed arms on his. "As long as you make me a fireplace with a cooking shelf."

Leather padded against the plank floor. They turned as one, watched Hope march around the kitchen holding her cloak back so she could admire her new moccasins.

Mitchel's arms tightened around her. "Thank You, Almighty God, for healing Hope. For giving her strength to walk and play again." His cheek pressed against her hair. "And thank You, Lord, for bringing us together in love."

"Amen." She blinked the film of moisture from her eyes and rested her head back against his broad chest.

"Anne."

"Yes."

"I'm leaving for Fort Vancouver tonight."

She stiffened, caught her breath. It wasn't that it was unexpected. But trips through the wilderness were so dangerous.

He cleared his throat. "It's time, Anne. The cabin is ready. And the church should be finished by the time I return." He grasped her shoulders, turned her to face him. "I'm not coming back until I have a preacher with me, Anne. I want you for my wife, and I'm not going to wait any longer."

Anne took a stitch on Hope's new dress, lowered her hands to her lap and stared at the door. He'd only left a few minutes ago and already she missed him, feared for him. It would be an eternity until—

"Mitch will be back soon, Anne."

She shifted her gaze to Zach, summoned up a smile she found hiding beneath her unshed tears. "I know. It's only that I'm not as brave as Emma. I try not to, but I keep hearing those terrible, tortured cries and re-membering that the Cayuse want—" She choked, looked down at her work, took another stitch on the ruffle.

Zach prodded the burning logs on the hearth closer, sat in the chair opposite her and dangled his hands between his knees. "Look at me, Anne."

She blinked her eyes clear, raised her gaze to him.

"I can't deny there is danger for Mitch. He's riding through a wilderness filled with hostiles. But there is a lot in his favor." Zach held his hand up between them. "Mitch knows the area and he knows the Indians—he's dealt with them since he opened the mission." He folded two fingers down to his palm. "He's on my fastest horse with the greatest heart—next to Comanche—" another finger folded down "—and that Colt he's carrying makes him the equal of ten men." He fisted his hand, rested it on his knee. "Most important of all, Mitch uses his head. He knows how to fight, or he never would have survived hand-to-hand combat with a Cayuse warrior, but he also knows wisdom avoids battles. He'll come home to you."

She nodded, dredged up another smile. "Thank you, Zach."

He nodded, rose and headed for the door. "When Emma finishes with her patient, tell her I went to check on that sick mare." He shrugged into his jacket, tugged on his hat and went outside.

The silence was terrible. She gathered her sewing and went to the bedroom. Hope was sleeping soundly. She glanced at her wedding dress smoothed out on top of the chest, knelt on the hearth and let her tears flow.

Anne dried the tureen, put the lid on it and set it on one of the shelves Mitchel had built in the corner by the dry sink. The few dishes looked so forlorn sitting there she moved the cups and saucers to another shelf. She wanted the cabin to look as warm and cozy as possible when Mitchel returned. *If he* returned. He'd had been gone three weeks and four days.

"This cooking shelf is wonderful, Annie." Emma chose one of the spiders out of the pile of iron pots Zach had carried in and placed it on the stone shelf, pretended to be cooking. "Gracious, no bending. Zach has got to make me one these!"

"Hello the house!"

Anne dumped the dirty water in the bucket with the charred edge, dried her hands and stepped into the parlor. "Hello, Lydia. What—" She stopped, stared at the women filling the bare room.

"We women had a meeting."

She smiled, she couldn't help it. She could imagine that John Hargrove, and a few of the other husbands, hated hearing those words.

"And we decided it wasn't fittin' for our pastor to move into a house with an empty pantry." Olga Lund-quist looked scandalized at the thought.

"So we brung some of our 'extras' to fill up them shelves." Lorna Lewis, looked down at her toddler daughter. "Jenny, you take these here biscuits and share 'em with Hope and Edward whilst we women are busy visitin'."

Anne glanced at the gifts in the women's hands and her throat constricted. There were no 'extras' on the frontier. "I don't know what to say."

"I do." Emma put her hand on her shoulder and waved the other through the air in the direction of the kitchen door. "This way, ladies."

"I feel terrible taking their food, Emma." Anne stepped to the bedroom door, checked on Hope. "I know things are scarce or unavailable on the frontier, and it will be difficult at first. But I have money to purchase staples when Mr. Swinton goes to Oregon City to re-stock his store."

"It's not about their food or our money, Annie. It's about helping and being a blessing to each other. The frontier has a way of making everything level. No one can make it alone out here. And those that try do so to their loss." Emma looked up from bandage she was roll-ing. "You will have your chance to bless them in return."

She nodded, looked out the window. "It's snowing again."

"Yes."

She wrapped her arms around her waist, went to the bedroom for her cloak. "I'm going outside. I want to see the church in the moonlight with the snow on the steeple." She smiled, reached deep for her faltering faith. "Mitchel will be so pleased to see the women 'had a meeting' about that steeple."

Emma laughed, sobered. "He'll be back, Annie. He's probably had trouble finding a preacher."

"Yes." She took a breath, fastened the button and loop at the neck of her cloak, pulled the hood up and opened the door. "I may go to the cabin, so don't be concerned if I stay a bit."

Large, fluffy snowflakes streamed from the sky, piled in abundance on rooftops and woodpiles. She strolled to the riverbank, looked across the whispering water. The church was an unpretentious log building, with only two windows, but it was beautiful to her. The townspeople had voted to put the windows they had purchased for their church in their pastor's cabin instead. She would write a letter home and tell them about it. And about the "extras" in their pantry.

It was so silent and still in the storm. Where was Mitchel? Was he on his way home to her and Hope?

She drew her gaze back from the church to the cabin. It looked small and cold and unwelcoming. The windows were dark, no smoke plume rose from its chimneys. What sort of welcome would that be if Mitchel—

What time I am afraid, I will trust in Thee.

She blinked the tears from her eyes, lifted her skirt hems and ran to the ferry. She stepped into the floating box, grasped the rope and pulled her way across the river. "I will trust You, Lord. I will start the fires and burn the oil lamp in welcome. You have only to bring Mitchel home."

She ducked her head against the snow and ran to the cabin.

The door hinges squeaked a protest at being made to work in the cold. She left the door open for light, ran to the kitchen fireplace and took the flint and steel off the mantel. Pressure built in her chest as she knelt and struck sparks into the laid fire the way Mitchel had taught her that day in the mountains.

The tinder smoldered. She leaned down and blew on it, smiled when it burst into flame and ate greedily at the kindling she fed it. She rose, lifted the chimney on the oil lamp and held a sliver of burning wood to the wick, tossed the spill into the fire and adjusted the flame. Golden light danced on the walls.

She added wood to the fire, slid a few pieces of burning kindling onto the fire shovel and carried it to the parlor fireplace. The fire caught, tossed sparks and flames into the air. She added wood, watched the dancing light a moment, then went to close the door. There was a wagon coming down the rutted path in front of the cottages.

She pulled her cloak close about her and watched it draw near. It must be the Suttons or the Murrays, one of the farmers who lived farther down on the plain. She shivered, stepped inside and closed the door.

The fire flared in the draft, settled to a steady burn. She could already feel the warmth spreading into the room. She picked up the fire shovel and carried it back to the kitchen, took off her cloak and hung it on one of the nails where her utensils would one day hang.

The door latch clicked. She frowned. Emma or Zach? Well, she was not leaving the cabin tonight! She raised her chin and went to do battle. Mitchel stood in the doorway, his handsome features furrowed in puzzlement.

She gasped, stared in disbelief. And then she ran.

Mitchel met her in the middle of the room, caught her up in his arms, crushed her to him. "Anne! Anne!" His lips found her eager ones, drank of the love they offered.

"Ahem…"

She opened her eyes, gaped over Mitchel's shoulder at the tall, lean man wearing a black suit and a fur hat with ear flaps.

Mitchel loosened his hold, lowered her to the floor. "Anne, this is Reverend Overbeck. He's come to marry us. Now stoke those fires, I've got a wagonload of furniture to bring in."

"So you expected the furniture?"

Zach sounded as flummoxed as Emma looked.

Mitchel took a sip of coffee and shook his head. "No. I received a letter some time ago telling me my uncle had died childless and left his estate to me. I knew he was comfortably situated, but I didn't know what the estate entailed. That's why, when I asked Anne to marry me, I told her to be fair I should wait. I didn't explain what I meant because I didn't rightfully know—" his gaze sought hers "—and I didn't want to wait. And I'm not going to. Not another day." He grinned. "I ran into the Lewis boys first thing this morning and told them to spread the news that our wedding will be this afternoon in the church."

They were all there. Every man, woman and child in town had turned out to help celebrate the first wedding in Promise. Her wedding.

Anne turned from the window, checked to make sure all of the tiny buttons on her fitted bodice made of Olga's lace tablecloth were fastened, then smoothed the long skirt made from one of Emma's silk gowns. She peered in the mirror over the washstand, slipped the wide strip of lace around her mass of red curls and tied it in a bow at the crown of her head. The long tails streamed down her back.

She was ready. She took a deep breath and left the cabin. Sunlight sparkled on the pristine snow. She lifted her hems and walked across the open space to the church, stepped inside the door left wide to let in the sunlight. She waited a moment for her eyes to become accustomed to the dimness of the interior, then walked forward.

Reverend Overbeck stood behind a crude wooden altar where two candles in pewter holders cast golden light on Mitchel's ink-stained Bible. Hope was in Emma's arms. She stopped, smiled at Emma and Zach, kissed Hope's cheek, then turned toward her beloved.

Mitchel, heart-stoppingly handsome in a black wool suit, white shirt and tapestry vest, reached out his hand and enfolded hers in its warm and strength. Together they turned and faced the altar.

* * * * *

SPECIAL EXCERPT FROM

🌿

LOVE INSPIRED
INSPIRATIONAL ROMANCE

An Amish man gets more than he bargained for when he moves next door to a large spirited family during the holiday season.

Read on for a sneak preview of
The Amish Christmas Secret
by Vannetta Chapman.

"Get back!"

Definitely a female voice, from the other side of the barn. He walked around the barn. If someone had asked him to guess what he might find there, he wouldn't in a hundred years have guessed correctly.

A young Amish woman—Plain dress, apron, *kapp*—was holding a feed bucket in one hand and a rake in the other, attempting to fend off a rooster. At the moment, the bird was trying to peck the woman's feet.

"What did you do to him?" Daniel asked.

Her eyes widened. The rooster made a swipe at her left foot. The woman once again thrust the feed bucket toward the rooster. "Don't just stand there. This beast won't let me pass."

Daniel knew better than to laugh. He'd been raised with four sisters and a strong-willed mother. So he snatched the rooster up from behind, pinning its wings down with his right arm.

"Where do you want him?"

"His name is Carl, and I want him in the oven if you must know the truth." She dropped the feed bucket and swiped at the golden-blond hair that was spilling out of her *kapp*. "Over there. In the pen."

Daniel dropped the rooster inside and turned to face the woman. She was probably five and a half feet tall, and looked to be around twenty years old. Blue eyes the color of forget-me-nots assessed him.

She was also beautiful in the way of Plain women, without adornment. The sight of her reminded him of yet another reason why he'd left Pennsylvania. Why couldn't his neighbors have been an old couple in their nineties?

"You must be the new neighbor. I'm Becca Schwartz—not Rebecca, just Becca, because my *mamm* decided to do things alphabetically. We thought you might introduce yourself, but I guess you've been busy. Mamm would want me to invite you to dinner, but I warn you, I have seven younger siblings, so it's usually a somewhat chaotic affair."

Becca not Rebecca stepped closer.

"Didn't catch your name."

"Daniel...Daniel Glick."

"We didn't even know the place had sold until last week. Most people are leery of farms where the fields are covered with rocks and the house is falling down. I see you haven't done anything to remedy either of those situations."

"I only moved in yesterday."

"Had time to get a horse, though. Get it from Old Tim?"

Before he could answer, a dinner bell rang. "Sounds like dinner's ready. Care to meet the folks?"

"Another time. I have some...um...unpacking to do."

Becca shrugged her shoulders. "Guess I'll be seeing you, then."

"Yeah, I guess."

He'd hoped for peace and solitude.

Instead, he had half a barn, a cantankerous rooster and a pretty neighbor who was a little nosy.

He'd come to Indiana to forget women and to lose himself in making something good from something that was broken.

He'd moved to Indiana because he wanted to be left alone.

Don't miss
The Amish Christmas Secret *by Vannetta Chapman,*
available October 2020 wherever
Love Inspired books and ebooks are sold.

LoveInspired.com

**IF YOU ENJOYED THIS BOOK
WE THINK YOU WILL ALSO LOVE**

⟨H⟩ HARLEQUIN

SPECIAL
EDITION

Believe in love. Overcome obstacles. Find happiness.

Relate to finding comfort and strength in the
support of loved ones and enjoy the journey
no matter what life throws your way.

6 NEW BOOKS AVAILABLE EVERY MONTH!

Before he testifies in an important case, businessman Michael "Mikey" Fiore hides out in Jacobsville, Texas, and crosses paths with softly beautiful Bernadette, who seems burdened with her own secrets. Their bond grows into passion...until shocking truths surface.

Read on for a sneak peek at
Texas Proud,
the latest book in
#1 New York Times bestselling author Diana Palmer's Long, Tall Texans series!

Mikey's fingers contracted. "Suppose I told you that the hotel I own is actually a casino," he said slowly, "and it's in Las Vegas?"

Bernie's eyes widened. "You own a casino in Las Vegas?" she exclaimed. "Wow!"

He laughed, surprised at her easy acceptance. "I run it legit, too," he added. "No fixes, no hidden switches, no cheating. Drives the feds nuts, because they can't find anything to pin on me there."

"The feds?" she asked.

He drew in a breath. "I told you, I'm a bad man." He felt guilty about it, dirty. His fingers caressed hers as they neared Graylings, the huge mansion where his cousin lived with the heir to the Grayling racehorse stables.

Her fingers curled trustingly around his. "And I told you that the past doesn't matter," she said stubbornly. Her heart was running wild. "Not at all. I don't care how bad you've been."

His own heart stopped and then ran away. His teeth clenched. "I don't even think you're real, Bernie," he whispered. "I think I dreamed you."

She flushed and smiled. "Thanks."

He glanced in the rearview mirror. "What I'd give for just five minutes alone with you right now," he said tautly. "Fat chance," he added as he noticed the sedan tailing casually behind them.

She felt all aglow inside. She wanted that, too. Maybe they could find a quiet place to be alone, even for just a few minutes. She wanted to kiss him until her mouth hurt.

Don't miss
Texas Proud *by Diana Palmer,*
available October 2020 wherever
Harlequin Special Edition books and ebooks are sold.

Harlequin.com